Where Love Grows

Jerry S. Eicher

HARVEST HOUSE PUBLISHERS
EUGENE, OREGON

All Scripture quotations are from the King James Version of the Bible.

This is a work of fiction. Names, characters, places, and incidents are products of the author's imagination or are used fictitiously. Any resemblance to actual persons, living or dead, or to events or locales, is entirely coincidental.

Cover by Garborg Design Works, Savage, Minnesota

Cover photos © Chris Garborg

WHERE LOVE GROWS

Published by Harvest House Publishers
Eugene, Oregon 97402
www.harvesthousepublishers.com

Library of Congress Cataloging-in-Publication Data
Eicher, Jerry S.
Where love grows / Jerry S. Eicher.
p. cm. — (Fields of home ; bk. 3)
ISBN 978-0-7369-3945-4 (pbk.)
ISBN 978-0-7369-4288-1 (eBook)
1. Amish—Fiction. 2. Weddings—Fiction. I Title.
PS3605.I34M48 2012
813'.6—dc23

2011044780

Printed in the United States of America

12 13 14 15 16 17 18 19 20 / LB-SK / 10 9 8 7 6 5 4 3 2 1

Chapter One

Susan Hostetler made her way to the barn to hitch the horse for the drive to the small farmstead where James and Teresa would live after their wedding next week. Susan smiled as she thought of Deacon Ray's struggle to get used to the idea that his son James was marrying an *Englisha* girl. *Nee*, it had not been easy for him. Of course, Teresa was Amish now. In the months since she had arrived with Susan, Teresa had turned into a model of submission and humility. Deacon Ray shouldn't complain even if Teresa's baby, Samuel, had been born out of wedlock before she came to the community. *Yah*, in an unwed state, but wasn't changing one's life for the better a commendable thing to do? Of course it was.

And Teresa was now properly baptized. She knew how to cook, wash clothes, and sew with the best of the women. She even had her own quilt completed and stashed in the cedar chest upstairs awaiting the day she and James would marry. She would spread the quilt on their bed and be able to say with complete honesty that she had done much of the work. There had been help from *Mamm*, five of Susan's eight sisters who lived nearby, and Susan herself. Between the work on the quilt, helping Teresa adapt to her new life, and now the plans for the upcoming wedding, the months had sped by.

Summer was waning, and it wouldn't be long until snow would be covering the Amish farms spread among these rolling hills of southern Indiana. But now was not the time to think of snow. The rest of summer lay ahead, followed by fall, and perhaps a glorious display of Indian summer. How appropriate that would be for all of them. And Teresa deserved a wonderful stretch of *gut* weather, both before and following her wedding day. It would be fitting after the hard road she'd traveled after arriving in the Amish community.

Mamm hadn't seemed worried back then by the attempt to match Yost Byler and Teresa. But Susan had been ready to panic before Yost finally decided, with Susan's *daett*'s help, that marrying Teresa wasn't a *gut* idea. Such a marriage would have been a disaster for Teresa and probably also for Yost. *Yah*, he needed a wife who had been born Amish to cook and clean for him. The *gut* news floating around the community was that Yost may have finally found an older widow as a potential *frau*.

Only a few days remained until Teresa's wedding to James. It would take place here on the Hostetler home place, just like *Daett* had provided for all Susan's sisters. How could things be more awesome than that?

Perhaps the icing on the cake was the love that was now beginning to stir afresh in Susan's heart for her old flame, Thomas Stoll. Who could have imagined such a thing? *Yah*, she had loved Thomas since their school days, but that love came to a halt the day she caught Thomas kissing Eunice outside a hymn singing one Sunday night. Thomas had claimed he'd just had a "weak moment."

After escaping into the *Englisha* world for a time, Susan was back now. And despite all the fuss, she and Thomas were getting together again. Of course, it hadn't hurt that Teresa had encouraged her to restore the relationship after Thomas's repeated apologies and continued attention. *Mamm* and *Daett* also gave their encouragement at every opportunity. But it was Teresa's opinion that had carried the real weight. How strange that an *Englisha* girl should have such sway in her life. But that was how things had turned out. Teresa was now the friend closest to Susan's heart.

Since Susan had returned from her flirtation with the *Englisha* world in Asbury Park, New Jersey, Thomas was the picture of repentance. Had he wanted to, he could be married to Eunice by now—or to just about any other young woman in the community. But Thomas hadn't pursued anyone but Susan in the months since her return. The result was that Susan felt some trust returning in her heart for him. Perhaps someday soon her heart would be fully restored.

In the meantime, there was no need to rush into setting a wedding date, even with Thomas's pleadings that they do. *Yah*, he loved Susan and wanted to marry her, but he also wanted to begin the work of taking over the farm from Susan's *daett*. In fact, he wanted it very badly. Thomas had no background in farming since his *daett* was a cabinetmaker, but he was anxious to learn.

Mamm and *Daett* were older now and tired. They both yearned for the comfort of the *dawdy haus*, which would be built as soon as the matter between Thomas and Susan was settled by marriage. Until then, *Daett* had hired young Steve Mast to help with the farm. He'd started in the spring and was a hard worker—no doubt due to his being raised on an Amish farm over in Daviess County. During the days he worked *Daett*'s farm, Steve took his supper and lodging at Susan's sister's place. Ada and her husband, Reuben, lived just down the road a piece.

Steve was a rare find, *Daett* said. A real answer to their prayers. Not many Amish men were available for hiring out once they became of age at twenty-one. Either they were married, were planning to get married, or had work on their own family places.

Steve didn't have work on his *daett*'s place, neither did he have a girlfriend or a prospect that anyone knew of. He was the second boy in a family of ten—six of them being boys. He wasn't that handsome or forward about himself, a good quality for an Amish man.

Susan stopped just short of the barn and looked up at the swaying branches of the old oak where she'd once had a swing and had climbed to its highest limbs. She sighed to think she was too old for that now. But at least she was here. She was home, hopefully to stay.

It was here she had played in the front yard with her cousins and older sisters during many a summer. Here she had watched *Daett* harness the horses in the first light of dawn. Here she had watched him take the teams to the fields, where his tall form moved in and out of view all day. Here her heart had taken deep enough root that she was pulled back after her time in Asbury Park. Susan sighed again. Was this why she was giving in to Thomas? Was this why she was allowing him to bring her home on Sunday nights again? Was she accepting his attentions although still feeling a little uncertain about their future?

No, it was more than that. It was high time she made up her mind and settled down with a husband. Steve couldn't work for *Daett* forever. And *Daett* was getting up in years. He and *Mamm* deserved to move into a *dawdy haus* and not work so hard. Was that how her love for Thomas would grow? Her desire to stay here in her childhood home, Thomas's desire to farm, and *Mamm and Daett*'s desire to settle in a *dawdy haus*?

It was possible, Susan supposed. Hadn't *Mamm* said love could grow anywhere? Anywhere it was allowed to, that is. Then Susan would allow it for everyone's sake. If love came slowly for her, then so be it. She and Thomas would have a lifetime for her love to grow stronger. That it was beginning small and uncertain for her would be her secret.

As Susan reached to open the barn door, a man cleared his throat behind her. Susan jumped and whirled around.

"Umm…I have the horse ready," Steve said. "He's tied up in the first stall."

Susan relaxed. "You didn't have to do that, Steve. I would have done it."

A hint of a smile crossed Steve's face. "It was no trouble. Happy to do it." He looked up at the clear sky. "It's sure a beautiful morning."

"*Yah*, it is," Susan answered. "Well, thanks for getting Toby ready. I wasn't expecting that. I know you're busy with the usual chores *Daett* gives you."

"Your *daett* is a *gut* man and a *gut* farmer." Steve tugged the hat rim down over his eyes more. "He's done a *gut* job keeping things up on the farm, even with his age." With that, he turned to go.

Without thinking, Susan asked, "Do you have any secrets, Steve?"

He stopped and looked back over his shoulder. "Me? Secrets? I'm a pretty ordinary fellow. No secrets."

"Really? I thought everyone had secrets."

"Not me. I'm pretty much what you see. No secrets and no roots. I'm kind of like the dandelions in the field. I grow where *Da Hah* blows me."

"So why don't you have a girl?"

His eyes twinkled. "Maybe I haven't found the perfect one yet."

"Is that why you moved to a new community? To..."

"Scout the land?" He finished her sentence. "Perhaps. Do you have anyone in mind?"

"*Nee*," Susan said. "And I don't know why I even asked something like that. Maybe it's that type of morning."

He smiled. "I'm afraid you'll have to look someplace other than myself for secrets. And no offense taken."

"Thank you," she said. "What do you think of Teresa and James?"

He raised his eyebrows. "They seem like a nice enough couple. Why do you ask?"

"Oh, no reason," she said. "I suppose you heard about all the ruckus before they got together."

Steve shrugged. "I don't pay much attention to rumors. They look like they're in love with each other. That should be *gut* enough for anyone."

"I want nothing more from life," she said, "than to settle down to a boring sameness, day after day, night after night, living in peace and love. Wouldn't that be wonderful?"

"I don't know about that," he said. "I'm not much into boring. I'm surprised you are. I heard you'd been with the *Englisha* for a while. That's not something a person does who's looking for boring."

"So now you're paying attention to rumors?"

Steve laughed. "I didn't really hear that much. People seem to think highly of you. And I'm sure your *mamm* and *daett* will be happy if you plan to stay. And Thomas, of course."

"What do you think of him?"

"Thomas?" He paused for a moment. "You want me to comment on your boyfriend?"

"*Yah*, I'm asking you. Coming from another community, you might have an unbiased perspective."

"What if I don't like him? Can I continue working here?"

She laughed. "I'm not going to chase you off."

"Well..."

"Come on now. Tell me the truth."

Steve tilted his head sideways. "Thomas comes from a good family, as far as I can tell. Of course, I don't know what secrets lie in his past. Maybe he ran off to the *Englisha* world for a while too. You know, something wild like that." His eyes twinkled as he spoke the last line.

"So you think that's a character flaw? You keep bringing it up."

"Depends on why a person did it, I guess."

"Let's just say I had my reasons."

"Fair enough," he said.

They stood silent for a moment.

Susan finally said, "Well, I better get busy or Teresa will wonder what's happened to me."

"And I better get busy in the fields before your *daett* thinks I've gone lazy on him." He turned and left.

Susan went into the barn thinking about the exchange. Steve hadn't given away much about his past. Not that it was any of her business. But a person just couldn't help wondering. Had some girl dumped him? He'd probably had his heart broken, and the wound was healing slowly and out of sight of the people who knew him.

She'd done much the same thing by moving to Asbury Park. True, it had been time spent among the *Englisha*. But *Da Hah* had brought good things out of the experience. That time of her life was nothing to be ashamed of.

Susan untied Toby and led him outside. Lifting the shafts of the buggy, she swung him underneath and fastened the tugs. Holding the bridle, Susan looked toward the house and waited. There was still no sign of Teresa.

Thoughts of last Sunday night buzzed through Susan's head. Thomas hadn't tried to kiss her yet. In a way she wished he would. It might hurry things along. But apparently Thomas wasn't willing to rush things until she agreed to a wedding date. To his credit, he seemed to ignore the fact that Eunice still made eyes at him almost every Sunday night at the hymn singings. *Mamm* was right though. Susan needed to trust Thomas and believe he wouldn't fall again just because Eunice batted her eyes at him. After all, Thomas claimed Eunice acted that way toward all the boys, which was partly true. To his credit, Thomas really didn't want Eunice. He was choosing her—Susan. That was worth something, wasn't it? Surely his persistence would arouse some of the old feelings she used to have for him.

And now here came Teresa, running across the yard, her face glowing with happiness. At least somebody had things figured out in this world.

Chapter Two

Susan drove the buggy on the main road, across the small one-lane bridge in the hollow, and continued until the fields opened up again. She looked at a red barn that belonged to the farmstead. It stood framed by the trees in the yard, their green leaves hanging over the roofline. In the background, a small, white, two-story house sat back from the road. A small front porch protected the front steps, and a broken concrete sidewalk led up to it.

"What a beautiful, beautiful, little place," Susan gushed. "I've been here several times now, and it still makes me want to move in! Even if the barn roof sags a bit."

"I still can't believe James and I are going to live here!" Teresa said, her voice catching. "Do you think it's all a dream, Susan? I live in horror I might wake up some morning and find it all gone."

"It looks pretty real to me," Susan said, pulling into the driveway. "I'd be more worried about all the work you still have to do on the place."

"James will work on it when he has the time. Right now it's good enough for me. And getting the farm going is more important than how the place looks."

"At least the barn and house roofs don't leak." Susan brought the horse to a stop by a small tree.

"You sure aren't very cheerful this morning," Teresa said, climbing down from the buggy. "Is something troubling you? I've been so wrapped up in my own world, I've about forgotten you. Is it trouble with Thomas again?"

"Not really." Susan tied Toby to a tree branch. "It's just not quite like old times. I suppose I'll get used to it."

"I know *Da Hah* will bless you, Susan. Look how He's blessed me beyond my wildest imagination. He'll do the same for you. I know He will."

"I hope so." Susan took the cleaning supplies out of the back of the buggy.

"You know *Da Hah* will," Teresa insisted. "Look at what kind of shape I was in when I arrived in the community. That wasn't so long ago. And just think, I could easily be marrying old Yost Byler instead of James—if *Da Hah* hadn't intervened."

Susan laughed and then frowned. "It's not funny, really. In fact, I have shivers running up and down my spine even now just thinking about it."

"He'll make that widow from Geauga County a good husband," Teresa said.

"*Yah,* he'll make someone a good husband. Just not you. I'm glad you came to your senses in time."

"I still claim Yost isn't all that bad. All he wants is someone to cook and clean for him. You know, we should go back and clean his house again just to be nice. Perhaps right before his wedding."

"I don't think so," Susan said, making a face. "One afternoon in his house was enough for me. Let his new wife take care of that."

Teresa laughed. "Poor man. But I do say, I'm glad things didn't work out between us. James needs cooking and cleaning like any other man, but there is also this wonderful love between us. I never thought it possible, Susan. I never felt such a feeling as this. Not even between Samuel's father and me. *Da Hah* is very kind. I don't deserve any of this."

"You're right. *Da Hah* has blessed you!" Susan opened the front door. It squeaked on the hinges, the sound echoing through the house. "Looks like you need oil on this door."

"I'm leaving it like it is unless James objects. That way I can hear the door every time he comes into the house so I can come running from wherever I'm working. Oh, Susan! I can't believe this is happening!" Teresa paused and tears sprang to her eyes.

Susan set the supplies on the hardwood floor and went to stand beside her. "I'm so glad you're happy, Teresa. You don't know how worried I was about you those first few months here. I thought Deacon Ray and Yost were going to mess your life up with their scheming. And you went along with their plans, having such a sweet attitude about what you couldn't control. I'm sure that's why *Da Hah* has chosen to bless you."

"He has blessed me," Teresa agreed. "And I'm not going to rest or stop praying until you're as happy as I am."

"You're a very precious friend, Teresa. I can never tell you that enough. If my attitude toward life's trials can become as pure as yours, I'm sure I'll be okay."

"I'll always be your friend, Susan. Please tell me if I ever do something that harms our friendship. I don't want marriage, or children, or busy days and nights to keep our hearts apart."

Susan wiped away her own tears. "Life changes things, Teresa. But, *yah*, I hope we will always be sisters in heart. In many ways you are much more of a sister to me than my eight real ones. They think I'm spoiled, pampered, and hardheaded. And they're probably right… which is why I like you—you're so nice to me in spite of how I act sometimes."

Teresa gave Susan a quick hug. "You liked me for some reason long before I was ever nice to you. I shudder to think how I must have looked going into Laura's bakery in Asbury Park. I was all swelled up and pregnant with Samuel. And then I asked you to help me arrange for my baby to be adopted by Amish parents when he was born. It's a wonder you didn't throw me back out on the street."

"Your beautiful heart was clear to me, Teresa. I could see it in your face. You just didn't know it. It would have taken a heart of stone to send you away. And mine wasn't quite frozen over. And now here we are. You have a beautiful baby boy and a soon-to-be wonderful husband."

"In some way I'll pay you back." Teresa sighed. "I'm going to do all I can to help you and Thomas get together. I want both of you to have what James and I have. Love is too wonderful to keep to myself, Susan."

"I won't object," Susan said. "Now, I suppose we'd better get to work."

"Yes...I mean *yah*," Teresa corrected. Both girls laughed.

Teresa continued. "I want to thank you and Thomas for agreeing to be an attending couple at the wedding. If you wouldn't have said yes, I have no idea who I would have gotten for my side of the family. James said it absolutely had to be one couple from each side."

"I'm glad to do it."

Teresa tilted her head. "You'll be a better-looking couple than James and I when you wed. I'm almost jealous."

Susan laughed. "You have nothing to worry about. Really you don't. The joy on your face will make you look like an angel. Okay, we really do need to get started."

"First I want to take you upstairs," Teresa said.

"I've already been up there."

"Not today you haven't. Come. Samuel's little room is ready!"

Susan followed Teresa up the steps and listened to the squeaking of the old farmhouse. The noises of these old homes soothed her spirit even after all these years. As a young girl she'd raced up and down stairs like this, just as Samuel soon would. How quickly time passed, and oh how the little things in life grew in value.

Teresa pushed open a door and walked into a light-blue room. A small bed was set up against the wall facing the window. A dark-brown knitted rug was on the floor. On the bed, a Texas star quilt lay. Teresa tossed back the quilt edges to reveal plain white pillows.

"It's adorable," Susan cooed. "Samuel will grow up exactly like you imagined before he was born."

"And he'll have a *real* father," Teresa whispered. "James has so taken to him. Samuel already calls him *Daett*."

"That's so wonderful." Susan ran her hand over the quilt.

"Come!" Teresa motioned for her to follow. "I want to show you the other three bedrooms."

"You have redone them already?"

"No, and we may not get to them for a while. That is, we may not need them for a while. You know what I mean...when we have...um... other babies." Teresa's cheeks turned bright red.

Susan laughed. "You already are a wonderful *mamm*, Teresa."

"I hope so. But these will be James's children. And what if I mess things up for him? What if I don't give him healthy children? Susan, do you really think I'll make a good Amish mother?"

Susan gave Teresa a warm smile. "Don't worry about it. *Da Hah* will give you grace just like He did with you and baby Samuel. You don't see James or anyone else in the community complaining about him, do you?"

Teresa took a deep breath. "No, I don't. But I wonder sometimes if people might be covering for my mistakes."

"*Mamm* and I would tell you if you were doing something wrong."

"Thank you. That so helps with my nerves. You have no idea how much." Teresa opened another bedroom door. Bare white walls and a high ceiling greeted them. Cracks ran everywhere across the plaster.

"Phew! This room does need work," Susan said.

"I know. What color would you make this room?"

"Hmmm...okay." Susan stepped inside. "The window faces the east, so the first sun rays every morning will be coming in. That will make everything look brighter. I'd go with a darker color. Maybe a nice blue... or red even."

"But those are boy colors," Teresa said. "Our first child together is going to be a girl."

Susan laughed. "You're awful sure of yourself, aren't you?"

Teresa blushed. "Just hoping. So I suppose we have to stay with neutral colors just in case. And I don't want to make it pink, right?"

Susan gasped. "Most certainly not! That would be very...well, it certainly wouldn't be Amish."

"Then a cream color, maybe a little on the dark side. I think I'd like that."

Susan turned to face the window. "I'd still go with a darker red or blue. Either way, it'll be wonderful."

"I know." Teresa beamed. "So many choices, but they can wait. There will be plenty of time after the wedding. Come on downstairs. I want to show you the main bedroom."

"Have you already fixed that up?" Susan asked as she followed Teresa down the squeaky stairs.

"Only the bed is in. I haven't brought over any bedding yet." Teresa pushed open the door, leading Susan inside. "We haven't painted in here yet, but that can also wait. I might not even bother right away. There's so much to do."

"But you have to!" Susan said. "You can't leave it looking like this. I'll come over and help with the work."

"You and *Mamm* have already done so much. I can't ask for more."

"But there are cracks all over the walls."

"I know, but it's an old farmhouse. James understands."

"I'm coming over this week to work on this. My sisters can help *Mamm* at home. Betsy and Edna were offering more of their time just last Sunday."

"Oh!" Teresa exclaimed. "Your help would be awesome. James is so wonderful. He deserves a fixed-up bedroom."

Susan laughed and glanced out of the window. "There's James coming now. I'm sure I didn't see his buggy when we arrived."

"He works here on the farm when he can get away. His buggy could be in the barn." Teresa was all aflutter now. "Oh, Susan, my neck and face are burning. He'll think I'm a total scatterbrain."

"He won't think anything like that." Susan took Teresa's hand and pulled her toward the living room. Teresa gathered herself together, smoothing her apron with little swipes of her hand.

"You just saw him Sunday night," Susan commented and giggled. "You're acting like a schoolgirl."

"You don't know how much like a schoolgirl I feel," Teresa confessed.

James burst through the doorway. "What have we here?" he said. "Well, if it isn't my lovely bride!"

"Not yet, she isn't," Susan corrected.

James laughed.

"Where were you?" Teresa asked.

"I was working in the back field," James said, sweeping Teresa into his arms. He kissed her several times on the cheek. "James, there's someone here!" Teresa whispered.

"I suppose Susan's seen boys and girls kissing before." James laughed and let go of Teresa. "I heard Thomas took you home again on Sunday, Susan. I'm glad to hear it."

"Thank you," Susan said. "Everyone does seem happy about it."

"So what do you plan on doing today?" James asked as he turned back to Teresa. He smiled ear to ear.

"Clean the house," Teresa said. "Or at least the parts we can get to. I don't know, though, if this house will ever be good enough for you."

"Ah, you're wonderful enough for me. Don't worry about the house," he said.

"I *am* going to worry about the house," Teresa retorted. "And I'm keeping it clean for you."

"I'm sure you will." James was still smiling. "Let me get back to my work before the horses take off. I left them standing in the field." He turned and headed toward the door. They watched as he opened it, walked through, and then shut it behind him.

Several moments later Teresa was still staring after James.

"Earth to Teresa!" Susan called. "Come on, girl! We have work to do."

"Oh, isn't it just a dream, Susan? A total dream. One from which I hope I never awaken."

Chapter Three

"I can't believe my mom is actually coming to visit," Teresa said. "It's been so long since I've seen her."

"Of course she'd come for your wedding," Susan responded. "What mother would miss her daughter's wedding? And besides, she hasn't seen Samuel since you left."

The two young women were waiting in the afternoon sunlight, and Toby was tied to a light pole at the gas station. The sounds of traffic rose and fell on the main road leading through the small town of Livonia. Vehicles coming into town slowed at the speed-limit sign, but accelerated when they caught sight of the open fields beyond the few houses.

Teresa looked down the street in the direction the bus would be coming from. She played with her bonnet strings until she noticed Susan looking at her with raised eyebrows. "Sorry," Teresa muttered. "But when Mom sees me for the first time in Amish clothing, it will be quite a shock. I feel like a completely different person now. She'll think I'm from Mars or something."

Susan laughed. "I'm sure she's seen Amish people before. You told me you used to watch movies about the Amish when you lived in Asbury Park. Your mom must have seen some of those."

"I guess so," Teresa said, crossing her arms and then letting them drop to her sides. "It's just that I'm so nervous. It seems like it's been years and years."

"It hasn't been that long," Susan said. "Calm down. We got here a bit early."

Teresa peered down the road again. "I can hardly stand it! What if the bus doesn't stop? This isn't a regular stop."

"We'll step further out toward the street when we see the Greyhound coming," Susan said. "The driver will see us. He'll know that someone from the Amish either wants to get on or is waiting for relatives or friends."

Teresa fidgeted as the minutes ticked past. "Mom never thought I could make it in your world." Teresa's face was pensive. "I think she didn't want to come until she was sure I wouldn't be racing back with her to Asbury Park."

Susan laughed. "Well, getting married to an Amish man certainly makes the move pretty permanent, I'd say."

Teresa smiled. "I guess it does. I so hope Mom decides to stay on for a while. That would be great."

"Does she plan to?" Susan asked, watching the road.

"I don't know, but it wouldn't surprise me. She doesn't have much reason to stay in Asbury Park."

"Well, you know she's welcome anytime. Ah, here comes the bus. Looks like your mother has arrived in Amish country."

"*Da Hah*, please..." Teresa's voiced trailed off as she stared at the bus. "Please let Mom still like me...even though I've changed."

"Come!" Susan pulled on Teresa's hand. "We need to stand closer to the road."

Trembling, Teresa followed.

The huge bus slowed to turn into the gas station and then stopped in front of them.

"Mom!" Teresa hollered as the form of a woman stood up inside the bus and walked forward. Teresa ran toward the bus steps, while Susan stayed a few steps behind.

This was Teresa's moment. Her first meeting with her mother since she had left Asbury Park after baby Samuel had been born. They should have a few moments to themselves.

Teresa looked up the bus steps, her face expectant. Maurice appeared and made her way down the steps.

"Mom, it's me!" Teresa cried out.

A smile started at the corners of Maurice's mouth and spread across her face.

"Teresa!" she said, pushing forward into her daughter's arms and exchanging kisses on the cheek.

The bus driver appeared and stood still for a few moments, watching as the two women, one in *Englisha* dress and the other in Amish attire, hugged each other. Finally he cleared his throat. "Excuse me, ma'am, but I need to get your luggage."

The two didn't seem to hear him, so Susan tapped Teresa on the shoulder. The two women parted, smiling at each other as they moved away from the side of the bus.

The driver opened the luggage compartment. "Nothing like mother and daughter reunions," he said to Susan.

Maurice stepped up and pointed out her suitcase.

The driver pulled it from the compartment and set it on the pavement. "You folks have a good day now," he said as he slid the large metal door shut. He climbed into the bus and closed the door.

"Thank you," Susan called after him.

The motor roared as the bus pulled away.

When the sound had faded, Teresa turned to her mom. "Mom, do you remember Susan?"

"I certainly do," Maurice said. "Susan, thank you so much for all you've done for my daughter. She looks very happy."

"You're welcome," Susan replied. "Teresa has taken great care of herself and baby Samuel. She's looking forward to telling you about the adventures she's been having since she arrived."

"Adventures? In Amish country?" Maurice raised her eyebrows.

"Believe me, Mom, it's not boring around here," Teresa said.

"Well, okay, if you say so," Maurice said with a laugh. "I assume you're not marrying some boring farmer? Since you didn't send me any pictures, how would I know? I can't even imagine what an Amish farmer looks like."

"James is the best-looking man around! And Amish people don't send out pictures with wedding invitations. In fact, they don't take pictures at all."

"Oh sure, I remember now. I really don't know that much about the Amish."

Susan stepped forward, picked up the suitcase, and carried it toward the buggy. She called over her shoulder, "Let's go! We can talk on the way."

"How was your trip on the bus?" Teresa asked as they followed Susan.

"Not too bad. I don't care much for buses though."

"Well," Susan said, "we have your room ready. You can sleep all night and all day tomorrow if you want. We plan to pamper you the entire time you're here."

Maurice laughed. "Let's start with instructions on how to climb into this chariot. I'm afraid this princess hasn't ridden in one before."

"Mom," Teresa said as Susan placed the suitcase behind the two bench seats, "it's very simple. Everything about the Amish is simple. You take a hold of this handle inside the buggy and pull yourself up. You're going to sit up front with Susan so you can see better. I'll ride in the back, but we can talk over the seat all the way home."

"Okay, here I go!" Maurice grasped the handle and pulled hard. With a groan she landed on the buggy seat. "My this chariot sits high in the sky."

"That's because you're used to riding in cars," Teresa said, jumping on the back step and then sitting on the seat.

"I like this!" Maurice said.

Susan climbed in, gathered up the reins, and slapped them gently on Toby's back to get him going.

"How far do we have to go?" Maurice asked.

"Only a few miles up the road. It will take us about twenty minutes," Susan said.

Maurice turned around to give Teresa another quick kiss on the cheek. "I still can't believe you're looking so well. Perhaps it's the country living."

"It's all the wonderful people. That and James. I can't wait for you to meet him! It won't be today though...or even tomorrow. James is out of town at an auction to buy some stuff for our place."

"I'm sure I'll see him soon enough, dear." Maurice looked down at the jeans she was wearing. "Looks like I'd better do some clothes shopping the first chance I get. I would have brought along a dress, but I don't own any. I didn't feel like visiting the Goodwill only to come away with something that still didn't look Amish enough to blend in. Susan, do you think your mother could perhaps lend me one of hers? At least until I can get into town? I doubt if I can fit into one of Teresa's or yours."

"We'll find something for you," Susan said. "But you don't have to dress like us. No one will mind. We understand that you come from a different world."

"What do you think, Teresa?" Maurice twisted to look over the seat.

"I think you should borrow some dresses," Teresa said. "They come with pins instead of buttons, but I'll help you figure it out. You'll feel much more comfortable during your visit if you feel like part of us. I'm sure you'll enjoy it more."

"I already know I'm going to enjoy it," Maurice said. "I want the Amish to feel comfortable around me."

"We'll accept you no matter what you wear," Susan assured Maurice.

"Mom, don't listen to Susan. If you want to experience everything, and I mean *everything*, you need to blend in as much as possible. You should even wear one of these *kapps*." Teresa pointed to her hat. "It's a unique and wonderful experience."

Maurice laughed. "I think you've sold me on the idea, Teresa. Bring out the Amish dresses and hats, Susan! This woman is getting into character!"

"Oh, Mom!" Teresa squealed. "This is going to be so wonderful. Why didn't I ask you here sooner? I just didn't have the courage. I wasn't sure if you'd come all this way."

"You didn't do anything wrong, sweetheart. I wouldn't have come a moment before this. I kept expecting to see you return with a look of defeat on your face. Only a wedding invitation convinced my hardened old soul that this Amish business wasn't a passing whim."

"Your heart isn't hardened, Mom." Teresa's voice caught. "You're very real...and very good. God has done so much more than I ever expected Him to do. And baby Samuel—he's going to have a father, a wonderful, real *father*."

"Yes, darling, that *is* wonderful." Maurice turned around in the seat again. "You know, all that time I listened to you talk about this Amish thing, well, I never in my wildest dreams ever thought it would come to this. I'm the one who should be saying I'm sorry because I didn't believe in you. I guess that's partly why I'm here. I wanted to say it to you in person."

"Mom, you don't have to apologize. I didn't expect you to believe in my dream. You did all you could. You allowed me to pursue it. A lot of mothers wouldn't have done that."

"That's nice of you to say," Maurice allowed.

"Are you still at that same house?" Susan asked, remembering the rickety stairs going up to the second floor and the peeling paint on the walls.

"No, I moved out soon after Teresa left. Where I am now isn't much better though."

"Have you thought about possibly staying here…longer?" Teresa asked as she leaned toward the front seat.

"I wasn't sure what it would be like. We'll have to see. But in the meantime, I plan to enjoy my daughter and grandson to the fullest."

"I sure hope you like it here!" Teresa exclaimed.

"We'll see," Maurice repeated and silence fell over the buggy.

Susan watched Maurice out of the corner of her eye as the older woman observed the passing landscape while Toby plodded along.

"Teresa and James have their own farm," Susan offered. "It's cleaned up now, but we're still in the process of fixing it up. Right now we're painting the master bedroom."

"I know how to paint!" Maurice exclaimed. "I certainly can help with that. Teresa, you never mentioned a farm. Do you really have one?"

Teresa laughed. "Yes, we do. What would Amish people do without their farms?"

"But you're so young, and this man of yours…is he much older?"

"He's my age."

Susan laughed. "You can be glad now you're not marrying old Yost Byler, Teresa. Your mom would have seen right through that one."

"Susan!" Teresa gasped. "Don't be saying stuff like that. Mom just got here."

"So you *do* have your secrets," Maurice said. "I can't wait for your adventure stories."

"They're *nice* secrets, Mom," Teresa said. "Nothing to be ashamed of or worried about."

Chapter Four

Mamm was waiting on the front porch swing when Susan turned Toby down the driveway. The rays of the early afternoon sunlight reached between the leaves on the shade trees and played on *Mamm*'s face.

Seated beside Susan on the buggy seat, Maurice gasped, her hand flying to her mouth.

"What's wrong, Mom?" Teresa asked quickly, leaning forward.

"It's just so *beautiful*...so Norman Rockwell like," Maurice said. "It's almost not real. And that woman on the front porch—she looks so angelic."

"That's my *mamm*," Susan said. "She's probably taking a short afternoon break."

"From the preparations for my wedding," Teresa explained. "These people have been working from dawn to dusk to give me a real Amish wedding."

"Well, God bless them!" Maurice said. "That's a very wonderful thing they're doing."

Susan pulled Toby to a stop by the house. Teresa climbed out and stood beside the buggy's front passenger door. She held her hand up to her mother. "Do you need help getting down?"

"I'm not an invalid," Maurice said. "I'll get down by myself."

Susan held the reins firmly, keeping Toby still as Maurice stepped down from the buggy, clinging to one side for balance.

When she touched ground, Susan said, "Good job! You'll be a pro at this in no time."

"No doubt about that," Maurice said.

Susan climbed out of the buggy and stood by Toby's head.

Mamm was already making her way to the buggy. When she arrived, Susan said, "Maurice, this is Anna, my *mamm*. *Mamm* this is Maurice, Teresa's *mamm*."

"Mrs. Hostetler," Maurice said, stepping forward. "I'm so glad to finally meet you. You have been taking fantastic care of Teresa. I don't think I've ever seen her looking better."

"We try." *Mamm* smiled and extended her hand. "And call me Anna. We go by our common names around here. It's simpler that way."

"Well, that's certainly in keeping with your simple lifestyle," Maurice said.

"So you came all the way from New Jersey?" *Mamm* asked.

"Yes. From Asbury Park. Thank you so much for inviting me."

"You're surely welcome. Tell me, did you see much of Susan when she lived in Asbury Park?"

"Only the few times she came over to help Teresa. She always brought us pies. Susan bakes awesome peach pies. You have a very wonderful daughter, Anna. Girls like ours don't come better."

Susan felt her ears grow red. She protested, "I'm not good all the time, you know."

"Well, *most* of the time," Maurice corrected with a laugh.

Anna smiled. "It's nice to hear Susan was behaving herself."

"*Mamm!* You know I was behaving myself," Susan protested.

"*Yah*, of course," *Mamm* added. "I'm just teasing. Now, Maurice, would you like to be shown your room? I'm sure you're tired after that long bus trip. I know I always am."

"Well..." Maurice cleared her throat. "Susan said something about getting me some appropriate clothing. Some Amish things. Do you think that's possible? I know the wedding's not yet, but I don't want to go around standing out so much. I see that plainly now."

"You want to wear our clothing?" *Mamm* looked surprised. "Did someone say you had to?"

"No, no one said that," Maurice said. "The truth is, I think I'd *like* to wear your kind of clothing."

"Oh!" *Mamm* said. "I guess we'll have to see what can be done then. Susan, why don't you drive on down to Ada's and see if she can spare a few dresses. Maurice looks about her size."

"Would that be a compliment?" Maurice asked with a hint of a smile.

"Believe me, it's a compliment," Susan said. "Shall I go now, *Mamm*?"

"Yes. Take the buggy; don't walk. You won't want to carry any dresses Ada gives you. They might be too heavy for that distance. While you're gone, I'll show Maurice her room." *Mamm* reached for the suitcase sitting on the ground.

"Oh no you don't." Maurice shook her head. "No maid service in Amish country, I'm sure. I'm starting this visit off right."

Mamm smiled and backed up. Maurice picked up the suitcase and the two women went toward the house.

"Looks like those two hit it off well," Teresa said, watching them cross the lawn. When they made their way onto the porch, *Mamm* held the front door while Maurice entered. They shared a laugh about something as they disappeared inside.

"Don't you just love when mothers get along?" Susan commented as she walked to the buggy, Teresa at her side.

"Beats them not getting along. Especially when she's going to stay for at least a week."

"Maybe longer," Susan said. "Too bad Yost has an Amish girlfriend now."

"Stop it!" Teresa laughed. "You're something else, Susan!"

"Well, it was a thought," Susan said with a wry smile. "Are you going with me to Ada's?"

"I'd better stay and get back to work," Teresa said. "See you in a little bit."

Susan climbed aboard the buggy and drove out to the main road, heading south a short distance before pulling into her sister Ada's driveway. She left Toby by the hitching post without tying him up. He was tired enough to stay put while she dashed into the house.

"Good afternoon!" Ada's eldest girl, Joan, greeted Susan at the door.

"Hi," Susan said. "Is your *mamm* home?"

"Upstairs." Joan pointed. "Shall I call her?"

"I'll just run up." Susan opened the stairway door. "What are you doing on this nice summer afternoon?"

"Baking cookies." Joan beamed. "Do you want one?"

"I'd better pass, but they do smell wonderful. I'd better get upstairs and see your *mamm*."

"Hello!" Ada called from the top of the stairs.

"Don't come down," Susan said, taking the steps up two at a time.

"What's going on?" Ada asked.

"Teresa's *mamm* arrived, and she's asking for Amish dresses to wear. *Mamm* sent me over to ask if she can borrow several of yours. She's about your size."

"*Yah*, of course." Ada followed Susan downstairs and then led the way into the main bedroom. "What's Teresa's *mamm* like?"

"About as nice as Teresa, if that's possible."

"Is she divorced?"

"I don't know. Neither she nor Teresa have ever said."

"Well, it doesn't matter," Ada said. "Here, take one of my dark-blue dresses, this dark-green one, and maybe my light-blue Sunday dress in case she wants to come to services."

"Thanks!" Susan said, her arms full.

"Do you want help carrying the dresses?"

"No, I've got it. And thanks again."

"Can I give you at least one cookie?" Joan begged as she followed Susan to the front door.

Susan stopped and opened her mouth. Joan popped a cookie in. Susan chewed while Joan waited for the verdict, her hands twisted behind her back.

"They're wonderful! Now stop worrying, silly," Susan said, giving Joan a big smile.

Joan looked relieved and opened the door.

Susan exited the house and hurried across the yard, placed the dresses on the backseat of the buggy, and then climbed up. She waved goodbye to Joan who was still on the porch and then urged Toby forward. He shook his head, and then they were off.

When she arrived home, Steve came out of the barn to help her unhitch. He had a curious look on his face. "So you have a visitor in the house? Teresa's *mamm*?"

"*Yah*, just in for the wedding. Teresa hopes she'll stay a little longer."

"Is she as nice as Teresa?"

"Now look here, Teresa's already taken," Susan teased.

Steve laughed. "She's still a nice girl. Let me take Toby to the barn for you."

"Thanks." Susan held the shafts while Steve led Toby forward.

"And I guess you're pretty nice too," Steve said over his shoulder before marching toward the barn and leading the horse by the reins.

"What's that supposed to mean?" Susan shouted after him. "You *guess*?"

"Just teasing," he said looking at her as he opened the barn door. Without a backward glance, he disappeared into the dark interior.

"Well," Susan said, turning to walk toward the house, "such a tease."

Chapter Five

The evening supper table lay spread with mashed potatoes, gravy, meat casserole, green beans, creamed corn, and a garden salad. Pecan pies had been cooling on the counter since early morning. Susan took one last look around before hollering, "Supper's ready! Will someone call *Daett* in from the barn?"

"You can go," *Mamm* called back from the living room. "I'll run upstairs and get Teresa and her *mamm*."

As she walked out the washroom door, Susan glanced toward the barn. Out of the corner of her eye she caught a glimpse of a figure coming down the lane. She looked closer. "Joan!" she exclaimed. "What brings you out this time of the evening?"

Joan ran toward her and handed Susan a brown paper bag. "*Mamm* said to bring this dress up. I guess she thought of another one Teresa's *mamm* could use."

"That was nice of her. Isn't it suppertime by now?"

"*Yah*, soon. But there's plenty of time to get back. *Mamm* said to ask if the dresses fit."

"I don't know. Teresa's upstairs right now with her *mamm*, who is trying them on. I think we would have heard by now if they didn't fit."

"Okay, that's good. I guess I'll see you then." Joan turned to go, but Susan stopped her.

"Tell your *mamm* that if Steve doesn't come home for supper, he's here. I'm going to invite him to eat with us since we already have company tonight."

"Okay. But tell Steve not to rush if he does come home. *Mamm*'s running late, and he always arrives hungry."

"I'll tell him." Susan waved as Joan ran across the yard and headed toward home.

Young people! Susan thought. They have so much energy. But she wasn't that old herself. It must be Teresa's wedding coming up that made her feel so ancient. The wedding was a reminder that she was old enough to be married...and even have children of her own by now. Most Amish girls were married soon after their twenty-first birthdays. She was well past that now and growing older by the minute. Should she marry Thomas? But nothing could be done about marriage unless she agreed to Thomas's plans. Maybe she would yet...perhaps next fall, but not sooner.

Susan walked toward the barn, glancing up at the setting sun in the west. Bright red and orange colors were splashed across the sky. She didn't slow down to take it in. Supper was on the table, and this wasn't the time to stare at sunsets and ponder problems. After supper and with the dishes done there would be plenty of time for dark thoughts.

"*Daett!*" Susan called, opening the barn door. "Supper's ready!"

There was no answer, so she walked in. Moving past the horse stalls, she noticed one of the back barn doors was swinging on its hinges in the breeze. She could see into the open barnyard where her *daett* and Steve were lying on their backs under a hayrack.

"Supper's ready," she repeated. "Steve, you're invited to join us, if you wish."

"I'd like to, but Ada will wonder where I am." Steve scooted out and stood, stretching his back.

"I sent word with Joan that if you didn't show up in time for dinner it's because you accepted our invitation to eat with us."

Steve smiled. "Then I'll stay. If nothing else than to get an earlier supper."

Susan laughed. "Joan said you always arrive starved."

"That's me," he agreed, his smile broadening.

"We'll be right in then," *Daett* said, still working under the large machine. "As soon as I get this bolt in."

"Supper's on the table now," Susan said. "Remember, Teresa's *mamm* is here. Joan came by to bring some dresses for her. Maurice doesn't want to draw attention to herself, so she asked if she could wear Amish clothing. We borrowed some from Ada."

"Looks like we'd better get inside, Steve. We can't have the women waiting," *Daett* said.

"That's what they say," Steve said as he handed Menno an adjustable wrench.

Susan hurried back to the house, holding her apron off to the side so it wouldn't flap against her legs. She arrived at the washroom door breathless, thinking she ought to run more often. It felt good to move like a young girl again. Entering the kitchen, she uncovered the dishes, transferring the lids to the sink with one hand held underneath to catch any drips. When she turned around, Teresa was in the doorway, a smile on her face. "You have to come and see Mom in her Amish dress! She looks absolutely darling."

"Ada's dresses fit then?"

Teresa beamed. "Perfectly. I didn't have to adjust anything. Come!"

Susan following Teresa into the living room where Maurice stood by the front window. She was clutching her hands together. "How do I look, Susan? It feels strange to be dressed this way."

"You look great!" Susan walked around Maurice. "I almost wouldn't have known you."

"I agree, Maurice," *Mamm* said. "Ada's dress fits you perfectly. You look good enough for Sunday services."

"Thank you." Maurice's face glowed. "That makes me feel so much better."

"You look so good you'll set old Yost Byler's heart pounding right out of his chest!" Susan said with a laugh. "Even if he's already made other plans."

"Susan!" *Mamm* gasped. "Don't say things like that."

"Who is Yost Byler?" Maurice asked.

"He's an older bachelor in the community. He has a history, let's just put it that way for now," *Mamm* said. "Susan, you shouldn't tease like that."

"Never mind Yost," Susan declared. "If we don't eat soon, supper is going to be cold...and moving toward frostbite."

"You're my kind of girl," Maurice said. "Lead us to the food!"

Susan laughed. "This way to the kitchen!"

"Where's Menno?" *Mamm* asked, pausing to listen for sounds coming from the washroom.

"I told *Daett* to come right away, and I invited Steve to join us. I hope that's okay."

"That's fine with me. But isn't Ada expecting him?" *Mamm* stepped outside the washroom door and hollered, "Supper!"

"I sent word back with Joan that he might be having supper with us," Susan explained after her *mamm* stepped back into the kitchen.

As if they'd been waiting for the final call, *Daett* and Steve came out of the barn and rushed across the yard.

Mamm bustled about the kitchen, double-checking everything while they waited for the men to wash up. Sounds of splashing water came from the washroom sink, followed by footsteps. *Daett* led the way in. Steve followed, his face still wet and red from the cold water and towel rub. Susan almost laughed. He must be nervous if he scrubbed that hard.

"It's good to meet you," *Daett* was saying as he extended his hand to Maurice.

"I'm so glad to be here, Mr. Hostetler," Maurice said. "My daughter hasn't looked better or happier in her life. I can't thank you folks enough."

"Please call me Menno. And this is Steve Mast, our hired hand. We've enjoyed having Teresa here. It is *Da Hah*'s doing." *Daett* continued. "We have Him to thank for what we have and for what we can give." He turned to *Mamm.* "Is supper ready or not?"

"It's been ready for a long time," Susan told him. "So don't be acting like we're to blame if it's cold."

Daett smiled, twinkles in his eyes.

"You have a lovely family, Mr. Hostetler," Maurice said. "And a beautiful wife."

"*Yah*, that is true," *Daett* agreed. "Anna's been a jewel all the years

I've known her. There couldn't be a better wife anywhere. And, please, it's Menno. We don't do mister and missus around here. At least not if you're part of the community or family."

"I'm honored to be considered part of your family and community, even if it is only for a week or so," Maurice said.

Daett nodded. "Now, let's eat!"

"We will as soon as you stop talking long enough to pray," *Mamm* said with a straight face.

They sat down at the table. *Daett* bowed his head, and the rest of them followed.

"Our gracious and heavenly Father, we give You thanks tonight for the rich and plentiful food on this table, for the willing hands that prepared it, and for the lives that are gathered here," *Daett* prayed. "Bless us, O Father, with Your Holy Spirit and guide us in our walk with You. We seek to do Your will and to obey Your Word. We give You thanks tonight especially for Teresa and her *mamm*, Maurice. You have blessed Maurice with a safe trip and with a daughter who has blessed our lives these many months. Bless them now as they have blessed us. In the name of the Father, the Son, and the Holy Spirit. Amen."

"Thank you," Maurice whispered when they had raised their heads. "That was a nice prayer, and you are such wonderful people."

"Well," *Daett* protested, "we're not all that wonderful. We're just flesh and blood. Give *Da Hah* the thanks if there is any to be given." He smiled to soften his words.

"That's right," *Mamm* added. "Please pass the potatoes, Susan. And you can start the gravy, Teresa. There's plenty for everyone. I know we've all worked hard today, and there will be plenty of work tomorrow."

"Wow! I haven't seen this much food in a long time." Steve rubbed his flat stomach.

Mamm glared at him. "Now don't tell me Ada doesn't cook up a good meal for you."

"He's teasing," Susan said, looking at her *mamm*. "And Joan told me he comes home starving every night. I'm sure he gets plenty to eat."

"*Yah*, I was just teasing," Steve assured *Mamm* as he took a large helping of potatoes. "A growing boy needs lots of sustenance! Where the food goes, I have no idea."

"A working man needs his food," *Daett* said. "You do more than your share in the fields. I know where the food goes." Everyone laughed.

Daett turned to Maurice. "How was your trip?"

"Just great, thank you," Maurice replied. "And when I got here, I realized I needed different clothes. Your daughter Ada was kind enough to lend me some dresses."

"Susan mentioned it." *Daett* laughed. "It wasn't necessary, but you look very nice. I thought perhaps Teresa influenced you."

"I suppose she has—perhaps more than I know," Maurice said. "I do know Teresa is really coming along well. I can't wait to meet this young man of hers."

"Oh, he's nice enough," *Mamm* said. "You'll like him, I'm sure."

"If Teresa likes him, that's good enough for me," Maurice said.

Minutes passed in silence while they ate. Susan broke the quiet. "Do you have to go back out tonight yet, *Daett*? Is the hayrack fixed?"

Daett looked up. "*Nee*, but we can finish in the morning."

"I'll stay and help. You know that," Steve said, looking down at his empty plate.

Daett shook his head.

"Anyone have room for pecan pie?" *Mamm* asked when everyone was finished.

Everyone eagerly admitted they did.

Mamm got up and brought the pie over. She sliced it and spooned whipped cream on top of each piece before passing it down the table.

After eating a bite of pie, Maurice said, "This is delicious. And it's so peaceful around here. You can almost hear yourself breathe."

"I guess I'm used to it," *Mamm* said.

Steve placed his napkin on the table, pushed back his chair, and rose. "Thanks for supper. I do believe you're as good a cook as your daughter Ada."

"I should be!" *Mamm* said with a smile. "I taught her all she knows."

Steve laughed and left by way of the washroom door.

"I want to help with the supper dishes, Anna," Maurice said. "I don't know much about the life you people live, but I do know how to wash dishes."

"You don't have to," *Mamm* told her. "You just arrived today. You should relax."

"Please, I want to."

Mamm smiled and pointed toward the sink. "*Yah,* then. You can wash while we clean off the table. One of the girls will dry the dishes." Noticing Menno heading toward the living room, she added, "Menno, there's a letter that came today for you on the desk."

Chapter Six

Menno sat in the living room, the latest copy of *The Budget* unfolded in his lap, the letter Anna had mentioned in his hands. He glanced at the return address. Carol Hale, PO Box 3716, Fairway, Kansas. Menno read the name again. Do I know a Carol? He froze. This surely couldn't be...could it? The Carol he knew years ago? He took a deep breath. Her last name wasn't Hale. At least it wasn't back then. But she could have married by now...

Menno's hand shook. He thought of the *kafuffle* over Teresa's arrival in the community months ago. Her arrival with Samuel had, much to his surprise, stirred up memories he'd tried so hard to forget. His nerves must still be on edge, he decided. He had never confessed his transgression to Anna. Some things were simply too awful to bring up. Dating Carol had been one such sin—and it led to even more sins. But hadn't *Da Hah* shown great mercy even before he'd fully repented of his sin? And then Carol had told him the baby had been lost. So what was there to confess now? He had confessed to *Da Hah,* of course. And He was the One who already knew everything.

With his hands still shaking, Menno opened the letter and read slowly.

> *Dear Menno,*
>
> *I apologize first of all for using the term "dear" in the greeting, but Menno alone sounded too impersonal. I couldn't stand it. I'm sure you're surprised—to say the least—to receive a letter from me, if indeed this letter finds you. I'm guessing you're still part of the Amish community in which you were raised, but*

perhaps not. If this letter does find you, I'll trust that it was God's will. I'm surprised that I'm even writing to you. I never thought it would come to this, but it has.

Our child has found me, Menno. I guess first of all I owe you a confession. I lied all those years ago when I told you I had miscarried. In telling you I lost our child, I thought I was doing what was best for you and for me. Even so, I should have told you the truth.

And now, Menno, I have advanced ovarian cancer. I'm nearing the end and trusting I will soon see the face of God. I wish to be clear of this matter before that day. Even without Donald showing up, I have been greatly troubled through the years by how I treated you and our son.

The truth is that I was afraid of what you would do if you knew. The demands you might make. Your community—the little I knew of it—seemed threatening to me. And I didn't know how our baby would be accepted. I know it wasn't fair of me to keep this from you, and I apologize.

Donald, our son, was indeed born healthy, and I put him up for adoption, believing that was for the best. I do admit that part of me hoped he might eventually look for me. I left the best trail behind I could through the legal documents. And when he searched, he found me. He's a good young man, Menno. His adoptive father passed away several years ago, and his adoptive mother, Ruthann Fry, encouraged him to find me if that was his desire. I wish I could meet her, but it's not likely to happen. She did a wonderful job raising our Donald.

Now that I have met our son, I truly know what I have missed. Even my marriage and the birth of my three children—two boys and a girl—did not ease the pain of what I lost with Donald. I feel I owe you and him at least an opportunity to meet. I'm coming clean on this matter, Menno. I'm leaving Donald my journal, and your name is in there.

I'm sorry, Menno, that this must come as such a shock. Perhaps I should have come to you in person to ask your forgiveness. Maybe I'm still not handling this correctly. But with my health, I'm not able to do anything beyond writing this letter.

I'm sure you've married and probably have a family of your own. I regret any pain and trouble this might cause you. But Donald has come to me, and I can't keep this secret any longer. Enclosed is Donald's address. I've told him about you, but I haven't revealed where you probably live.

He wants to meet you, Menno. And surely in your heart you wish to know him. Write to him, please.

With my sincere apologies again,
Carol (Henderson) Hale

Menno laid the letter aside, covering it with a page from *The Budget*. He closed his eyes. What would Anna think about this? An *Englisha* child! His *Englisha* child with his *Englisha* girlfriend from his service days during the war. He'd worked in a hospital in St. Louis instead of going to Vietnam as a soldier because he was Amish and, therefore, refused to fight. And what would Deacon Ray say? He couldn't confess it to him…not Deacon Ray.

Anna had to be told. He had no choice. But when? He couldn't tell her now. There would be time later. They had a guest in the house, and Teresa's wedding was coming up. Nothing should be done before that. His past shouldn't mar the festivities. Teresa deserved that much consideration.

Sliding the letter into his pocket, Menno tried to read *The Budget*, but the words kept running together on the page.

That same evening, across two state lines, Donald Fry held a package in his hands. Carol had said to open it after her funeral. And the service had been today. He was nervous. So much emotion happening so quickly, but he had to know. Too many years had passed already. So much had been lost. All those years he could have known his birth mother. He wouldn't allow the same thing to happen with his birth father.

Donald sat down at the kitchen table and opened the box. Inside was a hard-covered journal, its edges bent and worn, the cover faded. Little scuffs pockmarked the surface. Apparently someone had handled the book roughly or frequently. He took out the journal and flipped open the pages to the last entry, about three quarters of the way toward the back.

May 10, 1969

My dear Journal, I have great news to report today. News that takes my breath away. I'm expecting again. The doctor confirmed it, or I wouldn't believe it. I'm sitting here in tears, feeling like a total wreck. Why I should break down like this after so many years is beyond me. I do know the reason. Somewhere in the back of my mind I believed God would never allow me to have another child. Not after giving up my dear baby boy. Even though I felt I had no choice and it was the best decision possible, that's not much comfort when my heart cries for my lost child.

I sit here taking deep breaths, telling myself that it's true. That just as Benjamin is real to me as a husband—just as his love is real—so this child will be real. After all I have lost, I'm being given another chance. I have to believe...to hope...that the broken pieces can really be put back together. Surely God can do that. My mind tells me He can, even when my pain says otherwise. How can God be so good to me after what I've done? His grace is amazing.

I think this will be my last entry. There has been too much sorrow recorded in these pages. The record laid down of my transgressions...of my losses. I've kept the worst parts from my dear Benjamin, but I know I've allowed myself to wallow in them. That must stop, and so too must this journal.

Let today begin a new book, I whisper. Let this day of the news of our baby—Benjamin's and mine—be a new beginning. A day when I will again live life to the fullest. A day when I will drink in all it has to give.

Today I begin a new journey with Benjamin and our child. A journey hopefully without so many tears. I will be a mother again, and, if God is willing, again and again. Oh, God, I can't thank You enough for allowing this to happen. Thank You for Benjamin, for our love together, and for this child. Thank You, thank You.

Goodbye, Journal. Let me kiss you one more time and then that will be it. Good night now and sleep well.

Donald wiped his brow with the back of his hand. This was his birth mother speaking to him from across the years. A voice he'd only heard in person during the short time after he'd found her. The fault was his own because he'd delayed his search for so long. Caught up in the dramas of his own life—his marriage to Sonia, Charles's birth, his father's illness, and then the divorce. Regardless, he should have looked for his birth mother much sooner.

He stared at the journal. At least he had this now. A token of her love, if nothing else. A touch of her even though she was physically gone. An opportunity to know her better. So he would read more. He would find more of her here. Her sorrow written in black and white. The pain she'd experienced while he was a child growing up in a good family and totally unaware of her existence.

Flipping to the front, Donald read the first entry.

June 6, 1960

I'm fifteen years old today, the first summer of living on the farm Mom and Dad purchased outside the city limits. Dad's a doctor, and he's worked hard to save enough for our new place. Mom grew up in Iowa as a farmer's daughter, and she's always wanted to get back to something resembling what she was used to.

Dad joked many times that love was enough. They would laugh, so I was always sure it was enough. But maybe one does need more than love. Mom is sure happy about the move—or maybe love brings what the loved one wishes. That's a nice thought. And it even looks good written down on the page.

I think I will also start a new venture—one brought on by our move. I will keep writing in this journal. I think it will be fun many years from now to look back over my life to see the highs and the lows. Hopefully there will be only a few lows. One needs some, I suppose, to deepen the soul. That's what Father Frank says, anyway. He said sadness brings out the color in life.

I guess that's true, although my life has plenty of color right now, inside and out. The front yard is blooming with a thousand dandelions. I've never seen anything like it in my life. Mom likes them, but Dad said something about white fluff balls appearing soon that will mess up the countryside. I'm not sure what he's talking about, but we shall see. Mom gave him a kiss after his muttered remark, saying, "Thank you anyway, Joe. It's so nice of you to indulge me like this."

I hope I meet a man someday who indulges me like Dad does Mom!

The other evening I saw a gorgeous sunset. Such colors you have never seen in all your life. Nothing like what we had in the city. The sky was painted with yellow, red, blue, and even purple mixed all together in long streaks. For some reason I started thinking about my future husband—whoever he will be. Sometimes I feel so other-worldly. I wonder why the man I will love couldn't be from someplace else, like another world maybe. Perhaps Mars or Jupiter. He could at least be from someplace I haven't been. Wouldn't that be wonderful? He'd speak another language, maybe French or Spanish. We'd laugh together and tell each other tales of how we were brought up. It would take weeks and weeks just to cover all that. We could fill the time between kisses right well.

Mom wants me to help with the laundry now, so I'd better run. I will keep this our little secret and visit you as often as I can.

To a long and happy summer and to many happy years ahead of us!

Donald turned the page to the next entry. He read, skipped a few pages, and read again. He would return later for a more thorough reading. Somewhere in here was the information he wanted.

June 14, 1960

Hello there! I'm back. Not as quickly as I had hoped, but I haven't forgotten you. Life on a farm is much busier than I ever thought possible. Right now I'm so happy I could burst! I don't care how hard I have to work. This joy of country living is worth all the sweat and pain.

Mom took me into town today, a small place not far from us. It's nothing like the big city. We stopped in at a dusty old feed mill, its name written in faded letters over the front door. Inside they had a wire cage with three of the cutest little puppies inside, all bundles and bounces. Mom didn't say a word. She just took me up to the cage and pointed.

I stood there for a long time, not wanting to believe it. Was one of them going to be mine? I looked up at Mom, and she was smiling. I knew it was true!

"Which one will it be?" Mom asked.

I closed my eyes because I didn't know which one to pick. I couldn't stand taking one of them and leaving the others. It seems like one of those sins Father Frank is always speaking about. An awful one at that. How could one puppy be better than the others? So I opened the door, and all three of them looked at me. That's when I closed my eyes and stuck out my hand. For a long time nothing happened. Then one of them touched my fingers with its nose. I could barely feel it, so light and tender was his touch.

I opened my eyes and grabbed him. A kiss is always the true test of love. I know it! He's the cutest, most loving little bundle of fur you ever saw. I've named him Bosky for some crazy reason. Bosky is a late–sixteenth-century word used to describe a countryside covered with dense bushes. I feel like that—densely surrounded by love.

Mom lets me keep Bosky in the house only a few minutes at a time. Even then he has to be watched carefully for you know what. I told Mom I would house train him quickly, but she is having none of that. Bosky stays outside most of the time. "This is a farm," Mom told me. "And on farms the dogs stay outside."

"Well, Bosky isn't a dog yet. He's a puppy, and his kisses are the sweetest things I've ever felt moving across my face. I know I will always love him, and he will always love me. Even after we're both dead and gone our love will exist.

When I ran around in the yard with him after we came home, Mom had the biggest smile on her face.

"He'll be good for you," she said. "I'm glad you're getting to grow up in the country."

I'm also glad! I think I knew I'd be glad even before my world contained wonderful things like puppy kisses. I also think this is how I will find the perfect man someday. I will close my eyes and see if he kisses me. How can that ever go wrong? Bosky is my proof that it works.

Donald smiled at his mom's girlish enthusiasm. He flipped pages, pausing to wait for his eyes to clear before he scanned the words again. How old was his mother when she met his father? Was he mentioned in this journal? That was the burning question. Surely Carol wrote about him. She wouldn't leave out such an important point in her life. He wanted to know everything about her and him, even with the pain the knowledge brought. Who was his birth father?

He scanned the pages and stopped at the entry dated January 12. Carol would have been nineteen, he figured.

I'm working at a part-time job in a St. Louis hospital while I go to school. To say I'm excited is the understatement of the year. There are so many new and wonderful things going on!

First of all, thanks must go to Dad for helping me land this job. He won't admit it, but I know he pulled a few strings with his friends. Not that I'm complaining because even if he did help, I'm still feeling all grown-up and on my own.

For a farm girl, I'm sure enjoying the city. Perhaps I have more of Dad in me than Mom wants to admit. I know I love both of them. I suppose one can be like that, having two loves at the same time. Mom has been dreaming of me marrying a farmer. I know because she told me. Dad wants me to succeed at nursing and eventually marry a doctor. He doesn't say so out loud, but it's not hard to figure out.

Donald scanned forward a few pages, stopping on February 15.

Hi there! I'm back, after a long, hard day's work. Although I'm on my feet all day, everyone here is absolutely wonderful to work with and for. I wonder if Dad knew that when he asked me to choose St. Louis instead of Des Moines, which was my first choice. He hardly could have. I'm sure the people would have been just as nice there as they are here.

I finally took the time today to say hi to the cutest boy you can imagine. He's not a doctor, but he's quite fascinating. I'd seen him earlier and asked around. One of the other nurses says he comes from a closed religious community that doesn't believe in war. I guess he's serving his military time working in a hospital under an alternative government program instead of being a soldier and fighting in Vietnam.

I wonder what his home community is like. I'm told he's Amish. He's obviously a farm boy—from the looks of his hands, at least. One of the girls said there are several Amish boys working in area hospitals.

I found out this guy's name is Menno, which I think is cute. He's got the sweetest smile, and it's even sweeter when he's nervous. I think I make him very nervous when I walk by. Even though he must be from a strange community and very religious, he doesn't look weird. He looks wholesome, healthy, country-raised—all those things you think of when someone says he grew up on a farm. I should know since I was raised on one!

This boy is country all the way through. I can see it in the way he handles his hands, the way he smiles, his hesitation, even in his walk. I find myself liking him more every time I see him and he smiles at me.

I would like him to ask me out, but we haven't even spoken! We just exchange looks and smiles whenever I walk by. He does always smile at me though. That's a good sign! I hope he'll ask me out sometime! I hope he doesn't think our worlds are too far apart. I'm religious, aren't I? I never thought love and religion had much to do with each other, but I'm sure they do somehow. Devotion, giving of one's self, isn't that what religion is? Perhaps we have a lot in common!

Donald paused. Was this young Amish man his father? He read the next entry.

February 21, 1964

The girls are all abuzz about the new singing group that has come over from Britain. The Beatles they're called. I finally listened to their songs, and I could think of nothing afterward but Menno. I made a special trip past where he works on my lunch hour to say hi. I decided if he's too shy to talk to me, maybe I should start the ball rolling.

"Hi," he said with that crooked, boyish smile.

I felt giddy but I said, "So you're an Amish boy from Indiana."

He laughed and said, "How did you know? Do I have hay sticking out of my hair?"

So he has a sense of humor! I thought. Wow! This is getting better all the time.

"I didn't notice any hay," I said. "The girls told me there are more Amish working at the hospitals around here. Your people object to the war, right?"

His smile disappeared and he asked me, "Do you have a problem with that?"

"Of course not," I said. "I think that's wonderful. Vietnam is an awful war. Thousands of people are dying unnecessarily. I'm glad some people are taking a stand against killing."

"We Amish don't kill people," he said. "Never!"

Dad doesn't know how much I oppose the war. I've mentioned it only a few times at home. Mom sympathizes but Dad just gets this "parents know better" look. "You'll understand someday, Carol," he always says. "There are times for war, just as there are times for peace. The Bible says so. And this is the time for war. If we don't stand up for the country, who will?"

I don't mind standing up for countries, like when Hitler invaded Europe. But who did the Vietnamese invade? They're just trying to hold on to their own country. I think we ought to mind our own business, and let them live their own lives.

Donald skipped ahead a week.

February 28, 1964

We're having a doing at Bobby's place on Saturday night. I point-blank told Menno this afternoon, "You're welcome to attend. You can come with me if you want to go." This seems to be my lot in life—making the first move when it comes to boys. But the sparkle in Menno's eyes was quite a reward!

He said, "Really? You're inviting me?"

I told him, "Well, it's nothing special, really. But the boys will be playing Beatles records, and we'll be dancing and eating food and chips and stuff."

"So where is it at?" he asked.

"Bobby Russell's place. Do you have a car?" I was sure he didn't, but I didn't want to embarrass him.

"No, I don't," he said. "But I can take the bus or hire a taxi."

"Better yet, why don't I pick you up?" I said. "Outside the hospital at six on Saturday?"

Without hesitating he said, "I'll be ready!" So I have my first date with Menno the Amish man. Hopefully if all goes well, he'll have enough nerve to ask me out himself the next time. I think he will. He seems to be a good man—sweet, gentle, and thoughtful.

February 29, 1964

Wow! Menno was so good looking last night in a new pair of jeans. I picked him up at the hospital, and he admitted he'd gone out and bought them to wear to the party. He must have seen the puzzled look on my face because he said, "I don't have Englisha *clothing."*

*"*Englisha*? What is* Englisha*?" I asked.*

He laughed and said, "Anyone who isn't Amish or from the family of faith is referred to as Englisha*. Things outside the Amish world are referred to as* Englisha*. It's our way of talking, I guess."*

I didn't really understand, so I changed the subject. "Do you know who the Beatles are?"

He shook his head.

"I suppose they haven't made it to Amish country yet."

Menno laughed and said, "I think that's pretty certain!"

"Why?" I asked. "Don't you listen to the radio where you're from?"

"No, we don't. We live in a completely different world."

"Well then," I said, "welcome to my world. Would you like to hear one of their songs?"

"Sure!" he said.

I turned on the car radio. We listened to the Beach Boys, Ricky Nelson, and a couple of other singers I wasn't familiar with, but then my favorite song came on: "All I've Got to Do" by the Beatles. When it was over I asked Menno if he liked it. And do you know what he did? He looked perplexed! He said, "Well, it must be good…if you like it."

"I don't know about that," I told him. "But lots of people like the Beatles, so it's not just my opinion. I hope you learn to like them."

"I hope so too," he said. "If you like them, I want to like them."

He didn't seem nervous at all!

"Are all Amish boys this plain speaking?" I asked. "Or is it because you grew up on a farm?"

"I don't know," he said. "I've never talked much with girls."

"You look old enough to have gone out with girls."

"Perhaps."

"Did someone break your heart?"

He smiled at that one. "No, I just didn't want involvement with girls until this is over."

"This what?"

"My government service," he said.

I told him again how strongly I felt about the war. He didn't disagree, although he seemed more opposed to all wars rather than this particular one.

When we arrived at Bobby's, I introduced him around. He didn't seem to pay much attention though. I think he was too busy watching me! I've never been with a boy who stared at me as much as he does. It was a bit strange, but it was also nice. Menno seemed totally taken with me, and he looked at me like I was fragile and might break.

The boys started the music, and I danced a few times with friends. Menno sat on the sidelines, which didn't surprise me. I figured he'd never danced in his life.

"Come on!" I finally told him, grabbing his arm.

"I don't know how," he objected. But he came out on the floor.

He stumbled through the steps, but he didn't look too nervous.

"Relax." I told him. "You'll get it."

Menno had the sweetest smile on his face as we danced. I declare, he was soon better at it than I was. He's got natural rhythm or something. He squeezed my hand when we danced to a slow song. After what seemed like hours, Menno led me over to the sidelines to sit down.

While the others danced, he turned to me. Then he kissed me! Wow! He was so gentle. And he kissed me so slowly. It was like the touch of a breeze on my face. It was pure heaven. And I knew I loved him.

And I know he loves me. He told me so when I dropped him off at his apartment. He asked me to go out with him!

April 2, 1964

Spring has arrived in St. Louis, but I can think of little besides Menno and how much he means to me. How can someone love a man so much and be loved back so much? We never talk about what lies ahead of us. I know there are many differences between us, but why can't they be solved? Love can solve anything, can it not?

May 11, 1964

Another party—at my place this time. Menno came, of course. He still doesn't own a car, which bothers me a little. Does he think about the future and about us? We are so much in love, so why disturb the sacred with questions? It will always be enough to know that I was privileged to have once loved such a man.

June 16, 1964

Menno was here last night, and we had another of our sweet times together. When he was leaving, I almost asked him what he plans to do when his time of service is over. But I couldn't get up the courage. Menno must have sensed my troubled spirit because he finally told me he's returning home soon.

I know he was just talking for a visit, but I think he meant something beyond that. I could see it in his eyes. He's never going to leave what he grew up with. And I doubt if I can go his way. I could visit his folks and find out. But with the little hints Menno drops, I don't think such a life would be for me. We are worlds apart. Yet surely somehow love can bridge the gap, can't it? I think it will have to or my heart will be torn apart. And yet how? I cannot begin to imagine.

July 10, 1964

The worst thing has happened. I thought in my foolishness that this might even draw us together into a permanent union as man and wife. Perhaps that's why I was careless, but I don't even want to think about the reasons now. I will have to be strong and brave for the both of us. If I really love Menno, I will do what is best for him.

I will tell him what isn't true to save what is true. I love Menno too much to destroy what he counts so precious at home.

After all these months, I know him well enough to understand how he thinks. He's going back to a world I have never been a part of. And it's a world I know I never can be a part of.

I will tell him tomorrow what the doctor said...and what the doctor didn't say. That I am with child...and that I lost the child.

It will be sad for him. He will not want to think of a baby—his baby—dying, even if it means things will work out better in the long run. The fact is, Menno leaves in a few weeks. Not for a visit but because his term of service is over. I will not be showing before he leaves, and he never needs to know the truth.

I pray that God will give him a wife and children who will love him as Menno deserves to be loved. For me, it will be enough if I'm able to find a decent home for our child. I will then spend my life in sackcloth and ashes. That's all I am worthy of. This was never Menno's plan...it was mine. And I need to be the one to decide what will make all three of us the happiest.

Donald closed the tablet. So his father's name was Menno. But Menno *what*? He would look tomorrow for more clues, reading more thoroughly instead of skipping dates. He would look for a last name and, above all, a location. Surely Carol had mentioned it somewhere.

If not, he would still find his birth father somehow and approach him cautiously. Perhaps his birth father wouldn't be so anxious to meet him, especially if he now had a wife and children and perhaps even grandchildren. And certainly if he was still living in that strange religious community—the Amish—of his.

Chapter Seven

The next morning, with the wedding quickly approaching in two days, the preparations were fully underway. For her part, Susan was sweeping the cobwebs from the barn beams. Maurice showed up in a white apron and carrying a broom.

"Your mom sent me to help," she chirped.

"But this is dirty work!" Susan exclaimed. "And you're a guest."

Maurice didn't hesitate. "Nonsense. So how much more do you have to do?"

"I just started. All of this area where the service will be held has to be swept down."

"This is one thing I know how to do, and I'm helping," Maurice stated. "Your mom and sisters are baking up a storm, and I'm in the way in the kitchen."

"There must be *something* you can do in the house," Susan insisted. "Anything would be better than sweeping down the barn beams."

Maurice shook her head, taking in the long beams with a steady glare. "Spiderwebs here I come!" Maurice waved her broom like a weapon.

Susan laughed and resumed her sweeping.

Maurice pawed fiercely at the stubborn webs above her, pausing to say, "So, you really will be having the wedding in here. I'm having a hard time imagining it."

Susan stopped for a moment. "Well, the men will have the horses outside for the day. And they will either clean the harnesses or move them. The stalls will be all cleaned out and fresh straw put down. Things will look much better by the time James and Teresa walk in together."

"That's a nice young man your dad's got working for him," Maurice said, sweeping again.

"Steve? Yes, he is." Susan also resumed her work.

"Is there anything between the two of you? I noticed you invited him to supper the first night I was here."

Susan jerked to a stop. "He's more like a friend. I haven't known Steve that long because he's from another Amish community."

"You sure? I would declare he's sweet on you."

"Really?" Susan felt her neck growing warm. "Steve's just a friend. And I'm seeing someone else. Didn't Teresa tell you?"

Maurice smiled. "Teresa did tell me about a young man, and I guess his name isn't Steve. Well, it's none of my business. Tell me more about Teresa and James. She gave me only the bare details. I don't think she's telling me everything."

"So what did she tell you?"

"That James's father used to have objections about her because of Samuel. That I believe. I mean, you people are living pretty holy lives here. And then Teresa was supposed to marry this Yost fellow, but he dropped her for some reason. She wouldn't tell me why."

Susan grimaced. "I guess we're all a little embarrassed over what happened to Teresa because of Yost. And the reason she's not telling you is that she's trying to be nice. Thankfully, someone got everything figured out before it was too late."

"So was Teresa in love with this Yost? Did he dump her? I have a hard time imagining that. And she's never had much of a thing for older guys."

"No," Susan said. "Yost called off their relationship for…um…'personal reasons,' shall we say."

"You need to be more specific than that, Susan. Teresa's my daughter, and I think I have a right to know what happened. And what was Teresa doing with him in the first place?"

"Okay, but please don't tell *Mamm* this. I never told anyone else, and neither has Teresa, that I know of. The only reason I know is because

I was with Teresa the day we went to clean his house. That's when Yost told Teresa their age difference was simply too much for him. That he didn't want her bearing children far into his old age. Now, I'm not sure that was his real reason, but that's what he told us."

"That's funny." Maurice burst out laughing. "Why was the old fogy dating her in the first place?"

"They never really dated. They talked to each other a few times. You know how badly Teresa wanted to join the community. She was willing to do anything to accomplish that for baby Samuel's sake."

"It still makes no sense to me," Maurice whacked at some spiderwebs spun around a beam.

"I guess I'll have to tell you our secrets." Susan sighed. "There was quite an uproar when Teresa first came—about her having a child without a husband."

"I'm not surprised. I always thought Teresa's desire was a wild goose chase. But she had her heart set on her dream."

"The solution one of the ministers came up with was to have Teresa accept Yost's offer to marry her—once she was baptized, of course."

"Sort of nip any problems in the bud?"

"I guess," Susan said. "I'm sure you think this sounds old-fashioned and unfair."

"And Teresa went along with the plan?" Maurice wasn't sweeping any longer.

"Much too willingly, I thought. I guess she didn't think she had any choice if she wanted Samuel to be raised among the Amish. Even after the ministers saw how sincere Teresa was and backed off the marriage requirement, Teresa stuck with the plan. And then James stood up for Teresa, which upset his father. James's father is a deacon. He objected so strongly to James and Teresa's budding feelings for each other that Teresa was even more determined to avoid trouble by sticking with her plans to marry Yost."

"Oh, the ways of mice and men," Maurice muttered. "But I can't blame anybody really. I suppose an unwed girl coming in from the outside with a child in tow could seem to threaten your way of life."

"At least it got worked out satisfactorily," Susan said. "And Teresa's faith is awesome! She really trusts God. She's been a great example to me...and to all of us."

"You can sure say that! Even to her old mother." Maurice stopped to wipe cobwebs from her face. "I'm glad to see Teresa happy and living among such sincere people."

"We're not perfect," Susan assured her.

"You try to be," Maurice said. "That goes a long way with me. So what is this old man like? He must not be too bad for Teresa to tolerate him."

"She's a saint, remember?"

"I'll still be looking forward to meeting the old fogy. He must be something."

Susan laughed. "His house took about as much cleaning as these beams are taking. His place was a major mess, and he desperately wanted a wife to cook and clean for him. That was about the list of requirements. Trouble is, no Amish women wanted him. Sometimes that happens with certain people. They develop a reputation—justified or otherwise—and never quite succeed in shaking it. At least Yost finally has found someone, from what it sounds like anyway."

Just then Teresa jerked open the barn door and paused for her eyes to adjust before exclaiming, "I can't believe you're out here, Mom, cleaning barn beams for my wedding."

"It's good exercise," Maurice said. "And I had to get away from all those women with their Betty Crocker cooking skills. I was ready to burst into tears from shame."

"Mom, you don't have to impress anyone," Teresa said.

"Well, I have to do something. I didn't come here to just sit around while others work hard on your wedding preparations."

Teresa stared across the barn before taking a few steps forward. "Come over here, Mom. I want you to see where James and I will be getting married."

Maurice followed Teresa with a puzzled look on her face.

"We're going to stand right *here*," Teresa said, stopping to motion with her hand. "The barn doors will be open, the sunlight will be flooding in on people's backs. There will be women seated over on this side, and men seated over there. The little boys on the front rows there and little girls on the front rows here. Everyone will be looking at us! The bishop will take our hands, asking us the sacred vows. Then we will be man and wife forever, as long as both of us shall live. These people believe in what we'll be promising. Only death will ever separate us in this world, Mom."

"That's very wonderful," Maurice agreed. "I'm glad I'm here to experience your dream with you. You inspire me, Teresa."

Teresa blushed, answering only after a long moment. "It's God who worked it all out, Mom. I don't take any of the credit. Even I never dreamed of this. Just having Samuel grow up with an Amish father would have been enough for me."

"Sweetheart," Maurice said, taking Teresa's hand, "only the best is good enough for you. God knows I could never give it to you. Come, give your old mom a hug."

Teresa's face beamed as she wrapped her arms around her mother. "You're not that old, Mom."

"Soon you'll have me believing that," Maurice said over Teresa's shoulder. "I tell you, there's something about this life that makes a person feel younger."

"It's their wholesome living, Mom," Teresa said, holding her mother at arm's length. "It's their honest, open-faced lives that makes them the way they are. They speak the truth even when it hurts."

"You're going to make me blush pretty soon," Susan interrupted. "We're not nearly as wonderful as you think. Any good thing we have or do comes from *Da Hah* alone."

"I don't think anyone disagrees with that," Maurice said. "Now, let's get some work done or those women in the house will think I can't work at all."

"You have been working!" Teresa protested.

"So what's next?" Maurice asked, ignoring Teresa's remark. "Lead us to our next duty, Susan."

"You're already sounding like one of us," Teresa said with a laugh. "I really think you should sit on the front porch swing for the rest of the day."

"I will not," Maurice said. "These old bones will toil until the sun goes down."

Susan joined in the laughter. "The garden is next on the list of things to do. It needs weeding."

"So even the garden gets dressed for the wedding day!" Maurice exclaimed. "I do like this more and more."

"I told you, Mom," Teresa said as they followed Susan across the yard. Arriving at the garden, they began at the side near the house, moving along on their hands and knees, making sure to pull even the smallest weeds. The three women worked away until Ada appeared with glasses of freshly pressed lemonade.

"Time for a break!" Ada hollered, her face beaming.

The three women got up and made their way to the edge of the garden. Ada handed them all ice-cold glasses.

Maurice took a sip. "This is heavenly! How do you folks do this?"

"Thanks," Ada said. "Fresh-squeezed lemons. One of the young girls made it. I'll tell her you liked it."

"Please do," Maurice said.

Teresa and Susan drank from their glasses and smiled their appreciation.

Ada asked Susan, "Do you need help out here? We could spare another person right now. We're almost done with the pies."

"No," Susan said, "we only have a few more feet to go."

"Okay then." Ada turned to leave. "I'm going home in a few minutes. My family will be crying for supper if I don't get back soon."

After Ada disappeared around the corner of the house, Susan walked back to the end of the garden row where she'd been working. She resumed her weeding. Teresa and her mother stayed behind, their voices rising and falling out of hearing distance. Susan smiled. They were lost in their own world, and they surely had much to speak of. Not only because of their long separation, but also because of the many changes that had occurred.

Maurice could have easily rejected her daughter for abandoning their life in the city, pushing her away because of the choices she'd made. Yet, instead, the two were reaching out to each other in a way they never had before.

Chapter Eight

That afternoon, as Thomas Stoll drove his buggy south on the gravel road, the rays of the setting sun flooded the side of his face. He squinted, turning his head before pulling down the rim of his hat. Troubled thoughts raced through his mind. Susan had finally invited him to stop by their place this week. But why hadn't she done so sooner? Was she having doubts again? He would be best man for Teresa's side of the family at the wedding, so this should give him quite a solid footing with Susan for the foreseeable future. And he was taking her home from the Sunday hymn singings again.

A smile crossed Thomas's face. He settled back into the buggy seat as the sun went behind low-hanging clouds on the horizon. Things would be in an uproar of busyness when he arrived at the Hostetler place. The wedding preparations were in full swing, so perhaps he should offer to help with the work this evening. A little thoughtfulness on his part couldn't do any harm, and it might just warm Susan's heart toward him all the more.

Thankfully this was finally happening. He had apologized often enough for the brief attention he'd paid to Eunice. And for the kiss, which he never should have done, of course. Thankfully Susan hadn't learned that while she was away in the *Englisha* world he'd gone on a date with Eunice. That itself was a miracle of sorts in this tight-knit community. Perhaps he should have told her about that date. It might have helped soothe Susan's hurt feelings sooner if she'd known he had pursued his attraction to Eunice just to make sure they were only a passing fancy. And that's how it had turned out.

Susan was the woman he wanted to marry. He'd wanted to marry her since his early teen years. They would have been married already if Susan had accepted his explanation about Eunice and hadn't overreacted. There never had been a reason for Susan to rush off to the *Englisha* world like she had. Everyone knew the *Englisha* offered no better solutions to matters of the heart than what the community had to give.

Thomas slowed down as the Hostetler farm came into view. The fields were laid out behind the barns in long, even squares, the corn almost ready for harvest. The hayfields were already in their second cutting. Menno had hired a new man for the summer—a situation Thomas hoped was temporary. First, because he should rightly be living on the farm this summer, learning how to farm by working alongside Menno. It wouldn't be long before Susan's father, due to his advancing age, might not wish to put the energy into training someone who hadn't grown up on a farm. But he had always dreamed of owning a farm, expensive as they were. He would have to pay Menno a fair price after Susan and he were married. He couldn't afford to make many mistakes in his farming practices because they could be costly. Things like crops planted on the wrong week. Hay cut when the weather wasn't right. Ruined hay could mean a winter spent having to purchase feed for the livestock, taking a serious cut out of the farm's profit margin.

That, of course, explained why Menno wanted a hired hand until Susan was married. Steve no doubt helped not only with the labor, but also with minimizing the risk of mistakes.

Thankfully, Susan seemed unaware of the sideways glances Steve was giving her at the hymn singings or the way Steve's face lit up when she spoke to him. How Susan failed to notice was hard to imagine, but hopefully this was a good sign.

Susan was quite *gut* looking. It was surprising that some other boy, perhaps better situated than he was, hadn't already made a move for her attention. They would have, he figured, if it hadn't been for the ruckus surrounding Susan bringing home that *Englisha* girl, Teresa. Well, Teresa wasn't exactly *Englisha* any longer. She was now almost like one of them. She could even talk the language decently, and his friend James sure was taken with her.

With everyone in a wedding mood, now would be the perfect moment to get Susan's promise of marriage.

Pulling on the lines, Thomas turned Freddy down the Hostetler driveway. A few buggies still sat near the barn and horses were tied to the fence. He stopped and jumped out to tie his horse. He'd unhitch after he talked to Susan.

Walking to the house, he knocked on the front door. It was answered moments later by Susan's *mamm.* With a surprised look, she said, "Thomas! Hello. We were too busy to notice someone else driving in, I guess."

"That's okay," Thomas said, pushing his hat back on his head. "Is Susan around? She said I could stop by and help."

"Of course." Anna turned to holler toward the back of the house. "Susan! There's someone here to see you!"

Susan appeared moments later, her hair hanging in strings out of the back of her *kapp*. Thomas beamed. Susan was even better looking in this state, he thought, than she was all fixed up on Sundays.

"Ah, so you've come." Susan pushed the stray hairs out of sight under her *kapp*. "I had almost forgotten."

Behind Susan two of her sisters' faces appeared around the kitchen doorway. Betsy and Miriam, Thomas noted. So those must be who the two buggies tied out by the fence belonged to. They smiled and disappeared again.

"I thought perhaps I was still in time to help out this evening. We had a job in the cabinet shop that ran late."

"Menno's still out in the barn with Steve doing chores," Anna said.

Being in the barn with Steve wouldn't be quite what he wanted to do, but Thomas found himself saying, "If that's what needs doing, then I'll help."

"That can wait. Come with me!" Susan pulled on his arm. He followed her out the door to the swing hanging from the porch ceiling, where she plopped down. "I need a rest, and they have things under control with the chores."

"It's nicer out here with you anyway," Thomas said.

Susan ignored him. "We've been working hard all day. This

afternoon we cleaned the barn beams and weeded the garden. You could have helped with that earlier."

"I would've been glad to, but things got busy at work, like I said."

"And earlier in the day I looked decent."

"You look beautiful," he said. "You really do."

"That silver tongue of yours." Susan sighed. "I hope you keep it to yourself around Eunice."

"Now please, Susan." He lifted both hands in a sign of surrender. "You know that's behind us. It's been behind us for a long time. I've done everything possible to make things right. You know I have, Susan. I love you more than I love any girl...or ever loved any girl."

She looked sideways at him. "How do I know you won't change your mind again? Perhaps even after you've said the vows? It's not like a promise kept you from running after Eunice the last time."

"You know I wouldn't do that to you, Susan. Our people don't do such things."

"I don't think you're being honest with me, Thomas."

Thomas took a deep breath. Should he or shouldn't he? It would be a great risk, but he obviously wasn't getting through to Susan now. "I'll tell you something you don't know and would never have found out. I know it might make me look bad, but that's how much I care about you."

"Okay." She was looking warily at him.

"While you were living in Asbury Park, I took Eunice home from one of the hymn singings."

"You did!" She sat bolt upright on the swing.

"It was only once, Susan. I thought I should find out for sure what I wanted to do. And I did find out. I found out I really do love you! Can't you see that?"

Susan was staring across the open hayfield, her eyes on the last light lingering on the horizon. "I'm too tired to fight with you right now, Thomas. It's not going to change anything."

"But nothing will change the way I feel about you, Susan." He took her hand in both of his. "You know that, don't you? Can't you find forgiveness in your heart?"

Susan shrugged. "That does make me feel some better, I guess. And I forgive you, Thomas. I know I'm not perfect myself."

"But you are!" he protested. "You're too perfect for me, Susan, and yet I keep dreaming that you'll someday return my love again. With all your heart. Remember how it used to be between us? How much fun we used to have together? Teasing each other in school. Me hiding your papers until your temper exploded. I'm still the same person, Susan. And you also are. We still love each other."

"Maybe so. I just wish we had what Teresa and James have."

"We once did, and we will again!" he declared. "And you can't compare yourself with other people. Even someone nice like Teresa. And they have suffered a lot. Like we have. Suffering makes people better."

When Susan said nothing, Thomas continued. "Can you imagine what it must be like to have a child outside of marriage and face people with that? It would have to destroy you or make you a saint."

"That's nice of you to say, Thomas." Susan took his hand and squeezed it. "I'm sorry. I really am trying to control my temper. And we did have some sweet times together. Remember the time I succeeded in throwing a snowball into your face? You looked so surprised. Like you never thought a girl could do that."

"You have surprised me a lot of times."

She came closer to him, nestling against him, leaning her head on his shoulder.

He smiled, holding her hand, "I'm sorry for what happened, Susan. I really am. Do you think we can get a fresh start? Maybe this wedding will be a good place to begin. Especially since James and Teresa are such good examples for us."

"They are," she agreed. "And perhaps we can. I know I would like to if we could. It would be nice not to have this hanging over our heads all the time."

"I agree."

They sat in silence for a while until Susan closed her eyes and started to drift off. Thomas gently lifted her head. "Susan, you're exhausted. You need some rest and so do I. Since there's nothing for me to do here, I'll go on home."

"Aren't you staying for supper? You're welcome, you know."

"It's tempting, but I better go," he said.

"Okay. I'll see you at the wedding."

"Until then." Thomas kissed her on the cheek and turned to leave. When he got to his buggy, he untied his horse, climbed inside the buggy, and guided Freddy around toward the road. As he drove his buggy out the driveway, he turned to wave at Susan, who was still sitting on the porch swing. She was a wonderful girl indeed. No matter how hard he had to work, he would be a fool to lose her again.

Chapter Nine

Thomas had no sooner left than Teresa came racing out the front door, slamming the screen door behind her. She bounced down on the swing beside Susan. Saying nothing to each other, the two watched Thomas's buggy get smaller and smaller. When he turned west, Teresa glanced at Susan. "You look happier than you have in a long time. Did you get things worked out between the two of you?"

"I think so." Susan sighed. "We had a good talk, at least. Thomas seems to be making a real effort at being honest and everything."

"I'm so happy for you." Teresa leaned across the swing to wrap Susan in a hug.

"Thank you." Susan jumped to her feet. "Now, I've taken up enough time sitting around. Is *Mamm* ready for supper?"

"Almost. Your sisters are getting ready to leave."

"Then I'll see if I can help with something," Susan said. She went inside.

Teresa stayed where she was, watching the sunlight fade from the sky. The golden haze hung on the horizon, prolonging the onset of darkness.

Interrupting her thoughts, Susan's two sisters came bustling out of the front door, their arms full of cleaning supplies and dishes. Teresa leaped to her feet, running over to take several of the items from their hands.

"We're fine," they protested, but she walked out to the buggies with them, helped them load their stuff, and held the horse's bridles while they climbed in.

"Thank you so much for everything," Teresa told each one. "I appreciate what you're doing for me."

Hearing soft footsteps behind her, she turned toward the barn to see the faint forms of *Daett* and Steve coming toward her.

"Has it been a *gut* day for you, Teresa?" *Daett* asked.

"A very *gut* day," Teresa replied. "I'm tired and aching, but very, very happy."

"That's *gut*," *Daett* said. "Now if we can keep you that way until after the wedding, everything will be just fine."

"I'll be perfectly happy until then. And that will be the most wonderful day of my life," Teresa said.

Daett smiled and Steve laughed. "Do you know if Anna has supper ready?" *Daett* asked. "I haven't heard anyone calling us. I suppose they got all wrapped up in the wedding work and forgot about us poor starving menfolk."

"Oh, you poor dears," Teresa said, taking *Daett*'s hand and attempting to lead him toward the house.

He laughed and turned to Steve. "I'll see you tomorrow then. We need to set aside some of our chore time to work on getting the place ready for the wedding. We only have tomorrow and then the wedding. Susan swept the cobwebs from the barn, but there's still lots to do before the big day." He paused and smiled at Teresa. "I should know by now how to do this with my eyes closed, what with eight daughters wed already."

Steve laughed and said, "And you still have Susan ahead of you yet." With that, he left for Ada's, cutting across the garden, his shape fading out of sight in the darkness behind the house.

"He's a *gut* man," *Daett* said. "He'll make someone a good husband someday."

"I wonder why he's not married already," Teresa said. "I don't know that much about your ways, but isn't it a little unusual for a man his age to be unwed?"

"Not if you're Yost Byler," *Daett* teased.

"Well, he's definitely not Yost Byler!" Teresa said. "*Daett*, thank you again for this wedding you're giving me. You're making me truly feel as if I were one of your daughters."

"Well, you know you've become almost like a daughter to me," *Daett* said. "That's hard to believe considering the short time you've been with us. Yet in a way, it seems like years already. I'm glad for the way things have turned out for you."

"You don't have to be so modest," Teresa said. "Susan told me she suspects you had a lot to do with persuading Deacon Ray. You know he took such a hard line with me at first. And now he's to become my father-in-law and the man couldn't be sweeter."

Daett smiled. "I wish you nothing but happiness as you and James start your new lives together. But I do wish to tell you, Teresa, that I haven't always done everything right in my life. I too have secrets that few know except *Da Hah*. Maybe that had more to do with how I handled things than you can imagine."

Teresa shook her head. "I can't imagine you doing a wild thing in your life. I suspect the worst you ever did was roll someone's outhouse on Halloween night."

Daett looked serious. "I did do that once, but there have been… other things. Things I now wish had never happened. But we can't go back and change the past."

Teresa held the washroom door open. *Daett* walked in, but he waited until she had washed her hands in the bowl and was drying them before he began to wash.

The kitchen door cracked open, and little fingers appeared around the edge.

"Oh, you little sweetheart, you!" Teresa cooed, kneeling down to swoop baby Samuel off the floor. She smothered his face with kisses. "Have they been keeping you upstairs all afternoon? But now you've come down to Mommy!"

"Da…da…" Samuel said, turning his face away.

"He's already trying to say daddy," Teresa gushed. "What do you think that means? Will my next baby be a boy since he's saying *daett* before *mamm*?"

Mamm came to the open door and said, "Oh that's just an old wives' tale. They never know what they're talking about. Now would the two of you quit chattering like blue jays and come inside? Supper is on the table."

"I didn't hear anyone call," *Daett* protested as he continued to dry his hands.

"Sometimes an old horse can find his own way into the barn," *Mamm* said. "We've been busy all day. I haven't had time to think."

"Well, I'm here now," *Daett* said. "And let me ask you something that I keep forgetting. Have you put in our word for the church benches yet?"

"*Yah*," *Mamm* said. "It's all arranged. Betsy's boy is bringing over the wagon tomorrow, and we'll fetch the benches then. Stop worrying, Menno. Right now you need to eat. Come in and sit down before you fall over."

Daett acted like he was tottering to the table, scraping the chair on the hardwood floor as he sat down. *Mamm* sat down beside him. Susan watched them out of the corner of her eye as she brought the bread over. She tried to keep from laughing. Teresa seated Samuel in his highchair before sliding onto the bench against the wall to sit beside her mom.

"Let us pray," *Daett* said, leading out as they bowed their heads. "Now unto the most gracious and mighty God, we give thanks tonight again for this food set before us..."

Teresa listened, remembering the first morning after she'd arrived from Asbury Park with Susan. At breakfast she had first heard *Daett* pray. How his deep voice had thrilled her to the depths of her heart. What confidence it had inspired in her. What hope had risen that things could really be like she had dreamed they would be. And even in the worst of the trouble that had followed, that awakened comfort had not been taken from her. She glanced over and could see her mom was experiencing the same thing. Tears were rolling down her cheeks. Teresa reached under the table and squeezed her mother's hand. It was so unusual to see her mother cry. It had been years since Teresa had seen this, not even during the hard years in Asbury Park.

"...And now the name of *Da Hah* be praised and glorified both with our mouths and with the works of our hands. Amen," *Daett* said.

Mamm looked over and noticed Maurice's tears. She rose and left the room. She returned quickly. It's a touching time for all of us," *Mamm* said as she handed a handkerchief to Maurice. "After marrying off eight girls, I haven't cried much for the last few. But I suppose there will be buckets of tears tomorrow at Teresa's wedding and even more when Susan's time comes."

Daett nodded in agreement as he dished meat casserole onto his plate. When he was done, he passed the dish on. Teresa took the casserole from his hands and placed a small amount on Samuel's plate.

Maurice wiped her eyes and took the dish when Teresa was done. She dished out a small portion onto her plate and handed it to Susan. When the food was passed to everyone, they ate in silence, the weariness of the day's work on their faces.

When they finished, *Mamm* brought out the cream pies. They were passed out, with each person taking a piece.

"That was good enough for kings and queens," *Daett* pronounced after he finished his serving. "If we dine this well at the wedding, I'll be putting on a few more pounds."

"You will!" *Mamm* affirmed.

They all laughed and bowed their heads for a silent prayer of thanks. Afterward, Teresa took Samuel upstairs to settle him in for the night. She came down in time to help with the last of the dishes. Maurice was washing, her hands and arms covered with suds all the way up to her elbows.

"Mom," Teresa whispered, walking up behind her, "you look so lovely tonight. I've never seen you like this before."

"It must be the country living," Maurice said, tears threatening again. "And the hard work. It makes a body weary and the soul light."

"I know what you mean," Teresa agreed. "May I help with anything?"

"We're done," *Mamm* said from the kitchen table. "But thanks, Teresa. You know, we're going to miss you when you move in with James. I hope you know that. Perhaps James and you will come home once in a while to pay us a visit on Sunday afternoons."

"I would love that," Teresa said.

"You are to always consider us as your second parents—after Maurice," *Mamm* said. "Don't ever forget that."

"I won't forget," Teresa said. "How could I? And how can I ever repay you for all this?"

"Regular visits home will be payment enough," *Mamm* replied with a smile. "That and seeing you and Samuel on Sundays. He's going to grow up to be a strong Amish boy."

"And he'll never know he wasn't born Amish," Teresa said. "I've almost forgotten myself." Teresa glanced up to meet Susan's gaze when she felt a light touch on her elbow. Susan motioned with her head toward Maurice. Turning toward her mom, Teresa saw tears running down her cheeks again. Teresa stepped up beside her mother and wrapped her arms around her neck. "I'm so glad you're here to enjoy this time with me. I wish you never had to leave. Don't you just want to stay with these people forever and ever?"

Maurice stroked the strands of hair hanging out from under Teresa's *kapp*, smiling through her tears. "I would love nothing better, sweetheart. I just don't know how that would work. I certainly couldn't stay here forever, no matter how nice that would be."

"I'm sure everyone here would love to have you stay as long as you want. James and I will put you up at our little house."

"No, I won't be the kind of mother who hangs around her married daughter's house and pokes her nose into business that isn't hers. But for a little while—and *only* a little while, it would be wonderful to stay with you. Thank you for inviting me!"

"It's all *Da Hah*'s doing," Teresa said.

"With a little help from you, I'm sure." Maurice smiled and stroked Teresa's arm.

Chapter Ten

Menno stirred long before the first steaks of dawn lit the eastern horizon. He pushed back the bedcovers, swung his legs over, and pulled on his socks. He finished dressing in the darkness. He felt his way out of the bedroom, his fingers finding the familiar door jamb within an inch, with the framed window fixed in his side vision.

Behind him Anna moved under the covers, and he turned to look back. The bed was only a shadow against the wall, her form hidden under the heavy quilt. She would not be up for a while yet, even on this, the day of Teresa's wedding. Soon buggy wheels would be turning into the driveway, the excited wedding party and the cooks arriving, but for now she could sleep.

He was the one who couldn't sleep. It was that letter Carol had sent. He was wondering whether he should answer it. Did he wish to see his son? Of course he did. He still couldn't believe it. He had a son! He still hadn't told anyone, not even Anna. But if he didn't gain control of his emotions soon, Anna would notice the struggle on his face. Then the sorrow that tugged on his heart would be unmasked.

Anna would find out, as would his daughters. Even Susan, whose heart was still healing from Thomas's betrayal. What would this do to her? Against his own sin, Thomas's faults looked like child's play. Menno had sinned greatly and betrayed the love of an *Englisha* girl. He had promised what he had not been able to give—security for her heart, a life together, and a home among her people.

Was this sin to follow him to his grave? Hadn't he atoned enough? If he hadn't repented, Teresa wouldn't be here now, her wedding day here. Hadn't he fought for her with both Deacon Ray and Yost Byler? Was that not of some value? And now Teresa's mother was here. The daughter and mother reunited in a place where *Da Hah* could minister to both. They were doing so in his house, under his roof, with his blessing. Yet the past wouldn't go away. And now he must surely tell Anna. She would be angry, but in the end she would understand. After all, it happened before they were together. Anna would probably know the best thing to do.

Menno groaned as he reached for a match and lit the kerosene lamp. With the soft light playing on his beard, he stared out the living room window, seeing only darkness. The time had come to share his burden. He must speak of his guilt. Anna would forgive and say words of wisdom as she always did in matters concerning their family.

Menno found his way slowly back into the bedroom, taking the lamp with him. Anna's startled face came up out of the covers before he closed the bedroom door.

"Please," he said, "don't be startled, Anna. I have something I need to talk to you about."

"Is someone sick? Has something happened?"

"*Nee*." Menno sat down beside her on the bed. "Everyone is okay. It is my heart that is not okay."

Anna shifted, pulling herself up. She sat propped against the wooden headboard. "You are a good man, Menno. All the community knows this. As do I. What is troubling you?"

"*Nee*, I only wish it were so." He paused. "Anna, I must tell you of a great sin I committed in my youth."

She was silent, listening.

He looked away. "When I was doing my alternative service in St. Louis, Anna, I dated an *Englisha* girl."

Her hand found his. "But you came home to me. That's what's important. The rest doesn't matter."

"There's more, Anna." Menno halted, unable to speak the words.

"What is it, Menno? You can tell me," Anna said, her hand rubbing his gently.

"Anna, I fathered a child in the *Englisha* world."

"What? A child, Menno? And you are just now telling me after all these years?"

He shook his head and pulled the envelope out of his pocket. "The letter with the news, it only came the other day. I thought the girl had lost the baby. That's what she told me before we parted." He handed it to her.

"And you never told anyone of this?" The envelope hung limp in her fingers. "Not even the bishop?"

"I spoke a general confession before my baptism, but I didn't talk of specifics."

"You were…you did this…with an *Englisha* girl?"

"Please don't be angry with me, Anna. I'm no longer a young man, and I have repented of this a thousand times."

She didn't look at him as she unfolded the letter and silently read the handwriting. When she was finished, she looked up. "Were you around until the time when this girl should have given birth?"

"*Nee*, my service time was over, and I left soon after she told me she'd lost the baby."

"Do you know what this could mean, Menno? Your son—he might come here…looking for you."

"I know. And I don't know what to do about it. Our girls…they must be told, but how will I ever tell them? It will hurt them so."

"What about me, Menno? Do you think I'm happy to hear this? I know I'm an old woman, but I still have a heart beating inside of me."

"I know you do." He took her into his arms. "I'm so sorry for what I did. You don't know how many times I've wished it could be undone, but it can't."

"So this is why you risked so much for Teresa? You understood her pain?"

"*Yah*…but I also love her as my own daughter. This is not a feeling I made up."

"I believe you." She stroked his arm. "In a way, I'm glad I didn't know of this before I was old. I have come to know your heart by now.

"After all these years, *Da Hah* has had compassion on you, and I can do no less, Menno. And this took place so many years ago. We will bear this burden together."

"I'm so sorry. Would you have wed me if you had known?"

"Perhaps." She met his eyes. "I don't know."

"You've been a wonderful *frau*, Anna. You are everything I could have hoped for. I have no regrets about our love and life together."

"You loved her, this other woman?"

"*Yah*, I cannot say I did not love her. But it was a long time ago. And my heart couldn't live in her world nor would she follow me back into my world. We parted in sorrow. It was a thing that could not be."

"If you were a young man and I a young woman, Menno, we would have ourselves a *gut* fight over this. And perhaps we will after Teresa's wedding. But for now, I will comfort myself in knowing that this explains something I've often wondered about you. There always was a sorrow that hung on you the days after each of our children were born. Daughters all of them. Were you hoping for a son, Menno?"

"Perhaps." He looked away. "But I am satisfied with what *Da Hah* gave. I was always thinking of what the other might have been. Asking what if the child had been born."

"You've been a *gut* man and a *gut* husband, Menno." She wrapped her arms around him. "Even though you've sinned, you've lived honorably since then."

"And it was a great sin." He spoke into the top of her hair, the length of his beard falling over her shoulder.

"It was, but so was Teresa's, and you forgave her. Welcomed the girl into your home. Promised her a wedding like she was one of your own daughters. If you can forgive Teresa, then I can forgive you."

Menno smiled as tears ran down his face.

"You're a wonderful woman, Anna. *Da Hah* has blessed me greatly."

Anna pushed him away. "Now, I have to get dressed before someone finds me still in bed. And you have a letter to write. You must write to this Donald...to your son."

"Oh, Anna! I knew you would know what to do. It will be a much better day now. I'm so sorry I didn't confide in you before."

"It may have been for the best, Menno. So let's not question the timing of *Da Hah* in bringing this to light now. He knows what is best for us and when. I'm comforted that you have finally told me."

Menno got up and walked out into the living room, leaving the lamp behind. The first streaks of dawn were in the sky, sending a soft glow through the window. He lit another kerosene lamp and sat down at the desk. He had a child in the *Englisha* world. A son. And now it was time to write him a letter.

Dear Son,

Christian greetings, though I don't have much claim to call myself a Christian with how I handled the situation with Carol, your mother. I hope you can forgive me. I assure you that I did not know about you until she wrote to me just a few days ago.

Your mother was not to blame for bearing you out of wedlock. I was the one who wronged her and pushed her into this situation before you were born. She was a good person, and I'm sure Da Hah will meet her with mercy on the other side, even as I hope that mercy will be granted to us.

You are welcome to visit me anytime you wish. My wife, Anna, has been told about you, and she holds no ill will toward you. It would be with great joy that I behold your face. If you're not comfortable visiting at my home or if you would rather we meet someplace else, then Anna and I will gladly consider such a trip.

On my part, I do not wish to leave this world without seeing you.

Humbly, your father,
Menno Hostetler

Menno addressed an envelope, folded the letter, and slid it inside. He placed a stamp on the outside. Rising, he picked up the letter, found his way into the mudroom, and lit the gas lantern. Squinting, he walked back into the kitchen, setting the light on the kitchen table. Anna walked in, and her smile was soft in the lantern light. This woman loved him. There was no question about that. And he deserved none of her devotion, and yet it was his. It had been his before she knew of his sin, and it remained his now, and it would be so tomorrow and every day thereafter. Swinging the lantern by his side, Menno walked out to the mailbox and slipped the letter inside.

Chapter Eleven

Menno stood by the living room window and watched the dawn brightening into the early morning light. At any moment now buggy wheels would be rolling down the driveway as the cooks would be stopping in for brief instructions before heading on down to Ada's place where the noon meal would be served.

And here he was thinking of his son. He had mailed the letter, and now he had to practice patience. This was Teresa's day, and his tumultuous emotions must be kept out of the way lest he mar her happiness. This was as it should be. Teresa didn't deserve to suffer because of his sin.

Behind him he heard the stairway door open and soft steps coming down on the hardwood floor. Menno turned and smiled as he caught sight of Teresa. Her eyes were still sleepy, but she was dressed in her work dress, as if she planned a hard day's labor.

"Is *Mamm* in the kitchen?" Teresa asked.

He nodded.

Mamm popped out through the kitchen doorway at the sound of Teresa's voice. "You're not helping with breakfast. It's your wedding day."

"I couldn't sleep. And I want to help. Everybody is doing so much for me."

"You can come out to the barn with me," Menno offered. "I don't have any work for you, but it will do your nerves *gut* to get out in the fresh air."

Teresa smiled. "I guess it could do me some good. I'm up for it."

"Come…" Menno took the gas lantern from its hook, and Teresa followed him outside, the morning sky lighter but the lantern light still erasing some shadows. They crossed the lawn, and Menno pushed open the double barn doors, exposing the rows and rows of benches they had set up yesterday along with the tables set up at Ada's place. In the back, the horses nickered, their hooves rustling the straw in their stalls.

"It's going to happen right here, Teresa." Menno waved his hand about. "*Yah*, right here in a few hours you will be seated. And in a few more hours you will say the marriage vows with James."

Teresa stared in silence, her face glowing.

"Do you like how everything is arranged? Steve and I finished around midnight."

"How could I not like it? It's perfect. I can never thank you enough, *Daett*. All of you—*Mamm*, Susan, Steve, and everyone…for all you've done for me."

"And we can never thank you for what your life has brought to us," Menno said. "Remember, Teresa, none of us are islands in the sea. We all touch each other, and the *gut* effects from our lives go on and on."

"I still thank you," Teresa said. "Besides my mom, you are my family now."

"*Yah*, and we want you to always feel that way," he said. "We want you to come home for visits just like any of our other daughters whenever you wish."

"Oh, *Daett!* Truly *Da Hah* has given me the father I never had." Teresa threw her arms around his neck and pulled until he lowered his head. She kissed him on his cheek.

He laughed. "And now, my daughter, I must take care of the horses before the cooks arrive. It's going to be a very busy day, believe me."

Teresa gave Menno another kiss on the cheek and then turned and ran back toward the house.

Before Teresa disappeared inside, a buggy came rattling into the lane. Menno walked out to help the first cook unhitch. Before he finished tying up the first horse, two more buggies were waiting. The rush didn't slow for another hour. And his breakfast was little more than gulping of food in the kitchen and racing right back out again. Menno found himself standing in the field, helping unhitch horses from a long line of buggies that were flooding into the field. Teresa might not have been born Amish, he thought, but she was clearly fully accepted in the community. This was a credit to her even above the fact that she was marrying James, the deacon's son.

"*Gut* morning," several boys greeted him, coming up to offer their help.

"*Gut* morning," Menno replied.

"We'll take over now," one of them said with a smile. "We can't have the man of the house working on the day of the wedding."

"*Ah!*" Menno laughed along with them. "Then I'll go catch my breath over by the barn."

While the boys gathered around the next buggy, Menno walked across the pasture, stopping to check the line of horses tied along the fence. There was still room in this section, he decided, but the space was filling fast. Along the barn a few other drivers had tied their horses. They stood contented enough for now, but they might have to be moved later in case they started making noise during the service. He would move them now, Menno decided. Even a momentary banging of a horse bumping against the barn siding or a squeal of a horse squabble was something Teresa shouldn't have to deal with on her wedding day.

"I need some help!" he hollered to Ada's boy, Duane, who was standing with his friends in the barnyard. Steve stuck his head out of the barn at the same moment. Duane, his friends, and Steve all headed toward Menno.

"What do you need, *Dawdy*?" Duane asked.

"These horses should be moved down to the fence behind the barn," Menno told them.

They nodded, each grabbing a tie rope and leading a horse away.

"Anything I can do?" Steve offered.

"Not unless you want to do women's work in the house," Menno said with a laugh.

"I think I'll leave that to the women." Steve joined in the laughter as they walked over to the line of men gathered in front of the barn.

It was time he relaxed, Menno told himself. He shook a few hands when they arrived. The younger generation could take on the rest of the morning's duties. Before long Susan's wedding day would come, and all his daughters would be married off. Then he could settle down in a *dawdy haus* between here and Ada's place. What an easy life that would be. No more rising before the sun was up and thinking about farm troubles. All he would have to do was stop by the farm to offer Thomas advice. And maybe help out with the little things. A smile spread across Menno's face as he continued to greet arriving guests and shake hands with the men. Moments later Deacon Ray came out of the barn and whispered in his ear.

"Are you expecting any *Englisha* visitors today?"

"Not that I know of," Menno said. "Except for Teresa's mother, of course."

"Well..." Deacon Ray stroked his beard. "There was a fellow came by my place yesterday, asking where a Menno Hostetler lived. Did he stop by here?"

Menno shook his head. "How does he know me? Did he say?"

"He seemed to know you, but he didn't say much. Asked if you had worked in a St. Louis hospital during the war. What would that be about, do you think?"

Menno tried to ignore the jolt he felt. Surely this wasn't his...son! "How old was he, do you think?"

"Forties somewhere, I'd say. I told him you were in the middle of wedding preparations. But that he should stop by if he wanted to speak with you. I gave him directions to your place."

"Did he say what his name was?"

"Dennis...Dennis White, I think."

Menno looked away as he shook another hand held out to him. The *Englisha* man wasn't his son. The name was wrong. Besides, he had just written his letter this morning. It still waited for the postman to pick it up.

Behind Menno more buggies poured into the yard, stopping by the house for the women to climb out. As they made their way into the house, the men drove the buggies into the field. Menno forced himself to think of something other than an *Englisha* man asking for him.

He should be helping somewhere instead of dwelling on his worried thoughts.

Minutes later, a dark-colored car pulled in and parked beside the long-distance vans. This was not a relative of James's coming in from out of state, Menno decided. None of them would hire a car in which to travel. And Teresa hadn't mentioned having any family other than her *mamm.* Menno watched as a man in a dark suit got out and looked about the yard. Pain returned to his stomach.

"That's the *Englisha* fellow," Deacon Ray said, poking Menno in the ribs and nodding toward the car.

Menno jumped. "Did you invite him to the wedding?"

"I guess he could have taken it that way," Deacon Ray said. "You're giving the wedding, perhaps you ought to make him feel welcome."

Menno took a deep breath and walked across the lawn. What was he to say? What if this man was his son? "Good morning," Menno said when he was near the man. He offered his hand. "I'm Menno Hostetler."

The man met his eyes as a smile spread across his face.

"I'm Dennis White. I hope I'm not intruding."

"Of course not." Menno swallowed hard. "I believe you met Deacon Ray the other day. He's the father of the groom."

"I believe so." Dennis glanced over at the fast-approaching Deacon Ray. "I also wanted to speak with you. A little research I'm doing on the Amish. Hopefully we can talk after the wedding, if that's okay. I wasn't quite sure how to do this. I only arrived here yesterday, and then I found that a wedding was taking place this morning. I hope I'm not intruding."

"I understand," Menno told him. "And you're welcome to stay."

"Well, hello, hello!" Deacon Ray interrupted, coming up to offer his hand in greeting. "I see you made it."

"Yes, and thanks for the information yesterday." Dennis offered a smile. "Will I get to see a real Amish wedding?"

"*Yah,*" Deacon Ray said. "My son's wedding!"

"And you're the father of the bride, is that right?" Dennis asked Menno.

"I claim her as my daughter, *yah*," Menno agreed.

"As part of my research on the Amish, I'd certainly enjoy witnessing an Amish wedding. Do you mind?"

Deacon Ray laughed. "Observe all you wish. We're different on the outside, *yah*, but the same on the inside. We have lunch afterward, so don't forget to stay for that."

"That's kind of you, sir. I certainly will."

"Come!" Menno motioned with his hand. "The service begins soon."

Dennis followed Menno back to the barn. Already Bishop Henry was leading the line of men into the barn.

"Just follow me," Menno told Dennis.

The *Englisha* man stayed close as they moved down the tight rows of benches and found places to sit. They were no sooner seated than the washroom door opened and a line of women appeared and walked toward the barn. Behind them came a line of unmarried girls. Finally, when everyone else was seated, the wedding party came out.

Thomas and Susan were in the lead, with Teresa and James following behind them. They were followed by James's cousin Ben and his girlfriend, Mary.

Menno held still, wild thoughts racing through his head. Who was this man sitting beside him really? Could he be his son? But it couldn't be. It couldn't happen just like that.

"Was the girl in the lead your daughter?" Dennis leaned over to whisper.

"*Yah*..." Menno jumped on the bench. "Susan."

In front of them the wedding party paused, waiting. The boys stood, facing the girls on the other side. Only when James began to sit down did the others follow. When all were seated someone shouted out a song number, and the singing began.

Menno watched the *Englisha* man out of the corner of his eye. He seemed to be soaking in every sight and sound. His eyes watched the ministers as they filed in towards the house, followed by James and Teresa.

"They're going in the house for some last-minute marriage counseling," Menno whispered above the sound of singing.

Dennis smiled. "Nowadays everyone can use that."

Menno smiled at the comment. He shared the songbook with the *Englisha* man as the singing continued. Deacon Ray acted strange this morning, Menno thought. Did he suspect anything about his past? But how could he? After all, Deacon Ray had been there with him in St. Louis during those days, and he hadn't known about Carol. Menno settled on the bench, letting the memories from those days return.

Deacon Ray and he had both served their alternative service in St. Louis, their time overlapping by a few months. Deacon Ray hadn't been a deacon back then. He was simply a homesick boy who went out a few times with the sister of a boy Ray was friends with at the hospital. Menno wasn't supposed to know that, just as Ray wasn't supposed to know about Carol. Likely Ray had never found out his secret, let alone how deeply he had been involved with Carol. If Ray had known, he would have assumed it was the same innocent flirting with the world he himself was involved in. So he must be imagining things, Menno decided. Guilt was that way. It drove a man to extremes, forcing him to flee shadows when they were but tree limbs moving in the moonlight. Menno glanced over at Dennis. He was watching Teresa and James coming back across the lawn, walking side-by-side, smiling at each other, seemingly oblivious to all the people in the barn who were watching them.

"They're a sweet couple," Dennis whispered.

Menno nodded. Teresa and James *were* a sweet couple.

The two took their seats as another song number was given out. The music ended minutes later when the ministers appeared and walked single file across the lawn. They took their seats. Then the first minister stood and gave his sermon. He spoke in hushed tones of the great love *Da Hah* had for mankind. How that love is lived out in the relationship between husband and wife. How all should go home after the services and practice the love of *Da Hah* with their family members.

With the sermon ended, the Scriptures were read. Bishop Henry rose. He told the story of Abraham sending his servant to find a wife for Isaac. At the well, the servant had prayed that *Da Hah* would reveal to him in a special way which girl was to be the chosen woman for Isaac.

Da Hah had shown His will, moving Rebecca to offer water for all the camels. This was no small task, Bishop Henry said, and was an example to all that *Da Hah* loved those who were willing to aid others, whether they were men or women.

Menno watched Teresa's face as Bishop Henry finished his sermon and asked the couple to stand.

The questions began at once. "Do you promise, Brother James, to take this woman, our Sister Teresa, to be your beloved wife? To cherish, protect, and care for her through sickness and health until death do you part?"

James smiled and answered with a firm "*Yah*."

Teresa had tears running down her face when she whispered her answer to the question about taking James as her husband.

Dennis shifted on the bench beside Menno as Bishop Henry continued the questions and listened to the answers. He then joined James and Teresa's hands and declared that they were now man and wife. The couple sat down. Teresa was wiping her eyes with her handkerchief, her face glowing with happiness.

Behind them the last song was given out and begun. When it ended, Bishop Henry dismissed the service.

Menno turned to Dennis, "I hope you enjoyed your first Amish wedding."

"I did." Dennis smiled with great warmth. "Even though I didn't understand much, it was very wonderful. You're a tenderhearted people, I see."

"Thank you," Menno said. "I hope you'll stay for lunch. It's being served at the next place down the road. It looks like the women are already rushing over there to help get things going."

"I would be honored to stay," Dennis said. "Thank you."

"I'm available anytime you wish to speak with me," Menno added, wondering what questions he'd be asked.

"Ah, perhaps I'll wait on that," Dennis said.

"Okay," Menno nodded. "If you need anything, let me know." He turned and walked over to Deacon Ray.

"Well, they're married!" Deacon Ray said. He laughed. "I think they make a wonderful couple, Menno."

Menno nodded, his gaze on the *Englisha* man's back as he moved through the crowd, shaking hands and talking with the men. He seemed to be a natural people-person, Menno thought. Could this be his son? It seemed very possible.

Chapter Twelve

An hour later the wedding party was seated at the center table surrounded by relatives and friends, some already sitting at the tables that had been set up in the pole barn at Reuben and Ada's place. Susan sat to the right of Teresa, and Thomas was beside her, smiling at every opportunity, obviously enjoying himself fully.

Well-wishers were filing past the table, shaking hands with Teresa and James. In moments the call for dinner would be given. Already one of the ushers was coming toward them and directing people to their seats.

Tears were still falling down Teresa's cheeks making her look, if possible, even more beautiful than she had this morning. All was well now, and Susan breathed a sigh of relief. Her thoughts turned to wondering where *Mamm* might be. She hadn't been around since they walked down the road to Ada's. Her place was still empty beside *Daett* on the bench reserved for the family. *Daett*, too, seemed at a loss as to *Mamm*'s whereabouts. The worried look on his face gave evidence of his concern. Likely *Mamm* was keeping baby Samuel out of sight so Teresa would have the full enjoyment of her special day. Susan relaxed at the thought.

Maurice's glowing face was a close second to Teresa's, Susan decided. She was glancing often toward her daughter. This day was going as Teresa had dreamed but often thought impossible. Yet *Da Hah* had brought them all through it—especially Teresa. Her faith had been behind all of this. And Teresa was now a married Amish woman. Wiping tears from her own eyes, Susan leaned over to whisper to Thomas, "What a wonderful day this is! And Teresa looks so happy."

Thomas jumped, quickly turning his gaze toward Susan and away from the spot across the room he'd been staring at.

"*Yah*," Thomas managed. "They sure are. And I'm happy for James."

"Do you know those young people?" Susan had followed the direction of Thomas's gaze.

"A few of them are James's cousins," Thomas said as a long line of young people filed in to find places to sit. "The others I don't know."

Susan watched the boys and girls split off to different sides of the room. Why was Thomas watching them so intently? Her thought was broken as Thomas looked over at James and Teresa. "Good things do happen in this world, Susan." He reached under the table to squeeze her hand. "And they can also happen for us. I really do believe that."

Susan nodded. She had to trust Thomas again. And now was a *gut* time to start. Teresa was such a good example for all of them. And Thomas was trying.

Thomas whispered in her ear, "You look so beautiful today. I almost thought you were the bride."

Susan felt a hot flush coming up her neck. She whispered, "Shhh! Someone will hear you."

Thomas smiled even more. He squeezed her hand under the table again, and she dropped her eyes. Tightening her fingers would make his smile even broader, so she held still. If they didn't stop acting sweet on each other, people would think they were the couple who said the vows today. Thankfully Thomas had looked away and was quieting down—for a while at least.

In the pole barn doorway *Mamm* appeared and rushed to her seat.

Moments later Bishop Henry got to his feet and announced in a firm voice, "We are gathered here today to rejoice with Brother James and Sister Teresa on this, their holy day of marriage. On their behalf I have been asked to thank all of you for coming. Many of you have traveled a distance to be with them, and they welcome your presence with great joy. We wish to extend to this young couple *Da Hah*'s great and mighty blessing on this day and on all the days of their married life. No man knows how long those days and hours will be. They all lie in the faithful hand of *Da Hah.* So to James and Teresa, we wish a *gut* beginning, a steadfast life, and a safe ending in the arms of *Da Hah*. Now, let's bow our heads and give thanks for the meal laid out before us."

They all bowed their heads while Bishop Henry gave thanks for the food and asked for *Da Hah*'s blessing on the rest of the day. The meal began at once, each table assigned a serving couple. The food was brought through a side door where the cooks were measuring it into table-sized containers.

The center table—the table for the bride and groom—had a special serving couple—James's younger brother Henry, who rushed up, stumbling over his own feet. Susan smiled at his obvious nervousness at this great honor. Henry laughed and managed to pull himself together, handing the plate he was carrying to Teresa. Beside him a girl Susan didn't know was keeping her emotions under better control. She handed over a plate of mashed potatoes without a tremble in her hand. With the other hand she set down the brown gravy.

"Having a good time?" James teased his brother, who smiled then and seemed to relax. With the plates deposited, the two servers scurried back for more. James dished out food for himself, and then held the plates out for Teresa. She took what she wanted and passed the food around the table.

When Henry and the girl came back the second time with dressing, noodles, and the vegetable side dishes, they were talking to each other and sharing shy glances.

"Ah, weddings..." Thomas sighed. "It's such a great time to learn."

Susan couldn't help but laugh. She found Thomas's hand under the table again and held it. Perhaps he would make her a *gut* husband as she would make him a *gut* wife. They would love and grow old together. This was all that could be asked of any couple.

Henry and the girl returned with date pudding and cherry pies.

"There's pumpkin and pecan back there yet," Henry said. "So don't eat yourselves full before we get back with more."

James laughed. "Bring everything you've got. I'm going to eat until I pop today."

"Thank you for helping out today," Teresa leaned forward to tell the two of them. "This is so good of you. I can't thank you enough."

"It's a wonderful day," the girl said. Both servers smiled and turned to leave again.

"What's the girl's name?" Susan asked when they were gone.

"Lucy, I think," James said. "Henry knows her. She's from northern Indiana."

"There's quite a few young people visiting from there," Thomas offered. "At least that's what I heard."

"I think you're right," James agreed. "We have relatives from there. Today I'm thinking mostly about someone else though."

Teresa turned a bright red and covered her face with her hands.

"Ah..." Susan cooed, "you two are so sweet."

"I know," James said. "And Teresa is the best *frau* I could ever have found."

"James!" Teresa said, her face still covered, "There are people around."

"Then it's a *gut* time to say such things," James teased.

After a few seconds, Teresa took her hands away from her face, streaks of red still running across her cheeks.

Thomas laughed and leaned toward Susan. "This wedding day has been a very *gut* one."

"Weddings are always supposed to be *gut*."

"*Yah*, and ours is going to be very sweet and very *soon*."

When Susan didn't say anything, Thomas glanced at her. "Do you agree?"

"Maybe." That was the closest she had come lately to promising a firm date. She supposed Teresa's wedding must be opening her heart to the idea of her own special day.

Thomas seemed satisfied with the answer since he was digging deep into his date pudding. Susan nibbled at her cherry pie, watching the servers as they waited on the guests. None of her sisters were among the serving couples since they were all married. Now that Teresa had married, Susan was the only one still single in the family. Yes, it was time. It simply was time to make up her mind and stick to the decision. No more dashing away at the first sign of trouble. Perhaps tonight after the singing, when everyone else had left, she would tell Thomas for sure. Whisper *yah* in his ear. Begin to plan her wedding day on Teresa's wedding day. It would be a perfect ending to a perfect day, and they could put the past behind them once and for all.

"You look like you're thinking sweet thoughts," Thomas teased.

"Could be..." She offered nothing more. Let him wonder what she was thinking. Although from the satisfied look on his face, he had a pretty good idea.

Bishop Henry stood and announced that it was time to give thanks again. As silence settled across the pole barn, the people bowed their heads and the bishop prayed. "Now unto the great God of heaven and earth, we give thanks for this food that we have eaten. We also give thanks for the good fellowship we have had and will have this afternoon with family and loved ones and friends. We have been given much by Your most gracious hand, O *Da Hah*, and we do not wish to receive of these bounties without giving You thanks. And now we ask, by Your grace, for a full and fruitful married life for our brother and sister James and Teresa. Amen."

Rustling filled the large room as many of the people stood and the younger children raced outside to play. Ada appeared carrying baby Samuel, who was delivered squirming across the table and into Teresa's arms.

"Oh little sweet darling, it's so good to see you," Teresa cooed.

James was giving the child his full attention, trying to make him look up by tapping his head. Finally it worked, and baby Samuel's mouth formed one of his happy smiles.

"Come on, big boy!" James held out his arms, and Samuel reached for him.

"That's so sweet," Susan said to no one in particular, feeling tears welling up again.

"James really has taken to the child," Thomas commented. "I wish the best for all three of them. They're a very nice family."

"I know," Susan said. "*Da Hah* has really blessed them."

"We'll also be a nice couple, Susan. You know that, don't you?"

Susan looked at him. He was playing with his plate, turning it around and around. "We'll be our own kind of couple, I suppose," Susan said. "But it's nice to have such a good example to follow."

"It is. And I'm glad it's finally working out for us, Susan. Although I know we both get a little tired of the struggle sometimes. Once we're married and on the farm, it will be worth everything we've gone through."

She touched his fingers under the table, wrapping hers around his, and he squeezed back.

Moments later Thomas rose. "I'm going over to talk with some of the visitors. Make them feel welcome."

Susan also stood. She stepped back over the bench to let him exit easily.

As Thomas left, more people were coming up to shake hands with James and Teresa and to wish them well. Susan soon followed Thomas, stopping in front of Betsy and Miriam on the way out. Miriam was holding her youngest in her arms and feeding him the last bites of his meal.

"Is Nancy doing better today?" Susan asked Miriam.

"*Ach*, *yah*," Miriam said. "I think the flu had her ears hurting last week. But even if she wasn't totally well, this day would have done anyone *gut*. It was quite wonderful to see Teresa finally married. She's such a special girl."

"You can say that again!" Betsy echoed.

"It was a blessed day," Susan agreed. She left them to head outside. She decided to walk up the road toward home. She didn't see any sign of Thomas. Groups of young people were coming and going already. Some of them were entering Ada's house, while others were walking in the same direction she was going—back to where the service had been held and the buggies were parked.

Perhaps she could get in a short nap this afternoon in her bedroom. And if any of the girls she knew or one of the many visitors wished to do the same, there was room on the bed for two. And a few others could rest in Teresa's now-empty room. It would be a nice ending to the morning's service and a proper preparation for the hymn singing tonight, which could last until midnight.

Susan was walking up the steps of her front porch when she stopped short. Visible through the living room window was Thomas. He was sitting on the couch beside a girl. He had his head lowered down close to hers, talking and laughing.

What in the world is he up to? Susan almost burst through the front door, demanding to know who this girl was and why Thomas was speaking with her. But she stopped herself. That would be an overreaction. Surely Thomas knew this girl from somewhere. Perhaps she was even his cousin.

Susan looked through the window again. *Nee*, the girl wasn't Thomas's cousin. She had been one of the girls walking into the pole barn with the young people from northern Indiana. Pulling her gaze away, Susan walked off the porch and headed back up the road to Ada's place. What Thomas was doing he could explain to her later. Right now she just wanted to be someplace else. Anywhere but here, she decided.

Chapter Thirteen

The afternoon was winding down, and Teresa and James stood holding hands in the yard. Behind them the evening sun was sinking into the west. People were leaving, pausing to give the married couple last words of good wishes.

"Our wedding day is almost over," Teresa said into James's ear. "And it's been more wonderful than even I could have imagined. Looks like we're getting a beautiful sunset as another added blessing." They turned together and watched as the colors deepened in the sky. Long, golden streaks of light rose up from the horizon. Below that, a thin strip of clouds covered the sun, showing only the faint outline of the huge, red globe. All around were runs of orange and brighter reds.

"It's been a *gut* day." James squeezed Teresa's hand. "I couldn't have asked for a better one...or for a better *frau*. Even baby Samuel seems to have enjoyed himself."

"I think so too. I expected he'd make a fuss if he was away from me for so long, but he didn't."

"He's got lots of relatives who adore and cater to his every whim. He'll have a hard time settling back to normal life after these past few weeks of spoiling."

"But he will." Teresa looked up at her new husband. "And he'll have you as his *daett*. It's obvious he already loves you dearly."

"He's a little sweetheart," James said. "But when he misbehaves, we'll have to spank him just like our other children."

"He's already gotten a few spankings when he was naughty," Teresa said. "*Mamm* saw to that. But it made him the sweetest boy afterward."

"That's how it works with children. That and loving them."

"I know." Teresa sighed. "Do you know how long I've waited for this day? How I thought it would never come? How many things stood in the way?"

"Those things are past us now," James said. "When *Da Hah* allows us trouble, we'll bear them again, just like we've borne the ones so far—with humility and grace in our hearts."

"And together," Teresa added.

"Hello there again!" Maurice called as she approached. "If it isn't the happy couple themselves. Beautiful sunset! How could the day end any better?"

Teresa and her mom embraced. Then Maurice turned. "James, you'll make my daughter happy. Teresa couldn't have done better if I had handpicked her husband myself!"

"Well, thank you." James smiled. "I'm honored indeed."

"I don't know how you Amish men do this, but is it okay if I give you a hug?" Maurice opened her arms.

"From my mother-in-law? Of course!"

Maurice hugged and then kissed him on the cheek.

James laughed.

"That's enough, Mom!" Teresa said. "Things are done a little differently around here."

"I will kiss my son-in-law at least once on his wedding day," Maurice declared. "Regardless of what country I'm in."

"I guess no one is staring." Teresa looked around.

"Of course not," Maurice said. "So what happens for the rest of the evening? I hear there are more festivities to come. And here I'm thinking I'll collapse from all the goings on so far."

"Well," James said, "there's a hymn singing with supper for the young folks starting at six. The old folks just tag along. Then the singing starts at seven-thirty, going until nine. Afterward, we sit around and talk for a few hours yet. So the whole celebration might end by midnight."

"That *is* making a full day out of it!" Maurice exclaimed.

James grinned. "For most of us, this only happens once in our lifetime. So we celebrate newly married couples as much as we can."

"That's a wonderful thought," Maurice said. "So what does the mother-of-the-bride do to help? I feel like I'm doing nothing but stuffing myself with delicious food."

"That's exactly what you're supposed to do, Mother," James said.

Maurice looked at him. "Did you just call me mother?"

"*Yah*, that's what you are to me now. And if it will help keep you here a while longer, I'll call you *Mamm*."

"Well, for that you get another hug!" And with that Maurice took James in another embrace and squeezed tight.

"Mom, that's enough!" Teresa said with a laugh. "Any more hugs will be given at home, not here where people are watching."

"Oh, all right," Maurice conceded.

Teresa turned to James. "I'll walk Mom into the house and be right back."

As they walked across the lawn, Maurice asked, "So you really aren't going on a honeymoon?"

"No. *Mamm* and Susan will take care of baby Samuel for our first night together, and then it's back to normal. That's how the Amish do things."

"Well, if that's their custom, okay. I guess everybody looks happy around here with or without honeymoons."

"Husbands and wives love each other for all their lives." Noticing her Mom's frown, Teresa said, "I'm sorry, Mom. I wasn't trying to make you feel bad." Teresa took her mother's hand as they walked.

"I've never even had a wedding, let alone a honeymoon," Maurice said. "So yes, I do feel bad. Or perhaps just sad."

"Mom, don't cry. God can change everything if you will trust Him. Why don't you stay around for a while and see what it's really like here? James won't mind if you use the upstairs bedroom. And you can help us get settled into the house."

"That's very sweet of you." Maurice's wiped her eyes. "I will certainly consider it. After I've been around you and baby Samuel this week, I don't want to go back to Asbury Park."

"Then don't!" Teresa let go of her mother's hand and held open the washroom door.

Susan was standing inside by the sink, her face tear-stained. Maurice smiled at her as she moved into the kitchen.

Teresa lingered behind and took Susan's hand. "Mom thinks you're happy for me, but I know you, and this is about something else. You're crying your heart out. Tell me why."

"I saw Thomas talking with one of the visiting girls earlier at our house." Susan broke into more sobs.

"Oh no!" Teresa groaned. "Are you sure? Maybe it was someone he knew. Perhaps you're jumping to conclusions."

"That's what I keep telling myself, but I can't stop crying. He's betrayed me before, Teresa, and it feels likes he's doing it all over again."

"Shall we go find Thomas? Let's just ask him and clear this up."

Susan smiled through her tears. "I don't think that would be wise. I'll try to gather myself together. We have to go in for supper before long. And you'd better go back to James. It's *your* day, and I don't want this time to become something about me."

"Susan, I care about you. If it weren't for you, I wouldn't even be having this wonderful day."

"I'll be okay." Susan squeezed Teresa's hands and motioned her back out the washroom door. "I'll see you in a little bit."

Teresa gave Susan a hug. "It'll be okay."

Susan nodded as Teresa left.

Why did trouble have to haunt this day, Teresa wondered. Hopefully Susan was imaging things. *Please help Susan, dear God*, she prayed, pausing to watch James talking with an *Englisha* man. Her husband's back was turned toward her. The final rays of sunshine had broken through the thin clouds and were blazing over James's shoulders.

As she approached, James turned slightly toward her and then back to the *Englisha* man. "Dennis, please meet my *frau*, Teresa. Teresa, this is Dennis, who is visiting today."

"Hi," Teresa said with a nod, her gaze immediately turning back to James's face. She could almost kiss him right here in front of everyone. He looked so handsome and so glad to see her.

"I'm glad to finally meet you, Teresa," Dennis was saying. "I saw the others going up to shake your hand, but, not knowing you, I wasn't quite up to that in the crowd. Congratulations."

"Thank you," Teresa said.

"Dennis came looking for Menno and was asked to stay for our wedding," James explained. He's doing some sort of research on the Amish and wanted to see how we do things. A wedding was a good place to start."

"Yes, it was," Dennis agreed. "And thank you for allowing me to share your day. I thoroughly enjoyed myself! It's getting a bit late, though, and I do need to be going."

"You were going to ask Menno some questions," James said. "Were you able to do that?"

"No, but I'll return and do so at a quieter time."

"You're welcome to stay the evening yet," James assured him. "We have supper and then hold a hymn sing."

"Thank you very much, but I do need to leave. I did get to at least meet Mr. Hostetler. I've arranged to come back tomorrow to speak with him at length. With his daughter getting married today, it didn't seem quite appropriate to take up very much of his time."

Teresa laughed. "I'm not really his daughter. I've just kind of grown into the family."

"There's nothing wrong with that," Dennis said. "And, James, you take care of this lovely bride of yours."

"I'll do that." James slipped his hand around Teresa's shoulder. They stood watching the last of the sunset as Dennis left for his car.

Moments later someone hollered from behind them, "Supper's ready!"

Teresa smiled and pulled James toward the barn.

"Someone's in a hurry for supper," Minister Emery Stutsman muttered as they passed. "I hope the rest of the young people get themselves here this quickly."

"I'm sure they will." Teresa pointed toward the barn. "See, the boys are already coming."

"I hope the girls agree." Emery laughed. "It sure makes my task a lot easier."

By the time they were seated at the center table, Susan and Thomas had appeared. Teresa looked over at Susan. Was she still upset or had Thomas said something to soothe her fears? She was smiling at least, but then Susan was always able to put on a front if she felt she needed to.

Ben and Mary appeared moments later, taking their places on James's side of the table. The young people continued to file in through the doorway, the steady couples first, followed by those who had been paired up for the evening by the "hook and crook" of the matching team. Emery Stutsman didn't have to do any hard work to get people gathered, regardless of how much he complained.

Teresa smiled at the obviously nervous young couples. She hadn't attended many Amish weddings, and now she would never have to face the matchmaking boys again as they came around on wedding afternoons, carrying their pencils and notepads, taking all the girls' names down who still were without a date for the evening and then retreating to where the boys were scattered throughout the premises. There they began asking the boys which girls they wanted to be paired with. First come, first served, was the rule of the day. The girls' only option was to say no if the choice was too onerous. And few did. Susan had warned Teresa of the process at the first wedding she attended. It was better to appear submissive and swallow whatever distaste one experienced if the boy chosen wasn't your favorite. This was only for the evening. It wasn't like one had to be alone with the boy or endure long conversations. Some couples said only a few words to each other all evening as they sat at the tables.

Since James had been taking her home from the hymn singings, he had also escorted her to the tables at weddings. Now he would be her husband wedding nights and regular weekday nights! Teresa leaned against his shoulder and looked up into his face. He looked down at her, his eyes shining with happiness.

Minister Emery interrupted Teresa's thoughts by announcing the prayer time in a loud voice. He led out after they had bowed their heads. Then supper began. As soon as Henry and Lucy, the servers for the center table, appeared carrying their plates of food, the other servers began waiting on their tables to the eager smiles of the hungry young people.

As they started to eat, Teresa gave her mom a smile across the room. She waved, not knowing that Amish didn't wave at weddings. At least no one was looking at Maurice strangely. People were being so wonderful and understanding. Teresa took another bite as she looked across the gathered group of guests.

Soon the years would roll on, she thought. Someday Samuel would be sitting here at his own wedding with a lovely bride by his side.

Giving up all hope of keeping back the tears of joy, Teresa let them run down her cheeks. James kept on eating with one hand and, with his other, holding her hand under the table. No one stopped eating to stare, even though they had to have noticed.

Did Amish brides usually break down on their wedding day? Teresa wondered. Well, if not, they were being introduced to a new tradition. The weeping bride at the wedding-night supper before the hymn singing.

Chapter Fourteen

The hymn singing had ended an hour ago, but James and Teresa were still inside chatting with the guests, many who were wishing them a last "God speed" on their married life. Susan waited in the front yard. The gas lantern shining through the front window of the house sent warm light streaming across the lawn and up the side of the washhouse. Susan studied each buggy profile as the long line approached. Thomas's buggy hadn't appeared yet.

They could just as easily leave his buggy here. Her house was within walking distance. But his last whispered words had been "I'm getting my buggy," just before she had smiled at Teresa, giving her another hug before slipping out of the barn.

That Thomas was driving her home instead of walking wasn't a problem. It was the look on his face that was troublesome. All evening he had been that way. Even when he laughed at the right places, Susan knew something had changed. But what exactly?

Girls with their bonnets pushed back moved past her, climbing into the halted buggies. Most of the horses held their heads high, occasionally rearing back on their hind feet before the driver loosened the reins and calmed them.

Could it be the girl Thomas had been talking to this afternoon? She was up to no good. Or perhaps it was Thomas who was up to no good—just as he'd been up to no good the evening she'd caught him kissing Eunice. But this time she was going to trust Thomas until she knew otherwise. That was what *Mamm* and her sisters would say to do, and they were right. There was probably a perfectly logical explanation.

This time she wasn't going to fly off the handle. She was going to keep her emotions in check.

Through the shadows Susan caught sight of Thomas's buggy approaching. At least his horse didn't have that dashing streak his master had. Freddy was unexcitable and calm—descriptions that would feel *gut* when used to describe a man. Maybe those qualities would filter down to the horse's driver someday.

Thomas, of course, didn't like his horse. He was always complaining about how slow Freddy was. So what did Thomas want? A horse like James drove—high strung and able to pass every buggy on the road. But a body couldn't always have what he wanted. For one thing, such a horse wasn't what Susan wanted. And Thomas seemed set on having her in his life.

"Hi again," Susan said as she climbed up into the dark buggy. Thomas's familiar form took shape as she settled into the seat.

"Turning a little chilly tonight," he said, letting out the reins.

Freddy started forward, shaking his head. Thomas slapped the reins hard on his back. Freddy jerked his head up but didn't increase his speed.

"Summer's about over," Susan offered. "I should have brought my shawl."

"Getup!" Thomas shouted through the open window, but again he got no better response.

"I like your horse," she told him. "Freddy has a calming influence in an unstable world."

Thomas laughed. "How do you figure that? I'd give a lot for a decent horse, but I can't afford one yet. Plus *Daett* says the high strung ones are harder to keep."

"I still like him. I always have."

"Well, I don't, and I'm the one who drives him."

"I think you ought to be thankful for what you have," Susan said. "Look at us. We're both older, past the age when most young people wed. It's time to settle down, and a decent horse will fit right into the plan."

"Look whose talking now!" he snapped. "You were the one who

threw things up in the first place. If it had been up to me, we'd already be married and settled on your parents' place."

"So you don't think you had anything to do with our breakup?"

"Please, Susan, do we have to argue about this? I'm tired tonight."

"So you don't want to hear that I'm finally planning to join the baptismal class? I thought you would be glad to hear that."

He sighed. "I thought that was a given, Susan."

"I said I was *thinking* about it before. I never said I would for sure. And the way you were acting this afternoon with that girl who was visiting has me troubled. I'm trying not to say anything about it, but I can't help it."

"So you're worried about me and a girl again?"

"So you noticed?"

"I saw you giving her evil glances all evening."

"Thomas, I didn't. That is your guilty conscience seeing things."

"And why should I be feeling guilty about talking to Wilma?"

"Oh, so that's her name. I saw you talking to her this afternoon at my house. All cuddly and cozy on the couch."

He slapped the reins and stared into the darkness.

"Do you have anything to say about that?"

Thomas was silent. Finally he said, "Susan, I think you're right."

"About what?"

"About Wilma. And maybe about a lot of other things. To tell you the truth, I'm tired of all this back-and-forth stuff with you. I'm tired of you bringing up Eunice time after time. You'd probably even bring it up after we married! I can almost hear it the first time I might come home late from a trip into town. I'm ready to call it quits. I think meeting Wilma and having fun with someone who wasn't suspecting me of anything did me good. Made me think of some things I should have thought of a long time ago."

"You're dumping me, Thomas? Is that it?"

"See what I mean? You'll always be putting the blame on me."

Freddy shook his head, glancing over his shoulder before turning into the Hostetler lane. Thomas stopped by the house but made no effort to get out. The silence stretched between them while Susan gathered her thoughts.

"Will you explain yourself better, Thomas? I've been trying to make this work. I don't want to act like I did the time I caught you with Eunice. Maybe there is some *gut* reason you were talking with that girl, with Wilma."

He sighed. "There's no reason *you'd* ever call *gut.* I really think we should part in peace, Susan. If we got married, you'd be doing it because it's expected, not because you really want to. And I'd be doing the same thing. Sure, I want to take over your *daett's* farm. Learn to run the place like your father does. Such a life would be wonderful—at least I've always dreamed it would be. But perhaps I've been wrong. Or perhaps there are other things I want more. I think I need to stop pretending."

"You've been pretending that you like me?"

"No, I didn't mean it to sound like that. You're a wonderful girl, Susan. You'll make someone a wonderful *frau* someday. But not me. You're too good for me, Susan. I guess it's time I admitted it."

"Please, Thomas. I'm not saying anything like that. I just don't want you looking at other girls like Eunice and now Wilma. Not while you're seeing me. And certainly not after we're married."

Thomas looked away. "I'm sorry about Wilma, but it came so easily. She was so much fun to be with this afternoon. It left me wishing you and I had that."

"But we had it once, Thomas. You know we did. You had my heart back in our schooldays...and a long time after. I mooned over you like the lovesick girl I was. Maybe I overreacted by running out to the *Englisha* world when you kissed Eunice, but I'm trying to do better...to not jump to conclusions. And I know we can make this work. Especially with Teresa and James as an example. It's their wedding day, Thomas. Let's not let anything get between us tonight."

"Susan, please." He touched her arm. "I'm sorry, but I can't do this anymore. We can't go on like this. I'm too tired of trying."

"So it *is* Wilma?"

He looked off into darkness before answering. "I don't know. Maybe. I might as well be honest with myself and you this time. Perhaps it will turn out differently with Wilma than it did with Eunice. Wilma's a wonderful girl, Susan."

Susan bit her lip and reached for the side of the buggy. She climbed down and waited a moment, listening for the sound of his voice calling her back. But Thomas said nothing.

"Good night," he finally said as Susan moved toward the house. "And I really am sorry."

Susan held back the tears as she walked across the lawn.

He called softly after her, "Susan! I really am sorry. I didn't mean to hurt you."

Without looking back, Susan pushed open the washroom door and stepped in, knocking her knee against the wooden leg of the bench. She cried out in the darkness. With tears pouring down her face, she found the kitchen door, opened it, and went inside. Throwing her shawl on the floor, Susan collapsed into a chair. She wept hard but silently as the light of the kerosene lamp above her played on the walls and on her white *kapp*.

Soft footsteps approached. *Mamm*'s voice came to her softly. "What's wrong, Susan?"

"Thomas just dumped me—and on Teresa's wedding night."

"Oh, Susan, I'm so sorry." *Mamm*'s arm came around her shoulder.

"He was talking with another girl this afternoon. And right in our house!"

"Now, now," *Mamm* said. "Perhaps it's not all that bad. You've been through this before."

"But this time it's truly the end. Thomas is already thinking of another girl. Why does this have to happen?"

Mamm sighed. "You always were such a high-strung girl, Susan. You take things so much harder than some of the other girls did."

"How am I supposed to take this?" Susan lifted her head. "My boyfriend from my schooldays, the one I imagined all these years I would spend the rest of my life with, turns out to be a flirting twerp who says I'm wonderful but can't keep from wishing he was seeing someone else. Are all men like this?" Susan looked up at her *mamm*'s face.

Mamm hesitated before answering, "They aren't, Susan. You know they aren't."

When Susan said nothing, *Mamm* drew her close. "Susan, please.

I know you're taking this—whatever happened with Thomas again—hard. You're that way, I know. Your *daett* is a man, and he isn't like Thomas. He has loved us for many years now."

Susan groaned. "I think the whole world is nothing but a bunch of rotten people. If I didn't know any better, I'd go running back to Asbury Park again. But what a joke that was. All the good that happened is I brought home Teresa, who thinks we're all sweeter than summer's honey. She doesn't think anyone in the entire community could ever be bad."

"Teresa has had plenty of her own troubles, Susan. You know she has. But I'm glad to hear you're not leaving us again, even if you think it's over with Thomas."

"It is over, *Mamm*. This time it really is. I can't seem to find a boy who loves me."

Mamm touched her shoulder. "You'll find love again, Susan. You're too wonderful a girl not to. If you don't want Thomas, we'll stop insisting you see him. How your *daett* will handle this, I don't know. I guess he can keep Steve over for another season."

Susan got to her feet. "So what is *Daett* going to do about the farm? This will affect him a lot."

"I don't know. But don't worry about the farm. We can sell it, I guess. Keep a few acres for the *dawdy haus*."

"I'm sorry, *Mamm*. I tried but it didn't work out."

"I know, Susan. And now what you need is a good night's sleep. We have plenty to do tomorrow with cleaning up after the wedding."

Susan stood up and hugged her *mamm*. They walked to the stairway door and then parted ways. Susan found her way up the steps in the darkness, running her hands along the wall until she found the doorknob to her bedroom. She climbed into bed weeping bitter tears and thinking about Thomas. And about James and Teresa. They would be lying tonight in each other arms. Why couldn't she find that kind of love?

Chapter Fifteen

The morning after the wedding, the chores were done and breakfast had been served an hour before. The sun was climbing into the sky. Out in the yard, Menno and Steve were loading the last of the collapsible benches into the black church wagon. Standing back when they were done, they surveyed the empty barn.

"I can't believe it's over," Menno said.

"Me neither. It was a good wedding though," Steve said, leaning against the wagon.

"Did you find any prospects for yourself among the visitors?" Menno teased.

Steve laughed. "There was a nice girl from Ohio. I took her to the table at the hymn singing. Her parents run a little dry goods store in Berlin, but our conversation didn't go much further than that."

"Your time will come." Menno turned toward the road when a car pulled in.

"That's the *Englisha* man who was at the wedding," Steve said, pushing shut the door of the enclosed wagon.

"*Yah*, he told me he'd stop by today. He wants to talk with me about something."

"I'll get the horses ready for work then. Do you think you'll be done soon?"

"I think so. But it depends on what he wants to speak about."

"I'll take the corn cutter into the field then." Steve disappeared into the barn.

Menno cleared his throat as Dennis approached.

"Good morning." Dennis extended his hand.

Menno grasped it. "*Gut* morning to you. I hope you enjoyed the wedding yesterday. I saw you left a little early. There was still the youth doings in the evening you could have taken in."

"I enjoyed myself immensely," Dennis said.

Menno sat on a small bench next to the barn and motioned for Dennis to sit down next to him. "I take it you're back this morning about the matter that brought you here in the first place."

"Yes, I am, Menno. Would you be willing to answer some questions about the past? Say forty-some years ago in St. Louis?" He hesitated and then continued. "Do you have any idea what I'm talking about?"

Menno looked down for a minute and then looked into Donald's eyes. "I'm afraid I do. You are Donald, aren't you?"

Donald didn't look too astonished. "I supposed you might guess. Carol said she was going to write to you. Yes, I am Donald. I didn't want to walk in and just announce who I was yesterday. You had the wedding going on, which I didn't want to disrupt. I guess my guise was easily seen through though."

"When I received Carol's note, I wrote you a letter inviting you to come. But I just mailed it yesterday."

"Does that mean you are...you are open to me being here? To asking questions?"

Menno stood and leaned against the bench wagon. "You're my son, Donald. Of course you are welcome here. Until last week, I didn't even know you existed. Your mother...Carol...she told me back in St. Louis that she had miscarried."

Donald remained seated, motioning with his hand toward the half-empty barn. "Do you wish you didn't know about me? I don't exactly fit into all this."

"You're my son, Donald. I am glad I know about you. Very glad! You could have told me yesterday. I would have welcomed you into our home and invited you to stay."

"I wanted to be sure this was a good idea. I wanted to see what kind of person you were and find out what the Amish are like. Sometimes it's better not to know the secrets of the past."

"Not in this case. I say *Da Hah* be praised for you!" Menno drew closer. "But come, Donald. We must find Anna, my wife, and tell her this good news."

"Are you sure? I'm your son with another woman..." Donald was now on his feet.

"Come with me. I will take you into the house. Anna knows of my great wrong, and she knows of you. She encouraged me to write to you. She'll want to meet you."

Donald hesitated. "I think I'll wait while you tell her I'm here. Then if she wants to meet me, I'll come in. That way it won't be so sudden or abrupt."

"You don't understand, Donald." Menno took hold of his arm. "This is now your home too. You belong here. Anna and I both feel that way. Anna is a wonderful woman with a big heart. She will accept who you are."

"I'm afraid it's not that easy, Menno. I'm very thankful for this kind welcome. But please tell your wife I'm here and give her a chance to respond in private."

Menno took some time to think about it. "All right," he said. Then he ran across the lawn, his beard flying over his shoulder. He burst into the living room. Susan and *Mamm* were coming through the stair doorway, carrying baskets of dirty linens. They both gasped as he dashed in.

"The *Englisha* man from yesterday!" Menno shouted. "He's here, Anna! And, *yah*, he is my son like we suspected. Come now and meet him!" He held out his hand to his wife.

Mamm put the basket on the floor and took his hand. She was ready to head outside, but a sound stopped her.

She glanced at Susan, who was staring at her *daett*.

Menno urged Susan forward. "Come, Susan! This man who came yesterday and is outside now is your brother." Menno was crying and laughing at the same time. "You have a brother, Susan!"

"Menno, stop a minute. The girl knows nothing about this," *Mamm* reminded, tugging on his hand. "She may need some time to think about this before she's ready to meet your son."

"What are you talking about, *Daett*?" Susan asked while frozen to the spot.

"I said I have a son!" Menno repeated. "*Da Hah* has turned a great sin in my youth into a blessing. He has given me a son."

"How could *Daett* have a son?" Susan looked to *Mamm* for an explanation. "Did you have a son before my sisters and I came along? I thought there was only nine of us. Would someone please tell me what's going on!"

Menno approached Susan. He gently took her basket and set it on the floor. Then, taking both of her hands in his, he said, "My dear daughter, you know that I love you and your sisters with all my heart. I have tried to be a good *daett* and bring all of you up in the fear of *Da Hah*."

Susan nodded, her eyes not leaving *Daett*'s face.

"And you know that I have feared greatly for you especially. I trembled when you left to live among the *Englisha*. Yet *Da Hah* had mercy. You have returned safe and sound. Now *Da Hah* is also having mercy upon me."

"I still don't understand."

Daett looked at *Mamm*, his lips moving silently.

"You'd better tell her all of it," *Mamm* said.

Menno's smile ebbed. He let go of Susan's hands and slowly began speaking. "Before I was married and was living in St. Louis, I spent time with an *Englisha* girl. We thought we were in love, and I committed a great sin. Of this *Da Hah* knows and your *Mamm* knows. I've kept it secret all these years because Carol, the *Englisha* girl, told me she had miscarried. But now my son has sought me out. You and your sisters must met him. And soon the whole community will know what has lain hidden in my heart for so long. I pray this brings no sorrow upon you or your sisters. Please do not take this as a hurt into your heart, Susan."

"And you knew about this, *Mamm*?" Susan asked.

"Come, Susan." *Mamm* took Susan's hand. "Let us go meet this man who is your father's son. I'm an old woman, and I haven't always done what is right either. I have never lacked in love from your *daett*.

He has loved me as if there never had been another. That's enough for me. And you know he has loved you with all his heart too. I hope you can find forgiveness in your heart for your *daett* and also acceptance for this brother of yours."

"This is too much…too sudden."

"Then I beg your forgiveness," *Daett* said. "I know it is a shock. I was surprised too. It will be a shock to your sisters and everyone else too. But we must not hold my silence against Donald. We must welcome him into our family. He is my son."

Above them the cry of baby Samuel echoed through the house and Susan jumped.

"Come!" *Mamm* said. "Maurice will take care of Samuel for now. Please come with us to meet your brother."

Susan looked at both of them for a long moment before nodding slightly and following them out the door.

Menno led the way, with Anna on his arm. Susan stayed a few steps behind. *Mamm* opened her arms as they approached the middle-aged man standing beside the barn. She took Donald into them without a word. *Mamm* stroked his head.

Donald, much to his surprise, found himself crying on her shoulder.

"So you are Menno's son. Welcome to our humble home, Donald. You should have told us yesterday who you were. We would have welcomed you and kept you at the house instead of sending you on your way."

"It would have been too much," Donald said. "You were in the midst of celebrating a wedding. And I wasn't sure what would happen."

"*Yah*, it would have been a surprise. But it is *gut* that you're here," *Mamm* said. She turned to Susan and took her by the hand, leading her to face Donald. "This is Susan, our youngest of nine daughters."

"Hello," Donald said with an easy smile. "I think you were one of the girls sitting at the center table yesterday. A very nice wedding, I must say."

"Thank you," Susan managed. "Teresa and James make a wonderful couple."

Menno spoke up. "Let's go inside the house, and we can talk."

"Well, for just a while," Donald said. "I don't want to impose. And I really need to get back home again. I've been on the road for over a week tracking down the one lead I had to find you. To tell you the truth, I was nervous and almost went home last night. But then I decided I had to resolve this one way or the other."

"*Yah*, it's too bad my letter didn't get to you in time to save you some trouble," Menno responded.

Menno and Anna led the way to the house. While Menno and Donald settled into chairs in the living room, Anna and Susan went to the kitchen to prepare a bite to eat. "I want them to have some time to themselves," Anna explained.

"I still can't believe this," Susan said quietly. "How could *Daett* do such a thing?"

Anna stopped slicing the cherry pie and looked at Susan. "Someday you will look back and hope that *Da Hah* and those who love you will be able to forgive what you have done in your youth. We do not all sin alike, but *Da Hah* knows that we all sin. *Yah*, I have sinned, your *daett* has sinned, and you too have sinned. Forgiving a person who has sinned is to do what *Da Hah* asks of us. And we know when we forgive others, we too are forgiven, just as the Bible says. Now, get four plates and some forks."

Susan did as her *mamm* asked. She heard the two men in the living room laugh at something they were talking about.

Two hours and much conversation later, Donald rose to leave. "Well, this has been far more than I expected," he said. "You've all been very gracious."

"Perhaps you can come back at Thanksgiving or Christmas—and bring your son, Charles, with you," *Mamm* said. "It's one thing to find a son Menno didn't know about, but to also hear of a grandson is yet another surprise."

"I would like that," Donald said. "I know my being here might make problems for you. Are you sure it's okay? Are you sure you want me to come back?"

"*Yah*, we want you to come back. *Nee*, you will never be a problem for me," Menno assured him. "I love you...son."

The two men embraced, Menno with his long beard pushed over his son's shoulder.

Donald turned and gave *Mamm* a hug. "May I come back some other time to visit? Would that be okay?"

"Certainly," Anna said. "You will always be welcome here."

Then he turned to Susan, who had remained mostly quiet during the visit. "So what about this one?" Donald asked, coming toward her. "Do you think you have place in your life for a brother?"

Susan offered her hand. "You'll have to give me some time to get used to the idea. But you are welcome here."

"I understand," Donald said.

Menno and Donald walked to the car together, while Susan and *Mamm* watched from the porch. Susan was clutching *Mamm*'s arm.

"He's always wanted a son," *Mamm* said, wiping away tears.

"I can't believe this is happening! First Thomas and now *Daett*. What temptations and sins are going to show up next?"

"You must not believe evil can triumph," *Mamm* said. "*Da Hah* intends only for the good."

"What am I supposed to believe?" Susan cried softly. "It turns out my own *daett* sinned in such a way. *Yah*, I will forgive, but it's hard to accept this." She was silent for a minute. "You do know what this will mean, don't you, *Mamm*?"

"*Yah*, but I don't think your *daett* yet knows what all is coming," *Mamm* admitted. "But I still rejoice with him that his son has come. *Da Hah* would not have sent Donald here at this time without a reason. A son will add joy to your *daett*'s heart in his old age just as you girls have always done."

[illegible] with his long coat pulled over [illegible] shoulder.

Donald turned to [illegible]. "Was [illegible] the other [illegible]?" [illegible].

[illegible]

[illegible] to whoever [illegible] Donald [illegible]

[illegible] you have [illegible] for a [illegible]?"

[illegible] offered her hand. "You [illegible] to [illegible] tell [illegible] keep [illegible]?"

"I understand," Donald said.

[illegible] and I [illegible]

[illegible] walked [illegible]

[illegible] away [illegible]

"[illegible] believe this is happening? [illegible] what [illegible] going to [illegible] now?"

"You [illegible] before [illegible] start [illegible] the spot."

"What am I supposed to believe?" [illegible] "[illegible] will [illegible]

[illegible] you [illegible]

[illegible]"

[illegible], but I don't think [illegible]

[illegible] "But I [illegible]

[illegible] would [illegible] I [illegible]

[illegible] you

[illegible]

Chapter Sixteen

As Donald pulled away in his car, Menno walked to the barn, looking over his shoulder and seeing the retreating forms of Anna and Susan heading into the house. There wasn't much he could say to them right now. He had apologized again, and Anna had seemed to understand. But Susan? That was another matter. In the meantime, how could such sorrow and joy be racing through his heart at the same time? He had a *son*!

He quickened his pace. Steve probably wondered what had happened to him. He was in the field already cutting the corn. Menno took a quick look into the distance. *Yah*, Steve was busily at work, the corn binder throwing the sheaves out behind it.

Menno hesitated. Should he or shouldn't he? The thought raced through his mind. All these years he had never willingly neglected work, yet this morning had been different than any other morning. And it was not over yet. His other daughters needed to know the good news. After they were told, he would need to tell others. Deacon Ray would hear the truth from his own lips, Menno decided. And Deacon Ray would do what he wished after that. Yet even the thought of what might be coming did little to dim the joy in his heart. He had been given a son! No one could take that away.

Running across the field, Menno waved his hat at Steve, smiling at the startled look on his hired hand's face.

"Whoa!" Steve pulled back on the lines. "You must have very *gut* news to share," he said, turning to Menno

"I do! I have a son. The *Englisha* man is my son."

"Your son?" Steve was staring now. "How is that possible?"

"It is a long story, Steve, and in many ways a sad one. But *Da Hah* has brought good from a sin of my youth."

"I see," Steve said, understanding coming slowly. "Is this man staying around?"

"*Nee*, he's gone back to Missouri where he lives. And now there are some matters I need to take care of today. Can you go on with the corn yourself?"

"Sure. I'll start setting up the stacks when I'm done with the field. How long will you be gone?"

"It may be all day. There are things more important to me right now than the farm. I wish to speak with my daughters about the news. And then I will speak with Deacon Ray and the other leaders."

Steve shrugged. "Do what you need to. I will carry on the best I can."

"I will see you later then."

Steve nodded, slapping the lines. The horses lurched forward.

Returning to the barn, Menno harnessed Toby and tied him to the hitching post. He then hurried toward the house. Across the lawn, he saw Ada walking up the road from her place. And from the other direction another buggy was approaching. He recognized two of his daughters—Betsy and Miriam. They were arriving to begin the cleanup from the wedding, moving down to Ada's place afterwards. Already *Da Hah* was making the path clear for him.

Menno stopped and turned toward the driveway. He greeted Betsy and Miriam as they drove up and climbed out of the buggy. "*Gut* morning!"

"What are you still around the house for, *Daett*?" Betsy asked.

"We've had a lot going on this morning," Menno said as he undid the tugs.

"I see you have the benches loaded," Miriam commented.

Menno cleared his throat. "*Yah.* I need to speak with the two of you. And with Ada too. I'll meet you in the house as soon as I put your horse in the barn."

They glanced at each other as they took their cleaning supplies from behind the buggy seat.

This was going to be even harder than he had thought. Most of the excitement was gone that had been present when he'd told Susan. Taking the horse into the barn and putting him into a stall, Menno slid the bridle off. He shut the stall door and shoved a quarter of a bale of hay into the manger before walking back to the house. How would the girls take this news? The joy was indeed leaving his heart, seeping away under the weight of the words that lay ahead. Yet he could still see Donald's face. *Yah*, Menno thought, my sin had been great, but the goodness of *Da Hah* was just as great—*nee*, it was even greater.

Menno squared his shoulders and walked into the house. Betsy, Miriam, and Ada were standing in the living room with *Mamm* beside them.

"I'm not telling you a thing," *Mamm* was saying. From the tone of her voice, he guessed she'd said it before. "Your *daett* will have to tell you himself."

"What is it, *Daett*?" Miriam asked turning to face him when she heard the door open.

Behind them Maurice appeared in the stair doorway with baby Samuel in her arms. Silence fell over the living room.

"Am I interrupting something?" Maurice asked hesitantly.

"If you could give us a moment, Maurice." *Mamm* tried to smile. "Menno has something he needs to tell the girls."

"Sure..." Maurice was already turning, and one foot was on the first step.

"Wait, Maurice," Menno said. "I want you to hear what I have to say. I will not keep this secret any longer."

"But Menno!" *Mamm* protested.

"This is going to be more than a family issue," Menno told her. "It involves everyone. The entire community will know very soon."

"Okay," *Mamm* agreed, motioning Maurice toward the couch. She then turned and called toward the kitchen, "Susan, please come in here."

"I already know what *Daett*'s going to say," Susan's muffled voice answered.

"Come anyway," *Mamm* said, taking her seat on the rocking chair.

Susan appeared a moment later bringing a chair. She sat down, still wiping her eyes. The other daughters sat down and waited, worried looks on their faces.

Menno cleared his throat. "Girls, there is no easy way for me to say this. And yet it must be said, so I will waste no words. A man arrived this morning—well, he was here yesterday. I'm sure you noticed him."

"*Yah*," Ada said. "I spoke with him. He's doing research..."

"*Nee*," Menno said. "He is not really doing research. His real name is Donald Fry, and...and he is my son."

There was stunned silence.

"I know this will be hard to hear and believe," Menno continued. "I will explain. Forty-some years ago while I was doing my military alternative service in St. Louis, I went out with an *Englisha* girl. Her name was Carol and she worked at the hospital. We went to parties together, and...well, one thing led to another, and...I...I did something I shouldn't have. I committed a great sin. Then Carol told me she was pregnant. Not long after that, she told me the child had been lost. I believed her."

The women were still silent, so Menno kept going. "We had talked about our different worlds. She was raised Catholic, and I came from the community. Neither of us wanted to come the other's way. And we parted. Not in the best of circumstances, of course, but for what we thought was the best. Yet I found out a week or so ago that she had not told me the truth. She hadn't lost the child. She thought she was making it easier for me—and for her—by going her way and letting me go mine. She placed him for adoption when he was born. After he grew up, Donald contacted Carol, and she, in turn, contacted me. And he has come to find me."

"You really did this?" Ada finally asked.

"*Yah*, Ada. I repented of this sin years ago, but the consequences of sin are far reaching. And now I must face it in the open. I shared this with your *mamm*, and she has forgiven me and agreed to accept Donald. I told Susan when Donald came here this morning. Now I am telling you. I will be writing to your other sisters, and Anna and I will go to Deacon Ray this morning yet."

Betsy was the first to her feet. She walked forward to give her father a hug. The others followed. Susan stayed on her chair and Maurice stayed on the couch.

"I'm very sorry about this," Menno said for all their benefit. "I know this comes as a shock."

"When did *Mamm* know about this?" Ada asked. "I never heard a whisper about it growing up."

"I knew some of the story," *Mamm* offered. "But even your *daett* didn't know Donald was alive until a short time ago."

"May I say something?" Maurice asked. "I don't want to speak out of turn..."

When Menno nodded, she continued. "This might come as a surprise to all of you, but this story is the most incredible thing I've heard in my life. And believe me, I've heard a lot."

"I hope you don't think ill of our people because of this." Menno looked troubled. "Because I'm the one who sinned."

"Gracious no!" Maurice exclaimed. "You're human, that's all. Don't you think that makes me feel better, not worse? I was beginning to think you were all angels walking the earth in human form."

"*Nee*, we are not angels," *Mamm* assured her.

Maurice laughed. "That's what everyone kept saying, and now it's nice to have some evidence—and in language I can understand. Things like having a baby out of wedlock...a hidden pregnancy...an adoption too. Now that's my world."

"I'm very sorry about all this," Menno said again. "I beg your forgiveness."

"Not to trample on your piety, Menno, but thank you for letting me be part of this. I believe your God is more real after experiencing this confession. I was beginning to wonder. It's good to know He can handle the human failings part of life."

"I have sinned," Menno said. "But I have also seen my son this morning—my only son. I repented of the sin years ago. But even with the sorrow there is joy in my heart."

"Come, Menno." *Mamm* took his arm. "We have to speak with Deacon Ray. And then you must write to the other girls before the news reaches their communities." She turned to the girls. "While we are gone, you can get started on the cleanup work."

Together Menno and Anna walked across the lawn, Anna's hand around his arm. Helping her into the buggy, Menno untied Toby. He climbed into the buggy. Slapping the reins gently against the horse's back, he drove down the road without looking back.

The girls were at the window watching their *daett* and *mamm* leave.

Never again would they look at him quite the same, Menno realized. Sure, they had offered their forgiveness, but he would live with this disappointment for the rest of his days. The shame of it seeped into his very bones. Yet he would also rejoice over his son. He would welcome him home whenever he chose to come. The whole situation would lie in his heart in one irreconcilable bundle. Much like the wrath and the mercy of *Da Hah*. Unexplained, unresolved, and yet existing sid by side. *Da Hah* wouldn't fully undo, in this world at least, the dark deeds of men.

"I'm very sorry," Menno muttered again, the reins held tight in his weathered hands.

"*Yah*," Anna said. "And you should be. That was a very wicked thing you did all those years ago. You broke that poor girl's heart. She wouldn't have told you what she did if she hadn't loved you and wanted the best for you."

"We didn't belong in each other's worlds. You know that, Anna. I have loved you with all my heart."

She took his arm. "Some things aren't meant to be understood, Menno. As for me, it is enough that you came back all those years ago. And that you have been a *gut* husband to me. I wouldn't ask for our lives together to have been different."

His beard blew over his shoulder, as a sudden gust of wind rocked the buggy. Menno held on to the lines. "I am not worthy of you, Anna. You know I have never been."

She tucked her hair under her *kapp*, ignoring his comment. "You also realize what Deacon Ray is going to say about this, don't you?"

"I suppose I do. He'll now know why I worked so hard on Teresa's behalf."

"Was that the only reason?"

"She is also like a daughter to me. You know that."

"It'll make no difference to Deacon Ray. You'll be excommunicated. There's no question in my mind."

Menno sighed. "Even if I've repented?"

"It won't be enough, Menno. You've hidden the matter for all these years, and now the whole community will be shamed. They'll excommunicate you for a long time—months no doubt."

"I'm sorry for your sake, Anna. As for me, I'll be happy to sleep in the barn until my time is done."

"You'll do no such thing," she said. "I'll not have your side of the bed cold while mine is warm."

Menno glanced down at her face. "You would join me? Even in the great darkness outside the church?"

"We will be warm together," she said. "And the grace of *Da Hah* will not forsake us. Besides, Deacon Ray will never believe I didn't know. A woman supposedly always knows."

"And did you know?"

"I thought of it once, Menno. But I figured it was only my imagination. I did know there was a sorrow in your heart."

"I'm sorry, Anna. So very sorry."

Chapter Seventeen

Menno brought the buggy to a halt beside Deacon Ray's barn and climbed out. Anna stayed inside while Menno tied the horse. Wash hung on the lines behind the house, swaying in the morning breeze. The noise of a small engine running filled the morning air. Moments later Deacon Ray's wife, Esther, appeared as she climbed up the outside basement steps. In her arms she carried a hamper of wet wash.

"*Gut* morning!" Esther called across the lawn. She set down her hamper and came toward them.

Anna waved and climbed out of the buggy.

"You'd better go talk with her," Menno said, "while I find Deacon Ray."

"I will do nothing of the sort," Anna stated. "I'm staying with you."

"She needs to know why we're here."

"Is Ray around?" Anna called to Esther and put on her best smile.

"*Yah*, here he comes now." Esther looked over her shoulder. "He was fixing the washing machine motor for me."

A surprised look crossed Deacon Ray's face when he saw who was waiting for him. But he came toward them with a firm step. Esther turned back and picked up her hamper. With a quick nod toward Anna, she headed to the back of the house.

She knew this was church business, Menno figured. And Deacon Ray would tell Esther the news once they left. As well he should. Soon everyone would know he had a son among the *Englisha* people. But even when the shame came crashing down on his shoulders he would know he had a son. That was something he would never wish to change.

"*Gut* morning," Deacon Ray greeted them, smiling to Anna. "I hope you don't come with bad news on this morning after the wedding."

"*Nee.*" Menno tried to smile. "But we do have some serious business. There's no easy way to say this, so I'll just have it out. The *Englisha* man who was at the wedding yesterday stopped by this morning. It turns out he's my son. I'm here to let you know and explain the situation. I wanted to be the one to tell you."

Deacon Ray's mouth fell open. "Your *son*? But you have no son."

"It turns out I do. Do you remember the time you and I spent in St. Louis doing our alternative service? Perhaps you remember I was seeing an *Englisha* girl. Her name was Carol."

Deacon Ray nodded. Then he turned to Anna. "Did you know about this?"

Menno spoke up. "Deacon Ray, I didn't even know Donald existed until a week or so ago. So how could Anna have known?"

Deacon Ray turned back to Menno. "The *Englisha* girl didn't tell you she was...expecting?"

"Yes, she did. But later Carol told me she'd lost the baby. I believed her. Perhaps because I wanted to believe her? *Yah*, but this does not change anything now. We parted ways, Carol and I. She moved back to her hometown, and I came back here. I didn't hear from her again until she wrote me some time ago to tell me I have a son. His name is Donald. And I'm glad he has found me."

"You don't sound very repentant, Menno. I'm surprised at you. And you told no one of this matter? For all these years? Not even Anna?"

"How could Menno tell me about his son if he didn't know himself?" Anna asked. "I hope you use some common sense in handling this and don't go racing off on some wild judgment."

"Now, Anna." Deacon Ray gave her a stern look. "You know me better than that. I don't plan to go racing anywhere. But this is a matter of grave concern. Menno has been a member of the church since his youth. He has played a hand in many church matters, giving his counsel, which we took as coming from an upright man. Now we find out that he has a son in the *Englisha* world. That cannot be ignored, Anna."

"You can do with me what you wish," Menno told him. "I have met my son, and he's a blessing from *Da Hah*. Even if he was conceived in sin."

Deacon Ray nodded. "I wouldn't wish the man to bear any of your shame, Menno. The *Englisha* man I saw seemed decent. And now I thank *Da Hah* that I did invite him to the wedding. I see what lay behind all this. As the Scriptures say, the man who covers his sin will not prosper. It was nothing but *Da Hah*'s grace from the beginning to bring this out into the open. And you helped hide this, Anna? For all these years?"

"We've told you. Menno did not know of his son until a few days ago. He told me the morning of the wedding what there was to tell," Anna said. "Menno didn't know his *Englisha* son had been born."

"And I'm supposed to believe this? Coming from you, his wife? You shared your heart and your bed with this man for all these years, and yet you knew nothing of his sin with an *Englisha* girl?"

"There are things one does not speak of, Ray. And you of all persons should know that."

"Well, perhaps you aren't as guilty as he is, Anna. But you should have asked questions. That's what a wife is supposed to do when she suspects sin in the life of her husband. None of us are to turn a blind eye to evil."

"I saw a heart in Menno that sought after the will of *Da Hah*. It was not in me to question that, regardless of what sins lay in his past. It's not like any of us have always done what is right. And Menno has lived honorably all these many years. He has loved me, and I have no regrets for the marriage we've had."

Menno cleared his throat. "It's best we talk of this without harsh words. I will take whatever punishment you and the community see fit to give. It was my sin, and I will own it. I repented of the sin years ago with *Da Hah*, although I didn't talk of it publicly. I will not have Anna carry any of this on her shoulders. She knew nothing of it until a few days ago."

Deacon Ray looked down for a minute or two. Then he looked at Menno. "This is a great shame, Menno. I will take the matter up with the ministers and with Bishop Henry. Then we'll decide what is the right way to go."

Anna straightened her shoulders. "If you choose to excommunicate Menno, I will still share his bed. You should know that now."

"Anna, please!" Menno touched her shoulder.

"Anna, it would be best if you stayed out of this," Deacon Ray said. "This is the sin of Menno, and he should bear his own burden."

"I am his wife. Nothing that has happened changes that. I will stand by him."

"You would not forsake him for false doctrine?" Deacon Ray stared at her. "You would stand with Menno if he left the faith?"

"*Nee*, I wouldn't repent. And you know that. But Menno isn't leaving the faith. He is choosing to submit to whatever consequences the community leaders decide. You heard him say so. I will stand with him in this decision. Even if it means the darkness of being cut off from the fellowship of the church for a time."

"I will speak with the others on this matter." Deacon Ray stroked his beard. "This news will be a great sorrow. All of us will walk with bent shoulders for many days. I wish you had brought this up years ago, Menno. Perhaps at your baptism. It would have been dealt with much lighter there."

"What one should have done is not what one always does," Menno said. "In my heart I did repent at that time, and I spoke with *Da Hah* about it. But now my son has found me. I accept him, and I accept what must be done. In that I will be satisfied. You and the church leaders will let me know what is decided. I will not protest whatever is chosen to do."

"At least I'm thankful for that," Deacon Ray said. "But this won't be an easy decision for any of us. I know it has broken my heart already this morning. The others will feel the same. The shame of this will be a heavy burden on the community."

"As well it should be," Menno agreed. "And now we will be going. I'm sure you have things to do, and we have cleanup from the wedding to tend to."

"May *Da Hah* have mercy on all of us," Deacon Ray said, stepping back from the buggy. Menno helped Anna climb in. He then untied Toby and got into the buggy. Menno turned the horse, and they drove away. Esther, returning from the wash lines with an empty hamper, waved to them as they drove out of the driveway.

A mile down the road, Menno put his arm around Anna's shoulder, pulling her tightly against him. "You didn't have to do that, dear. I would have borne my shame alone."

She leaned against him and burst into tears. "Why did you do this sinful thing, Menno? I know you were young and still thinking about whether to join the world or not. But an *Englisha* girl? How could you? Is that why you never told me? Because she was more beautiful than I? Is that why I never asked questions? Because I feared the answer? Did you ever wish you stayed in her world, Menno? Did you want to? Tell me the truth. I need to know."

"Anna, please…" Menno soothed her. "It was none of those things. Nothing but my shame has followed me from those days. I never wished to go back. I could have if I'd wanted to. I wasn't forced to leave my work at the hospital. Carol would have stayed with me."

"Are you telling me the truth, Menno?"

"*Yah.* And you'll just have to believe me because I don't know what else to say. I love you, Anna."

"I don't know what to believe right now, Menno. I could have said something before now about the sorrow I saw in you. I could have asked about the little things. Like how troubled you were when Susan left for the *Englisha* world. And, especially, when she brought Teresa back. Or when our children were born. You seemed to have a sadness inside. And all of them were girls. Do you regret that, Menno? Did that bring you sorrow? I knew there were questions in your mind. I knew something from your past haunted you."

"Anna…Anna..." He drew her close. "It's not your fault. This problem lies with me. This was my sin…my doing. And it's only by *Da Hah*'s grace that any good has come out of it."

Anna looked at him. "Do you think the darkness of being separated from the church will be a small matter? We're both old, Menno. What if our souls are called home during those weeks? How will we explain that to *Da Hah*?"

"That is why you must not walk with me through that valley. And, Anna, *Da Hah* knows what has happened. He knows I repented of this sin and talked to Him about it many years ago."

Anna sighed. "Perhaps Deacon Ray will have some sense and keep a level head about him."

Menno snorted. "I'm afraid that's not going to happen."

Anna ignored him. "We will pray. We will pray hard. So much *gut* has already been done by *Da Hah* in these past years. Susan has come back, and Teresa is now married and in the community. Perhaps *Da Hah* will do more. We should not imagine evil where there is none, remember? You always look on the dark side of things, Menno."

"It must be my old age and my sins," Menno said, pulling into the driveway and coming to a stop by the barn.

"We will not speak so anymore," Anna said, climbing out of the buggy. "Let's count our blessings and be thankful for what *Da Hah* has given."

"You are a *gut* wife, Anna. Too *gut* for me."

She smiled, reaching up to rub the last of the tears from her cheeks before walking toward the house. Menno watched her before unhitching. He led the horse to the barn, where he unhooked the harness and hung it on the wall. He put Toby in his stall. Through the open double doors he saw Steve still working in the cornfield. Sheaves of corn were kicking out of the back of the cutter and falling to the ground.

"*Da Hah*," Menno prayed, "what am I going to do? What do You want me to do now?" Slipping behind the manger, he threw his hat on the floor and fell to his knees beside a bale of straw. He buried his face in his arms. The face of Donald came into focus. There were questions in his eyes, and Menno groaned. He saw each of his daughters after they were born, one by one. Each one precious. They had been his and Anna's. Why had he been allowed such joy after what he had done? "Please spare Anna from the pain of my sin," he prayed. "And change her mind about walking through this darkness with me. It's not her fault, dear *Da Hah*. You know that. She was pure when I married her. It was I who wasn't honest. And protect my daughters from the shame of what I've done. Help them bear this. Let the worst fall upon my shoulders. But I do thank You that Donald has found me. I thank You that he's my son. And that he lived to see the light of day. I give You thanks that he walks on the earth. Be with Donald as he returns home. And allow him to view me with forgiveness in his heart."

After a few moments of silence, Menno rose and put his hat back on. He walked across the field to Steve. Sorrow and joy had arrived together in his heart, and they were at war. And this was as it should be. *Da Hah* was revealing what had been long hidden. If the pain was more than he could bear, *Da Hah*'s grace would be made available. And Menno could blame no one but himself. This was all his own fault.

"How did things go?" Steve asked after stopping the horses at Menno's approach.

"As well as could be expected. There will be difficult days ahead as everything is sorted out."

"My heart has been heavy thinking of Susan and how she will handle this."

"I know." Menno bent over to stack corn sheaves. "So have I...and also of the other girls. This will hurt all of them."

"I'm glad you met your son," Steve said. He nodded and then commanded the horses to move on. They stepped forward.

Menno watched Steve go. Now there was a *gut* young man, he thought. One who knew what to say in times of sorrow.

Chapter Eighteen

Donald watched the rolling Missouri hills pass by his car window as he drove toward his mother's house. She would want to know about his adventure. In fact, she had called again last night asking for news. Of course Mom has a right to know. To share in the news of how he had found his biological father. But how would he explain everything to her? This feeling he had from visiting the Amish community—it was like he had sleepwalked into another century. What a life the Amish lived. In his short time there, he'd noticed they were disciplined, hardworking, punctual, and deeply devoted to doing the will of God on this earth. Ironically, his biological father was one among them. All men had weaknesses, he supposed. Even godly ones. Menno had certainly given him a welcome, which couldn't have been easy. Everyone at the wedding festivities had been friendly. But underneath he'd felt a current of something, perhaps a streak of hardness that wouldn't bode well for people stepping outside the Amish traditions. And his birth father certainly was a transgressor. He might not fare that well when the news of his son's visit reached the ears of the community. Perhaps he should have stayed away? Kept this to himself? Especially after he realized his birth father was Amish. Yet driven by a need to know more, he hadn't been able to help himself.

Approaching the edge of town, Donald slowed down as he wound through the streets of the small burg. His mother's house appeared on the right. A small, blue, single-story his parents had purchased twenty years ago, soon after his father's first stroke. Now that his adoptive father Charles was gone, Ruthann kept the place up on her own. That would end soon, whether either of them liked it or not. She would need to move to a retirement home so she wouldn't have to deal with cleaning, laundry, and cooking meals.

He pulled into the driveway and parked. Ruthann was sitting on the front porch in her wooden rocker, her favorite place on sunny summer afternoons. The chill of autumn was already in the air, but she would keep the ritual going for a while, hoping to draw the last warmth from the Indian Summer days.

He walked up to the porch and bent over to kiss her on the cheek before sitting down on a rocker next to her.

She smiled. "Good to see you, Donald. Sorry to bug you last night. How did it go? I want to hear everything."

He smiled back. "Well, I found him."

"I knew you would. I'm glad for you, son. What is he like?"

"Have you ever heard of the Amish?"

"Yes, of course."

"My birth father is Amish, Mom. How strange is that?"

"That's interesting. Did they chase you off their property when you arrived?"

"Not at all!" Donald laughed. "They were friendly, really. I got invited to a wedding. Their deacon's son was marrying one of my birth father's daughters. Only it wasn't his real daughter. She was sort of adopted, they said. It was all nicely done. And it gave me a chance to observe them before I dropped the news of who I was."

"What did he have to say?"

"He was a little incredulous, of course. But Carol had written him. He said he wrote to me, but he'd only mailed the letter the day before. He said he just received Carol's note a week or so before. He remembered Carol."

"Did he try to convert you to his religion?"

"No." Donald laughed again. "No one made any pitch at all for me to join their community. I think you would have liked them, Mom."

"Well, maybe. At any rate, I'm happy for you, Donald."

"Thanks, Mom. I knew you would be."

They rocked on the porch in silence until Donald said, "You know what, Mom? Being with the Amish gave me an idea. A solution to the problem of you living alone here."

"Donald." She held up her hand. "I appreciate your concern. But I can get around fine. I'm not going anywhere—especially to some adult care center."

"Mom," he protested, "that's not where I was going."

"Plus your father didn't leave me a rich woman, Donald. And don't tell me you'll pay for a better place. I'm not falling for that line, regardless of how loving a son you are."

"Mom, please. What I want to say is that I could move here or you could move to my place. Either way is fine with me. We can rent out the extra house to get some cash-flow going. It's ridiculous that we're living alone in separate places when we have plenty of room to share."

She wasn't looking at him. "You should get married again, Donald. The single life isn't good for you. And I don't want to be in the way when you find the right woman."

"I'm not seeing anyone, Mom."

"Well, you should be. You were seeing someone a while back, weren't you?"

"Yes, but that doesn't change anything now. We're family, you and I. If Mandy and I ever get back together and get serious and marry, well, she'd be joining our family. In the meantime, you can have one of the bedrooms at one end and I'll take the other. Surely we can get along with each other, Mom. The Amish do it all the time."

"That's very sweet of you, Donald." She patted his arm. "I'll have to think about it. It would mean moving to your place, since your house is better situated for that arrangement."

"When you're ready, I am." Donald rocked gently in the chair.

A smile crossed her face. "So tell me about this Amish man who is your father."

"You and Dad will always be my true mother and father," Donald assured her.

"I know that, Donald. But tell me about your birth father."

Donald spoke without hesitation. "His name is Menno Hostetler. He's medium-height, gray-haired, has a long beard down to the middle of his chest, friendly face, and seems quick to smile. Your average, loving, Amish grandfather, I suppose."

"Is he married with children?"

"Yes. And his wife was very understanding. He has nine daughters. He was very excited about having a son."

"Where do they live?"

"In southern Indiana. It's a place of rolling hills. Not unlike here, only better farming country. I can't imagine it getting quite as hot during the summer. I noticed Menno has a large farm and a hired hand."

"You're not thinking of an inheritance from the man, are you, Donald? Because you shouldn't."

"Of course not." Donald chuckled. "I wanted to meet him, that's all. And Menno must feel the same way. He and his wife, Anna, invited me to come back for Thanksgiving or Christmas."

"And you're going?"

"Yes, I would love to go. They're wonderful people—not to mention that they're family."

"What did his wife have to say about her husband having a son from another woman? And out of wedlock, at that."

Donald sighed. "She was nice enough. No hostility that I could see. She seemed to know something about me, so he must have told her before I arrived."

"Good for him. There's nothing like hiding a sin to make things worse."

"I have a bad feeling though." Donald grimaced. "I think my visit to Menno will result in serious problems for him. I got the impression the Amish aren't the kind of people to sweep things like my existence under the rug. He mentioned that he hadn't told anyone about Carol."

"Well, that's interesting." She settled back in her rocker. "It might do the man good to suffer for what he did. Forsaking a young girl in the hour of her need."

"Carol told him she miscarried, so he didn't even know about me until a week or so ago. And I believe him, Mom."

"I still don't think he was very eager to find out he was going to be a father. That's probably why she told him what she did."

"Possibly, but we'll never really know. And that's in the past. It's the future, I'm thinking about. Say, would you like to go back with me for one of the holidays? I'm sure they would welcome you. And I'd love to have your company."

"I think you'd better go by yourself. I doubt I'd fit in very well with the Amish from all I've heard."

"I suppose not." Disappointment flashed over his face. "But you'll consider moving in with me, won't you? That much Amishness you can accept, right? And you know it's time. You could fall and hurt yourself. Or you might need something, and I wouldn't be here to help you. Think of the benefits of being at my place. And I wouldn't be around during the day, so that would give you time alone."

She smiled. "I'll have to think about it, Donald."

"Well, I haven't even been home yet. I stopped here first. I'd better go." He got up and kissed her on the cheek.

"I'm glad you found your birth father, Donald."

"I know you are, and I appreciate it," Donald said. He turned and walked to his car. He got in, started it up, and backed down the driveway. On the way home, Donald ran the idea of his mother moving in with him through his mind. The longer he thought about it, the better the idea seemed. How wonderful this was. Already good was coming out of his visit to Amish country. The idea to bring his mom to his place seemed so simple now, so obvious. Why hadn't he thought of it on his own?

Was modern life like that? So far removed from the ordinary, from the idea of a home place, that common sense no longer grew? It certainly seemed so. Having seen horses working in the fields and Amish buggies from another era driving up and down gravel roads, even he had changed. And wasn't that singing at the wedding something? It had stirred feelings in him he didn't even know were there.

Was this his Amish blood coming forward? Donald laughed at the thought. Half Amish, that's what he was. That didn't make sense either. One wasn't born with such things. They had to grow in the heart, had to be cultivated with silence, with prayer, with humility, with the virtues of another time and place. One didn't just drop those desirable qualities into one's life by right of birth.

But one thing was certain. His son could use some of what the Amish had. All of the decency he and Sonia had tried to plant in him were being cast aside right now. The music his son listened to was awful. The boy had been named Charles because Donald's adoptive father had been so upright and law abiding. And now the boy was turning into a rebel, even wearing his pants down over his hips and hanging halfway to his knees. Charles and his buddies were into being cool. Acting like ghosts traveling through life...and arriving at nothing.

Structure. That's what Charles hated. And so quickly he had turned from the likable boy into this person who wasn't very likable at all. Could he get Charles to go to Amish country with him at Thanksgiving? What a clash of culture that would be! The essence of structure running into its most bitter enemy. Donald sighed. Somehow he would have to convince Charles to go with him. Lure him with tales of the quaintness and uniqueness. Perhaps talk of the weirdness of Amish life. After all, the Amish *were* a little weird, and Charles did weird.

Chapter Nineteen

On Monday morning Susan hitched Toby to the buggy and climbed in. She waited, holding the reins loosely in her hands. Maurice's suitcase was already behind the backseat, but she hadn't come out yet, no doubt taking her time saying goodbye to *Mamm*. Not that Maurice was going far this morning—only over to James and Teresa's place. Maurice had grown close to *Mamm* in the short time she'd been in the community. How long she was staying was still anyone's guess. If Teresa had anything to say about it, her mother wasn't leaving anytime soon.

Finally the door on the porch swung open and Maurice came out, followed closely by *Mamm*. They embraced, lingering for a moment before Maurice came across the yard.

"Sorry I didn't help with the horse." Maurice paused to wipe her eyes. "But we got to talking. I'll miss your mother even though I'll only be down the road a bit."

"You're always welcome back for a visit." Susan leaned down to give Maurice a hand for her step up into the buggy.

"Whee! I'm still not used to getting into these things." Maurice settled onto the seat. "And thanks for what all of you have done for me in the time I've been here."

"You're welcome," Susan said, guiding the horse toward the main road. "Have you decided yet about staying in the area?"

"I still don't know." Maurice sighed. "It's hard. I can't stay at Teresa's forever."

"You know our house is open, but I'm sure *Mamm* already told you that."

"Yes, she did. But I can't stay around here forever, either. You people have your own lives to live. And I need to make a living."

"Well, it's been *gut* to have you be part of our lives here."

They rode in silence, the fields of cut corn passing by to the sound of the horse's soft hoofbeats on the graveled road. Sheaves were stacked at irregular intervals, their long stalks pointing into the air. The random pattern flowed together until it looked designed, as if someone had placed each stack with great care.

"It's so beautiful here," Maurice gushed. "Not at all like Asbury Park."

"I guess that's why I came back. For that and for Teresa's sake."

"What a dear you are." Maurice put her arm around Susan's shoulder. "Your mom told me about your boyfriend dropping you for another girl. I'm so sorry."

Susan smiled, the effort weak. "What is it with the men in my life?"

"Now, don't be blaming yourself. You're a wonderful girl. Believe me, I wouldn't just say so. Somewhere in these hollows lurks the perfect fellow for you. I can almost see him coming now. Running out of one of these lovely farms to take you as his bride."

Susan laughed. "You must be dreaming! But it's nice of you to say so."

"We all need to dream a little. It's what keeps us going."

"I don't think I'll be dreaming much anymore. Not after mine keep getting popped like balloons."

Maurice sighed and fell silent. After a few minutes she said, "I hope you're not sore at your father."

Susan kept her eyes on the road. "Perhaps. I don't know."

"Being upset would be normal, dear," Maurice assured her. "Although I don't know from experience. My father was never around to be anything good or bad."

"I'm sorry. I didn't know that."

"I'm not asking for sympathy; I'm just giving you perspective. Mine only, that's true. But it is a perspective. And I'm not your mother, so maybe you'll believe me when I say that your father is a very wonderful person. Don't hold against him something he did a long time ago, and he has spent a lot of effort making right. Look how he's lived his life since his youth. I'd give a million dollars and then some to have such a father."

"Thank you," Susan said. "I'll try to remember that."

Maurice smiled and watched the passing farms.

Susan took a deep breath before speaking. "If you're staying around much longer, you're going to hear this anyway, so I'm not spreading rumors. *Daett* will face some kind of discipline from the church. Our people don't look kindly to keeping things hidden. Especially not something like this and for so many years."

"My, you people are a bundle of contradictions!" Maurice exclaimed.

"Yes, we can be. We are human, after all."

Maurice shook her head. "Yet who am I to say how a whole community is to be run? Perhaps you have to make hard choices for the common good."

"Something like that," Susan muttered as she turned Toby down Teresa's driveway. She forced her thoughts toward more pleasant subjects.

The homey little place took her breath away this morning. Even more so now that she knew baby Samuel and Teresa were actually living here. This was one time when dreams had become reality. Perhaps there was hope for her own dream? She would have to keep up her hope. Teresa had done so even when the road had been long and hard.

"I see my little sweetheart at the window!" Maurice proclaimed, interrupting Susan's thoughts. "Waving from his mamma's arms at his grandma as she arrives in a buggy. Who would have ever thought this possible?"

"Not me," Susan said, climbing down and then reaching back to give Maurice a hand. Maurice waved it off, placing one foot on the round step and then leaping to the ground with a shriek.

Susan laughed. "You're getting quite good at this, but don't try that at church on Sunday morning. The leaders don't appreciate noisy women climbing out of buggies."

"Then I will be decorous, prim, and proper on Sundays. Only in front of my daughters will my real self be shown to the world," Maurice announced.

Susan tied Toby up, and together the two women walked to the front door. Teresa pushed it wide open with one hand before they arrived. The wiggling Samuel was in her arms and reaching out to Maurice.

Susan waited while the three hugged. Then she gave Teresa a hug while Maurice held Samuel and smothered his face with kisses.

"You'd think we haven't seen each other in years, you little dear," Maurice cooed. "I just saw you on Sunday."

"I think the days are longer, fuller, and richer in Amish country," Teresa said. "It seems like more life has gone by than really has."

"I do believe you're correct," Maurice agreed. "Now tell me, how is this husband of yours treating you?"

"Oh, Mom, you have no idea how sweet he is!" Tears sprang up in Teresa's eyes. "He's too wonderful for words."

"Then let's hope he stays that way." Maurice laughed.

"Everything stays wonderful around here," Teresa declared. "At least it seems so."

"Ah, the rosy eyes of young love." Maurice gave Teresa a kiss on the cheek. "Now let me put this little boy on his blanket before he climbs out of my arms."

Baby Samuel kicked his feet after being put down, reaching up with both arms for Maurice again.

"You'd better hold him, Mom," Teresa said. "I don't think he's had enough of you yet."

"Oh, you little sweetheart!" Maurice picked Samuel up for another round of smooches.

When the kissing and cooing had stopped, Teresa said, "You can have the room upstairs, Mom. The one facing east. That way you can watch the sunrise each morning."

"You're spoiling me," Maurice said. "And my suitcase? I do declare! I left it in the buggy."

"I'll get it," Susan said. "We'll blame Samuel that we forgot. It was his grinning in the window that distracted us."

Susan ran across the lawn to the buggy and returned with the suitcase. She paused on the porch, remembering the day she'd first come here to clean with Teresa. It wasn't that long ago, but already it seemed like life had changed dramatically. Now it was better. Teresa was married and happy. Susan smiled at the thought. But was life better for her since she'd lost Thomas? With a sigh she went back into the house. Teresa and Maurice's animated voices were coming from upstairs.

Maurice would be happy here, Susan figured. Teresa could teach her the ways of the community, which Maurice wanted to learn. But was she really going down the same path Teresa had? Possibly joining the community? It could happen. Maurice had never said one way or the other. She loved the life, that much was clear. But joining was another matter.

Taking the steps one at a time with the heavy suitcase, Susan made her way upstairs. On the top of the landing she went toward the sound of the voices. The two women were in the east room, unfolding a quilt on the bed when she walked in. Baby Samuel sat on the floor. He looked up and laughed when he saw her.

"We should have helped you carry the suitcase up the stairs!" Teresa exclaimed as she turned around.

Maurice grabbed the suitcase as if to make up for the lost opportunity.

Susan grinned. "I didn't grow up on a farm for nothing."

"Well, that's true," Maurice agreed. "Being in good shape is one of the privileges of country living. I was just telling Teresa that I want her to start looking for a small house I can rent. Preferably close by so I can visit back and forth easily. And I think I'll start looking for a job in Salem since it's the closest city. That is, if Teresa can take me there in the next week or so."

"But, Mom," Teresa interrupted, "you know you're welcome right here. And it would be much cheaper than renting your own place."

"Cheaper but not practical," Maurice said. "I need my own place if I'm going to stay a while."

"Well, let's take this one step at a time." Teresa sighed. "For now, we're going to make you at home here. And baby Samuel and I are going to enjoy your presence fully."

"I really have to get back home," Susan said. "Work awaits."

Teresa gave her a hug, and Maurice kissed her cheek. "You be a good girl now!" Maurice said.

"Oh, I will," Susan said with a laugh. As she made her way downstairs and through the living room, she caught sight of James in a field behind the barn. He was driving a wagon and glancing toward the house. When she got out on the porch she waved, and James lifted his hand in greeting, his hat pushed back on his head.

How different James had turned out to be from his friend Thomas, Susan thought as she untied Toby and got into the buggy. James was loyal and faithful, sticking by Teresa's side even when his own father wouldn't give his blessing. Now things had turned around for them, almost like the *Englisha* fairy tales she'd read in the school library.

Susan drove out of the driveway, turning to cross the bridge that spanned the little creek nearby. The running water made a soft gurgling sound, reaching her ears now that she was alone. It was strange how one heard things when alone that were missed when in the company of others. Had she perhaps been missing something else in her life? Something that was near at hand but drowned out by the racket? Susan laughed at the thought.

What a silly mess she was in to grasp at such straws. Life was exactly the same now as it had been before. She was apparently the problem, not the boys. That had to be the answer. Maybe she didn't have what it takes to be an Amish wife. Painful as that idea was, perhaps it was time to face it. Was life among the *Englisha* what she really needed? The driver's license was still hidden in her upstairs drawer. *Mamm* would have a fit if she knew she had it, especially with what she was going through now.

Allowing Toby to take his time, Susan thought the matter over and came to a decision long before she arrived home. There would be no more running away. It was time she faced the worst. Even if the worst was Amish life as an old maid. Perhaps that was all *Da Hah* had in store for her.

With another sigh, Susan pulled into the driveway at home and stopped beside the barn. While she was climbing down, Steve appeared from the doorway, his hat pulled down to shade his eyes.

"Did you get Maurice dropped off safely at Teresa's place?" he asked with a smile that was barely visible under his hat.

Susan laughed. "Well, I certainly didn't lose her along the way." She undid the tugs on her side.

"Didn't drop her in the creek then?" he joked as he unfastened the tugs on his side.

"No, I like her better than that. Now some boys I know…maybe that would be a good idea."

"I understand," he said, leading the horse forward while she held a buggy shaft. "I think you're holding up really well, considering. And also with your *daett*'s situation."

She stared at him in surprise. "Well thanks, Steve. That's nice of you to say."

"I think your heart belongs here, Susan. I hope you stay." He took off toward the barn with the horse and didn't look back.

Now why in the world would he say that? Susan wondered as Steve disappeared into the barn. How could he know what her thoughts had been on the ride home?

Chapter Twenty

A few evenings later, Susan was washing the supper dishes and looking out the window at the field of stacked corn sheaves. The setting sun turned the brown leaves golden on one side and dark on the other, while casting long shadows behind the shorn cornstalks.

This is like my life right now, she thought. Sunny and bright on one side with the memory of Teresa and her wonderful wedding. On the other side was Thomas leaving his shadowed mark. Even *Mamm*'s best attempts to cheer her this evening hadn't helped. Everyone had their problems, *Mamm* had said. It was all in how people dealt with them. Look at *Daett*. His joy in his son was still present even though the threat of church discipline hung over his head. Burdens were placed on people's shoulders by *Da Hah* to strengthen their faith. It was part of life and must be borne with as much good cheer as one could muster.

Last night Susan had almost taken a small step in that direction. She had held her driver's license between her fingers in one hand and the scissors in the other. In a way it would have felt *gut* cutting the thing in half and then melting the plastic in the fire of the stove. She could even have told *Mamm*—after the fact, of course—and watched her smile grow wide at this final victory.

But she hadn't.

The questions racing through her mind wouldn't let her. Was this the life she wanted? Was she willing to accept life as an Amish old maid? Was that the lot *Da Hah* had for her? The search for answers was leaving her with a throbbing headache. She had to stop thinking like this and find some resolution. She was growing older every day, and being an old maid was not the life she had always imagined for herself.

Perhaps she could do something really unexpected, like run the farm for *daett*. Plowing the fields of the farm by day and keeping the house by night. That would surprise people. Susan choked back her laughter at the thought. A woman simply couldn't do such a thing. Not run a farm by herself. It would be unacceptable, even if she somehow managed to handle all the hard field work. There had to be another answer.

Daett had been extra quiet this morning at breakfast. Did he blame her for Thomas giving up on her? Surely not. *Mamm* would have explained by now. Maybe he was thinking only of his own problems, which were coming into sharp focus as pre-communion Sunday drew near. Surely the leaders were contemplating some form of punishment for his youthful transgression and keeping it a secret for so many years.

Being disciplined by the church was much worse than having no one to take care of the farm. *Mamm* at least was practicing what she preached. She had smiled at *Daett* this morning and chattered away about what Ada's children were doing, even as she hovered over *Daett* like a hen watching her warm nest. In a way it was *gut* that Maurice was no longer staying here. The coming dark time was best walked through without visitors in the house.

If excommunication really happened, *Mamm* said she planned to walk the path with *Daett*. Her courage was admirable if a bit misguided, Susan thought. *Daett* could make it on his own, even if he had to sit at a table in the living room by himself. Susan shuddered. This was going to be more than awful. Like watching a star fall from heaven. Her own father, the one she had always looked up to, the one whose word was law in the house, shoved off into a corner to eat alone.

Washing another plate, Susan heard *Mamm*'s soft steps behind her. "What's that, Susan? Outside the window?"

Startled, Susan looked up and out. She could see nothing but open fields with the corn sheaves no longer golden now that the sun was lower in the sky.

"There's a flickering on the dark side of the sheaves," *Mamm* said. "It can't be anything but a fire reflection. But where is the fire?"

"A fire?" Susan paused with a dish halfway to the drainer.

"It's not from our place. Could it be coming from Ada's? But why would they have a fire going this early in the evening?"

While they both stared out the window, a loud patter of feet came from the outside. The sound rushed across the front porch and the door burst open.

"Our barn is on fire!" Ada's daughter Joan shouted, terror in her voice.

Mamm gasped. Susan and *Mamm* twirled around together. As they ran out of the kitchen, Susan hit the edge of a kitchen chair, sending it clattering across the floor. In the living room *Daett* was on his feet, hopping around as he quickly pulled on his shoes.

"Let's go!" *Daett* hollered, waving them out the door. He followed close behind as Joan led the way, still gasping for air. In the distance the sound of sirens pierced the air. Coming around the corner of the house they could see flames leaping from the eaves of their neighbor's barn.

"What happened?" *Daett* asked as he ran past them.

"I don't know," Joan hollered after him. "*Mamm* told me to run and tell you. We just saw the fire a few minutes after supper."

Susan, *Mamm*, and Joan soon slowed to a walk while *Daett* ran on ahead. His figure was a strange sight with his shoe laces flying, his beard pushed off to one side, and his head hatless. Taking Joan's hand, *Mamm* slowed even more.

"It's just the barn," *Mamm* told both of them. "There's nobody in there. The men will get the livestock out. At least no one is in danger."

"I'm going to help." Susan didn't look back for approval as she took off after *Daett*. She caught up with him at the barnyard gate where he'd stopped to catch his breath and tie his shoes. The angry glow of flames danced on the grass.

Someone was shouting inside the barn as smoke poured out the open door. Ada and the younger children stood close to the house, but there was no sign of the men.

"We have to help!" *Daett* hollered, seeming to see Susan for the first time. "There's another door in the back. The horses are still inside."

Following him, Susan helped push open the sliding door. Smoke tumbled out, and from somewhere above them the fire crackled.

"It'll take a while for the fire to burn through those floor timbers," *Daett* yelled, pulling off his shirt and tearing it in half. "Here, take this. Smoke is our main problem, so stay low. Remember, the horses are scared and won't move unless you cover their eyes."

Menno plunged into the rolling smoke, almost crawling on his hands and knees. Susan followed him, the sting and smell of smoke choking her. Bending over, she ran toward the stalls. When she arrived, *Daett* already had the first stall open, appearing in the ghostly smoke with his half of the shirt wrapped over a Belgian's eyes as he yanked hard on the halter.

Daett was choking, and his eyes were barely open. Tears were running down his face. Lowering his head, he moved past her. Susan waited for only a moment before entering the next stall. A driving horse stood near the back, slamming its back feet against the wooden slats. The sound repeated like rapid gunfire.

"Come on, girl." Susan reached up to stroke the horse's nose. She jerked her head around and rolled her eyes back. Wrapping the shirt over the horse's face, Susan pulled on the halter. Slowly the animal followed her, a few steps at a time, shying when loud cracks came from overhead.

"I'm going back in again!" *Daett* hollered in Susan's ear when he appeared suddenly in the smoky air. "Don't come in after me. It's getting too dangerous."

Susan said nothing as she continued to pull on the horse's halter. *Daett* would say such a thing, of course. But he was going back in...and she would follow—especially if he didn't come back out by the time she had this horse away from the barn.

Bursting into the fresh air, Susan gasped for breath and wiped her face. For the first time she felt the wetness of her tears. Leading the horse to the gate separating the barnyard from the pasture, she took her through before taking the shirt off her head. The animal glanced back at the burning barn before racing along the fence toward the other horses.

Ada and Reuben's son Duane came around the other side of the barn leading a horse, and Susan waited until he was through the gate before closing it. The ends of his hair were burned, and wild pieces of it curled skyward.

"You're hurt!" she shouted, pointing at a bleeding wound on his head.

"I hit a beam, that's all."

"Where are Steve and your *daett*?"

"They should be out by now. There…"

Susan turned to see Reuben and Steve come around the corner of the barn, each leading a horse. Steve handed the lead rope to Reuben and dashed back into the smoky interior.

Behind her the loud roar of a fire engine sounded at the end of the driveway. The blast of its horn filled the air, just as she turned and watched it careen into the area in front of the barn. Susan turned and ran toward the barn. Steve was going back to look for more horses. Taking a deep breath, she plunged into the inferno. She stopped a few feet inside. The burning in her eyes and mouth were too much to endure.

Gasping for air, she staggered outside and fell to her knees as coughs racked her body. The ghostly form of *Daett* appeared in the doorway leading another horse. His bare chest was soaked with sweat, his beard black with cinders.

"Where's Steve?" she screamed, choking from the effort.

Daett shook his head and fell to the ground. With a cry she grabbed the halter of the Belgian, who reared in fear. Susan fought him, pulling him sideways away from her father's gasping form. The work animal's huge hooves landed inches from her father's leg. She pulled again, guiding him toward the gate.

Two firemen came rushing around the corner of the barn, their faces hidden behind smoke masks. Both were clad in heavy, flapping suits. Behind them another fireman raced, his face uncovered, shouting, "Is anyone still inside?"

"Steve is!" Susan yelled, hanging on to the horse's halter. The horse reared again and she let go, diving sideways to escape its dropping hooves. Out of the corner of her eye, Susan saw Duane and her *daett* rush between her and the horse, their arms outspread. Shouting like wild men, they herded the animal toward the gate. The fireman without the mask was shouting into a mike on his shoulder and pointing toward the billowing smoke pouring out of the barn door. Steve was nowhere in sight.

"He's gone back inside!" Susan screamed again, struggling to get to her feet. Waves of weakness rushed over her. Another coughing fit drove her to her knees. What would Steve be experiencing inside the barn if the air was this bad just a few feet outside? Nothing could be done but watch and wait as time passed slowly. She kept her eyes on the smoke billowing out of the barn door.

The fireman without the mask was still shouting, running back and forth in front of the barn door. A gurney appeared, pushed and pulled by two men who must have been taking orders from the unmasked fireman. From inside the barn came the shrill scream of a horse cutting above the crackle of fire.

Susan stood up and felt the firm grip of *Daett*'s hand on her arm.

"We must pray!" *Daett* said as Susan stood frozen. *Daett*'s voice murmured in prayer, "Keep us all safe, O dear *Da Hah*. Help the fireman inside the barn and Steve. Allow him to live to see another day. Protect any animals still inside."

Susan tore herself away from the sound of *Daett*'s praying when *Mamm* and Ada appeared around the corner of the barn. She ran toward them even as they were shooed back by a fireman. Susan stopped short. Nothing good could be happening inside the barn. Would the fireman be coming out of the barn bearing Steve's body? If he did, would Steve be overcome by smoke inhalation or worse? How tragic the night had become. Steve, with his shy smile and gentle jokes. Surely he couldn't be gone. But who knew what *Da Hah* planned? He might very well decide this was Steve's time. At least he didn't have a *frau* whose heart would be torn by sorrow and grief at the news of his passing.

Susan pushed the horrible thoughts away.

Two firemen appeared in the smoking doorway carrying Steve between them. They placed him on the gurney.

Susan rushed forward, trying to reach him. The fireman in charge raised his hands and told her to stay back. One fireman caught her and kept her from getting closer to the gurney and the barn. She watched as men strapped a plastic mask over Steve's face and rushed the gurney toward the waiting ambulance that had arrived shortly after the fire trucks.

"Steve!" Susan shouted, but he gave no response as he was wheeled by.

"He should be okay," the fireman without a face mask said as the gurney disappeared around the corner of the barn. "We think it's just smoke inhalation."

Susan stared after the gurney and didn't move.

"Are you his girlfriend? His wife?" the fireman asked. "If so, you can ride along in the ambulance."

Susan shook her head. But there ought to be someone riding with him, she wanted to shout. Steve was a decent man. He shouldn't have to ride alone to the hospital without someone holding his hand.

"Come!" *Daett* took Susan's arm. "We have to move away from the fire. Thank *Da Hah* Steve wasn't injured more severely. The boy shouldn't have done what he did. No horse is worth such a risk."

"Amen!" Reuben agreed from behind them. All around them streams of water from the firemen's hoses hissed when they met the flames.

The attempt was futile, Susan figured. The barn would burn to the ground. But they were trying, just as Steve had tried. They were all good men, and that was what good men did. They tried. She broke down and wept, leaning against *Daett*'s shoulder.

Chapter Twenty-one

Three fire trucks were parked in the yard. The one between the house and barn was still spraying water on the utility shed. Susan stood with *Mamm* and Ada on the front porch while the men milled around the pasture, being kept away from the area by the ever-vigilant firemen.

The ambulance had long since departed. Duane had gone along to keep Steve company. Susan had almost offered to go at the last minute, but that would have been unseemly, even though it might have been understandable. Steve needed a woman's touch and he was her *daett*'s hired hand. Perhaps she should have been bold enough to go, but it was too late now.

Buggies were coming down the road now, the horses urged on by heavy slaps of the reins. A few *Englisha* vehicles had parked alongside the road, the neighbors getting out to stare at the aftermath. *Mamm* and Ada went down to the road to meet the Amish as they arrived to see if they could help. They talked for a few minutes with the people as they pulled to a stop. There wasn't much anyone could say or do at this point. Showing their concern was the main thing. And it did feel *gut* to have the community gather in support. At least it was only Reuben and Ada's barn that was burning to the ground. To lose the house would have been much, much worse.

No reason had been given for the cause of the fire yet. That would come out in due time. Meanwhile, more buggies were arriving. Susan walked out to join *Mamm* and Ada by the road.

Daett and Reuben headed across the pasture to direct buggies to pull in where they would be safe and out of the way. Even from a distance many of the horses looked wild-eyed and acted as if they were on the verge of bolting or shying into the roadside ditch.

"What happened?" one of the women asked Ada. Susan turned her attention toward them to hear Ada's reply.

"I haven't heard," Ada said. "Reuben hasn't said anything. We were in the middle of supper when Joan got up to take the pies out of the cupboard. She saw the fire through the kitchen window."

"That must have been quite a shock," someone said. "Do you think the men left a lantern burning in the barn?"

"No, they were done for the night," Ada replied. "Steve Mast works for Menno, so he hadn't been in the barn all evening. He came straight into the house from work."

"It looks like there was no chance to save the barn," one woman observed. Just then they heard the sound of large timbers crashing to the ground. "That must have been the barn's main beams," she added.

Ada clasped her hands. "Thank *Da Hah* no one was inside. That would have been awful—losing someone at a time like this."

"Didn't an ambulance leave with someone in it?" someone asked.

Ada nodded. "Steve inhaled too much smoke trying to get the last of the horses out. The paramedics think he's going to be okay."

"Did you lose any livestock?" the woman asked.

Ada shrugged. "I don't know. At least one horse, I think. I was too worried about Steve. Horses can be replaced."

They all nodded and turned to watch as another beam fell, seemingly in slow motion, an eerie sound filling the air. A spray of water from fire hoses arched through the sky and drenched the trees near the house.

As some of the people drove out, the women moved to the house porch. They hadn't been standing there long when one of them suggested they make sandwiches and prepare drinks for the firemen.

"That's right!" Ada said. "And there are still pies on the table. That will be a good place to start in helping the men recover from this ordeal."

Susan followed them inside and squeezed lemons for the lemonade while others got out pitchers and glasses. Other women sliced pies and put the pieces on plates.

"That will do while we make egg-salad sandwiches." Ada waved toward the door. "Take out what we have."

One of the women was already heating water over the stove when Susan left with her hands full of servings of pie. Joan and two others followed with lemonade and glasses.

Walking down the porch steps to the picnic table, they spread the drinks and pie out for the firemen.

Susan took a quick look around. The food ought to be safe here from the still-floating cinders. How should she get the firemen's attention? Perhaps they didn't want to be disturbed in their work. Seeing Reuben out by the pasture fence, she walked over to him. "Ada has drinks and food ready for the firemen. Sandwiches will be ready soon. I'm not sure how to let the firemen know."

He nodded. "I'll let them know before long." Reuben's face looked drawn and distracted, which was understandable. His barn had burned to the ground. Gone in the matter of an hour or two.

Already it seemed like years since Susan had stood in front of the kitchen sink thinking her moody thoughts. "Have you heard how Steve is doing?"

Reuben didn't say anything. He just stared at the embers where the barn had once stood.

Susan was ready to repeat the question when he shrugged.

"I don't know, but I think someone should check on him."

"I'll go into town," Susan offered without thinking. "Maybe someone needs to sit by his bed for the night. Duane will probably want an update on what's happened out here too."

Reuben nodded. "You shouldn't go by yourself. Take Joan along."

"Okay, I'll ask her."

Reuben turned around. "Come with me first. I'll see if I can find someone to drive the two of you to the hospital."

Susan tagged along as Reuben approached the crowd of neighbors. "Anybody willing to drive Susan and Joan to the hospital so they can check on Steve Mast?"

"I'll drive them," an elderly *Englisha* neighbor offered.

"Thank you, Rodney," Reuben acknowledged. "They took Steve to Scott Memorial."

"I'll be back in a minute." Susan smiled her thanks before running toward the house. She found Joan among the woman gathered on the porch. "Your *daett* said you could go with me to see how Steve is doing. If he needs us, we'll stay for the night. Do you want to go along?"

"Of course," Joan said at once. "But I should ask *Mamm.*"

Susan nodded and went to find her own *mamm.*

Meeting back on the porch, they nodded at each other and walked across the lawn and out to the road.

"Are you ready to go?" the *Englisha* neighbor asked as they approached.

When they nodded, he said, "My wife is waiting in the car. Do you need to stop to pick up anything at your house, Susan?"

"We're fine," Susan told him, imagining sitting in a chair all night as the worst-case scenario. They wouldn't need more than what they had on.

"Is the young man your sweetheart?" the old fellow asked on the way to the car.

Susan shook her head. "Thank you for taking us," she said. "Steve's our hired hand."

"I see." He didn't sound convinced as they arrived at the car. "Lydia, this is Susan and Joan. I just offered to take them into town to check on the young man who was taken to Scott Memorial."

Lydia smiled at Susan and Joan. "I'm glad we can help. I appreciate the way your people look after your own."

Susan opened the back door and motioned Joan in first. While they fastened their seat belts, the old fellow climbed in, groaning as if he were in pain.

"Tough getting so old," he said as he turned the key in the ignition. "It's tough losing a barn in this economy too. Tough anytime, as far as that goes."

"Do they know how the fire started?" Lydia asked.

"I haven't heard," Susan replied.

Rodney turned the car around and headed toward town.

"Surely it couldn't be arson?" Lydia glanced at Rodney.

Her husband cleared his throat. "I heard the men talking. Reuben thinks it must have been the last batch of hay. It was rained on before he baled. He thought it had dried sufficiently, but maybe not. The fire could have been caused by spontaneous combustion. And from how fast the fire advanced before it was first spotted, that makes sense. Much of the loft would be involved before there were visible signs from outside."

"I was the one who spotted the fire from the kitchen window," Joan volunteered. "I couldn't believe it at first. Smoke and flames were coming out of the eaves."

"You poor thing." Lydia reached over the seat to pat Joan on the arm.

"It was awful." Joan shuddered. "Then *Mamm* said to run up to Uncle Menno's place to tell them. *Daett* said he was going to run across the road to call the fire department from the phone shack."

"You never know when tragedy will strike." Lydia sighed. "I suppose the Lord has His reasons."

They rode in silence along the rolling southern Indiana hills. The trip was made in a fraction of the time it would have taken a horse and buggy.

"We'll come inside to make sure everything is okay," Lydia said after Rodney parked the car.

"That's awfully nice of you," Susan told them. "Are you sure you have the time?"

"Believe me," Rodney replied, "we don't have much left but time. If we go home, we'd just be watching *Jeopardy* on TV."

With Rodney still chuckling, they climbed out of the car. Susan led the way into the low, one-story hospital. She hadn't been here for years—not since Joan had broken her arm in the eighth grade. Susan had ridden along to the hospital with Ada and an *Englisha* driver then too.

"I remember this place," Joan whispered, looking up at the round, glass-enclosed top of the building as they walked in.

"I was just remembering the time you broke your arm," Susan whispered back.

In front of them, Duane jumped up from where he'd been sitting in the waiting room. A smile filled his face. "I thought I'd been forsaken and abandoned by everyone."

"You know we wouldn't do that," Susan said. "How is Steve doing?"

"I was in the room with him until a few minutes ago. He's awake now and ready to go home, he says. I didn't know what to do about that. No one answered the phone at the shack when I called."

"That's good news about Steve." Relief flooded Susan's face.

"That is good news!" Rodney declared. "We'll wait here until he's checked out and take all of you home."

"I'd better go back and see for myself," Susan said. "I just realized that Steve being ready to go home may not be the same as the doctor being ready to allow him to go home."

"Talk to the nurse up front to see if she says it's okay for you to see Steve," Duane said. "They don't like people wandering around without permission."

"I'll do that."

Susan walked up to the nurse's small window. "May I please see Steve Mast?"

The young woman disappeared for a moment, and Susan heard the murmur of voices. The nurse returned and quietly said, "The doctor said it's okay. I'll take you back." The woman led the way to a room with several curtained-off spaces. Motioning with her hand toward one of them, she said, "He's in there. Go ahead. One side's open."

"Are you sure?" Susan asked. What would Steve think if she just barged in?

"Oh, he's decent, don't worry." The nurse smiled and then turned to go to her station.

"I didn't mean that," Susan said, blushing red she was sure, but the nurse had already left.

Taking a deep breath, Susan walked around the edge of the curtain and stopped. Steve lay on a bed, his eyes red and swollen. He was propped up in a sitting position.

He turned his face toward her, and a slight smile played on his face. "Hi, Susan."

"Hello," Susan said. "You look awful."

"If you're going to tell me that, please go home."

"If you're going to be grouchy, I will."

He tried to smile again but grimaced instead. "Who came with you?"

"Joan. And Duane was already here, of course. Rodney and Lydia, Ada's neighbors, brought us in their car."

"I saw Duane, *yah*. Hopefully he told you I'm ready to go home."

"Will the doctor let you go?"

"They want to keep me for the night, but I'm not going to. I can't afford to stay here. It's expensive. How stupid of me to hit my head and end up here. I feel fine."

"But it was something," Susan protested. "You were trying to do a very brave thing. And you should stay here if the doctor thinks you should. What if something serious is wrong?"

He grimaced again. "There's only a knot on my head from one of the barn beams as it fell. It was a glancing blow, so it's not too serious."

"Where?" Susan asked, walking closer to run her hand over his head.

He held still, allowing her hand to find the bump.

Susan stopped. "You really should stay. What if there's a concussion?"

Steve made a face. "I've already talked with the doctor, and the X-rays showed nothing. So I'm going home. Just give me some time to get out of this hospital dress."

Susan laughed but Steve didn't join in.

"Will you please tell that nurse I want my clothes back?"

"I'll see what I can do." There really was no sense in arguing with him, she decided. That might do more harm than good if Steve got stressed. And home was the best place to recuperate—even from a serious injury.

"Did the horse I was trying to get out survive?" Steve asked before she was out the door.

Susan shook her head, stopping to turn around. The expression on his face fell. He shouldn't have asked right now, Susan thought. There were already enough things on his mind.

"I'm sorry," she said.

"It's not your fault," he said. "I suppose it's really no one's fault. But I wish I could have succeeded."

"You tried," she assured him, and his face relaxed. Leaving the room, Susan found a nurse in the hallway and told her what Steve wanted.

"I was expecting as much." The young woman laughed. "I'll go see what the doctor has to say, but it shouldn't be any problem as long as Steve will sign the no-fault papers."

"He'll sign," Susan said. "He wants to go home."

Chapter Twenty-two

While Steve was signing his release papers, Susan stood at the door of the waiting room and watched as Rodney's car pulled out of the parking lot. Joan waved from the backseat and smiled. Duane was seated beside her. Since the car wouldn't hold six people, Rodney had decided a second trip would have to be made. No doubt Joan was enjoying her ride in the *Englisha* car. She didn't often get a chance to do that. Even the reason for the trip didn't dampen such simple pleasure.

Not that long ago, Susan would have greeted a ride into town with great excitement too. Now it didn't seem like such a big deal. Was she getting old? Or had she already seen too much of the world? Likely both, she decided. She held up her hands and looked at them closely. Were they the future hands of an old, single, Amish woman? What would these hands do in the years ahead? Would they ever change diapers on a *bobli* of her own? Would they ever steer a car again?

A man cleared his throat behind her, and Susan jumped and whirled around.

"Steve!" she exclaimed. "You should make yourself known before you creep up on a soul."

He winced, his face still puffy. "So, it looks like we got left behind."

"We all wouldn't fit, so Rodney said he would come back for us. He'll be here before you know it."

He nodded. "Did you burn your hands getting the horses out?"

"No, why do you ask?"

"Because you were staring at them."

Susan blushed. "That's because I was feeling sorry for myself. But it had nothing to do with the fire."

He smiled but pursued the matter no further. His gaze drifted to the parking lot.

"By the way, that was brave of you to try to save the last horse."

"Maybe stupidity more than anything," he muttered. "And if you ever tell anyone you saw me in a dress, I'll have to resort to violence."

Susan laughed. "You looked as harmless as a butterfly, Steve. Like you couldn't hurt a kitten."

"I can breathe fire if I have to," he said. Then he winced. "I think I'd better sit down. Maybe 'breathing fire' isn't such a great idea after all."

"You should stay overnight like the doctor wants you to." Susan took his arm and helped him to a nearby chair. "If you pass out here in the waiting room, I'm going to scream for help."

"I've never heard you scream. That would be interesting," he said with a grin.

"Well, if you had been listening, you would have heard me scream outside the barn. But, being a man, you were too busy breathing fire."

"Do you always torture injured patients with such harsh words?"

"You're not a patient anymore, remember? You're on your feet, so it's open season."

"Why do I get the feeling that it wouldn't make a difference?"

"I can be nice and sweet when the need arises, but running into burning barns trying to be a he-man and then leaving the hospital against doctor's orders doesn't qualify you for tender treatment."

He smiled. "I am rebuked and chastened by your words. I will repent in sackcloth and ashes."

"Well, you've had enough ashes. Sackcloth will do. Does that mean you'll stay the night in the hospital like you're supposed to?"

"Nope. I'm not *that* repentant."

"That's what I thought. Stubborn to the core."

"Hey, I'm injured. I could use a little sympathy here. And you did see me in that stupid dress they made me wear."

"It wasn't a dress, it was a 'gown,' Steve. And it's nothing to be ashamed of."

"Still, I'm glad it was you and not some other girl."

"Any other girl would say the same thing."

"Perhaps." He shrugged. "It was nice of you to come."

"You're welcome."

"I'm sorry about Thomas," he said, not looking at her.

"Now where did *that* come from? We were talking about today and the fire."

"There are more fires than the kind that burn down barns." Steve touched her hand. "You didn't deserve what you got. But it's Thomas's loss and not yours."

"You shouldn't say things like that." She choked for a few seconds, and his grip on her hand tightened.

"I really mean it," he said. "Thomas doesn't know what he's talking about when it comes to you."

Susan tried to keep breathing evenly although her heart was beating faster. Where was this emotion coming from? How did the conversation take this turn? She'd said nothing that would bring Thomas into the conversation. But here he was. "Maybe Thomas *does* know what he's talking about."

Steve shook his head. "He doesn't, Susan. And the sun will come out again for you. *Da Hah* has a perfect future for you. He will lead you there when the time comes."

"That's easy for you to say. You haven't had your heart broken."

He hung his head for a moment. "I can imagine Thomas would be hard to lose. He's good-looking, dashing, every girl's dream, I'm sure."

"No, no...I didn't mean it like that at all. Steve, you are..."

He waited quietly when her words stopped.

She couldn't seem to pull her eyes away from his.

His smile broadened and his still-red eyes twinkled a bit. "Were you actually going to say something nice about me?"

Susan laughed. "You're jealous of Thomas, I do declare."

"Maybe." He looked away.

"But there is no need. You are quite..." Again she stopped.

Again he waited.

Blushing this time, she let the words rush out. "You have a nice horse. Your buggy is in good shape. You work for *Daett*, and he likes you. That's quite an accomplishment right there."

"I guess I ought to be thankful. And I am the one here next to you."

The moment hung between them.

Susan refused to look at him. She felt she should say something. He was being so nice. "Thanks," she finally managed. "Thanks for the compliment." Susan was sure her neck and face were getting even redder. What had she been thinking, jumping on his words of praise? Was she hoping Steve was wishing he could take her home on Sunday nights? What a bloated sense of self-importance she'd worked herself into. The sun didn't rise and set on her. Maybe that was the first lesson she needed to learn during this time of trial.

"You'll be okay," Steve said. He touched her arm again.

Susan jerked herself out of her trance. "Now look here, you're the one who needs comforting, Steve, and here you are giving me aid and advice."

"Sorry," he said. "I just wanted you to feel better about...things."

After another awkward silence, Susan said, "I'll go see if Rodney's here." Rodney wasn't back yet, but Susan needed to get away from Steve for a few minutes. She walked outside. She could feel herself blushing again and wondered why. After all, she was here because she felt sorry for Steve. This was her duty—a simple act of kindness to her *daett's* hired hand. There couldn't be anything between the two of them. Steve knew about her dash into the *Englisha* world, and he hadn't seemed too impressed. Now, why was she worried about what Steve thought anyway? After a few minutes, Susan saw Rodney drive into the parking lot. She went back inside and told Steve, "Time to go. They're here."

Steve got to his feet and groaned. "I think I need Ada's soft bed for my poor, beaten-up body."

"Here, let me help you." Susan stepped forward to grab his arm with one hand while pushing open the front door with the other. Rodney had the car waiting by the curb, the rear passenger door open. "Everything okay there, young man?" he asked.

"Yep." Steve groaned again as he climbed in. Susan shut the door and then ran around to the other side, sliding in beside him. Steve was holding his head like it hurt.

"You sure you're okay?" Lydia asked, turning around to study Steve's face. "You look a little green."

"Nothing that a good night's sleep and a glass of Ada's apple cider won't cure," Steve asserted, trying to smile.

"Tough people, the Amish are," Rodney commented as he turned the car onto the main blacktop road leading back to the community.

When Steve groaned again, Susan reached over in the darkness to take his hand. He could think what he wanted. She didn't mean anything by it, but he needed mothering right now. If he didn't like it, he could push her hand away.

"The fire department was pulling out when we left," Rodney said. "The barn's pretty much down flat."

"I was expecting that," Steve said. His hand wrapped around Susan's. "Did Reuben lose any livestock other than the one horse?"

"I don't know," Rodney replied.

Susan moved her fingers, feeling the calluses on Steve's palm. She stopped when she sensed him looking in her direction. "Are you okay?" she finally whispered.

He nodded, still looking at her.

She pulled her hand away and turned to stare out the window, watching as the shadows of trees whipped past.

They drove by the small burg of Livonia, turning north on the state road. Minutes later Rodney pulled onto the familiar gravel road that led to Reuben and Ada's place. No one said anything as he pulled into the driveway. He stopped in front of the house. A few buggies were still lined up in the pasture, but all the *Englisha* vehicles were gone.

"Do you want us to drive you home?" Rodney asked Susan.

"Thanks very much for the offer," Susan said, "but I need to see if *Mamm* is still here. I can walk up to the house in no time."

"Thanks for bringing me home," Steve said, his hand on the door handle.

"We were glad to be of help," Lydia assured him. "One can feel so helpless in times like this."

"Thanks again," Susan said as she climbed out. She walked around the car and waited for Steve to get out. He looked a little weak, so she took his arm.

"Stop babying me," he ordered. "People will think I should have stayed in the hospital."

"Well, you should have, you stubborn mule."

"Do you like stubborn mules?"

Susan remained silent, and Steve didn't offer anything more as he worked his way up the porch steps one at a time. At the top, she let go of his arm and held the door open for him. He winced as the light from the lantern hit his eyes. He ducked his head to enter and shield his eyes.

"It's Steve and Susan!" one of the smaller children hollered.

"Well, if it isn't our hero," Reuben said as he stood up. "Thank you, Steve, for trying to save the horse. I didn't want you to risk your life though."

"I had to try," Steve said, holding his head with one hand.

Ada came over and lifted Steve's chin with her fingers. "*Lieber kinder!* The boy is on the verge of collapse. Reuben, help me get him up the stairs and into bed. Joan get a jug of apple cider from the basement. That's the best thing for him right now."

"That sounds delicious," Steve said just before moaning. "That and getting into bed."

"Why didn't you stay in the hospital?" Ada demanded. "You didn't have to be so stubborn."

"That's what Susan told me," Steve said, making it as far as the rocker before he sat down.

Ada rushed to the kitchen and returned with a glass of apple cider, which Steve drank in long, deep swallows before taking a breath.

"It doesn't look like *Mamm*'s here, so I'm off to home," Susan said, turning to leave. She glanced over her shoulder and saw that everyone was still gathered around Steve. He had the glass of apple cider tilted up high, draining the last drop. Closing the door behind her, Susan stepped out onto the lawn.

Chapter Twenty-three

Susan sat anxiously on the bench as Bishop Henry stood to close the Sunday morning service. Today was pre-communion church, and she would have to leave in a few minutes, along with the other non-members. Oh, if she'd only taken the baptismal class with Teresa last year! Then she could stay and hear what Bishop Henry and the leaders had decided to do about *Daett*'s situation.

Bishop Henry was speaking in a soft voice. "And now that the brothers have given testimony on the Word of God shared today by the ministry, I'm glad that all could give a *gut* word. So let's be dismissed. Those who are members, please stay behind as we prepare ourselves for our communion time in two weeks."

Bowing his head, Bishop Henry waited as the nonmembers left. Susan stood with the younger girls and moved down the aisle. The other young women her age had stayed seated because they were members. Some of them were even married, their husbands sitting across the room in the men's section. Even Steve was still seated. He was considered a visitor, but because he was baptized, he could partake in communion. He was a member in good standing in his home community.

Now what was she supposed to do? She could perhaps help prepare lunch for the children. Susan reluctantly made her way to the kitchen and got busy helping set up the children's table in the washroom. She listened for any unusual sounds coming from the living room. Walking past the kitchen opening, she caught brief glimpses of Bishop Henry standing in front and speaking in his quiet preaching voice.

He would be going over the *Ordnung*, she knew. Touching on points he thought needed refreshing. And the other ministers would soon be adding their own points. Afterward, everyone would express their unity with what had been said. Not that she had ever sat under such instruction, but the years of listening in kitchens and hearing her older sisters talking about what had been said gave her a fairly good picture.

Bishop Henry's voice droned on, and Susan served the meal with the help of the school-aged girls. In the basement, the young boys took full advantage of their privileged status of getting to the first table, whooping it up as loudly as they dared.

"Quiet down!" Susan ordered. "Your *daetts* will be coming down if you disturb the meeting." This produced the desired result for a few minutes, but they were soon at it again.

"I can hardly get two sandwiches down," one of them moaned in pretended agony. "Normally I can handle three. I think I'll wait until later next time, when the preachers have the members sitting in."

"Maybe you can sneak to the table with the grown men when they come out," one of his friends teased. "We can paste some straw on your face for a beard."

"That would work," another said, and they all roared with laughter.

"Benny's got enough stubble of his own, if he'd let it grow," the first boy added when they quieted down.

"You mean he's getting ready to ask Ben's Rosanna home from the hymn singing and forgot to shave because he was in such a rush."

Benny made a face at first but soon joined in the laughter. Susan gave up and retreated upstairs. Let their *daetts* come down and tell them to quiet down if they wanted to. She had done her part. Boys this age weren't exactly controllable by someone they considered little more than an older sister.

In the kitchen again, Susan heard her *daett*'s name mentioned. She walked to the kitchen opening and listened. Several of the young girls looked at her, and she whispered, "They're talking about my *daett.*"

That seemed to satisfy them. They would also want to listen if their *daetts* were being discussed at pre-communion church. Only people in trouble were personally talked about on this day, so Susan's *daett* must be in deep, deep trouble.

Susan's attention perked up as she listened to the Bishop.

> It has been revealed to us that Menno Hostetler has a son in the *Englisha* world. We can tell you that Menno, along with his wife, went to Deacon Ray to confess this sin. An action of repentance for which we are quite grateful. But what is troubling to us is that Menno did not reveal this matter prior to the *Englisha* man making himself known to the community and revealing this sin in such a public fashion.
>
> The revelation has brought great shame upon all of us, and has placed our testimony to the outside world in question. As the ministry, we do not believe this matter can be ignored. Although Menno has straightened this matter out with *Da Hah* and his wife, it has now become a matter for the community to deal with.
>
> I don't need to remind any of you that we are all a community. What affects one of us, affects us all. Perhaps this is a *gut* lesson to be reminded of. And that sin cannot be covered forever. *Da Hah* will see that it is revealed and laid before the eyes of all to see. We as the ministry believe that Menno has been in grave sin all these years by hiding this matter from us.
>
> With that in mind, it is our decision to refuse communion to Brother Menno when we observe it in two weeks. And we also believe it would be best if some further punishment were given in order that all may know the seriousness of this sin. Accordingly, we have taken counsel together as the ministry. Deacon Ray spoke with Menno and Anna last night about this.

Susan held her breath. So this was what that visit had been about.

She'd guessed right, but both *Daett* and *Mamm* had refused to say a word about the matter.

Bishop Henry continued.

> Sister Anna has requested that she also be included in this punishment, which at first glance seemed unnecessary to us. But upon further consideration, we see her point. She has lived with Menno all these years and has admitted that at times she wanted to ask him about his past life but chose not to. What these reasons were, we did not think necessary to inquire into. It is enough that Anna wishes to share in her husband's punishment because she is his *frau*.

"Is it something terrible?" one of the younger girls whispered in Susan's ear.

Susan nodded, pressing back her tears.

Bishop Henry was clearing his throat again.

> It is the decision of the ministry that Menno Hostetler be put on a six-week *bann*. During this time he is to have no communion or fellowship with the community. Menno and Anna are to be seen by all as having been placed outside the church. We are to accept nothing in material or spiritual aid from either of them. If they should pass over to the other side during this time, we pray only for their souls. We ask that *Da Hah* would understand the special circumstances and will have mercy on both of them. So let us now vote on this matter, as well as on having communion in two weeks.

Low sobs came from the living room. A few women's voices were raised in agony.

Susan heard the shuffling of feet. Deacon Ray and the other ministers would be going around the aisles and asking each member for his or her vote. Clutching the doorjamb, Susan tried to stay upright. It wouldn't do any *gut* to go crashing across the floor in a dead faint. She'd known this was coming.

What was Teresa going to say about all this? She was in there, and she didn't understand their ways yet. Still, she had to vote, and she loved *Daett*. What if she objected? "Oh, dear *Da Hah*, help her," Susan whispered, turning to find a chair at the kitchen table. "Why didn't I go over to her place last night and talk with her?" But perhaps James would have told Teresa, if he had thought of the matter.

"What's happening to your *daett*?" the same concerned girl was back, standing a few inches from Susan's knees.

"Something awful," Susan managed. "*Daett* sinned years ago, and he didn't confess it to the community."

"He has an *Englisha* son," the girl said, more statement than question. Obviously she knew already. "How could your *daett* have done something like that?"

"It was before he was baptized," Susan said. Hopefully that would satisfy, but the girl wasn't moving away.

"My *daett* didn't do anything like that before he was baptized."

"I know," Susan said, trying to smile. "And you can thank *Da Hah* he didn't."

The girl nodded and then disappeared to her chore. Susan turned to the implications of the *bann*. *Mamm* and *Daett* were being thrown out into the darkness to walk without the blessing of the church for six weeks. Why was there bitterness and anger rising up in her heart? Thankfully she hadn't spoken those words to the young girl. That would have been awful indeed. Perhaps she was feeling anger because she had been out in the *Englisha* world herself, becoming polluted by their way of thinking. Out there, being obedient and compliant wasn't the way people lived.

Susan walked over to the kitchen sink and offered to help dry the dishes. A girl handed her a towel, and Susan forced herself not to listen to the murmur of voices in the living room. Instead, memories floated in her mind. Visions of Laura and the bakery shop. Of laughing and joking with Robby and the time they ran along the shores of the ocean at Asbury Park after dark. Of sitting on the sand watching the moon rise over the ocean with the wind blowing in their hair. How free it had all felt, and how different from this life.

No one here knew all the things she had done. Were they sins? The thought jolted her. Was the day coming when she would need to confess what had happened before she was baptized? All of a sudden, she had to leave. She dropped the dishcloth and dashed outside. The children playing in the yard looked up as she went by and headed for the barn. She stopped halfway there. She couldn't go there. That was where the young boys gathered to talk, telling their stories after lunch until it was time to go home. Where else was there to go? Turning toward the line of buggies, she saw theirs. Almost running there, she climbed inside and pulled the buggy robe over her head. This is foolish, she told herself. But let it be foolish. So what if someone saw her? Let them think what they wanted. *Daett* and *Mamm* were inside being excommunicated. This felt like a winter night's nightmare. Dreams she had suffered through as a child. Night torments of bears chasing her in the woods. Huge fish that came leaping out of ponds with their mouths wide open, sharp teeth bared to sink into her skin. Screaming hadn't been an option then, and screaming wasn't an option now either.

Susan controlled herself, breathing slower. She thought about Teresa. The poor girl. What had she said when asked to vote? If Teresa objected to the excommunication, they would no doubt have Deacon Ray over the next Saturday night for a visit.

Susan placed her hand on her mouth. She had to think sanely about this. James was Teresa's husband, and Deacon Ray was James's father. They would have thought of this very thing, and Teresa would have been warned. She had to have been. Neither James nor Deacon Ray were that careless.

Sobbing, Susan stayed under the blanket. The buggy door was tightly shut, but she peeked out once in a while to see if church had been dismissed. When the men spilled out into the yard, she pushed the blanket down, dried her tears, and marched back toward the house.

As she neared the washroom door, it burst open and Steve came out.

"There you are!" Steve exclaimed. "I was looking for you."

"For me?"

"We'll make it through this, Susan." Steve took both of her hands in his. "Just be strong and don't get bitter. It will come out right in the end."

"Why do you care?" Susan asked, amazed that right there in front of everyone he'd taken her hands.

"I work for your *daett*. Of course I care."

But Steve cared about more than *Daett*. She could see it in his eyes. He cared about her.

Chapter Twenty-four

Susan wiped her eyes as she stood in the washroom listening to the women moving around in the kitchen. She shoved her handkerchief back into her dress pocket. *Mamm* would likely be in worse shape than she was, as would Teresa. She needed to be with them instead of out here nursing her own pain. Her privacy wouldn't last long anyway. Soon some young girl would come bursting through the washroom door and catch her crying.

Susan opened the door slowly. The kitchen was packed with unmarried girls preparing to serve the adult tables. Keeping her head down, Susan made her way through, catching a glimpse of Teresa seated on a bench in the living room. She had her face in her hands and her shoulders were shaking.

James's *mamm* was seated beside Teresa, speaking in a low voice so Susan couldn't make out what was being said. Bishop Henry's wife was standing beside them, her hand on Teresa's shoulder.

Susan took a deep breath. Clearly Teresa was distraught. But she must have voted to follow the church leadership's recommendation, otherwise the two women wouldn't be comforting her. Or perhaps James found a way for Teresa to excuse herself.

Susan gasped as *Mamm* and *Daett* came out from the back bedroom where they must have fled. They had their heads bowed as they walked to a small bench table set apart against a wall. Taking their places across from each other, they waited as others filled the long main tables. Silence settled over the house as Bishop Henry got to his feet and announced the prayer.

Bishop Henry's voice trembled. "And now that we are gathered again to eat, let us bow our heads and give thanks."

Susan closed her eyes, the tears stinging again. Bishop Henry completed the prayer, and Susan slipped onto the bench beside Teresa, placing her arm around her friend's shoulder. The sobbing started again. Long moments passed as Susan held Teresa close, the dinner conversation rising and falling around them.

"You should have gone to the table," Susan whispered.

"I can't eat anything," Teresa choked out, muffling her cry with her handkerchief. "This is awful. Why are *Mamm* and *Daett* sitting over there by themselves?"

"Didn't James tell you what was going to happen?"

"The voting, yes. James said to say I wasn't objecting, but he didn't say anything about them having to eat alone."

"It's the way it's done," Susan said. "They are separate from us now, and we can't eat with them until it's over in six weeks."

Teresa stared at Susan for a few minutes before whispering, "I'm coming over tonight to visit. Surely that's allowed."

Susan nodded.

"James will come with me. I know he will."

"Some of my sisters will be coming too, I'm sure. But we'll all just sit around and cry. Are you sure you want to be part of that?"

"I'm a part of whatever's happening with your family."

"You're way too sweet." Susan gave Teresa a quick hug. "Now, let me get you on the next table. You have to eat something."

Teresa didn't protest as they stood together and waited as the first meal neared a close.

"I'm glad Mom wasn't here today to see this," Teresa whispered. "James found her a nice little place to rent in Livonia, and she's settled in. She bought a car this week and found a job in Salem at the little Christian bookstore. I think her connections with the Amish helped."

"Maybe so. I think the *Englisha* admire us...in spite of our imperfections," Susan said, glancing over at *Mamm* and *Daett* still seated at the little table.

Bishop Henry rose to announce the final prayer for the meal.

However much it hurt inside her, the pain had to be even greater in *Mamm*'s heart.

Teresa clung to Susan's arm as Bishop Henry began the prayer. With her head bowed, Susan dared to peek again at *Mamm* and *Daett*. They looked so calm, so at peace with what was happening. Not at all like she had expected. How had they found such grace while she was so torn up? *Mamm* must be burning up inside from the shame, yet on the outside she was serene. And communion would be in two weeks. For the first time that she could remember, *Mamm* and *Daett* wouldn't participate. This knowledge must even now be tearing at their hearts. And ahead of them lay six more weeks of this. Tonight they would probably weep in each other's arms. But they would also keep presenting accepting faces during the day like they were now. Committed to enduring what *Da Hah* had seen fit to send their way.

At least *Mamm* was standing with *Daett*. That was much to be thankful for. She didn't have to. No one would have blamed or required it of her. What a heart of gold *Mamm* had. Such love for *Daett* that went beyond mere feelings. *Mamm* knew what *Daett* had done in his youth. How could she do this?

Could *she*, Susan Hostetler, ever so love a man? Had she not failed completely with Thomas? Perhaps if she had been more understanding of his faults she wouldn't have left for the *Englisha* world or driven him away. Feeling the tears sting again, she wiped them away as Bishop Henry came to the end of his prayer.

"Come," Susan said, pushing the dark thoughts away and taking Teresa by the arm. "You're going to sit down and eat with me because I haven't eaten either."

Teresa followed and they sat at a table Susan chose for them. They waited as the young girls cleaned it off.

"I need coffee," Teresa muttered, "to brace my soul."

"I think I do too," Susan agreed. "It takes coffee on a day like this."

They looked at each other and then quickly looked away. They both turned to look at *Mamm* as she walked past them toward the kitchen. Alone. The women she passed nodded to her, but no one spoke.

"I hate this," Teresa whispered. "I want to scream."

"It will pass like all our troubles eventually do," Susan whispered back. "That's what we tell each other, and it usually works."

"How did I ever get accepted into the community with baby Samuel, when your *mamm* and *daett* get treated like this for doing the same thing I did?"

"They look at things differently once you're a church member."

Bishop Henry's voice interrupted them, announcing prayer again, and they bowed their heads. Susan watched Teresa out of the corner of her eye. She seemed to be collecting herself well. When the prayer was over, Teresa spread butter on a piece of bread and then added the peanut butter with slow motions of her hand.

None of the girls on either side offered conversation. By the looks of things, they were wrapped up in their own talk. They meant no disrespect, Susan figured, but were giving Teresa and her space. And for that she was thankful. When they had finished eating, Susan whispered, "I have to go. *Daett*'s been waiting for me to finish, I think."

"I'll see you tonight then," Teresa said, forcing a smile.

Sure enough, when she got to her feet, *Daett* made his way outside. He picked up his hat by the front door and pulled it low over his eyes. *Mamm* was already in the mudroom looking for her bonnet when Susan arrived.

"Let me help you, *Mamm*," Susan said.

Mamm nodded, swallowing hard.

Susan searched for both of their shawls. When she found them, she helped *Mamm* slip hers around her shoulders. *Mamm* was no child and knew how to pull on her own shawl, but right now she looked frail and weak. Susan took her arm and helped her through the washroom door and down the steps. *Daett* hadn't driven up yet. He was still out by the buggy getting the horse under the shafts. Should she wait here or walk out to the barnyard? Susan looked to *Mamm*, but she wasn't much help. She wasn't saying anything or looking at anyone. They would walk over, Susan decided.

A few of the little girls waved and smiled as they went past. That would all change by next week. Right now they didn't know what sitting at a small table by yourself meant. Someone would soon tell them and whisper of the pain felt by a soul cast out to wander in the darkness for sins they had committed. Now they only saw what they had always seen. Susan and her *mamm* going past. People they had always looked up to.

Susan helped *Mamm* climb into the front seat before she pushed in the tug on her side. *Daett* wasn't looking at her, and his hat was still pulled low over his eyes. He wouldn't cry, she supposed. He would save his tears for the haymow or his times alone with *Mamm*.

"I'm sorry, *Daett*," Susan said across the shafts and Toby's back.

He nodded and threw the lines into the buggy, still not looking at her. She climbed into the back of the buggy while he pulled himself up the front step. They drove past the walk by the washroom door. They were the first buggy to leave. This was as it should be. Such pain could only be borne to a certain point.

The little girls waved again, shouting out "Bye!" The sound was faint above the clatter of the buggy wheels.

"I'm sorry you had to see this day," *Daett* said, giving a brief glance over his shoulder toward Susan. "I can never say how sorry I am for putting you and the rest of the girls through this. If you want to leave home tonight for the *Englisha* world, Susan, I would understand."

Mamm gasped in the front seat. "Don't speak such awful things, Menno. This day is bad enough without losing Susan yet."

"I'm not going anywhere," Susan responded.

Daett didn't seem to hear her, but *Mamm* gave a sigh of relief.

"Anna," *Daett* started slowly, "I can never say how very sorry I am for what I've done, and now you're bearing the burden with me. I wish you wouldn't have chosen this path. It wasn't necessary. I could have walked this road alone."

Mamm said nothing, but she leaned against *Daett*'s shoulder as they drove toward home.

Susan waited a while before speaking. "Teresa and James are coming over tonight. And I'm sure some of the other girls are also coming. Did you know this, *Mamm*?"

Mamm nodded before choking out, "I can't feed them in this condition. And they can't eat with me—or eat any food I make."

"I'm sure they'll bring food along," Susan assured her. "They'll know that."

"I don't think I can bear the thought of my own daughters forbidden to eat with me in my own house," *Mamm* said through fresh tears.

Daett slipped his arm around *Mamm*'s shoulder, the lines limp in his other hand. Toby slowed, looking over his shoulder as if he couldn't figure out what was going on.

Daett did nothing, as they plodded down the road. They were still the only buggy in sight. Susan wanted to get out, run across the fields, hide in the woods—do anything but stay here and watch this pain tearing her *mamm* and *daett*'s hearts apart. But she was frozen in place. And where was there to run, anyway? The *Englisha* world wouldn't understand or heal this. She didn't even understand.

Not until they were near the house did some peace come. *Yah*, just as she told Teresa, this trouble too would pass. All trials in life passed. Such was the faith of her people. *Her people. Yah*, she was one of them and, though it was painful now, these were her people and these were their ways. How strange that it had taken the pain on this day to finally feel the depth of her devotion. But it had.

Daett pulled into the driveway. When he stopped out by the barn, Susan climbed out and helped *Mamm* step down.

"You shouldn't stay around the place while we're in this condition." *Mamm*'s voice broke.

"I'm going nowhere, *Mamm*," Susan said. "This is my home."

Mamm sobbed, clinging to her arm as Susan helped her into the house and then to her rocker in the living room.

Chapter Twenty-five

That evening the house was full, even the folding chairs were set up along the living room walls. *Mamm* and *Daett* were ensconced in their rocking chairs. Betsy and Miriam were making sure that popcorn bowls and apple cider glasses were kept full. Ada and Esther were in the kitchen slicing ham and cheese for finger food. Already plates were laid out on the table from where the food would be served. Apples and oranges lay beside the plates. Slices of pie sat ready.

The smaller children were racing through the house. None of the adults made any attempt to slow them down or keep them outdoors. A game of prisoner's base was being organized in the yard by some of the school-aged boys. They would play as long as there was light enough to see, switching to another game once darkness fell.

Clearly Susan's sisters were making the best of the bad situation. They would stay around until late this evening, giving *Mamm* and *Daett* as few moments alone as possible on this their first night of being in the *bann*.

All the food being offered had come with the buggies, including the popcorn *Mamm* and *Daett* were eating. Ada had brought cider from her basement. If one smiled, it was possible to forget for a moment what had happened today. One could almost become lost in the sweet tangy taste of Ada's cider and the crunch of the fluffy popcorn. At the moment, no effort was too great to cheer everyone's spirits.

"Come, come!" Betsy was saying. "It's time to eat."

Silence settled on the house, falling into place like a quilt tossed on the bed with its corners askew. What was to be done about prayer?

The question raced through Susan's mind. *Daett* always prayed, but he couldn't tonight.

"Let's pray," Betsy's husband announced, interrupting her thoughts. John led out, not waiting to see what anyone thought of his offer. "Now unto the great *Hah* of heaven and earth, we give You thanks for this food prepared before us. Bless it, O Father, and the hands that brought it to us. Forgive us our sins as we forgive others their trespasses. Make this an evening in which we can experience Your forgiveness and grace. Amen."

Daett had kept his head bowed the whole time, keeping it down a moment longer once John was done praying. There was a sad-but-resigned smile on his face. He seemed to be at peace. *Daett* was accepting their efforts, clumsy as they were. He must know they were trying and wished them well.

"Okay, the food is ready," Betsy announced.

The children looked perplexed about being shooed through first instead of their grandparents. But finally they shrugged and stopped asking questions. They helped themselves, piling the food high on their plates.

Susan glanced at Miriam. There was no reason to explain things to the children. It wouldn't make sense to such young minds as to why *Mamm* and *Daett* couldn't go through the food line. In time, the ones who needed to know would be told. Tonight was about making *Mamm* and *Daett* comfortable. Miriam or one of the other sisters would soon slip them a plate of food, and none of the children would be the wiser.

As the adults began to file into the kitchen, Susan happened to glance through the living room window just as Steve walked past. What was he doing here? It made no sense even if Ada's family was here. Steve wasn't family. But it was *gut* to see him, she acknowledged. And he needed to be welcomed now that he was here. Susan ran to the front door and opened it before Steve could knock.

"Hello" he said as the door opened, his voice rising above the ruckus in the house.

"I'm surprised you're here," Susan said.

He raised his eyebrows. "I do work here, don't I?"

"Well, of course. But not tonight."

"No, you're right. Not tonight. The real reason I came is because I think you should come with me to the hymn singing. You shouldn't be cooped up here with the older folks."

Susan looked over her shoulder before protesting, "But *Mamm* and *Daett* need me."

"They have all your sisters with their husbands and children."

"But—"

"Come on, Susan. You'll be with your *Mamm* and *Daett* during the week."

He was persuasive, there was no question about that. And a drive with him was appealing. Already the day seemed like it had lasted a week with all the pain she'd seen and experienced.

"What do you say?"

Steve was waiting. Susan's face brightened, making up her mind as another buggy pulled in the lane. "There's Teresa now. I'll speak to *Mamm*, and then I'll tell Teresa why I'm leaving. Then I'm ready to go."

"Have you had supper?" Steve looked into the house at the line of people near the kitchen.

"I'll bring a plate along," she whispered. "Is that all right?"

Steve nodded and her fears fled away.

"Have you eaten?"

"Yes, I ate before I came. Thank you for asking. I'll wait for you in the buggy."

After he left, Susan went over to *Mamm*. "Steve invited me to the hymn singing, and I'd like to go. Is it all right?"

Mamm looked at the clock on the wall. "But they've already served supper by now, and you haven't eaten."

"I can take a plate along."

"In the buggy?" *Mamm* looked perplexed.

"*Yah*."

A moment passed before *Mamm* smiled. "Then go, and please don't worry about us."

How like *Mamm*, Susan thought as she slipped into the kitchen where everyone seemed to understand and make room for her. She filled her plate and left through the washroom.

"Where are you going?" Teresa asked, already halfway across the lawn when Susan met her. Behind Teresa, James was leading his horse to the barn, giving a brief wave to Steve sitting in his buggy.

"Steve invited me to the hymn singing, and I couldn't resist getting out of the house. We've been crying all afternoon. Now things are a little cheered up with my sisters here, but still..."

"Oh, you poor thing." Teresa gave Susan a hug. "And here you were comforting me after church when I should have been comforting you. But how am I going to comfort you if you leave?"

"It'll be comfort enough knowing you're here," Susan said. "I know *Mamm* and *Daett* will be blessed. And remember, when you go inside, just do whatever my sisters are doing. It's okay and a little crazy in there right now."

"Like how?" Teresa was looking worried.

"It has to do with eating food and being in the *bann*. Like the meal today at church."

"Okay..." Teresa didn't look convinced.

"Remember, don't worry. Just eat with the rest, and if you make a mistake, they'll understand. You weren't raised in the faith."

Susan dashed toward Steve's buggy. She handed him her plate of food and then climbed in. "Sorry to keep you waiting." She reached for the plate and sat carefully, balancing it on her lap.

"Be careful with that food. You might spill it."

"Steve!"

He laughed and slapped the reins. "I'm glad you're coming with me."

"I guess I didn't know how much I needed this. Thank you for asking me."

"Glad I could be of assistance."

They drove in silence as Susan ate. Thankfully, it was mostly finger foods.

"This buggy feels different." Susan paused for a moment. "It drives funny or something."

"I did bring it up from Daviess County," he allowed. "We don't drive quite the same styles."

"But I do like it," she decided.

"You've not ridden in it much."

"I know, but I like it already. It feels solid."

"Okay." He chuckled.

She *did* like it. And she liked some other things too. Like being able to eat in the buggy with him and not feel uncomfortable about it. And she liked his stability too. Plus, he was simply a very nice man. *Yah*, he was clearly being nice to her tonight out of sympathy for her family's plight, but that was *gut* enough. Soon her thoughts wanted to drift to other possible reasons for him being so nice, especially when she glanced at his face in the falling darkness. But no, he was doing this only for friendship's sake, she reminded herself, and she shouldn't mess things up by thinking otherwise.

"What are you going to do about working for *Daett* now that he's in the *bann*?" Susan asked, forcing her thoughts in another direction.

"Well," Steve wrinkled his brow, "I've thought some about that, but what can I do? We're in the middle of threshing and filling the silo. I can't just up and leave your *daett* with all that work."

"The community would help him out."

"It's not the same," he said. "Your *daett* needs someone working alongside him, not just a group of men coming in for a few days."

"You know *Daett* can't pay you while he's in the *bann*."

Steve shrugged. "There are worse things than not getting paid. Things like leaving your duty when the road gets tough."

"But it's not your fault!" Susan exclaimed. "How were you to know *Daett* would be placed in the *bann*?"

He looked at her. "I'm staying, Susan. I'm working on your *daett*'s farm during these six weeks."

"Well, I..." she started. Then she changed her mind and left it at that. He must have his reasons for doing this.

He seemed to read her thoughts. "You're a suspicious soul, Susan. And I can't say I blame you. But I'm not up to anything other than helping your *daett*."

"I'm sorry." She touched his arm with her fingers. "I guess I'm a little touchy."

"I can see why," he said. "Your boyfriend drops you, and your *daett* turns out to have a child with an *Englisha* woman. I'd be a little jumpy myself." A soft smile crept across his face.

There it was again, Susan thought. That smile. She didn't have an answer, so she said nothing.

"What?" He interrupted her thoughts.

Blushing, she grasped for anything to say. The first words she found were, "You do have secrets, Steve, don't you?"

He laughed. "I think you've asked me that before. And the answer is still the same. I'm an ordinary fellow. And ordinary people don't have secrets."

Still finding nothing better to say, she asked, "Are you sure about that?"

"I think so. Why should I have secrets?"

"I was beginning to think all men had them." She tried to sound angry.

"I can understand that, but there's none here. I'm just an ordinary Joe who wanders the earth by himself."

"You are much too modest, if you ask me."

He laughed and pulled into the driveway where the hymn sing was. He stopped at the end of the walk. "See you after the hymn singing."

"Thank you." Susan climbed down and watched him drive off out of the corner of her eye. He made it sound so casual. *See you after the hymn singing.* Like he didn't care one way or the other. Did he really feel that way deep inside? Or was there interest for her stirring in his heart?

Glancing up she saw a buggy pull in behind her. She could see clearly that it was Thomas's horse and buggy. A girl climbed out. Wilma, of all people. Thomas's new girlfriend. Thomas was laughing as he drove the buggy on. The nerve of him, Susan thought. They must have missed supper like she had, only for a different reason. They had been enjoying themselves enough to show up late. Susan plunged toward the house and grabbed the washroom door. She jerked it open.

What gall the boy had, and so quickly after he left her. Taking up with another girl as if they had never spoken of love.

Throwing her bonnet and shawl on the floor, Susan entered the kitchen, ignoring Wilma behind her. There was no sense in torturing herself with a fake smile and a "*gut* evening." Not just yet. Perhaps later when the pain wasn't as intense. But why was she even so upset over Thomas and Wilma? She hadn't wanted a relationship with Thomas when she came back from Asbury Park. She had been talked into it, her hope revived that perhaps they could make something of their shattered relationship. It had never really been possible. She'd known that down deep all along. That was where the pain was now coming from, more than anything. The knowledge she had dreamed things that would forever remain dreams.

This was no way to act. She was worse than Deacon Ray when he insisted on placing *Mamm* and *Daett* in the *bann.* She had to stop this. Making a sudden decision, she turned around and went back. Susan slipped into the washroom and greeted Wilma with a warm smile and a "*gut* evening."

"*Gut* evening," Wilma replied, a surprised look on her face. "You're Susan, aren't you?"

"That's right."

Wilma hesitated. "I hope there aren't any hard feelings between us. I mean about Thomas. I'm not from around here, and I really didn't try to break anything up between the two of you."

"I know." Susan said. "It was just time. Let's put it that way. I hope things go well with the two of you."

"That's what Thomas said you would say. But sometimes boys say things like that when...you know."

Susan smiled. "Let's not talk about that, okay? Are you staying long? I didn't see you this morning at church."

"I was there, but you had your parents' problems to deal with. Are they doing okay?"

"As well as can be expected," Susan said, holding the kitchen door while Wilma walked inside.

Thomas was a skunk, Susan thought, but Wilma would have to

find that out on her own. And perhaps by some miracle Thomas had changed. Perhaps with the right girl a skunk could at least lose his stripes—and his odor. Wouldn't that be a miracle? Now, if she could find such a miracle, how happy the world would be.

Chapter Twenty-six

The morning of Ada and Reuben's barn-raising dawned without a cloud in sight. Susan was up before the first streaks of light touched the horizon, peeling potatoes for the casserole and rolling dough for the pies. Everyone would be bringing food, and the Hostetler household's contribution would remain the same even without *Mamm* helping.

Mamm had prepared *Daett*'s breakfast earlier, and the couple had eaten in the living room by themselves. *Mamm* was there now, sitting on the couch crying. Yesterday she had offered to help with the food, whispering that no one would ever know. But Susan had shaken her head. *Mamm*'s help wasn't a matter either of them wanted on their conscience. So even if *Mamm* wavered in her dedication to the rules of the *bann*, she had to be strong. Even if no one asked, if *Mamm* helped they would have to pretend she hadn't, and that was too much to add to the load they carried with the sorrow already on them.

Looking out the kitchen window, Susan saw Steve walk up to the barn door, his hat pulled down over his ears. The air must have a chill this morning. Strange that *Daett* hadn't said anything when he came in from doing the chores. Perhaps he had his mind on other things. Why was Steve here this morning when there was so much to do at Ada's place? Likely he was making a last-minute check on the farm before being gone all day at the barn-raising. It would be the most logical explanation, and Steve would do something like that. And he had stayed true to his plans so far of not accepting pay from *Daett*. Every day he showed up for work like usual, taking no money even when *Daett* offered. Steve had even turned down the money owed him for the week prior to the *bann*.

Steve really shouldn't be working without pay. So what if *she* paid him? Susan smiled. That would be a joke. She didn't have the money. Certainly not enough to pay Steve fair wages. And if *Daett* paid her back after the *bann* was lifted, that would be the same as violating the *bann*. How could Steve afford to lose his wages? He hadn't exactly come over from Daviess County to work for nothing. But then it wasn't like he was a married man who had to supply for his family. Maybe Steve was trying to impress her? Not likely, Susan decided. He didn't do things to impress people. Even so, Susan had to admit she was impressed anyway.

Steve had dropped her off with a simple goodbye the night he took her to the hymn singing. And he gave no hints of anything more after that. Not even the comment that he would like to see more of her or take her to the hymn singing next time.

Maybe he was interested but deliberately taking things slowly, giving her time to adjust, to get over Thomas. But that didn't seem like Steve. Well, at least she wasn't yet dreaming about Steve—if she ever would. She could remember back in school sitting at her desk for long stretches while thinking only of Thomas. Studying his face across the room until Thomas would look up. And then the red would rush all over her face. Steve didn't inspire any of that.

Susan stopped short, remembering where she was. What would *Mamm* think if she knew what she was thinking? Probably *Mamm* would think the work and the sorrow were addling her mind. And maybe they were.

Steve had worked here since the spring of the year, but Susan had never given him a thought as someone like...a potential husband. The thought sent a shiver up her back. Such a thing was completely out of the question. And even if Steve had an interest in her, which he probably didn't, was she really interested in him that way? Not really. Not when it came right down to it. There weren't enough stars in his eyes or in hers. Not like Teresa had for James. Now there was a couple to model a life after. Sweetness in a person or in two persons. And so in love with each other.

Did *Da Hah* make such unions twice? Not likely. They were probably the only ones privileged to experience such devotion for each other. James and Teresa...and perhaps Thomas and Wilma. They had looked so in love the other Sunday night at the hymn singing. Sparks flew between them.

Hearing a noise, Susan turned around. *Mamm* was in the doorway of the kitchen, wiping her eyes.

"I really should be helping," *Mamm* said. "I can't stand sitting out there while you work in here all by yourself. Maybe I can bring things up from the basement for you. That's not the same thing as making the food."

"*Mamm*," Susan kept her voice firm, "I know how you must feel, but no, you can't help. I don't want to pretend you didn't all day. You know how that would feel. So please don't think about it. You need to find something else to do, like the wash or something. In fact, that would be a great idea. Put some wash on the line."

"This isn't right," *Mamm* muttered, leaving to come back with a hamper half-full of laundry from her bedroom.

"You can't take mine from upstairs," Susan reminded her.

"I didn't get your wash. My sins would find me out if I did, you know. Hanging your things on the line for all the world to see." *Mamm* went out the washroom door, and Susan heard her clump down the basement steps.

A while later, the washroom door behind her opened, and Susan started. She whirled around to see *Daett* standing in the doorway.

"My poor, brokenhearted daughter." *Daett* walked up to place his hand on her shoulder. "How many times I have said this, but I will say it again. I'm so sorry, Susan. None of this is your fault, and yet you have to suffer along with us."

"You and *Mamm* mustn't go to the barn-raising today," Susan said. "It would be too painful. All you could do is stand around and watch."

"I've been thinking the same thing. I'll go tell *Mamm*. She's in the basement from the sounds of it. She'll be disappointed."

"*Yah*, but it can't be helped. She's doing the wash."

Daett's eyes swept over the food preparation before he left. "Perhaps I can help her with a load of laundry. It seems that's all I'm fit for anymore."

"Oh *Daett*!" Susan threw her arms around his neck. "Can't we all just go away someplace? Somewhere until this is over? We wouldn't have to see anyone, talk to anyone. Please, can't we?"

"You know I don't run away from my problems," *Daett* said, holding her tight. "It's not the way *Da Hah* would have us handle things. Bearing our sorrow is part of what this is about. It cleanses the soul, Susan. Even though you may not understand now, this is for the best."

"Why do I always want to run away, *Daett*? I ran away from Thomas, and it didn't help. I can't seem to stop wanting to run again."

"*Da Hah* will have His way, Susan. What He's doing in your heart, I don't know. I can only say I'm sorry for the pain I've caused. I wish I had never sinned. But I have, and now others must suffer with me. May *Da Hah* give all of you a rich reward for your love for me. And also for your *mamm*. She is a woman I never deserved, and now I know I never will."

"We all love you, *Daett*, so please don't be so hard on yourself."

He smiled and held her at arm's length. "You're my sweetest daughter, Susan. The wild one, *yah*, but the most loved also. You have always been like a young filly who loves the open field with the wind blowing through her mane as she runs. Someday you will find a man worthy of your heart."

"So you don't hold it against me that I couldn't keep Thomas?"

"*Ach*, Thomas." *Daett* smiled. "Maybe it's a relief off my mind that I don't need to train that young boy as a farmer. Watching Steve work has set my mind to seeing things I hadn't noticed before."

Susan grimaced. "Perhaps your lack of vision came from having only girls around?"

"*Yah*, perhaps. A boy, in order to run a farm, should be raised on a farm. He should feel the dirt between his toes from the time he can walk. He should be up with his *daett* to help with the milking before he goes to school. Those were things Thomas never experienced. I believe losing Thomas was for the best, Susan."

"Oh, *Daett*, thank you!" Susan flew into his arms again.

He held her, clucking with his tongue until she laughed.

Susan pushed herself away as a thought rushed through her mind. "Do you know what you should do soon, *Daett*?"

He looked at her, tilting his head.

"Write Donald and invite him for Thanksgiving Day. All this horribleness will be over by then. We could have a big meal with Teresa and James and all our family. We can invite as many as will fit in the house."

"You think this would work?" *Daett* asked.

"Of course it would," Susan assured him. "And we'll have something to look forward to."

"What if Donald finds out about this...about what we're going through? He will feel responsible for our misery."

"No one has told him, and no one will."

A trace of a smile crept into his face. "You do think of the most wonderful things. I will think about it."

"I think *Mamm* will agree. Do you wish me to ask her?"

"No, I will." *Daett*'s face darkened. "But if Donald is too much for her, we will not do this. Otherwise, I will write the letter soon so Donald can prepare for the journey. That is, if he sees fit to come."

Susan said nothing more as she watched her *daett*'s bowed back disappear out the washroom door and heard him move down the steps. Low voices soon came from the basement, and she closed the door, rushing about again. If the pies were to be done in time, the dough needed to be in the oven right now.

Taking out the pie pans, she thinned the dough with the roller. With a few quick glances, she guessed at the size. She cut the dough into squares and flipped the thin sheets over the pan. After trimming the edges, she was pressing the ridges in by hand when she heard a knock on the front door.

Whoever it was would either have to wait or come in without being asked. And sure enough, the door opened and footsteps soon came across the hardwood floor. Steve appeared in the kitchen opening, peering in.

"*Gut* morning," he said.

She smiled. "I saw you came by this morning."

"I had to see if everything was okay since I won't be back today."

"*Daett* could have taken care of things."

"*Yah*, I guess." He was studying the pie crust. "Those are nice. Even my *mamm* couldn't do better than that."

Susan didn't look at him. "But you haven't tasted them."

"They look good from here."

"Looks don't make a pie."

Steve laughed. "Looks help. So can I take anything over to Ada's for you, since I assume your *mamm* and *daett* aren't going today?"

"No, but thank you. I'm not close to ready yet. And I would think you'd want to be down at Ada's when they start building."

"I suppose so. The yard is already full of buggies."

She didn't say anything more as she rushed about.

"This will all be over soon," he said. "And *Da Hah* will make us all better for it. That's the promise He gives."

She started to say something, but Steve was already gone, the sound of his footsteps going out the front door. How does he understand? she wondered. He was such a *gut* man.

Chapter Twenty-seven

Two hours later Susan drove the open buggy the short distance to Ada's place, her pies in the back, along with a casserole wrapped in a quilt. The day had kept its promise, the sun beating down without a cloud in the sky. Reuben couldn't have chosen a better day for his barn-raising. Already the men had the skeleton of a wall up.

Teresa came running out of the house before Susan stopped at the end of the walk. "Oh, Susan, I was so worried about you. Ada said you would still be working on the food and not to worry, but I almost walked over to check on you."

"You should have!" Susan said, jumping down from the buggy. "I miss you around the house."

Teresa gave her a hug. "Where's *Mamm*?"

Susan winced. "It's better if she and *Daett* don't come. They wouldn't be able to help with anything."

"This is still so awful, Susan. I can't get used to it."

"I hope your *mamm* hasn't heard about this."

"I haven't told her anything. I'm sure she wouldn't understand."

"Sometimes I don't understand myself." Susan loaded her arms with pies. Teresa grabbed the casserole from under the quilt, and they made their way to the house, leaving the horse standing in the driveway with the reins hanging loose.

Ada met them at the door and ushered them into the kitchen. Susan and Teresa squeezed through the crowd of women and deposited the food on the counter. When they returned to the buggy, one of the young nephews was standing by the horse's head and holding the reins.

"Thank you, Jonas," Susan said. "Toby usually stays in place, but you never know with all this racket going on."

"It's noisy," Jonas agreed. "And *Daett* had his horse run out to the barn last week. I didn't want you to wreck your buggy."

"Did your *daett*'s horse harm anything?"

Jonas shook his head. "We caught him pretty quick."

"This was thoughtful of you. Do you want to lead the horse out to the fence after we've unloaded everything?"

"*Yah*!" Jonas's face was shining. "I've done that before for *Mamm.*"

While Jonas waited, Susan and Teresa took the last of the food out of the buggy. With their arms full, they watched for a moment as Jonas left, leading the horse with the buggy bouncing over the rough field beyond the lane.

"Do you think he'll be okay?" Teresa asked. "He's so young."

"Our boys grow up fast," Susan said, turning to lead the way into the kitchen where they set the rest of the pies on the counter.

Ada had followed them into the kitchen. She now ordered, "Okay, out you go! You've worked hard all morning. Go out and watch what the men are doing."

Susan stood her ground. "I want to help where I can."

Teresa pulled on her arm, and after a moment Susan gave in. The two walked out to the porch. Spending time with the community women felt *gut*, Susan thought. Even if *Mamm* and *Daett* were shut away at home. That was a terrible feeling to have—and selfish no doubt. But there it was.

Ada had followed them and now whispered in Susan's ear, "Did *Mamm* make any of the food?"

"No, I made sure of that."

"Just checking. It's just that I noticed you brought the same amount *Mamm* usually brings."

"That's what I tried to do," Susan said. "But I worked hard, and I made the food myself."

"Okay, I believe you. I had to ask in case someone asks me."

"Come." Teresa pulled on Susan's arm again when Ada was gone. "Let's go watch the men work. I want to see James working on the barn."

Susan took in deep breaths of the fresh air, allowing the tension and guilt to flow from her body. Perhaps this good weather was *Da Hah's* way of saying He had everything under control. Well, it was *gut* that someone did. She really needed to spend more of her days outside, perhaps helping Steve and *Daett* around the farm. But that would be difficult to manage now with *Mamm* unable to help with the normal household chores.

Teresa was pulling on her arm again. "Let's go see if we can find James."

"*Daett* may invite Donald for Thanksgiving dinner," Susan said, as they came to a stop near where the other girls were standing. All of them were watching the swarming group of men pull the timbers up for the roof of the barn.

"Really? May James and I come too?"

"Of course you can. Thanksgiving wouldn't be Thanksgiving this year without you."

"I'll bring pies...if you trust me with them," Teresa said. Then she pointed and said, "There's James. Clear up on the top."

"Are you sure? How can you tell?"

"Now what woman couldn't pick out her husband?"

Susan laughed. "This is like trying to find the right buggy at the Sunday night hymn singings when it's pitch black."

Teresa glanced sideways at Susan. "So tell me about Steve taking you to the hymn singing and bringing you home again. Is there something I should know?"

"No, there isn't, Teresa."

Teresa didn't look convinced. "Like I'm not going to notice? You walked out of the house right in front of me."

"There's *nothing*, Teresa, really. Steve felt sorry for me and offered. He dropped me off in front of the house when we got home."

"Maybe he's taking it slow."

"Or maybe he doesn't care about me in that way. Lots of people are feeling sorry for us right now."

"I don't believe you." Teresa didn't wait for an answer before she began waving, hollering, "That *is* James." The figure on top of the barn beam studied her for a moment and then waved back.

"He's still looking at you." Susan said, moments later.

"What if that wasn't James?" Teresa giggled. "He'll never figure out who was waving at him. He'll probably think it was his long-desired sweetheart admiring his climbing abilities."

"They can climb, that's for sure. I think they like to show off on a day like this."

"Something like that," Teresa agreed.

The two stood watching the long center rafters being pushed up. The pieces would dangle for a moment in mid-air, followed by a loud shout from someone below before a final push completed the effort.

As the morning wore on, Susan and Teresa mingled among the girls, talking and chatting. Eventually, close to one o'clock, Ada hollered behind them, "Lunch! Would someone tell Reuben?"

Two of the smaller boys took off running, their pant legs a blur as they raced each other. Susan watched them go. How full of life the young were and bursting with energy. Of course she was still young, wasn't she? *Yah*, Susan told herself with a firm set of her chin. And she would remain so now and for always.

"Let's go help get lunch out." Susan nudged Teresa. Teresa nodded but lingered for a moment, taking one last look toward the new barn. She turned and caught up with Susan. Several of the women were pulling the long benches from the church wagon, so they stopped to help. Before long the yard was full of set-up tables, and the women brought the hot food from the house.

The men lined up at the makeshift water basin by the water pump, throwing their hats on a growing pile beside the bench wagon. They splashed water on their faces and scrubbed down with soap before they flopped down on the grass under the shade trees.

Reuben hollered for another washbasin and started a new line when it arrived. The men jostled each other playfully, pulling the occasional hat off the head of the owner who hadn't yet added his to the growing pile. The hat usually went sailing across the lawn, producing a chase by the younger boys, who then returned it, usually receiving a pat of thanks on the head from the grateful owner.

Several of the teenage boys gave chase themselves, apparently not high on preserving their dignity in front of the girls. Or perhaps preserving it by not accepting the offered help from the younger ones.

Susan couldn't imagine Steve chasing his own hat. He was keeping a close eye out while he approached the line. He kept his hat on his head until he arrived at the bench wagon. Thomas, on the other hand, lost his and chose to stand there until it came back. Susan looked away. She no longer cared to think about Thomas. Wilma could take care of that problem.

When the last man was through the line, Bishop Henry called out, "Let's pray and thank *Da Hah*."

They bowed their heads, the women on one side, standing behind the steaming array of food. The men on the other, grouped together in a half circle.

"And now, O God of heaven and earth," Bishop Henry prayed, "we pause to give You thanks for this day, for those who have gathered here to lend a helping hand. Grant that Your most gracious protection continue over us, keeping us safe from harm and from the dangers of body and soul. We give You thanks for this food and for those who have prepared it. Bless their hearts and hands. In Your great name, we pray. Amen."

The teenaged boys elbowed each other but stayed in line behind their elders. Bishop Henry led the way past the steaming food. Susan watched the men move along the tables, heaping their plates high. These were her people, she thought. And they were also *Mamm* and *Daett*'s people. None of the men were asking anything of *Daett* they wouldn't be willing to go through themselves in a similar situation. She had to grant them that. Somehow thinking such thoughts helped quell the bitterness rising up inside her.

Plus she was still young, and they were old. Sometimes the young had to trust the wisdom of age, did they not? Bishop Henry said so all the time. But here the question was real, a test in actual living. Did the older people know things the younger ones didn't? Susan looked away from the benches full of men with their plates on their laps. Somehow she had to believe they did. Perhaps not in matters of book learning, where the *Englisha* thought wisdom was hidden. But in matters of living, *yah*. They had been through things she couldn't imagine. Many of them had experienced the deaths of parents or the loss of young children.

Beyond the suffering, they had lived life in joyous celebration of the love they believed in. The love for the land. The love for their life companions. The love for their children. The love for the traditions handed down to them for more than 500 years. And above all, their fervent love for *Da Hah*. Did not that count for something?

Teresa pulled at her elbow. "Get in line with me. The boys are moving through."

"I'm not married," Susan protested. "The girls aren't going through yet."

"Then perhaps today you can pretend," Teresa said, her voice teasing.

Susan gave in, falling in line with the young married women. No one looked at her strangely. They probably knew this was Teresa's doing. And *Mamm* and *Daett* weren't here, so everyone would go out of their way to make things easier for her.

Susan and Teresa took their plates to the front porch and sat on the benches that had been set up. Over at the young married men's table someone must have been telling a hilarious joke because laughter was rising in a roar.

"Sounds like someone still has plenty of energy left," Teresa commented.

"I'm sure the foremen are watching and remembering for the work this afternoon," Susan said.

"I have to tell you something," Teresa leaned over to whisper.

"*Yah*?" Susan waited.

"Mom's seeing someone in town."

"Your *mamm*?"

Teresa smiled in glee. "Someone she met at the bookstore. I haven't met him yet, but Mom claims he's a *gut* Christian."

"But she can't possibly know him very well so soon."

Teresa shrugged. "Mom's a wise woman."

"Then she's staying around. At least that's *gut* news."

Teresa took a drink of her lemonade. "Honestly, I can't believe how blessed I am. Samuel has a *daett*. I have a husband. And now mom is living near here and making friends."

"I'm so happy for you. And I can take any *gut* news there is right now, believe me."

"It will happen to you. I know it will," Teresa said. "And now, I'd better check on Samuel. I left him with all those babies upstairs."

"Give him a kiss for me," Susan said as Teresa disappeared into the house.

In front of her, the men were stretching out on the lawn, their hats pulled over their eyes. Some of them looked sound asleep. Soon they would be hard at work again, and the women would have a chance to catch their breath. By nightfall the barn would be completed. Not that unusual a thing really. It happened because they all worked together. Here there was hard work, but there was also great joy. If she could endure her own pain, this would all be over before long. *Mamm* and *Daett*'s time of trial would be completed. And when the Sunday after communion came she would make the big choice. She would join the instruction class, taking the first step toward her baptismal vows.

Today was a strange day to decide such a thing, Susan figured. But she had decided, strange day or not. And she would not be changing her mind this time. Not because of Thomas or anyone else. Not if she had to live as an old maid all her life. The time had come to join the community in a real way. The road now lay before her, clear and open.

Mamm and *Daett* would be so happy. Even with their aching hearts they would urge her on the way. That was the way life was supposed to be here in the community. Lived together in pain, in sickness, in health, and in joy. It was time she became one with them. It was high past time.

Chapter Twenty-eight

On Sunday morning, Steve lowered his head against the wind as he shook hands with the long line of men standing beside the barn, all the while hanging on to his hat as the early morning gusts sailed across the barnyard.

"Doesn't look like it'll rain," one of the men offered.

"No, I don't think so either," Steve agreed.

"Silo filling's up for this week," another added.

Steve nodded, taking his place at the end of the line. The murmur of the conversation rose and fell around him. Other men came down the line to shake his hand, muttering the occasional "*gut* morning" to him.

Steve watched as Menno pulled in with his surrey. He stopped at the end of the walk, and Anna climbed out. Moments later Susan came from the other side of the buggy, and the two women went up the sidewalk. Their shawls moved with the wind, the flayed ends flapping as the two clung to their bonnets. With their heads turned sideways against the wind, they disappeared into the washroom.

Would Susan be among the new baptismal class this morning? Steve wondered. All week he had wanted to ask what her plans were. Perhaps tell her of his feelings for her. Hoping that if he did, his words might influence her to take the final step. But this couldn't be done that way. Not if he wanted to live with himself. Not if he wanted to trust her completely. He must see what Susan chose on her own with no influence from him.

And there were plenty of reasons why Susan might choose otherwise. She had already been out in the *Englisha* world once, and now she had plenty of reason to do so again. Thomas had dumped her. Her *daett* and *mamm* were in the *bann*. He was close enough to the family to see how much it was hurting all of them.

Menno's drawn face after communion still lingered in his mind. The man seemed to have aged years in those few hours, his back stooped even more after the service ended. Likely Menno hadn't missed partaking in a communion service since he was baptized—unless for a bodily illness, but not for reasons of his soul. And Menno's heart had clearly gone out of the farmwork. Oh, he came out every morning as always, but the strain showed.

Steve had done what he could to show his intentions to Susan these past few weeks without revealing too much. The woman had attracted him from the time Menno had taken him on as his hired man. But she had been dating Thomas then. And he wouldn't have even considered interfering with another man's relationship. Plus, Susan hadn't noticed him. At least not in that way.

But now with the double blows of Thomas and her *mamm* and *daett's bann*, perhaps he should have moved in at once and made his feelings known. Any normal man would have done so. But he was much too cautious. And this time he might have waited too long. What if Susan didn't join in the instruction class this morning? Would he always wonder if he should have done this differently?

He could have asked Susan home officially from the hymn singing after Thomas dropped her instead of just giving her the little ride on that one night. But he hadn't. Was it because he hung on to some obstinate conviction about doing things the right way? What if he lost Susan? The one girl who had finally caught his full attention?

"You'll have to settle down someday," his *mamm* had told him many times, but he had never wanted to. Until now. Not that he had that much to offer a girl. He wasn't outgoing like Thomas. He couldn't crack a joke after church and have the young boys roll on the benches in mirth. He ought to have settled for the first girl who would take him, but he hadn't. He had held out for something. And now he knew what it was. Rather, *who* it was—Susan Hostetler. The bright, sunny, smart girl who had spent time in the *Englisha* world.

"Bachelors turn weird after a while," his *mamm* had warned. "Old and tattered and messed up in the head. You need a woman to soften your edges, Steve. Do you want me to pick one for you? Or I can get your sisters to ask a girl for you."

He had laughed and ignored her. *Mamms* were made to be ignored; at least when one became a certain age and on certain subjects. Instead, he had prayed about a wife. But nothing had happened. Except he had received an offer to be a hired hand for Menno Hostetler in a neighboring county.

Taking the job with Menno had seemed more a choice made out of boredom than anything else. His *daett* no longer needed his help at home with the younger brothers coming up. But there would have been many things for him to do in Daviess County other than farming. Jobs that paid better money than Menno offered. But he didn't want to leave farming.

Was this the hand of *Da Hah* guiding him? Placing him in the right place at the right time? Then why was he wasting time with waiting? Susan belonged in the community. He didn't need more evidence. Look at how she had been holding up under all the pressure. Standing by the side of her *mamm* and *daett* during their time of suffering. Sure there had been the stories he'd heard. Stories of Susan's travels in the *Englisha* world. Stories of Susan dating *Englisha* men. But they were stories. And even if true, they were likely exaggerated. He shifted on his feet as he stood in the line of men.

Had Susan really gone out to fancy restaurants with an *Englisha* man? Had she spoken of love with him? It seemed so impossible, so completely different from what she was. And yet it could have happened. The signs were there in the way Susan freely threw her head back when she laughed in those moments at the supper table when a faraway look crept into her eyes. It was there in the way she drove her buggy at times—with a touch of recklessness, pushing the horse hard.

Steve shoved his thoughts away long enough to shake another hand and mutter, "*Gut* morning." He must get himself out of this frame of mind. Was this how love affected people? Causing them to wander in their mind? If it did, he must be deeply in love the way his mind was going all morning. Tensed up and all emotional about a girl. His *mamm* would be smiling from ear to ear if she knew and getting her hopes up. But the big question remained. Would Susan go along to the baptismal class this morning? If she did, he would ask her home from the hymn singing tonight.

He took a deep breath at the thought. Susan wouldn't be surprised, would she? Somehow he figured she already knew. Indeed, she probably was waiting for him to make up his mind. Well, today it would be made up one way or the other.

Steve jerked his head toward the main road as a buggy came racing in the driveway. Someone driving a surrey with a sharp, peppy horse was a little late. What would a man with a family be doing with such a horse?

A smile broke across Steve's face as the buggy dashed up to the walk. The driver was James Troyer. Teresa already had a child, so James must have invested early in a surrey, expecting other children to follow soon.

Teresa was climbing out of the back, her shawl wrapped around the little boy in her arms. A gust of wind caught Teresa's bonnet and sent it flying back so it was hanging by the strings tied under her chin. James jumped out of the buggy and took the child in his arms while Teresa got her bonnet back on her head. He had left the lines inside the buggy, and there was no way such a wild horse would stand alone without a tight hand on the reins. Someone must still be inside. The Troyers had visitors this morning?

James climbed back inside the buggy and waited for a moment until Teresa arrived safely at the washroom door. He then let out the reins and the horse lunged forward. As he drove closer, the visitor's face and shirt became visible through the windshield. A young *Englisha* man? Who could he be? He must be from Teresa's side of the family. Perhaps one of her mother's friends.

When James pulled to a stop, the visitor climbed out of the buggy and briefly fumbled with the tugs on his side, obviously wanting to help but clearly not knowing his way around horses and buggies. Steve smiled and ran forward to offer his help. But another boy was already holding the shafts for James when he arrived.

"*Gut* morning!" Steve offered his hand to the *Englisha* man. Behind him, James dashed toward the barn, hanging on to his prancing horse.

"Good morning!" The man smiled. He turned his head sideways as the wind blew through his hair. "Kind of gusty out in the country this morning."

"*Yah*, it is. Feels like a storm blowing up. But Mullet over there claims it won't rain. I guess his old bones have been right more often than wrong."

The *Englisha* man laughed. He was tall, handsome, and dashing. Exactly the sort of man Susan might have gone out with in the *Englisha* world. Surely Susan didn't know this man. After all, he hadn't arrived with the Hostetler family.

"Robby's the name," the man said.

Steve put out his hand. "Steve Mast's my name."

"So this is where you have church?" Robby looked over the gathered men. "Susan said yesterday I was welcome to attend. But I couldn't make up my mind until this morning. Thanks for giving me a welcome right away."

"Susan?" Steve was staring. "You know Susan?"

"Quite well," Robby said. "She stayed with us while she was in Asbury Park. Well, not really at our house, except for the last few weeks. The rest of the time she rented the apartment above my mom's bakery."

"I see." Steve swallowed hard. "Are you visiting?"

"I've been visiting my aunt in Livonia," Robby said. "I thought I'd stop by since I know Teresa and Susan. Teresa offered me a ride to the service this morning, and I accepted.

"When did you arrive?"

"Yesterday."

"Are you staying long?"

"Well, I hope to spend more time with Susan before I leave. Catch up on old times. Teresa said perhaps she could have Susan and me over for supper on Monday night. I really can't stay longer than that."

"I see." Steve cleared his throat. He motioned with his head toward Bishop Henry, who was leading the long line of men to the front-porch door. "It's time for church to start. You can follow me in if you wish. Sit with us young men, even if you're married."

"Oh, I'm not married," Robby said. "Am I allowed to sit with the girls?"

He must be joking! Steve thought, glancing over at him. The man clearly had a twinkle in his eye.

"I might get you a seat with the married women," Steve replied. "I think they'd trust you there."

Robby laughed. "I like you people, that's for sure. You have a great sense of humor. Susan always was like that. I had more fun with her than I've had with almost any girl I've known."

"What do you mean?" Steve asked. But he didn't wait for an answer as he blended into the line of young men, Robby staying close behind him. He wasn't sure he wanted to hear the answer to that question.

Robby stayed with Steve as they moved toward the house. Steve's mind raced with questions. When had Robby been at the Hostetler place? He hadn't worked on the farm yesterday afternoon. Was that when Robby arrived? *Englisha* cars came and went all day because Anna was still selling the last of her garden produce, so Steve wouldn't have noticed even though he worked on the farm. Surely nothing was unusual here. Susan wouldn't do anything inappropriate, would she? Of course not. He had to keep believing that. Robby couldn't have been the man she used to go out with in the *Englisha* world. He wouldn't dare walk in here like this, as if nothing was wrong if that were the case.

Steve followed the line of boys into the living room, sliding sideways on the hard bench as he sat down. He took several deep breaths, trying not to look toward the girls section. Abe Troyer's house was warm this morning, and sweat beads crept out under his shirt collar.

When the first song was announced, Bishop Henry stood up and led the line of ministers upstairs. Two boys got up to follow, and three girls after that. Steve forced himself to look. He had to know if Susan was among them. At least that would supply some comfort. His gaze caught sight of her familiar face, with her head bowed low and her gaze on the floor, leading the girls upstairs. So he had judged Susan's character correctly. He let out a sigh of relief. But why was this Robby guy sitting beside him?

Chapter Twenty-nine

Three hours later, Bishop Henry was still preaching the closing sermon. Steve glanced over at the clock on the living room wall. A few more minutes and the bishop would surely wrap up his thoughts. Robbie shifted again beside him on the hard bench; obviously trying for a more comfortable spot after sitting longer than he was used to. Robby could get over his discomfort on his own, Steve decided. Steve had been stealing glances at Susan and keeping track for the entire service. Not once had Susan looked their way from where she was seated in the unmarried girls section.

Was something wrong? Was Susan ashamed of letting him know she knew Robby? Susan didn't normally look his way during the church services. Though with Robby beside him, surely her eyes would have strayed over once or twice if she knew the *Englisha* man? If Robby meant anything to her, that is. Since Susan hadn't looked, did that mean Robby hadn't been her boyfriend in that *Englisha* past of hers? He really was being a jealous old coot, Steve told himself. He hadn't even asked Susan home yet. He had no right to stake a claim on her. Yet he couldn't stop the questions. Perhaps Susan only knew Robby as a friend? There certainly was no devious air around the *Englisha* boy. And would he have come to church if he planned to lure Susan out into the world again? Not likely.

Steve's eyes had followed Susan when she came down the stairs after the instruction class. She cut quite a striking figure, as she always did, but today even more so in her new, dark-blue dress, no doubt made especially for the occasion. The new dress meant the baptismal class had not been something Susan decided overnight. She planned to stay in the community. And if all that was true, perhaps *Da Hah* could bring about feelings between them that could grow into something serious. If this Robby didn't make trouble anyway.

Steve forced himself to look away from Susan as Bishop Henry wrapped up his thoughts. Minutes later the bishop asked for testimony from two men before taking his seat.

Deacon Ray cleared his throat and spoke first. "I can say that all we have heard here today was from the Word of God and is the Word of God for us. The many warnings given today against the world have pierced our hearts again, reminding us that we are only pilgrims and strangers on this earth. Let us remember this in the days and weeks ahead as we seek to walk in the fear of *Da Hah*." He paused and then continued, "I want to mention our baptismal class that began today. I know that those in the class no doubt wrestled long and hard with this decision. And yet they have made the choice to forsake the world with all its lusts and join the church that dwells on this earth."

Deacon Ray stopped to pull his handkerchief out of his pocket and blow his nose. Why was the deacon so emotional? But, of course, Steve knew. How had he forgotten? Today was not only the first day of the new baptismal class, but also the day of Menno and Anna's restoration. He had been so busy thinking about Susan, he hadn't remembered this. He ought to be ashamed of himself. No wonder Deacon Ray was in tears. Today was a day of new beginnings in more ways than one. Susan had chosen to begin the instruction class the day her *mamm* and *daett* would be taken back into fellowship.

"We are not a perfect people," Deacon Ray continued. "We all know that, and yet we believe *Da Hah* sanctifies the hearts of those who believe. I wish to welcome the class and to hope for the best as they continue down the path toward baptism. I also hope that any bitterness in our hearts caused by the discipline sanctioned by the church may not allow the devil an open door to torment us.

"I know that suffering of this kind is not pleasant but necessary at times. Old Bishop Mullet used to tell us the story when we were growing up of the shepherd who had a young lamb. This lamb often strayed from the shepherd. No fence was high enough or gate strong enough to keep the lamb inside. One day when the young lamb was again lost on the mountains, the shepherd found him just in time. That day the shepherd broke the leg of the lamb and carried him home on his shoulders.

"We might think what a cruel thing this was, and yet as the shepherd carried the young sheep with him for the weeks it took the leg to heal, a bond of love formed between the two of them. When the time came for the young lamb to run again, he no longer strayed because he had learned to love.

"I pray from the bottom of my heart that we also may have learned of love during these weeks of suffering. I hope the bond between *Da Hah* and us has been made stronger by this injury. More than that, I cannot wish for. So may *Da Hah* bless this day and the rest of what is said."

Abe Troyer, in whose house the services were being held, coughed. He gathered himself together and spoke. "I too can say that all I have seen and heard today was from the Word of God. I am blessed to be part of such a privilege—that of being ministered to by heaven. I confess that I'm but a pilgrim and a stranger on this earth, though often my eyes are drawn away toward the world. I ask that you pray for me in the hour of my temptations, so that together we may arrive safely at home on the other side. Beyond that, I have nothing more to say. May *Da Hah* continue to give His blessings."

Bishop Henry stood up, waiting a few moments before speaking. "I am thankful that the preaching of *Da Hah*'s Word has been testified to as having been done under His grace. Now at this time, as many of you know, it lays upon our hearts to receive brother Menno and sister Anna back into our fellowship as they have not been a part of us these past six weeks.

"It has grieved our hearts greatly to see this happen, and yet we as a ministry couldn't see any other way to keep the purity of the church without taking this measure. So now will brother Menno and sister Anna please come forward and kneel before the congregation?"

Menno got up first and moved out of his aisle. His back was bowed as he waited for Anna to join him from the women's section. Together they approached Bishop Henry and knelt at his feet.

"Will both of you confess before the church and before *Da Hah*?" Bishop Henry asked. "That you have failed and sinned greatly in this matter, and that you ask for forgiveness from the bottom of your heart?"

"*Yah.*" Menno's voice was low.

Anna's answer must have followed Menno's because Bishop Henry continued.

"Do you, brother Menno and sister Anna, commit yourself to forsaking once again the world, the devil, and the lust of your own hearts, and to give your minds and souls to the love of *Da Hah* and to the building of His church on this earth?"

"*Yah*, I do," Menno said.

"*Yah.*" Anna spoke louder this time.

"Then I give you the right hand of fellowship." Bishop Henry extended his hand. Menno took it, his knees trembling as he stood up. Bishop Henry kissed him on the cheek.

"And now to our sister Anna, I also give the right hand of fellowship."

When Anna stood, Bishop Miller stepped aside, giving Anna's hand to his wife, Ruth, who had come up to stand beside him. She kissed Anna's cheek and tears ran down her face. Anna threw her hands around Ruth's neck and hugged her. The two women stood together weeping as Bishop Yoder waited. Around them the room became quiet, the clock ticking loudly on the living room wall.

After long moments, Bishop Henry cleared his throat. Anna let Ruth go. She turned to look up at Menno, who still had his head bowed. He reached over to take her hand in his. Together they walked back down the aisle, parting at the women's section.

When Menno was seated, someone shouted out the song number, and the last song began. When the number was completed, Bishop Henry spoke from his seat on the minister's bench. "And now may the blessing of *Da Hah* be on the rest of the day as we are dismissed."

The younger boys moved for the door, grabbing their hats on the way. Outside in the yard, they ran for the barn like spring calves let out in the pasture after a long winter shut up in their pens.

Robby turned to Steve. "So that's an Amish church service."

"*Yah*. And you even got to see a baptismal class and a man and wife received back into fellowship."

"I saw Susan go upstairs. So that's what was going on. I'm glad to see she's settling down."

Steve said nothing as he watched the older girls get to their feet and move toward the kitchen. They would be helping prepare dinner. Susan had been one of the first ones to go, as always, willing to help. She would be a jewel of a wife if her heart could be captured. That was the question, really. Would she allow him or any other man close to her again? But here he was, thinking about his own matters again when Menno and Anna had only been taken back into fellowship a few moments ago. His heart should be rejoicing for them. They certainly must be praising *Da Hah* for having preserved them during the short time of darkness.

Robby leaned over. "You mentioned being received back into fellowship. Was that about Susan's parents…when they were on their knees? If ever I wished I could understand the language, it was then. I guess it teaches one to pay attention in school during German class."

Steve thought a moment before answering. "Menno and Anna had something to take care of with the church. That's how we do things in the community…when confessions have to be made and discipline given."

"I see," Robby said, although he clearly didn't.

Well, he would just have to wonder, Steve thought. He didn't feel like explaining how things worked in the Amish world to an *Englisha* man, even if he was a friend of Susan's. And there was no sense in embarrassing Menno and Anna by telling strangers about Menno's sin.

"I'm going out to the barn for a few moments," Steve said. "You're welcome to come along or you can wait here. Lunch will be served soon."

"I'll wait and talk with some of these older fellows," Robby said. "I'll get some good, old-fashioned farm wisdom, I'm sure."

Steve nodded and left Robby, who was already moving toward the benches full of older men. They greeted him with handshakes and broad smiles. Robby would get his ears full of wisdom, Steve decided. There was no doubt about that. All he would have to do is ask.

As he walked to the barn, Steve wondered how he was going to get a chance to speak with Susan. It was time he did. Especially since today had been such a day of new beginnings—even of miracles. He ticked them off in his mind. Menno and Anna were restored. Susan had joined the baptismal class. *Yah*, today he would also take the plunge. He could do no less. He would ask Susan home from the hymn singing. Officially and with intent.

He thought hard about how to go about this, but the solution didn't come to him until he was on the walk back from the barn. The way was to send one of the younger girls playing in the yard to ask Susan to come outside. He would speak a few words with her beside the washroom door, and whoever saw them could think what they wished. He was asking Susan home, and this was nothing to be ashamed of.

Steve approached the group and asked the tallest girl, "Will you go tell Susan Hostetler someone wants to speak with her? You don't have to tell her who it is."

The girl looked at him, a wide smile spreading across her face. Several of the others covered their mouths and giggled. Steve felt the burning of his skin under his collar.

"Will you please?" he repeated.

The girl nodded and ran off. Steve left the snickering group of girls. He figured it wasn't every day that older boys provided live entertainment for their young funny bones. Well, Susan was worth the effort. Now if she would only say *yah*. But would she? The question made his neck burn even more. He should have thought of this much earlier. Maybe his *mamm* was right. He should have let her pick his girl.

The young girl came bursting out of the washroom door, grinning ear to ear, followed by a puzzled-looking Susan. The girl ran off with a quick glance over her shoulder.

"What do you want right this minute? We're at church."

"I want to ask you something."

"You see me almost every day. It couldn't wait?"

"*Nee*, it could not. Susan, may I take you home from the hymn sing tonight?"

Susan stared at him. "Like a real date?"

"*Yah*, of course."

"You want to take me home?"

"Come on, Susan," he begged. "I'm asking you, I'm standing here looking like an idiot with a bunch of girls giggling about it. Just say *yah*, please?"

A trace of a smile teased her face. "Maybe I have to think about this."

"No, you don't!" He was glaring at her now.

She laughed. "Of course you can take me home. Now get out of here!"

He glanced toward the house. "Does that *Englisha* boy mean anything to you?"

"Who?" Her smile was teasing again.

"You know who. That Robby guy."

"You wouldn't be jealous now, would you, Steve? I'm surprised at you."

"Who is he, Susan?"

"Go!" She waved her hand. "I'll explain tonight."

He smiled as she turned, went inside, and closed the washroom door behind her.

Chapter Thirty

After the Sunday night hymn singing, Susan came out into the windy night hanging on to her *kapp*. She waited as another girl came down the steps behind her, walked past her, and climbed into her boyfriend's buggy. There had been whispers and smiles among a few of the older girls during supper, with a few quick glances sent her way. Someone must have seen Steve and her talking after church today, and apparently everyone approved so far. Steve was a decent man. Not that she was planning to marry him or anything, but allowing Steve to take her home could lead, well, in that direction. But she ought not to think such things. She should just relax and enjoy the evening.

And here came Steve's buggy. Susan walked toward it and climbed in.

"*Gut* evening!" Steve's voice was muffled by the noise of the wind against the buggy sides. He pulled out and drove around the other waiting buggies until he reached the main road. When Susan still had said nothing, he glanced at her with raised eyebrows.

"*Gut* evening," she said. "I was just teasing you."

He laughed. "I thought the cat might have gotten your tongue. Or is your heart pounding so hard at my glorious presence that you can't breathe?"

Susan joined in the laughter. "How refreshing! A truly humble man."

"Do you always verbally assault the boys who take you home?

"That was a compliment, really. If you only knew."

"I think I do know," he said.

Silence settled in the buggy. A comfortable enough silence, Susan thought. But then they had always been comfortable around each other since the beginning, although she had always thought of it more as a friendship. Not exactly *this*... She let the thought hang as the buggy was buffeted in the wind.

"Some night to take a girl home for the first time," Steve said. "Well, it's my first time, so have a little mercy on me."

"Is it really? I'm not sure I believe that."

"*Yah*, it is. Are you going to hold it against me?"

"No, of course not. But why haven't you before now?"

"Because I've never really wanted to before."

"Time to settle down maybe?"

"Now quit being so mean. You're much nicer during the week."

"At least you're honest," she said as another blast of wind shook the buggy.

He laughed. "I suppose that does count for something."

"It counts for more than you know. Not like a certain man we both know."

"At least he was dashing."

"Maybe I'm tired of dashing."

"Is that supposed to be a compliment? Me being boring and all?"

"No, it's just that...that..."

"You don't have to explain." He slapped the reins as they went around a corner, and the horse ran into the wind for the first time.

"So am I really the first girl you've taken home?"

"*Yah*, but let me ask you a question now. Who was that *Englisha* boy who showed up today? You said you would explain."

"You shouldn't be jealous, Steve. Robby has a girlfriend. They're getting married this spring."

"So you never really dated him?"

"No, Steve." She found his arm in the darkness. "We had some fun together, but I never thought of them as dates. I did date an *Englisha* man while I was away. Only he wasn't half the man you are."

She listened to his breathing inches from her face.

"That's *gut* to hear, although I don't know about the last part being true."

"It is true. All of it."

He didn't answer as they pulled into the Hostetler driveway. A light still burned in the living room, casting a soft glow across the front porch and into the yard. Steve came to a stop by the hitching post.

For a long moment they sat on the buggy seat until Steve said, "I think we'd better go inside, don't you?"

Susan said nothing but climbed out of the buggy. Steve got out and tied his horse up. He took Susan's hand and they walked to the house. As they entered the living room, there was no sign of *Mamm* or *Daett*, and Susan seated Steve on the couch. "I'll get you something from the kitchen. I'll be back in just a minute."

"I don't need anything really."

"*Yah*, you do," she countered.

She returned moments later with a piece of cherry pie with a scoop of vanilla ice cream.

He smiled. "Treats for a king, huh?"

"Of course!" she said as she sat beside him.

"You did *gut* today," he said, eating his pie. "Joining the baptismal class. I'm glad you did."

"Thanks."

"There's so much about you I admire, Susan. How you stuck with your parents through this whole excommunication thing. And that you're still here after Thomas let you go. You could have run back to the *Englisha* world. Robby kind of made that point. You have friends out there."

"Shhh...stop talking." She nestled up to him. "I just want to be with you."

"I'll be as mum as a bear in his winter sleep," he murmured.

"You don't listen to a word I say, do you?"

"Nope. A man has to be the head of the house, you know." He dipped his spoon into the ice cream.

"So already you're talking about being the head of the house? On the first date? Is that supposed to be a proposal already?" she joked.

He laughed. "Just sayin', that's all."

"Ah…so it's like making sure your woman understands? No wonder you've never taken a girl home before."

"You still don't believe me, do you?"

Susan shrugged. "I think I do, but I'm still surprised."

"And why is that?"

"You could have any girl you choose. Well, almost. I guess you are a little plain."

He made a face. "That cuts deep."

"You asked for it."

He laughed. "*Yah*, I guess I did."

"Did I hurt your feelings?" She touched his arm.

"I'm smarting to the depths of my soul. Soon I'll have tears gushing down my cheeks."

She laughed. "You're nice to be with, you know. I'm glad it's come to this, though I've always thought of you more as a friend."

"Being a friend isn't a bad thing. It can be a solid foundation."

She waited until his pie and ice cream were finished before turning to him. "Tell me about your plans, Steve. What do you have in mind when *Daett* lets you go?"

He raised his eyebrows. "Is he letting me go?"

"Well, you can't stay here forever. Something has to be done sometime. *Daett*'s not getting any younger."

"Perhaps, but I hadn't thought about it much."

"Don't tell me you're after the farm. Is that why you're seeing me?"

He laughed. "Marrying the farmer's daughter to get the farm?"

"Well, they do kind of go together."

"I'm not like that. Surely you're not thinking so?"

She shook her head. "Of course not. I was just thinking of someone else. Please forgive me."

"It's okay, Susan." He took her hand. "I understand. You haven't offended me."

"Oh, Steve, you have no idea…"

"The worst is over now." He squeezed her hand.

They sat in silence for a few moments until Steve said, "It's late. I'd better be going."

She glanced up at the clock. "It's not that late."

"Farming duties come early," he said. "I don't want my work to suffer just because I'm seeing the farmer's daughter."

He stood and walked to the front door. Susan followed. He turned, a smile playing on the corner of his face. "And may I come back next Sunday night? I think that's what I'm supposed to ask. Of course, I'm not sure—this being my first time and all."

"Oh Steve!"

"So it's *yah*?"

Susan nodded, her face blushing now. Steve had never succeeded in so disconcerting her before. But then he had never asked her home either.

"Just checking." He smiled, obviously enjoying himself. He turned and disappeared out the door.

Susan watched him go across the lawn, untie his horse, get into the buggy, and then she followed the shadow of his buggy as it drove out of the lane.

Chapter Thirty-one

The following morning, *Mamm* and *Daett* were beaming as they sat at the kitchen table for breakfast—their first meal with Susan since the *bann* was lifted.

As soon as *Daett* left through the washroom door, *Mamm* jumped up, filling her hands with empty plates and utensils. The joy on *Mamm*'s face brought tears to Susan's eyes. How deeply she must have felt the pain of the time they had just walked through.

On the way to the counter, a fork slipped off the stack and crashed to the floor. *Mamm* gasped, nearly losing her grip on the plates. Susan leaped to her feet and rushed to *Mamm*'s side. She took the plates from *Mamm*'s trembling hands and placed them on the counter.

She turned back to *Mamm* and took her hands. She guided her back to the table.

"Sit down right now," she ordered. "What is wrong? Shall I call *Daett*?"

"No!" *Mamm* said trying to smile. "My nerves are collapsing, that's all. The last few weeks have been harder on me than I realized."

"It's over now," Susan said, keeping her hold on *Mamm*'s hands. "It's over."

"I know." A soft smile flitted on *Mamm*'s face. "I feel such relief, such peace in my soul. We were spared, Susan. From the awful darkness. I can never say how grateful I am to *Da Hah*. One of us could have died during that time. And I would not have wanted to cross over while living away from the church. And neither would your *daett*."

"But *Da Hah* would not have allowed that," Susan said. "He knew your hearts. And even if you had gone, *Da Hah* would have understood that you had already sought repentance."

Mamm nodded. "I know that in my head. And Bishop Henry told us the same thing. But it feels different once you're living there yourself."

"I hope I never find out," Susan said with a shiver.

"So do I," *Mamm* said. "I certainly never thought I would find out."

"You really should sit and rest for a while," Susan said. "I can do the dishes."

"*Nee*, I can't sit around with all the household work to do," *Mamm* protested. "And the threshing crew is coming this week. And then Thanksgiving is coming up."

"Speaking of Thanksgiving," Susan said, "did you ever hear back from Donald? Can he come?"

"*Yah.* The letter came yesterday. He is coming."

"Oh, *Mamm*, that's such *gut* news."

"*Yah*, it is," *Mamm* agreed. "And now that we're out of the *bann*, I should be up and rushing around the house instead of dropping forks on the floor. I'm an old woman, I guess. I can't take things as well anymore."

"You'll be okay," Susan assured her. "My sisters and I will help with the work for Thanksgiving. And what would you think of inviting Steve?"

"Oh, my!" *Mamm* beamed again. "*Yah*, of course. *Daett* and I noticed Steve brought you home last night. Here I am all wrapped up in my own troubles, and I forget about the wonderful things happening with my youngest daughter. Yesterday you started baptismal class, and now Steve has brought you home. Is he coming again?"

"Do you want him to, *Mamm*?"

"What kind of question is that, Susan? Of course I want him to."

"You don't wish I was still seeing Thomas?"

"*Ach*, Thomas," *Mamm* said, waving her arms. "I'm not the one who would have had to marry him. And he did drop you, and I'm on your side. Steve will make a fine husband for you."

"We're not marrying yet, *Mamm*. Please."

"I know," *Mamm* said, patting Susan's arm. "Now let me get on my feet again. Didn't you plan to visit Teresa today?"

"*Yah*, if it's okay. Are you sure you'll be all right?"

"Is that *Englisha* boy going to be there? Robby, was that his name?"

"*Mamm*, please. I'm over that. I'm not going back to the *Englisha* world. Robby is a friend, no more."

"Are you sure, Susan?" *Mamm* was looking at her.

"*Yah, Mamm*."

Mamm was clearly not convinced. "Does he have a girlfriend?"

"*Yah*, and he told me Saturday they're getting married in the spring."

Mamm sighed. "Then I'll have to trust you. I guess you could have run away a long time ago if you'd wished to. It's not like we didn't give you plenty of reasons of late."

"You don't have to feel bad about it." Susan gave *Mamm* a hug. "I understand."

"Now, now," *Mamm* muttered, getting to her feet. "Don't be treating me like a *bobli*. I'm still your *mamm*."

"*Mamms* need hugs just like everyone else."

Mamm smiled. "Why don't I start the baking for the threshing crew, and once you're finished with the dishes you can leave for Teresa's place?"

"I'll be back as soon as I can," Susan said as she rushed around the kitchen. *Mamm* wiped the table clean and brought the flour from the pantry. Susan was through with the dishes by the time *Mamm* had the bread dough rising. Putting the last dish away, Susan raced for the barn.

Hopefully Steve was working in the back field this morning instead of repairing something in the barn for the threshing crew. It might be embarrassing seeing him around after last night. And he might still be a little jealous if he knew where she was going. Not likely, but why take the chance? She pushed open the barn door and walked inside, pausing to peer around in the dim darkness. No sign of Steve. She breathed easier, letting the memories of Teresa's wedding rush over her. The preacher had stood right over there. It seemed like years ago, and yet it wasn't.

Would this be where she would get married…soon? With Steve instead of Thomas? How many times over the years had she dreamed of standing here with Thomas, her cheeks blushing, saying the sacred vows with him? Even after she had caught him talking with Eunice, she had managed to hope. Now that dream was dead. Susan sighed. Perhaps it was best things were going like they were. She was tired of dreaming, of imaging how great things might be, only to have them dashed. Steve certainly caused no dreaming. He was solid. Wholesome. And a little funny in his own way. And he was a *gut* man. There was no question about that. And he was also sweet. That was the maddening thing about Steve. You liked him just because he was so good. It was all very confusing.

Calling to Toby, Susan caught his halter and led him outside the stall to throw the harness on. When she was done, she led him to the buggy, bending down to pick up the shafts.

Someone unexpectedly rounded the corner of the barn, and Susan jumped.

"I'm not trying to scare you!" *Daett* said when she whirled around. "I thought I'd help you get on your way."

"I thought you were Steve!" Susan said, trying to catch her breath. She was even weak in the knees and that was embarrassing.

"Would that have been such an awful thing?" *Daett* asked. "Steve seems happy this morning. Happier than I have seen him in a long time. Is it possible my last daughter has finally found the man of her dreams?"

"*Daett*, don't tease me," Susan said, holding up the buggy shafts. "I'm trying to make sense of this myself."

"Well, you have my blessing," *Daett* said swinging the horse between the shafts.

"Thanks for your approval. But I don't know myself yet what will happen. Remember, I was seeing Thomas not so long ago."

"*Da Hah* moves in mysterious ways," *Daett* said.

"*Yah*," Susan said.

"And there's something else I want to tell you, Susan," *Daett* continued. "I want to thank you for the way you stood with us during our time of trial."

"You know I couldn't have done anything else," Susan said as she threw the lines through the buggy front. *Daett* held Toby's bridle while she climbed into the buggy. As Susan pulled out, she and *Daett* exchanged waves.

Daett had seemed so calm all morning, Susan thought as she guided Toby onto the main road. It was like peace followed him around today. Or perhaps it was simply relief that the *bann* was over. And yet it was more than that. *Daett* had grown during his time of suffering. He was even gentler than before. The wrinkles around his eyes had grown deeper, but inside his heart was larger. He wouldn't always have taken her loss of Thomas with such grace. Unlike *Mamm*, *Daett* had really liked him.

Susan slapped the reins, and Toby picked up his pace as they drove along the back roads. Signs of autumn were already showing on the leaves of the maples and oaks. Soon they would be turning bright red and orange and then falling to the ground in preparation of winter. Strange how she was in the process of opening her heart to the possibility of something new while the world around her was preparing for snow and ice. Was this a warning perhaps? A sign of the foolishness of her attempt to find love again? Surely it wasn't. She hadn't gone looking for it this time. And *Da Hah* had been with them through their great trials in the past weeks as He surely would be with them for the rest of the journey. She needed to trust that perhaps Steve was the man who fit her heart perfectly.

Ahead of her, the little concrete bridge below Teresa's place came into view. Susan slowed down. She took the ride across leaning out of the buggy to listen to the running water, just like a schoolgirl who didn't have better sense. Well! Susan thought, pulling her head back inside. In more ways than one she still was a schoolgirl at heart. Steve would just have to deal with that. If he only wanted a practical, decent woman to work on the farm with him and raise his children, then he could find someone else. "There!" she said out loud. "That's how I feel about it."

Driving into Teresa's driveway moments later, Susan burst out laughing. Here she was fighting with Steve, and he wasn't even here. What an odd couple they made.

Robby's car was sitting beside the barn, so he must have driven up early from his aunt's place in Livonia. Unless he had stayed here for the night, which was also possible. Teresa was probably eager to practice her newfound skills as an Amish hostess.

Susan tied Toby to the hitching post and made her way to the porch. Teresa met her at the front door, flying into her arms for a big hug. "Oh, it's so *gut* to see you again!"

"You saw me only yesterday!"

In the background Robby was laughing. "I think she's a little crazy myself."

"How can you say such a thing?" Susan stepped around Teresa to look at him. "She's like a sister to me."

"Look at this!" Robby pointed to his stomach. "She had me staying the night when I could have stayed at Aunt Bonnie's place. Last night she filled me up with mashed potatoes, gravy, meat, corn, pumpkin pie, cherry pie, and other things I can't even remember. Then this morning it's biscuits, gravy again, oatmeal, bacon, eggs, and orange juice. The woman is killing me."

"And it was so much fun!" Teresa said.

Robby was patting his stomach and shaking his head. "Thankfully I'm leaving in a little bit."

"You wouldn't have gone without seeing your old friend again, now would you?" Susan questioned.

"No! I knew you were coming this morning," Robby said. "So tell me, Susan, are you staying here or can I give my mom the good news that you'll be back to work in the bakery?"

"Hey, if you're going to lure Susan out to the world again, you're out of here!" Teresa huffed from the kitchen door opening. "No more *gut* cooking for you."

"Well, I wouldn't do that," Robby protested. "I thought maybe I didn't need to entice her. Maybe she's ready to come back."

"No, I'm not going back," Susan said. "Lure or no lure. I've come to the conclusion that I'm Amish through and through. Now tell me about your girlfriend and the wedding."

"Well, there's not much to tell yet. I knew her back when you were there, Susan. It just wasn't love yet. More like friendship, if you know what I mean. Some romances start that way."

Susan started to turn red. "*Yah,* I know what you mean."

"Remember all those pep talks you gave me about love?" Robby asked.

"Of course I do," Susan said. "Love is out there for everyone. We just have to find it."

"Susan said that?" Teresa looked strangely at both of them.

"Yes, she did," Robby said, grinning.

"I suppose I was a little carried away in those days," Susan admitted. "But I do still think it's true. Just not in the way I thought before."

"Speaking of that, how did it go last night with Steve?" Teresa asked.

"Okay, I guess."

"What are you two talking about?" Robby looked puzzled. "Mind cluing me in?"

"A man from the community took Susan home after the hymn singing," Teresa said, beaming.

"Well, that's probably a good sign," Robby said.

"I think so too," Susan said. "And he's nice as can be."

Robby laughed. "You'd be the expert, right? At least that's what I always thought."

"No, I'm definitely not an expert when it comes to love," Susan said.

There was a brief silence, as if the conversation had played out. Then Robby said, "Can I at least tell Mom that you might come to visit sometime? I know she'd love to see you."

"I don't know," Susan said. "A visit might happen, but not a move. I'm home to stay."

"Surely you still have your driver's license though? I worked too hard helping you get it to have you throw it away."

Susan said nothing, and now Teresa was staring at her. "You still have your license, Susan? You have to get rid of it. What if someone finds out?"

"What? Is this a secret?" Robby looked perplexed. "What's wrong with having a driver's license? Like for emergencies? I think that would be wise."

"That's because you're not Amish," Teresa told him. "Susan is going to get rid of that thing—and quick! Aren't you, Susan?"

"*Yah*, I will," Susan said, unsure of when she would muster up the courage to do it.

"I have some cookies to take out of the oven," Teresa said as she disappeared into the kitchen. She returned moments later with a full plate of macaroons.

"Wow!" Robby said, taking a bite of one. "If Susan doesn't come back to work for Mom, you sure could! These are delicious."

They all laughed at the idea even as Susan and Teresa assured Robby that neither of them would be working in his mother's bakery.

An hour later, the plate was long empty. Susan jumped to her feet after a glance at the wall clock. "I have to go. It's getting late."

"Is this all the time I get?" Robby complained. "We just started talking."

"Only until your next visit," Susan said. "And next time bring your new wife."

"Well, maybe, but it won't be on our honeymoon," Robby said.

Susan reached up and gave him a goodbye peck on the cheek.

Teresa was staring at both of them.

What if Steve found out about this? Susan wondered. Her kissing an *Englisha* boy...even if it was only on the cheek.

"The best to you, Susan!" Robby said with a warm smile.

"And you too," Susan said. She gave him a quick hug and then went outside. She ran across the lawn, untied her horse, and climbed into the buggy. Robby and Teresa were both waving to her from the front porch as she drove past.

It had been *gut* to see Robby again, she thought. He truly was like a brother. But things were even clearer now than before. It would never be the same if she went back to Asbury Park. Already she could tell they were drifting into separate worlds.

Driving across the bridge again, Susan looked down at the water and wondered about the future. About Steve. Were they to be man and wife someday? The question sent no thrill through her, but maybe it didn't have to. They were the same in so many ways. They both loved the farm and the community. And they liked each other as friends. Perhaps that could be the basis of their love. It would grow like a tiny seed out of the ground. It would be wonderful if this were true. Very wonderful indeed.

Susan slapped the reins. It was high time to get home. She'd already been away from her duties much too long.

Chapter Thirty-two

On the following Wednesday, the roar of the silo-filling machines filled the barnyard as Susan carried a large thermos of lemonade to an open buggy. She set it, along with glasses, on the floorboards. Off to her left she could see black smoke pour out of the steel-rimmed tractor exhaust. The contraption sat a dozen feet from the silo filler, and a drive-belt connected the two.

Several of the men were standing on wagons piled high with corn sheaves. They turned to look at her, broad smiles spreading over their faces as they noticed the thermos and glasses. One of the men pulled off his hat and wiped his brow with his sleeve.

"Come and get it!" Susan hollered, her voice not rising above the racket. They would know what she said, she figured. She turned to walk back to the house when a loud clang came from the silo filler. She stopped and turned, watching as the tractor groaned and slowed. The smoke pouring out of the muffler stack was even darker than before.

"Hold off!" A man's voice rose above the noise, and someone standing on the wagon waved his hand. The steady stream of corn sheaves stopped moving. The tractor sputtered and then returned to normal strength. With another wave of the man's hand, the bundles were heaved again, each one landing heavily on the metal conveyor belt to disappear into the spinning blades of the silo filler.

Susan shivered. Silo-filling day was a glorious time of action and noise, but it was also dangerous. The men would be careful, but even so, there were often accidents. *Daett* had prayed this morning for the safety of the crew, and now Susan had an extra reason to be glad that

Da Hah heard every prayer. Yesterday Steve had joined the crew for the first day of the fall season. Today and tomorrow he would be filling in for *Daett*, going along for the other stops. This was the first year *Daett* wouldn't be going with the crew. Steve was already fitting in so well, it almost seemed like he had always been here.

All that had been happening was a little scary. The world had almost taken on a mind of its own, and she was just along for the ride. She and Steve had only just begun seeing each other, but still... Well, she'd better not stand here gawking at the line of wagons unloading or the men would think she was a young teenager who had never seen a silo-filling day before.

Susan walked toward the house, pausing again when she saw Teresa's buggy coming down the road. James had arrived at the break of dawn with his team. He was helping to bring the sheaves in from the fields. He hadn't said anything about Teresa coming, but it was wonderful that Teresa had taken it into her head to arrive, hopefully for the entire day. The buggy rolled into the driveway, and Susan went to help unhitch. Samuel was sitting beside his *mamm* on the buggy, all dressed up in a new pair of pants with suspenders.

"*Gut* morning, little fellow," Susan said, sticking her head inside the buggy to pat Samuel on the legs. He looked amused even with all the racket coming from the barnyard.

Teresa was staring at the workers. "I still can't believe it. Even after I saw this last year. It's such a glorious mess."

"It's silo-filling time. That's how it's done."

Teresa was still staring at the sight when she climbed out to undo her side of the tugs.

"I'll take your horse to the barn," Susan offered, leaving Teresa standing beside the buggy. Turning the horse loose in one of the stalls, Susan threw a small bundle of hay into the manger. When she went back outside, Teresa was still standing beside the buggy with baby Samuel in her arms, her face pained. "It looks so very dangerous. And James is in there somewhere."

"*Yah*, but the men are careful. Steve is out there too."

Teresa's glance went down the long row of wagons.

"He's used to it." Susan assured her.

"*Da Hah* protect him...and Steve," Teresa whispered.

Susan took her elbow and led her toward the house. "They'll be okay," Susan said again.

Teresa continued looking over her shoulder. "I can't see James."

"Let's pray right now." Susan stopped to hold Teresa's hand. Why was this fear also rising in her heart? The men worked around these machines all the time, and they were very careful. Still, it would be *gut* to pray.

Teresa bowed her head and prayed out loud. "O dear *Da Hah*, watch over all the men today as they work so hard. Keep them safe—especially my dear James and Susan's Steve. I don't want to be selfish, but I do so love James. I don't know how I could live without him."

Susan waited until Teresa lifted her bowed head and was ready to move on. As they went to the house, baby Samuel peered back over Teresa's shoulder at the men. Susan glanced back and saw that they were now gathered around the lemonade. As the two women came up the porch steps, *Mamm* opened the front door. "*Ach*, Teresa, it's *gut* to see you again. But you didn't have to come to work in the kitchen. Betsy and Ada are due any time."

"I couldn't stay away," Teresa said. "I had to see what filling the silo looks like close-up. And from what I can see, it's dangerous and exciting at the same time."

"That it is," *Mamm* agreed as another buggy pulled into the driveway. "Here are Betsy and Ada now."

"They can unhitch by themselves," Susan said when Teresa looked toward the buggy.

"So I get special treatment? Is that it?"

"You'll always get special treatment around here!" Susan held the front door for Teresa. Once inside, Samuel kicked his legs and reached for the toys *Mamm* must have spread on the floor as soon as she saw Teresa's buggy. Teresa set Samuel down and checked his diaper. She scrunched up her face.

Susan laughed. "We'll be in the kitchen when you're done. You know your way around upstairs." In the kitchen Susan got busy. Kettles of peeled potatoes, still steaming, were set on the table after the hot water was poured out. Susan separated them into smaller bowls and began mashing them. Teresa appeared again moments before Betsy and Ada entered the house.

"*Gut* morning, Samuel!" they cooed, their voices reaching into the kitchen.

"Come in and help us!" Susan hollered.

Both women huffed in exasperation and were taking off their shawls as they came in.

"Look who's sitting down and yelling at us to come work," Betsy teased.

"She's always been that way," Ada added. "She can't help herself."

"Would someone be nice to me this morning?" Susan said with a laugh. "Or did you two climb out of the wrong side of the bed?"

"If things were that easy to fix, I'd go home and climb out the other side, I do declare!" Betsy said. "Joel started today with his first cold of the season, and Mary looks ready to join him. Thankfully they were still well enough for school today, as I would hate to have missed *Daett*'s silo filling."

"Then get busy and work your blues out on these potatoes," Susan ordered. "There are two kettles to go, and my arms will soon be ready to fall off."

"My, my! Look who's snappy this morning," Ada said.

"*Yah*," Betsy said. "Susan should be in a *gut* mood from what I hear. Ding, ding, ding, wedding bells are ringing. Looks like the girl's finally settling down."

"So is this finally it, Susan?" Ada teased.

"Stop tormenting me!" Susan snapped. "Steve only brought me home once."

"Now who crawled out of the wrong side of the bed?" Betsy chided.

"Do stop bugging her," *Mamm* ordered as she came up from the basement. "Let *Da Hah* work things out in His own *gut* time. We're all glad Susan is patiently sticking things out the way she is."

"I have to agree," Ada said. "I've seen a lot of maturity in Susan lately.

She's even joined the baptismal class, which was highly overdue in my opinion."

"Do you want me leaving for Asbury Park again? I can, you know," Susan warned.

Betsy and Ada looked at each other, raising their eyebrows.

"She won't go!" Teresa asserted. "She's just threatening. Susan's heart is here with us."

"Well, *Da Hah* be praised for everything!" *Mamm* declared. "That's what I thought Susan's plans were, but it's *gut* to hear this from someone else."

"And how are you doing, *Mamm*?" Betsy asked.

"I'm doing fine. What do you mean?"

"You know what we mean," Betsy said. "It hasn't been that long since the *bann* was taken up. We know that was very stressful."

"Well, it was awful, as I've told you before," *Mamm* said. "But *Daett* and I made it, and I sure wouldn't have wanted him to go through it alone."

Ada, standing nearest *Mamm*, gave her a hug. The others reached across the table to touch her arm.

By eleven o'clock most of the food was done, and Susan went out with Teresa to set up tables in the yard. There was no church wagon filled with tables and benches today, so they used sawhorses *Daett* had set out yesterday by laying sheets of plywood across them. Boards rested on firewood logs for benches. Over them went white table covers, followed by the food.

Mamm went out to tell *Daett* lunch was ready, and the racket in the barnyard died down. The crowd was much smaller than the day of the barn-raising, so the men were soon through washing up. *Daett* led out in prayer since neither Bishop Henry nor any of the other ministers were present. When the men had gone through the line and were sitting at the tables eating, *Mamm* motioned for the women to get their food.

Betsy and Ada went first, with Teresa following. When Teresa had filled her plate, she took her food over to the table where James was sitting. He gave her a smile and made room for her. A few of the men stared, but the teasing soon started.

"Where's my wife?" one of the men hollered. "This isn't fair in the least."

A roar of laughter went through the small group.

Did she dare? Susan wondered. It would be a bold thing to do, but she wanted to. Seeing Steve bent over his plate, the back of his shirt soaked in sweat, slivers of cornstalks hanging in his hair drew her to him. He looked so, well, so like a farm boy. So down to earth and yet so sweet. How that was possible she didn't know. She wasn't blushing like Teresa had when she'd been dating James. Still, she wanted to sit with him. He'd be asking her to be his steady date before long, so why shouldn't she? Betsy and Ada were already joining their husbands, following Teresa's lead, so she wouldn't really stand out.

Walking across the lawn with her plate of food, she looked down at Steve's surprised face. He seemed so humble, so grateful, as she sat down beside him.

"Now this really isn't fair," one of the men said. "I will have to speak with the bishop about this."

In the noise of their laughter, Susan looked at Steve. "Is this okay?"

"It's okay with me," Steve said, rather pleased with himself now.

Chapter Thirty-three

Donald stirred in bed and listened to the strange sounds in the predawn light. Where was he? He sat up, pushing aside the heavy quilt and breathing in the unheated air. The room smelled fresh, though it was colored with the faint scent of corn and farmland. The soft bumps and bangs below him continued. Across the hall the hinges of a door squeaked, and soft steps went past his room.

That he was in the house of his birth father raced through his head. Laying his head back on the soft pillow, he allowed a smile to spread over his face. The welcome had been fabulous last night. His return had been all that he'd hoped. His father had taken him into his arms and wept on his shoulder.

"You have to come more often, Donald," Menno had said. "We're so glad to have you here with us for Thanksgiving."

Susan and Anna had shaken his hand, along with that of Charles, Donald's son. They had welcomed them with broad smiles on their faces. Last night there had been pies and baked items laid out all over the kitchen counters. A raw turkey had sat on the table, and the supper dishes had been put away when they arrived.

"You should have come for supper," Anna had protested.

Donald said he'd wanted to, but there hadn't been enough time in his visitation schedule with Charles. Anna had insisted they sit down and eat large pieces of pie.

That Charles was even along was a miracle of sorts. And there hadn't been the expected objections from him. No long stories on how unique or weird Amish life was had been necessary. Even assurances of how much Charles would be missing if he didn't come weren't needed. After only the barest of details, Charles, the rebel, the contrary one, had consented to come along for the trip. The fourteen-year-old boy who couldn't wait to get out from under the authority of either of his parents had agreed to come to the disciplined Amish community.

Last night when they arrived, it had been too dark to see much, other than what the car lights revealed of the barn and front yard. Beyond those lay the open fields Menno owned and had kept for years—likely since he'd married Anna.

Donald rolled over and got out of bed. Sleep was impossible. Too many thoughts and strange feelings were running through him. And the noise from the kitchen continued. My, these people get up early. The sun still wasn't up. He could only see a soft glow on the horizon when he looked out the window. He pushed back the curtains for a better view and watched the light grow in the east.

What would it have been like growing up Amish? Not that such a thing would have happened for him, even if Menno had known of his birth. Carol would never have come to this strange culture. But the question still begged to be asked. He was half Amish, wasn't he?

Maybe that was the missing piece of life that had always eluded him. Instead of being a lawyer, he was supposed to be a farmer. Tilling the soil and bending over to run the plowed ground through his fingers. The thought was comforting in a way, as wild and impossible as it was. After all, farmers weren't the most prosperous people in the world, especially on the small farms. But that was his non-Amish mind thinking. The Amish continued to make successes of their small farms, passing on their acres to the next generation with great anticipation. Susan and her boyfriend probably had plans to take over this place now that Menno was up in years.

A loud bang came from downstairs, followed by a faint gasp. Another smile crossed his face. Apparently Amish people weren't above making mistakes. But he'd noticed they were the first to admit such a thing. They even made the big mistakes, such as fathering children out of wedlock. Yet they also seemed to have a system in place that took care of whatever problems—big or small—arose.

What did Menno have to go through for correction when it became known he'd fathered a child before he was married? He would have to ask if the question didn't seem too uncomfortable. There had to have been something.

Donald dressed by the faint light from the window and carefully made his way downstairs, feeling his way along the walls with his hands. The small shaft of light coming from under the door below helped, and he made his way safely to the bottom without tumbling head-over-heels.

The living room was empty, but a gas lantern was hanging from the ceiling. Its soft hiss filled the room. Donald peeked into the kitchen and saw Susan and Anna fixing breakfast. He cleared his throat.

"*Gut* morning, Donald," Anna greeted him. Neither of the two women slowed down or turned around. They must have heard him coming, he figured. The silence of the country house was something he wasn't used to.

"Where's Menno?" Donald asked.

"Out in the barn doing the chores," Susan said. "Do you want to tag along?"

Like a little boy would, Donald thought with a smile. He felt like a little boy. Susan had captured the feeling exactly.

"I think I will," he said. "Do I go out the front door?"

"Either that way or through the washroom," Anna said, motioning with her head.

Donald imagined hats and coats hanging in his way with boots scattered by his feet in the darkness. "I think I'll use the front door. If Charles wakes up, tell him where I am."

"Do you think he's settled in and sleeping well?" Anna asked.

"He's okay," Donald assured her. "He liked the place before he even got here."

"That's kind of you to say," Anna said. "How is your mother doing while you're gone? You said last night she had moved in with you."

"You know how those things go. Mom thinks she can live by herself even when I'm there. So a few days of me gone will pass quickly. She might even enjoy having some time to herself."

"It's hard to let go," Anna said, a sad smile on her face.

Donald turned to leave, thinking that Anna also knew what she was talking about. Doubtless a life of this kind required a lot of letting go. More than he could possibly imagine. When he went outside, he noticed the barn windows were lit with a soft glow. He took his time crossing the lawn, stopping to look at the sweep of stars overhead. They twinkled with a brilliance undimmed by city lights. A person felt closer to God here, as if a connection was ready-made between the Creator and His created. Why did men move so quickly to places where the feeling was diluted?

Donald shook his head as dawn broke. Pretty soon he'd be packing up and moving here himself. Like that would ever happen. He was too old for such a move and too much a creature of his own world. But that wouldn't keep him from coming here once in a while. He would take advantage of this contact with his birth father. It was a precious gift he would value all his life.

As he pushed open the barn door, Donald peered around, catching sight of Menno throwing hay into wire racks hanging inside the stalls. Menno saw him approach and turned to meet him, a smile covering his face.

"My son!" Menno said. "You've decided to get up with the birds, I see."

"I couldn't sleep. The air is too fresh."

Menno laughed. "Keeps a man healthy, it does. I wouldn't live anywhere else unless *Da Hah* asked me Himself."

"I hope to come here often," Donald said. "Not to live, but to visit. Is that okay?"

"You're welcome as long as I own a roof over my head," Menno said as he split a bale of hay, throwing half of it into each manger for the Belgians.

"Your own hay crop?"

"*Yah*," Menno said. "The pastures are thinning out a little early this year with the cold snap, but thank *Da Hah* we have plenty of hay stored in the barn."

"So was it a good year this year—for farming?"

"One of the best. It seems *Da Hah* blesses where and when He pleases. But we are glad when the crops turn out well. Did anyone tell you my daughter Ada's husband down the road lost his barn? Burned to the ground! Thankfully we have a good crop so we can replenish his supply and have enough for this year. We had a barn-raising, so he has a place to put the hay again."

"No, I didn't hear that. What happened?"

"Reuben must have gotten in a rush on the last hay cutting and put it up still damp."

"Lit on its own, then?"

"*Yah*, the fire was already well on its way by the time anyone noticed. The fire department saved all the other buildings and even the tree by the house. We had much to be thankful for."

"Don't let me keep you away from your chores." Donald stepped back and leaned against a wooden stall. "In fact, I'd be glad to help."

"You're a city boy," Menno said.

"I know, but I am half Amish. Doesn't that count for something?"

Menno smiled. "I was just teasing. I'm through with what has to be done this morning. We don't milk anymore, and there won't be any work in the fields today. The man who helps me, Steve, doesn't come up on mornings we aren't working. There's nothing an old man can't take care of."

Donald took a deep breath. "Tell me something, Menno. Did you have trouble with your church after I came for the wedding?"

"Why do you ask?"

"I got to thinking about how you people do things. You seem to have a plan for everything in life. A simple plan, but a plan. Seems to me your people probably also have one for this type of problem."

"I don't look at you as a problem, Donald," Menno said, motioning for Donald to sit on a nearby hay bale. Then he sat on one himself. "Let's be clear about that first, okay?"

"Yes. Thank you. You've never given me the impression I was."

"Nor are you one in spite of what I'm about to tell you. It's just that our ways might seem strange to someone from the outside."

"I'm half Amish, am I not?"

"*Yah,* and you are my son, Donald. I didn't do my part with you when you were small, and I apologize. But I am glad *Da Hah* and Carol were able to find a *gut* home for you."

"Mom and Dad did a great job."

Menno sat on the bale saying nothing for a long moment.

"Back to your church," Donald prompted. "They disciplined you once I left, didn't they? Even after all these years?"

"*Yah,* but it was not just discipline for my transgression. What *gut* would that have done when what I did could not be undone? It was also done out of love for me. And for Anna. For all of us. For our way of life. Such a sin had to be commented upon. Otherwise it grows like a cancer until it fills the community."

"Okay. But they did more than talk about it, I'm sure."

Menno sighed. "Only the harshest of measures are *gut* enough when the sins of the body and soul threaten. What I did was a great sin. Against Carol. Against you. Against *Da Hah.* And against the community. If I had come home and confessed, perhaps they would have understood better. But I didn't. I told no one, not even Anna. Covering one's sin can be as large a thing as the original act."

"So what did they do to you?"

"I spent six weeks cut off from the fellowship of the church. We call it the '*bann.*'"

"I'm sorry I caused that." Donald hung his head.

"There's nothing for you to be sorry about. I do not wish you had stayed away."

Donald nodded. "It seems like I've heard of such a practice somewhere. Aren't you then considered lost to God and man during that time?"

"We walk in the darkness, *yah.* But even then we have hope."

"You said 'we.' Who else was involved?"

"Anna walked through it with me, even though she didn't have to."

"I'm feeling worse all the time. Maybe I shouldn't have sought you out."

Menno shook his head. "You must not think so. I had already told Anna on the day you came, on the day of Teresa's wedding. This would eventually have become known to all, as the sin was heavy on my heart. If you hadn't come, I would have walked alone without seeing for myself how *Da Hah* had brought *gut* out of the situation. You have lightened my heart, Donald. I have a son! You don't know what joy that brings to me."

"I'm glad I got to meet you." Donald touched his arm. "I'm glad I found my birth father."

"*Yah*, so am I." Menno stood and wiped his eyes. "We must not think *Da Hah* doesn't know what He's doing. But now we had better go in for breakfast. Anna will think we got lost in the barn."

"How are we going to eat breakfast and still leave room for the big meal I heard is coming at noon?"

Menno laughed, patting his stomach. "This is one of those days when there is always room for more. We must eat and be glad for what *Da Hah* has blessed us with."

Chapter Thirty-four

Donald glanced at his watch as the first of the buggies came rolling into the driveway. It was ten o'clock, and Anna had said lunch was at twelve sharp.

"Or thereabouts," Menno had added with a laugh.

"*This* year we will be on time," Anna had shot back, waving her hands to send them away from the breakfast table. "Now scoot! We have a lot of cleaning up to do yet."

Charles, sitting on the back bench against the kitchen wall, had grinned, still sleepy-eyed in the midst of this exchange. It was amazing, the change that had come over the boy. When Charles stayed at Donald's house in Missouri on weekends, it was a struggle to get the boy up before noon.

As soon as *Mamm* had banished the menfolk from the kitchen, Charles had said he was going to explore the barn.

"Be careful around the horses," Menno had cautioned with a smile.

Donald had almost offered to go with the boy, but he'd decided not to. Perhaps this was some freedom Charles needed. "Freedom" seemed a strange concept for an Amish farm, but it was nonetheless true. There *did* seem to be more latitude here in the quiet openness of the fields, the unadorned buildings, and the minutes that ticked by without a radio, TV, computer, or electronic toy in sight.

Menno, sitting in his rocker, stood up. "Reckon I'll go out and help unhitch. That looks like Betsy's buggy. They must be coming early to help in the kitchen."

"Mind if I tag along?" Donald asked.

"Not at all," Menno said, holding the front door open for him.

As they walked across the lawn Donald was wishing he had a set of Amish pants to wear. Not that anyone was looking at him strangely, but just for the experience and to blend in a bit. He hadn't felt this adventurous in years.

"*Gut* morning," Betsy greeted them as she climbed out of the buggy. She offered her hand to Donald with a smile. Her husband, John, was already unhitching on the other side as their children raced across the yard toward the barn.

"Good morning," Donald replied, shaking her hand and nodding to John. "It's good to see you again."

"I hope *Mamm* put you up well for the night. And your son...where is he?"

"He's exploring the barn. Enjoying himself, I think."

"Farms have a way of doing that," Betsy said, waving a hand at the disappearing backs of her children. "They have a barn at home, but they love to come here to *Dawdy*'s place." With that, Betsy headed inside to help with the food.

After Menno and John unhitched, Donald followed the men into the barn, the two Amish men's low voices rising and falling as they spoke German. People from the community seemed to do that, Donald remembered from the wedding. It didn't strike him as a sign of disrespect toward him. It just happened. When they'd moved three feet from him, they'd changed from English to Pennsylvania Dutch. It was like throwing an electric switch to another circuit.

Charles was coming down the ladder from the haymow when they walked in. His hair was messed up and hay covered. A huge smile was on his face.

"You can really do it, Dad!" he hollered. "You really can."

"You can do what?" Donald asked.

"Jump from way up top down to the bottom of the haystack. It's just like in the movies."

"But you shouldn't! You could break your leg or something."

Menno laughed from where he stood near the horse stalls. "The children all do that. Don't worry, Donald. It's part of growing up around here."

"See!" Charles said, as a thump came from overhead. "The other kids are the ones who told me it was safe. I just took one jump. Come up and watch me take another one."

Donald looked up at the ladder. Strings of hay were hanging on each step. The end stretched out of sight in the dim light above him.

"Go on," Menno encouraged him. "I'd come join you myself if I weren't so old and brittle."

"Come, Dad!" Charles tugged on his arm. Donald couldn't remember when he'd seen such excitement shining in his son's eyes. He allowed himself to be led to the ladder, and they both climbed up. Above them the children's excited exclamations grew louder.

Strings of hay tickled his nose and his eyes. Donald almost sneezed as he pulled in air. At last he was through the chute. He filled his lungs with the sweet smell of seasoned hay. His eyes watered, but the sneeze tickling left. He craned his neck to look at the rafters towering above him. Spiderwebs and bird nests were plentiful around the wooden beams. Bales of hay were stacked all the way to the top like stairs stepping skyward. On the loft floor, a mound of loose hay billowed up for a dozen feet or so.

"Yee haw!" a small voice hollered from the heights above. A small body of a young boy suddenly appeared. It seemed to hang suspended in midair before tumbling into the loose hay.

"Are we ready?" The hollered question from a girl came from the same place the boy had just left.

The boy in the hay rolled sideways until he ended up on the haymow floor, kicking his legs in high glee. "Ready!" he yelled.

"Coming!" the girl cried. Her body appeared in the dusty air. Her dress flying with her skinny legs extended. She landed softly with a rolling fall on the mound of hay.

"Isn't that fun!" Charles exclaimed, running up the stacked bales. "Come on and try this, Dad."

"I'll watch you go first," Donald said, watching his son climb up the rickety hay bales. The two youngsters approached him after climbing the ladder, pulling hay out of their hair and staring at him.

"I'm Donald," he said, extending his hand.

Their exuberance from moments earlier had vanished like fog in the bright sunlight. They both nodded, not offering to shake his hand.

"Coming down!" Charles yelled from high above them. Donald saw their smiling faces turn upward before his did. His son's body appeared, his arms flaying, sweeping through the air as he landed smack center on the mound of hay, disappearing up to his armpits. Charles came up laughing with delight.

"He likes our haymow," the young boy said.

"*Yah*," the girl agreed. "He's having fun."

How unaware they were of the great privilege of their birthright, Donald thought. They had done this a hundred times in the few short years of their lives. The wonder of it was probably even now growing dim. It must seem strange to them to see a teenager experience such a sensation for the first time.

"You've got to try this, Dad!" Charles called from the top of the mound.

"I'll break a leg," Donald said, envisioning being rushed off to the hospital by ambulance, lights flashing and siren blaring. What a way to end Thanksgiving Day—and the meal not even eaten yet.

"No you won't," the two beside him said together, shaking their heads.

"Really?" Donald glanced sideways at them.

They looked innocent enough, but who knew? Underneath the calm demeanor might dwell twisted minds who would take delight in seeing a middle-aged man wrestled down the haystack and screaming in pain from smashed body organs.

"Dad, come on! It's safe." Charles had arrived at the bottom of the mound. Hope glowed in his face.

He couldn't turn that down, Donald thought. There hadn't been anything like hope written on his son's face for over a year now.

"Then the old man will jump!" Donald called. He turned and began climbing. There was silence below him, which didn't help. Cheers might have been more in order. Arriving halfway from the top, Donald stopped and looked down at the faint outline of the mound of hay below. This was high enough and then some.

"Higher!" Charles yelled.

Donald shook his head. At least he might live to recover from his injuries at this height. Then, with a whispered prayer, he launched himself, feeling the sinking feeling of nothing beneath his feet and air moving past his ears without a sound. His arms went out by themselves, his feet churned under him. This was clearly not a graceful way to pass from this world to the next. The impact came like landing on a featherbed, only the bed didn't stop him. His body kept going and going. Hay filled his eyes, his ears, and his mouth as he hollered in fright...or was it delight? The following bounce put him on his backside, sprawled across the hay mound, the sound of three voices in high mirth all around him.

"That was awesome, Dad!" Charles said. "You need to do that again. The second time is even more fun."

"I'm not doing that again." Donald groaned, moving each limb in turn. At least they all seemed to work.

Charles scrambled up the mound to peer into his father's face. "Are you okay, Dad?"

"I'm splendid!" Donald said. "Now I'm getting myself into the house before you children kill me for good."

They slid down the haymow together. The two children on the floor still had smiles on their faces when he walked past them. Apparently they didn't see non-Amish parents airborne every day.

The barn was full of men when he walked into the next room. He paused to pull hay out of his hair. They grinned and offered to shake his hand. He couldn't remember all their names, but their welcome felt good. Almost like he was part of them, even in his outsider clothing. *How amazing!* he thought. Such a little thing like jumping off hay bales could break down such large barriers.

The men worked their way toward the house, speaking his language when they were close to him. In the house, the living room was full of women who gave up their seats when the men appeared. They paused to shake hands with Donald before disappearing into the kitchen. They all gave their names, their faces familiar from the wedding, but he had a hard time keeping track. He did remember the young man who said his name was Steve. Wasn't he Susan's boyfriend? He looked like the type of man she'd go for. Solid, kind, and tenderhearted.

"Not all the girls made it home today," Menno said. "Some live out of state. But someday we hope to have the whole family here at the same time."

Menno's face almost glowed with happiness, Donald thought. From their talk earlier in the barn on what Menno and Anna had been through, Donald looked for some bitterness to be present. But he saw no signs of any.

The morning passed in busy chatter about farming and how each of the men's families was doing. Donald looked up to see Anna standing in the kitchen doorway.

"Menno!" she called. "It's time to set up the tables."

Menno surveyed the people in the room. "I think everyone can fit in here. What do you women think?"

A few of the women looked in from the kitchen, appraising the space with their eyes.

"The children can eat at the kitchen table," Anna decided. "Let's bring up the large table from the basement. And with the leaves extended, we'll be set."

Two men stayed behind and moved the living room furniture. Menno went with three others and Donald to the basement. While one man held the door open, the others collapsed the oak table and wrestled the main frame up the basement stairs and into the house. Once there, all the leaves were put back in.

The women spread out the tablecloth and set the silverware. Food followed. The turkey was placed in the middle with a large carving knife sticking out of the center. Behind that came the mashed potatoes, gravy, dressing, cranberry salad, caramel sweet potatoes, and a five-layer salad. For dessert there were pumpkin and pecan pies.

Donald stared as his stomach growled.

Standing beside him, Menno laughed. "See! I told you. There's plenty of room left in a man's stomach for *gut* foot. Anna makes the best in the community, I'm telling you that much."

"I believe you." Donald was still staring. This almost outdid the spread at the wedding.

Anna was glowing and standing by the table. "We're ready, Menno. You can call in the children."

"Time to eat," Menno hollered through the open front door. Quick feet came running from outside. As they entered, the children were herded toward the washroom, where the women oversaw their hand and face washing.

Charles came in. "What on earth is this all about? I thought we ate a huge breakfast."

"It's food, Charles!" Menno boomed. "*Gut* Amish food made by willing and able hands. It's the blessing of *Da Hah*."

"Wow!" was all Charles managed as he stared at the overloaded table.

Outside the sound of another buggy pulling into the driveway reached them. All heads turned to look out the living room window.

"It's James and Teresa!" Menno said.

"Her mother is along, so that's probably why they're late," Anna added, going to the front door. "Here I've been so wrapped up in my own work I hadn't noticed Teresa and her family hadn't arrived."

Menno and Susan joined Anna at the door. They waited as their company approached.

"Hi, everyone! Sorry we're late!" Teresa called as she came across the yard.

Anna laughed. "We just have the food out. Hurry and come inside."

"It's all my fault," Maurice said, following Teresa. She gave Anna a hug on the porch.

"You still made it in time," Anna assured them.

"Goodness gracious!" Maurice exclaimed as she entered the living room. Her hands flew to her face. "This spread! It's like heaven on earth!"

"Not quite," Menno said. "But it sure looks *gut*."

"Hello," Donald greeted Maurice and Teresa. "So how are the newlyweds?" he asked Teresa.

"Splendid!" Teresa said with a blush. "Couldn't be better."

Behind her the front door opened and James came in, shaking hands all around.

Anna took her place at the table again, repeating the announcement. "The adults will eat here in the living room, and the children in the kitchen. Would everyone please be seated."

They found places, the men pretending to jostle for the best seats but ending up beside their wives.

"And now let's pray," Menno said when the room had grown still. They bowed their heads as Menno led out. Donald listened to the German words, understanding only a few. It was an honor though, he thought. They were including him as if he were one of them. A prayer in English would have made him feel like a stranger.

"Thank You, Lord," Donald whispered, "for bringing Charles and me among these wonderful people."

The day passed with long conversations and much food. Donald and Charles spent the night again, and early Friday morning said their goodbyes. Even young Charles seemed reluctant to leave. He did manage to give *Mamm* a kiss on the cheek with a sincere "thank you." He shook hands with Menno, and said, "It's good to have met you, sir."

Menno tousled his hair. "You behave now, son."

Charles grinned.

As the car pulled away, *Mamm* said, "*Da Hah* brings happiness out of sorrow...and even out of our own sins."

"*Yah*, He does," Menno said. "He surely does."

Chapter Thirty-five

The half-moon hung low in the sky as the buggy drove home from the Sunday night hymn singing. Steve allowed the horse to take his time, the lines hanging loose over the storm front. Susan was leaning out of the buggy door to look at the broad sweep of stars overhead.

"They look so peaceful," she said. "So settled. Like they don't have a trouble in the world."

"They're nice tonight, aren't they?" Steve pushed his hat back on his head to look out the other side of the buggy.

"Like the hymn sing was," Susan said. "I thought everyone was extra happy tonight."

"I know I'm happy tonight."

"You should be. You're driving home with me!" Susan said with a laugh.

He joined in but didn't say anything.

"I'm glad you are." Susan slipped her hand around his arm. "I'm glad so many things are behind us. Like Donald's first holiday visit, and the hard things, such as *Mamm* and *Daett*'s *bann*. And Thomas too."

"Forget Thomas. Another good thing to mention is your joining the baptismal class," Steve added.

"But that wasn't hard. Not like I thought it would be anyway."

"How's it going?"

Susan shrugged. "It's going okay. I'm staying within the *Ordnung*, and Deacon Ray doesn't bother people who are in the *Ordnung*."

"I wasn't talking about keeping the *Ordnung*. I know you do that. I was asking about joining the church."

Susan waited a few moments before answering. "I think I'm okay. I haven't had any doubts lately. Why? Are you trying to give me some?"

"No." Steve laughed. "Of course not. I think you did really well during your *mamm* and *daett*'s hard time. That could easily have driven you back into the world."

"Do you think that's where I was…in the world….when I lived in Asbury Park?"

He stared at the lines, the silence long before he spoke. "It is the world, Susan. You know that. You could have been in great danger."

"Of what, Steve?" She turned to face him, his outline faint in the light of the stars. Why did Steve have to bring up this subject tonight just when everything was looking so much better? She didn't want to deal with the memories and ramifications of her time in the city. Asbury Park was over, and she intended to settle into the community for *gut.* Steve was a decent man and would make a decent husband if he asked her to marry him.

Steve reached over to take her hand. "Tell me about that time. You've never told me much."

"What do you want to know?"

"Everything," he said.

Susan drew in her breath. "Are you worried I did something I wasn't supposed to? Like what *Daett* did?"

"No, I know you better than that."

She took another deep breath. "Is this really necessary then?"

"I would like to know." His fingers moved in her hand.

"Well," she began, "I worked for Robby's mom in their bakery. I lived in an apartment above the bakery. Basically I minded my own business. Eventually Teresa came into my life and took up a large part of my time from then on."

"You're an amazing girl, Susan. Have I told you that before? I'm glad you came back."

She leaned against his shoulder and watched the stars outside the buggy.

"What else?" he asked in the silence.

"Okay…" Susan stayed where she was. "I'll tell you what might be considered 'the worst.' I studied hard and passed a high school diploma equivalency test—what's called a GED. And…" she hesitated. "And I got my driver's license. In fact, it's hidden in my dresser. I also dated an *Englisha* boy a few times." She looked up at his face to see his reaction. Would he be satisfied now or rush over to Deacon Ray with this information? If he did, would she have to make a confession in front of the community to continue with the baptismal class? She did trust him. He wasn't like that at all, she was sure. Still her hand trembled in his. When he didn't say anything, she asked, "Do you think I sinned while in Asbury Park? Are you going to talk to Deacon Ray?"

"I love you, Susan. I wouldn't do anything to bring trouble on you or your parents. It's us that I'm concerned about."

"So you don't care that I got my GED and a driver's license?"

"Perhaps, but not for why you think I do."

"What do you think is the problem then?" She sat upright on the buggy seat.

He sighed. "It's a matter of the heart, Susan. That's the only thing that troubles me. You're still looking back, remembering it as a good time and keep going back as an option, I'm afraid."

She said nothing, not moving on the seat.

He studied her face until she looked over at him.

He took her hand again. "It's not words that you need from me, Susan. Your heart has been betrayed by Thomas and by your *daett*. I don't blame you for feeling the way you do. Yet even with such hurts, a heart must one day make a choice to go forward. Don't look back, Susan. That's not the direction to go."

Susan found her voice. "So you think a driver's license in my dresser drawer means I have the freedom to run away again? To go *back* to the *Englisha* world?"

"It's what you think that matters. Why do you still have it, Susan?"

"Well," she said, "it doesn't mean a lot to me. I just keep it as a… well…a memory of something I accomplished, something unique for an Amish person."

"You don't have to prove anything with me." He squeezed her hand. "But you'd better get rid of the thing."

She sighed. "I will before too long."

He was still looking at her. "This *Englisha* thing, why did you do it?"

"I think I wanted to accomplish something. Remember, this was right after the first breakup with Thomas. My heart was hurting, and it felt *gut* to get away and do something Thomas couldn't do. And the *Englisha* people thought I was right to dump Thomas, unlike *Mamm* and *Daett*. I could be someone else out there. Someone who didn't need Thomas. Someone who didn't have to stay with a man who was unfaithful."

"But you didn't have to do that. You were already your own person. That's what I like about you."

"*Yah*, I see that now. But it's hard to see when your heart is hurting."

The Hostetler driveway became visible in the dim buggy light, and Steve turned in. He pulled to a stop at the hitching post. The two sat unmoving, silently staring out at the night.

"It's still a lovely night." Susan broke the silence first. "Even with all our troubles."

"We don't have any troubles," he said. "At least I don't when you are with me."

She nestled against him. "You say such nice words, and I believe them. Isn't that something?"

"You mean trusting what I say even after Thomas proved that men could be fickle?"

She moved beside him. "*Yah*, but let's not talk about him."

They sat close to each other, listening to the soft night sounds buzzing in the field.

"Do you think we should go in?" she finally asked.

"I like it here," he said.

"*Mamm* and *Daett* are going to wonder where we are."

"They can look out the window and see the buggy."

"Come in." She took his arm. "I have ice cream and pecan pie inside. I'm sure you need strength for the ride home."

He laughed. "I only live down the road."

"All the more reason you can stay a while and eat."

He climbed down and tied the horse to the hitching post.

Mamm had left a kerosene lamp burning in the living room, and Susan motioned for him to sit on the couch. She returned in minutes, carrying two plates of pecan pie with vanilla ice cream.

"I think I see lots of this kind of food ahead of me," he said. "I think life will be *gut* indeed."

"That's all you're here for? The food?"

He laughed, pulling her down to sit beside him. "You know better than that."

She stared into his face, trying to keep breathing. The ice cream and pie were forgotten.

He reached for her face, his fingers touching her cheeks. His arm came around her shoulder and pulled her closer.

Was he going kiss her? Thomas, with all his boldness, had never been very bold about this. But Steve's face above her seemed to hold no doubts. She found herself trembling.

"You're beautiful." He traced her lips with his finger.

She tried to speak but no words would come. He was much too close for that. She closed her eyes as his lips found hers. She slipped her fingers around the back of his neck, pulling him toward her. He held his shoulders firm, lingering only for a moment.

"You're more than beautiful," he whispered. "You're gorgeous."

"You shouldn't say things like that."

"Oh *yah*..." He laughed softly. "I should say lots of things like that."

She gave up and nestled against him. "Eat. Your ice cream is melting."

Reluctantly he ate the pie and ice cream. And then they talked...and talked...and talked until past midnight. Conversation about little and about nothing. Reuben's delight in his new barn. The upcoming Christmas dinner. Donald's happiness when he left with Charles after Thanksgiving. They made plans to attend Christmas breakfast in a few weeks at Steve's parents' place in Daviess County. Then, with that settled, Steve left a little before one o'clock. Susan walked out to the hitching post with him.

He kissed her goodnight before getting into the buggy. She stood in shocked silence and watched him drive away into the night. She had definitely never felt anything like that with Thomas.

Chapter Thirty-six

The last load of wash hung on the line, swinging in the brisk morning air. Susan burst into the kitchen through the washroom door, blowing on her hands. Steve had waved at her from the field behind the barn where he was driving the team of Belgians in front of the wagon. Thankfully the blush on her cheeks could be explained from working outside since daybreak or *Mamm* would be drawing conclusions that weren't quite warranted—even with that good night kiss a few Sunday nights ago.

In that time, Susan's respect for Steve had been rising. Wasn't kissing supposed to make a woman respect a man less? she wondered. She'd felt that way when Thomas kissed her. But with Steve she hadn't, though the real reason for respecting Steve more was likely related to the driver's license issue.

He had mentioned nothing further, apparently being willing to give her time to work through the issue on her own. With the driver's license still lying in her dresser drawer, Steve could get in trouble himself if Deacon Ray found out she had it and that Steve knew but chose to do nothing about it. The last few Sunday evenings with Steve had been quiet and nice. Not heart pounding, but *gut* enough.

"Is it warming up outside?" *Mamm* asked from where she was bent over the stove cooking.

"It should before long." Susan blew on her hands again. "What shall I do next?"

"Well..." *Mamm* paused, her face warm from the heat of the stove. "There is all the upstairs to clean before Christmas, though we don't have to do everything this week. But certainly by next."

"What are you and *Daett* going to do for Christmas?"

"Well, with you going with Steve to Daviess County, and Betsy and Ada both having plans, *Daett* and I have been talking, and we thought we'd do something special this year. We want to have Deacon Ray and his family over for Christmas dinner, along with James and Teresa. This would do all of us good after the *bann* Menno and I went through."

"You're considering having Deacon Ray over? But, *Mamm!*" Susan stepped closer. "Isn't it too soon? Maybe next year, but this just happened. How can you have him, of all people, here at the house during a celebration?"

Mamm sighed. "That's the best time to do such things, Susan. Before the wounds have time to fester. Not that they are festering, but you know what I mean. Deacon Ray and *Daett* were close. And there's no reason things can't go back to what they once were. At least we want to do our part to reach out."

"Then I'm glad Steve is taking me to see his parents."

"For Steve to take you to see his parents, he must be getting serious."

"I guess he might get serious, but only if his parents like me and don't throw me out."

"Susan!" *Mamm* said. "Don't talk like that. They won't throw you out. They will love you like Steve does. That's why he's taking you home. My guess is he's never taken a girl home for Christmas."

"He never even dated a girl before me, *Mamm*."

"He never did?" *Mamm* raised her eyebrows. "He's kind of old to just be starting, isn't he?"

Susan winced. "*Yah*, it seems Steve had his standards set pretty high and never could find a girl who met them."

"Then you should be honored," *Mamm* said.

Susan looked out the window at the distant horses working in the field and the man who was holding the lines. "I don't know, *Mamm*. I'm afraid it doesn't quite work that way. I think Steve's finally decided to go with his feelings instead of his head. And that would be dating me, the flawed one. The wild girl who raced around the *Englisha* world for a while."

"Steve told you this. Just like that?" *Mamm* looked horrified.

"Not in those words, but he has thought them, I think. One thing is of comfort though. He does like me."

"I'm sure he does," *Mamm* agreed. "You have yourself all *fahudled*, Susan."

"I don't think I'm confused this time. I know Steve's solid, steady, and in love with me. Maybe I'm flattered if not honored."

"Susan..." *Mamm* took both of her hands. "I've seen the two of you together. Don't doubt yourself. All those feelings are coming from *Da Hah*."

Susan dropped her eyes. "I suppose so."

"Then they are *gut* enough." *Mamm* turned back to the stove. "Love is like a little seed that gets planted in the heart. It takes time, and rain, and pulling weeds. And lots of care for love to grow. All of our people are that way, remember? We don't always have to see everything before we believe."

"Do you think I'll ever feel for Steve what I did for Thomas?"

Mamm came back to sit on a kitchen chair. "You've always been my dreamer, Susan. *Daett* even called you a young filly while you were visiting the *Englisha* world. Like a horse who loves to run in the wind. I didn't like the idea then, but I knew he was right."

"I suppose so," Susan murmured.

Mamm went on. "You spent many years growing your feelings for Thomas, most of them apparently on your side of the fence. This time Steve already has the crop well underway on his side. So let some of his seeds drift over. Don't pull them out when they sprout. You don't know how the ear of corn will look by what first comes out of the ground."

Susan looked away. "I do have feelings for Steve, just not like I used to with Thomas."

"You'll be okay." *Mamm* got to her feet.

Susan waited a few moments. "Will you and *Daett* be okay with Deacon Ray over Christmas?"

"Susan, Deacon Ray only did what needed doing. We can't hold that against him. Bishop Henry and the other ministers also agreed, remember?"

"I think Deacon Ray could have done a lot to help out, and yet he chose not to."

"We must not judge a man's heart, Susan. Only our own. And you should ask *Da Hah* to help you forgive the man if you have this bitterness in your heart."

"*Yah*, I know."

After a few minutes of comfortable silence, Susan broke the stillness. "Should I start the upstairs cleaning?"

Mamm smiled. "That would be *gut.* And I will help when the bread is done."

Susan gathered the cleaning supplies. Starting in the back bedroom, she began sweeping, making sure the corners of the rooms were clean. She pushed open the bedroom closet door. There she saw the old cedar chest, its varnished surface glowing in the early morning sunlight pouring through the window. She drew in her breath as memories flooded over her. Here she had come that long-ago day to put away the wedding dress, the drive to burn it strong as she smarted from Thomas's betrayal. But she had overridden the urge, held back by Amish thriftiness. Even if Thomas never said the vows with her, someone else could use the dress. It had lain here all this time, forgotten. And now she was remembering on this cold morning. Was this a sign? Perhaps of *Da Hah*'s good pleasure? Susan lifted the lid on the chest, the hinges making no sound. She dug to the bottom, finding the dress by the feel of its soft fabric on her fingertips. Its dark-blue color shimmered in the sunlight when she held it up to the light.

"My wedding dress," she whispered. "It's still so beautiful."

This was a dress that needed wearing in the spring, when the winter had made its first turn toward changing seasons. Her heart pounded at the thought. Would it happen for her? Had she found love again? Could she trust a man again? Or would she come out some Sunday night after the hymn singing and find Steve standing in the shadows talking with another girl? That would be too awful to bear. Her heart couldn't live through that again. The dress slipped from her fingers and fell to the floor. It lay crumpled, the rays from the sun highlighting the dust motes moving around the cloth.

Long moments passed. This was just a dress, she told herself. She shouldn't read too much into finding it. Were not hearts meant to bond, meant to hold on to promises held by hope, by trust, by the goodness they contained? Thomas had broken the sacred trust, and before him, her own *daett* had done worse. Gentle, loving *Daett* had a child before he knew *Mamm*. How did *Mamm* live with that knowledge and even join him in walking through the darkness of penance?

Mamm must be more of a saint than she appeared to be or else what she shared with *Daett* was what real love was made of. Susan picked up the dress and held it to the light again. She remembered the hour she had spent picking out just the right color at the fabric store on a trip to northern Indiana. The care she had taken sewing, marking twice and then checking again before proceeding. She wore out the measuring tape, *Mamm* had said laughing. She had wanted this dress to be just right. But the dress hadn't been enough to keep her dreams alive. She'd needed more.

Could what *Mamm* had be hers with Steve? Did it help that she hadn't pursued him? Was he capturing her heart? The least she could do was keep it open. Susan sighed. Hanging the dress on the closet rod, she stood back for another look. Strange that she wasn't crying buckets of tears, sobbing her heart out, but she wasn't. The dress was just something to wear now. Should she wear it on Christmas Day? *Yah*, she decided. Steve wouldn't know the history and probably wouldn't care if he did. *Mamm* might raise her eyebrows, but she would get over it.

Then bitterness lifted its head for a moment. "Stupid dress," she whispered. "You betrayed me too. I worked on you for all those hours, dreaming and hoping—and all for naught. You ought to be burned." Tears stung her eyes.

The door opened behind her and *Mamm* entered.

"What's wrong, Susan?"

Susan turned to face *Mamm*. "I found my old wedding dress."

Mamm walked over to lift the dress from the closet rod, holding it up to the light.

"I'm going to wear it for Christmas at Steve's parents' house."

"You will do no such thing. It will stay right here on the hanger until we iron it for your wedding day."

"*Mamm*, I can't do that."

"Come, come." *Mamm* took Susan's arm. "We have work to do. Enough of these tears. You're a grown woman now, almost ready to marry. It's time you grew up. You don't wear a wedding dress for anything but a wedding. Trust me, it will be okay. Steve will love it."

"He hasn't asked me to marry him yet."

Mamm smiled. "Don't worry, he will. When it's time, he will. And Steve will know when that is."

Chapter Thirty-seven

The headlights of the car cut through the early dawn, flooding the Hostetler house and barn with light as the *Englisha* driver turned into the driveway. At its honk, Susan came racing downstairs, taking the final two steps in a flying leap.

"Susan!" *Mamm* called from the kitchen. "Slow down before you injure yourself."

"I'm so nervous!" Susan gushed, standing in the kitchen opening. "How do I look?"

"You look fine," *Mamm* said, not even looking at her.

"Can you handle things by yourself today? I've done everything I know to do. And I'll be back tonight."

"Get going!" *Mamm* pointed out the door. "And have a *gut* Christmas with Steve's parents. Don't worry, they will love you."

"I do hope so," Susan said, heading for the door.

"Now remember," *Mamm* hollered after her, "I can handle things. Even if I'm an old woman. And Teresa will help me if I don't get dinner ready in time."

"See you!" Susan said as she dashed outside.

She slowed going down the steps. Steve would laugh if she came running across the yard. He'd know she was nervous.

"Good morning," the driver of the van said through his open window.

"*Gut* morning," Susan replied, going around to the other side. The van door was open, and the dome light was on. There was only one seat left—beside Minister Emery's wife, Lois. Steve was sitting in the front seat, but now he climbed out.

"Who wants to trade seats?" he asked.

"Now why would anyone want to do that?" Minister Emery asked, laughing. "I didn't 'get up' this load. The one who gets up the load sits in front."

"It makes no difference to me who got up the load," Steve said. "I'm sitting with Susan!"

"Ah love, love, love…" Emery grumbled. "How they make old people go here and then go there."

"Thank you," Steve said, motioning for Susan to climb in. She sat on the seat beside Lois, whispering, "*Gut* morning. Sorry to chase Emery away."

"Oh, he likes the front seat," Lois said. "Don't pay him any mind. His bones ache in the morning, that's all. He'll get better as the day warms up."

"It's not going to get all that warm," Susan said as the driver rolled up his window and pulled out of the driveway.

"Well, it could be snowing and blowing like it was last year on Christmas Day," Lois replied. "We had a trip planned to northern Indiana but had to call it off."

Susan smiled. "I'm glad it's not snowing. Do you have relatives in Daviess County?"

"*Yah*, a sister. And Emery has a couple of cousins. Neither of us grew up there, but both of our families are scattered around. Not like some people, who all stay in one place."

Susan nodded. "*Mamm* would have loved it if all us girls stayed around, but moving happens."

"And what about you? Are you staying around?" Lois teased.

With Steve sitting beside her, what was she to say? They hadn't agreed to marry yet, let alone discussed where they might live.

"I'm sorry." Lois laughed. "I really wasn't trying to make you uncomfortable."

Beside her, Steve cleared his throat without looking at her. Apparently he wanted some kind of answer too.

"I'd love to stay on the home place," Susan finally said. That was a safe enough answer, and Steve could do with it what he wished. Her big concern today was facing his folks for the first time. If they didn't like her, it would be a nightmare of grand proportions even if Steve managed to smooth things over. How would she marry Steve if his parents didn't like her?

Steve leaned forward on his seat to speak to Lois. "Menno hasn't said what he wants done with the farm other than to say he'd like me to work for him next year."

"Oh." Lois smiled. "I know Menno better than that. He's itching to get into his *dawdy haus*. But there's nothing wrong with that. Emery and I are loving our new *dawdy haus*. I wish we'd moved there two years ago instead of hanging on like we did."

"I'm sure *Daett* can't wait," Susan agreed as Steve settled back into his seat.

"I told Emery not to make our *dawdy haus* too big," Lois continued. "I just needed two bedrooms, one for us and one for visitors."

"I'm sure *Mamm* has her own ideas about the *dawdy haus*," Susan replied, mostly to make conversation as she watched the Christmas lights on the houses race by.

"What time do we tell the driver to start picking everybody up?" Steve asked Emery a few minutes later.

"Ask Lois," Emery said, not looking back. "I'll stay as late as she wants to."

"You'd better ask the others," Lois said when Steve looked at her. "I agree with Emery."

Steve turned around and asked the question again. A lengthy conversation ensued, with eight o'clock receiving the most votes. Steve passed the information on to the driver, who grunted his agreement.

The rolling hillsides soon gave way to flat, open land. Susan watched for signs of buggies as they drove through a town and out into the countryside again. The first one they passed, the man and woman inside waved, apparently noticing the load of Amish-dressed passengers.

"Do you know them?" Lois asked Steve as she craned her neck to look back.

"I don't think so," Steve said. "It's a huge community with lots of districts."

"Time for directions," the driver said. "We're coming up on the main part of the community."

Several people hollered out road names, and Steve took the driver through the turns for each place. When they had reached the last stop, Steve gave directions to his parents' place. Five minutes later they pulled into the farm. Two silos rose high in the air behind the barn. The house was tall, white, and two-story. Lines of buggies were parked beside a huge earthen ramp that ran up to the second floor of the barn. Children were playing in the yard, but they stopped to stare at them.

"Home," Steve said with a broad smile on his face. "Don't worry, Susan. Everyone will love you." Steve offered Susan his hand, helping her down as if she were a rich *Englisha* woman climbing out of a fancy limousine instead of a plain Amish girl stepping out of a simple passenger van. Like always, Steve had known how nervous she was but had waited to say something until the right moment. His words helped her breathe easier.

"See you at eight," Steve told the driver.

Susan clung to his arm as they walked across the yard.

"Hi," Susan said to the children as they walked past them. They smiled at her and looked ready to return to their play.

"No tricks today," Steve told one of the taller boys, who laughed and shook his head.

"This is a huge place," Susan said. "You never told me."

"It's pretty normal for around here. Now relax, okay?"

If this were an *Englisha* house, Susan thought, she would march in without any fear at all. Why all the nervousness now? It was time to get ahold of herself. So what if she was about to meet the parents of her *perhaps* future husband. That was no reason for feeling so nervous.

"You said there were eleven of you, but you're almost the oldest. Where do all the buggies come from?"

"My older sister, Martha, is married, and also two of the ones after me. A couple of the young people are in *rumspringa*. And I think *Mamm* invited some of the aunts and uncles. They're nice people, so don't worry."

"I'll never remember everyone. That much I know."

"You don't have to," Steve said. "You only have to remember me."

She laughed and muttered, "Conceited, just like a man." Steve's teasing did make her feel better.

He squeezed her hand as they approached the front door and a round woman rushed out, wiping her hands on a white apron.

"Well, if it isn't Steve and Susan!" she gushed, wrapping her arms around Susan. "I'm Steve's *mamm*, Elizabeth. Oh, it's so *gut* to finally meet you! Steve hasn't said much about you, and I see why. He couldn't have said it well enough even if he tried. Steve's not much with words, as you already know I'm sure."

"He has a way with words around me," Susan said. Then she wondered if that was the right thing to say. She breathed a sigh of relief when Steve's *mamm* took it in stride.

"If you can get him talking, then I'd say Steve's finally found the right one," She said as she ushered them inside and waved her hand toward the interior of the house. "Come meet the others. I'm sure you won't remember all the names. I don't remember my own half the time."

"*Mamm*, it's not that bad." Steve took ahold of Susan's hand. He didn't let go until they were inside, making the rounds, and had shaken everyone's hand. The living room was crowded, with long, double tables filling the length of the house.

They all said their names and where they belonged. Susan listened to each one, filing it away, hoping the names stuck with the faces somewhere in her brain. Some of the names she already knew. Abe was Steve's *daett*, who shook her hand warmly. Martha was the oldest sister who was married. The brother after Steve, Emmanuel, was also married and standing beside his smiling young wife, Ruby. The other names would have to wait, she figured, until she learned to know the people better.

Martha took Susan under her wing and led her out to the kitchen first and then upstairs. "There are six bedrooms on the second floor," Martha said. "Two on the first floor, and two more in the basement. *Mamm* and *Daett* added on to the house twice."

"It's so big!" Susan said.

Martha smiled. "And this is Steve's room—or was. His brothers have taken it over now."

Susan looked inside. There didn't seem anything unusual about it. Just bare walls with two beds and dressers. Some Amish boys kept books around or deer heads on the walls, but these two didn't. The Mast boys must live like Steve did, simple, direct, and to the point.

Martha took her downstairs again, and Susan joined in with the food preparation. Everyone chatted as they worked, with most of the news mentioned being unfamiliar to Susan. Who among the young people was seeing whom. Which of the women in the community were expecting. What plans they had for their gardens in the coming year.

By ten o'clock, breakfast was spread out on the tables in the living room. Ham sliced by Elizabeth. Bacon, great bowls of it, cooked to golden perfection. Biscuits with gravy, chunks of sausage swimming in the depths. Blueberry pancakes, fresh maple syrup, eggs fried so the yolks trembled on the plates. Butter piled high in double-layered stacks, raw and sliced apples, peaches, and pineapple. And, last but not least, jars of hard candy, homemade taffy, licorice, buckeyes, and double-layered chocolate bars.

"Will everyone please be seated?" Elizabeth said. "It doesn't matter where, but keep your children with you. And no little ones into the candy until we've eaten our eggs and pancakes."

Steve came out of the crowd and took Susan by the hand. "Come over here."

"Where are you taking me?" she asked.

He motioned for her to be seated off to the side but near the head of the first table. "Right here."

"But everyone will see us."

"No, they won't," he said. "They'll be too busy eating. I want you to be able to talk with *Mamm* and *Daett*."

Susan felt warm inside. Now that she had met his *mamm* and *daett*, she could see what an honor this was. They were very nice people, and Steve was clearly thrilled to have her here. What a wonderful day this was turning out to be. These were common people like her own *mamm* and *daett*. She would be okay.

Elizabeth and Abe took their places at the first table, and Abe opened the large Bible he was carrying. He cleared his throat and said, "We wish to thank everyone for coming today. It's *gut* to have you all in our house. But especially we want to welcome Susan, who is here with Steve for the first time. For those of you who thought Steve would never settle down, well, it looks like you were wrong."

Susan felt her ears grow red. She ducked her head as the others chuckled and laughed. Steve reached under the table for her hand.

"Now I wish to read a short few verses out of the Gospel of Matthew," Abe said. He then began reading the verses in German. When he was done, he closed the Bible and prayed. "Our Father which art in heaven, hallowed be thy name..."

Susan closed her eyes and listened to the sound of his voice quoting the familiar words. This was so like the words her *daett* prayed at home, and no doubt like his *daett* before him. She was becoming a part of all this, a wonderful and *gut* part with Steve. It was so wonderful it hurt all the way down to her toes.

"Amen," Abe said, reaching the end of the prayer and sitting down in his chair.

"Please start passing whatever food is in front of you," Elizabeth said. "Don't be afraid to eat."

Susan smiled as Steve again squeezed her hand under the table. "They like you," he whispered. "And I like you too."

She looked away, knowing her face was bright red again.

Chapter Thirty-eight

When the driver dropped Susan at home that night, she figured she had experienced the best Christmas Day ever. Her worries about meeting the Masts had been needless. She already felt like part of the family. Now, if Steve would just ask me to marry him...but she pushed the thought away. That would happen in its own *gut* time, like *Mamm* said.

Mamm and *Daett* were in bed when she arrived, and she crept silently up the stairs and fell into bed exhausted, not waking once during the night. It was still dark when she did awake to the noise of *Mamm* banging around in the kitchen downstairs. Why was *Mamm* up so early on the morning after Christmas? They ought to be sleeping in for another hour. There were no cows to milk, and the chores could be done by *Daett* after a late breakfast.

Had something happened between *Mamm* and *Daett* and Deacon Ray? What else could be waking *Mamm* at this hour and causing her to be so noisy?

Susan threw off the covers with a wild fling. She lit the kerosene lamp and dressed quickly. With lamp in hand, she went down the stairs, pausing a moment at the bottom to still her beating heart. Whatever had happened, she had to be strong for *Mamm*'s sake. *Daett* would be okay, but this might be the straw that broke *Mamm*'s endurance. Why hadn't she knocked on their bedroom door last night to check on them? The least she could have done was ask how their day had gone. But no, she had been on cloud nine about her day in Daviess County and the wonderful attention Steve and his parents had paid her.

Susan tiptoed into the kitchen and set the lamp on the table. *Mamm* was obviously crying as she stood over the stove.

"*Mamm*, what's wrong?" Susan asked.

"Oh Susan!" *Mamm* groaned as she turned to face her daughter. "How could you do this to us?"

"What are you talking about? I was in Daviess County yesterday with Steve. What did I do?"

"Susan—an *Englisha* driver's license? And upstairs in your bedroom all this time? And you attending the baptismal class!"

Susan sat down abruptly. "How does anyone know about my driver's license?"

"It doesn't matter how anyone found it. What matters is that you have it."

"It doesn't mean anything, *Mamm*. I was just keeping it for the memory. Believe me, please. I'm staying here."

"Does Steve know about it?" *Mamm* was looking at her sternly.

Susan's mind raced. Was she going to get Steve in trouble? Yes, she might, yet she couldn't lie.

"I see," *Mamm* said, reading the answer in Susan's face. "So the two of you have been in this secret together?"

"No, *Mamm*." Susan leaped to her feet. "Steve has nothing to do with this. He dug the information out of me, but he's been nice by not saying anything. He understands I need time to heal. To get over Thomas's betrayal...and everything else that has caused such trouble."

"And you think keeping an *Englisha* driver's license upstairs is okay? How is that helping you get over anything? It's more like an escape door in case things get rough. Something you can always fall back on if you need to or want to."

"You think that's the reason I've kept it? I can't believe you would think such a thing of me. I've never been more settled in the community than I am right now."

"It doesn't matter what I think." *Mamm* sighed. "It's what Deacon Ray thinks, and I'm sure he knows by now."

"You told him?"

"Your *Mamm* didn't tell anyone anything," *Daett*'s voice said behind her. "Teresa found the license when she went up to change into one of your dresses because Samuel threw up all over hers. Deacon Ray's daughter, Rachel, went upstairs with her to help. She saw the driver's license."

"Teresa knew it was there," Susan said, the kitchen walls swimming in front of her eyes. "What did she do, wave it around for all to see?"

"Teresa did nothing of the sort," *Mamm* said. "She didn't tell me until Deacon Ray's family left around eight. The girl understands me. She knew it would have been difficult for me to make it through the day knowing what had happened. And I'm not sure she would have told me about finding it if Rachel hadn't seen it."

Daett was shaking his head. "You're not blaming others for this problem, are you, Susan? Teresa didn't go looking for the license. She didn't bring it downstairs and thrust it in anyone's face."

"It dropped to the floor as she pulled out the dress," *Mamm* said. "It was hidden in your clothing, I guess. Rachel picked it up. That wasn't Teresa's fault. You shouldn't hide things in the first place. You know sin always comes to light, Susan."

"So what am I to do now?" Susan buried her face in her hands as her tears flowed.

"You can start by burning the license," *Mamm* said. "And then by taking a trip over to Deacon Ray's place to confess."

"The sooner you do that the better, Susan," *Daett* agreed. "It's time you make your choice about staying or going once and for all."

"Not like this." Susan groaned. "It wasn't supposed to happen this way. Steve and I were working our way through this. Why does someone else have to interfere? Why does it have to be such a big deal?"

"We're a community," *Daett* reminded her. "We're not people who live alone. What one person does affects us all. You should never try to work through these things by yourself. It doesn't work."

"Go get the license, Susan," *Mamm* ordered. "There's no use waiting around. I have the stove hot."

"You weren't preparing breakfast?" Susan stared at the bare stove.

"I was trying," *Mamm* said. "But my heart was too torn. How could you put us through this, Susan? And right after we are healing from our own wound?"

"I'm sorry." Susan rose. "I'll go get it."

Susan took the kerosene lamp with her, its light dancing off the narrow walls of the stairway. Tears stung her eyes. Now would be the time to make a stand, to refuse to turn over the license and face the consequences. She would have to leave home...and leave Steve too. She walked to her bedroom window and looked out over the dark fields where the dawn was breaking in the sky.

Fiery colors of red and orange hung low on the horizon. There was a storm coming in the next day or so, but inside the house it was already here. Did she want to leave all of this again? *Mamm* and *Daett*, the home place, Steve? This time there would be no easy return. And no Teresa to bring her home.

Sobbing, she walked over to the dresser drawer and pulled out the driver's license. Holding the piece of plastic up to the light, her photo stared back at her. A memory of all she'd accomplished and what she'd been through. But there was too much to lose here. Even the painful trip to Deacon Ray's was worth choosing to stay. Had not *Mamm* and *Daett* gone through much worse?

With the lamp in hand, Susan returned to the kitchen. *Mamm* took the license, opened the stove lid, and dropped the piece of plastic inside. It curled on the edges and shriveled until it was a small mound of goo. The flames leaped up, and it disappeared.

"There!" *Mamm* said. "That's done. Now for the trip to see Deacon Ray."

"I'm going to ask Steve to go with me," Susan decided as the tears stung her eyes.

"I think I'd better go with you," *Mamm* said. "Deacon Ray might listen to an older voice of reason."

"First, we will eat breakfast and pray," *Daett* said. "After that I think it's Susan's choice. She will know what is best."

"But, Menno," *Mamm* protested.

Daett laid his hand on *Mamm*'s shoulder. "We have already interfered enough for one morning. Susan will find the right road."

A sob shook Susan as *Mamm* hung her head. "I'm sure you know best, Menno. I'll fix breakfast then."

"Thanks, *Daett*," Susan said as she wrapped her arms around her father's neck.

"Now, now," he said. "Your *mamm* loves you too. She's just worried and wants to help."

Susan went to *Mamm*'s side. "I'm so sorry."

Mamm turned toward her with a weary smile and opened her arms. They embraced. "You don't have to help with breakfast," she whispered. "You've been through a lot."

Susan said nothing, but she helped with the bacon and eggs anyway. *Mamm* worked beside her, glancing up once in a while, the hint of a smile on her face. "You've turned into quite a fine woman, Susan. I know you'll do the right thing."

Susan nodded, not trusting her voice. They finished the meal preparations and called *Daett* in from the living room. He sat down and began praying, "O dear *Da Hah*, all-knowing God, help us this morning to praise Your name even in the midst of our troubles. We give You thanks for the breath of life You have placed within us, for the love we feel from our families, and for the joy we receive from being in Your presence. Help Susan this morning, and all of us, to face our lives with courage, with humility of heart, and with thankfulness for all You have given. Bless this food now. Bless Anna and Susan for preparing it. We receive it with thanksgiving. Amen."

"Amen," *Mamm* echoed. She looked up and handed the plate of eggs to *Daett*. He slid off what he wanted and passed the plate to Susan.

They ate in silence, and *Daett* prayed again when they were finished.

Susan stood to help *Mamm* clear the table.

"I'll get the horse ready," *Daett* said as he left for the barn.

Mamm and Susan worked side by side in silence. Over their heads the lantern hummed. "Go now," *Mamm* said when she caught sight of *Daett* coming out of the barn with the horse.

Susan kissed *Mamm* on the cheek and then grabbed her winter coat in the mudroom. She put it on and slowly walked outside.

Daett had Toby under the shafts when she arrived. After fastening the tugs on her side, Susan climbed in. *Daett* threw her the lines and slapped the horse on the rump. Susan looked back as she turned south toward Ada's place. *Daett* was walking across the lawn, his back bent, but he waved. Susan pressed back the tears. At Ada's place, she stopped by the hitching post and waited. Now what? Would Steve even go with her? Had he eaten breakfast yet? Would he risk getting into trouble himself? Gathering her courage, she left the lines hanging over the dashboard and walked up to the front door. She knocked, the sound loud in the still morning air.

Ada opened the door, a questioning look on her face.

"May I speak with Steve?" Susan asked. "Out here?"

"Can he at least finish his breakfast?" Ada asked. "We're almost done."

Footsteps came across the hardwood floor, and Steve appeared in the doorway, slipping on his coat.

"I'm done," Steve said with a smile. He stepped outside.

Ada shut the door behind him, still looking puzzled.

Ada will have to figure this out later, Susan decided. Right now explaining to Steve would be hard enough.

"Is something wrong?" Steve wasn't smiling anymore.

"My driver's license was discovered yesterday," Susan blurted out. "Deacon Ray knows, and I have to go talk to him about it. Will you come with me?"

"Whoa!" Steve said, holding up his hand. "Where is the driver's license now?"

"*Mamm* burned it this morning after we all talked about it."

Steve looked at her but said nothing.

"So will you go with me? I plan to ask his forgiveness and see what I can do about patching things up."

"Let me tell Ada I'll be gone for a while."

He disappeared into the house. The moments seemed long before he reappeared with his hat on his head.

"Did you tell Ada and Reuben what is going on?"

"No. You'll have to tell them later."

"Thank you." She climbed into the buggy. Steve followed, taking the lines without asking. It felt *gut*, Susan realized, to have him take charge. But it might take more than that to persuade Deacon Ray to go easy on her. Yet what could Deacon Ray do? They had already destroyed the license. She might have to do a public confession, but that was bearable...providing Steve stuck with her.

Steve drove for a mile or so before taking a turn down a side road.

"Where are you going?" Susan asked.

He said nothing, driving on and bouncing to a stop under some trees overlooking a pasture. Beyond the field, a small stream ran, the cold waters tinkling over rocks. The edges of the banks showed small feathers of ice streaking outward.

"I'm having this out right here," Steve said.

"Having what out?"

"Will you marry me, Susan?"

"Steve!" she gasped. "On a morning like this?"

"Just answer the question."

"Do you think this will make things better? Must I prove my loyalty before you support me in front of Deacon Ray? Don't you know I can always get another driver's license? The *Englisha* people keep those records."

"*Yah*, I know that. But that's also where you're wrong. I want your heart, Susan. Any of us can break the rules, run off to wherever afterward. The question is where our hearts lie. Do they lie here in this land of the people, among those who love us, among others who fear *Da Hah* as we do? Where is your heart, Susan? Does it lie with us? Does it lie with *me*?"

Tears stung Susan's eyes as she studied Steve's serious face. She reached up to brush his cheeks with her fingers, "My heart has been with you for a long time, Steve. It's just been slow in knowing it."

"Then you're saying *yah*? *Yah* to us? To our life together?"

She nodded.

Where had the love for this man come from? she wondered. Had *Mamm* been right? Did it spring up from things unknown?

He touched her face, his lips coming toward her. She lifted her face to meet his, clinging to him with both hands. He lingered in the kiss a long time.

"Now we are ready to meet Deacon Ray," he said, taking a deep breath. He turned the horse and gently slapped the lines against Toby's back.

Susan nestled against Steve's shoulder, tears running down her cheeks. Why was she crying? There was nothing but happiness bubbling up in her heart. More happiness than she had ever known in her whole life.

Chapter Thirty-nine

The early morning sun warmed the inside of the buggy as Steve pulled into Deacon Ray's driveway. Susan sat up straight, taking her head away from the comfortable position on his shoulder. Her heart was still beating hard, and her head felt dizzy. How strange her life was turning out, with so many unexpected twists and turns. Who would have thought all those years ago, when she dreamed of Thomas with her head between her hands and elbows propped up on the school desktop, that a hired hand would be the one to win her heart?

Now here they were at Deacon Ray's on an unpleasant errand. She had arrived for her first church confession, and she wasn't even a member yet. It figured. This was how her life had always gone. Taking the road others stayed away from. It might as well keep on this way. With Steve standing with her, surely she would survive this too.

Susan caught her breath as Deacon Ray walked out of the barn. He had his wool hat pulled down low over his forehead and his heavy winter coat wrapped around him tightly. Pushing his hat up, he squinted in the bright morning sunshine, surprised to see them.

Susan waited while Steve tied up, and then she climbed down to stand beside him. Deacon Ray was coming toward them at a slow walk.

"*Gut* morning," Steve greeted him.

Deacon Ray nodded. "*Gut* morning. What can I do for you two?"

Steve cleared his throat. "Susan has a matter that needs taken care of."

Deacon Ray didn't waste time. "I suppose this is about the driver's license."

Steve glanced at Susan.

Susan found her voice. "*Yah*, it is."

"Is the finding of the license the problem or the fact that you had one?"

"Having one, of course," Susan said at once. "I need to confess the matter. I know I do. It was my doing. No one else is to blame. I was keeping it as a memory of what had happened to me in the *Englisha* world."

"I see. Did Steve know about the license before this morning?"

Susan opened her mouth to speak, but Steve answered first. "I did, Deacon Ray. I tried to talk Susan into getting rid of it, but she needed more time. I felt it was better to exercise patience in this situation."

"You are a young man," Deacon Ray said, squinting at Steve. "Do you profess to know what needs doing? Especially when such a thing concerns your girlfriend? It might have been better to tell the ministry. The flesh of man is very weak."

"I take care of those I love." Steve's voice was firm. "I made the best choice I knew how, with her best interest in mind. And I will continue to do so when she becomes my *frau.*"

"I see." A hint of a smile crossed Deacon Ray's face. "Where is the license now?" he asked Susan.

"*Mamm* burned it after we talked this morning," Susan said.

"That's *gut*," Deacon Ray said, nodding.

"I'm sorry for the trouble and worry this has caused," Susan said. "I really am."

"Are you willing to say this in front of the church?"

Susan opened her mouth to agree, but again Steve spoke first. "I don't believe that is an appropriate measure to take in this instance."

"You don't?" Deacon Ray was looking at him.

Steve didn't hesitate. "Susan isn't a church member. She hasn't been using the driver's license nor has she tried to influence anyone else into getting one. Don't some of the sins of *rumspringa* get forgiven without a public confession?"

"You wouldn't have been talking with Menno now, would you?" Deacon Ray asked, staring at Steve.

"No," he said, looking a bit puzzled. "Susan came to me this morning about this, and we came straight here. I haven't seen Menno since the day before yesterday."

"And you, Susan?"

"*Daett* and *Mamm* spoke to me this morning about the license, but I'm not sure I know what you're getting at."

"Did Menno advise you about what you should say or do?"

"Beyond destroying the license and coming to talk to you, neither *Daett* nor *Mamm* gave specific instructions. *Daett* said I would know the right thing to do," Susan told Deacon Ray while looking into his eyes.

"*Ach*, then I am ashamed of myself." Deacon Ray lowered his head. "Menno is indeed a better man than I am. You see, there is a matter I have never confessed publicly either. Menno and I were working together in St. Louis, putting in our time of service for the government. While there, I not only obtained a driver's license, but I purchased an *Englisha* automobile, hiding it at a friend's house. Your *daett* knows this, Susan."

Susan stared at him nervously. "*Daett* told me nothing of this."

"Menno is a *gut* man," Deacon Ray said. "Perhaps we had better follow what I think his advice would be and forget some of these things that are done when we were young. The ones that harmed no one, at least. Those we will confess to *Da Hah* and forsake in our hearts."

"I think that would be a wise plan," Steve said. He cleared his throat.

"What about you, Susan?" Deacon Ray was looking at her now.

"I have forsaken the world in my heart," Susan said, taking Steve's hand.

Deacon Ray smiled. "Then we will leave the matter as it is. Please tell Menno he has my highest respect."

"*Yah*, okay then." Steve was still holding Susan's hand. "We thank you for your time this morning, Deacon Ray."

He turned and helped Susan into the buggy. He untied Toby, threw the reins into the front, and climbed up. Deacon Ray was walking to the house as they pulled out. He turned to waved from the front porch.

"I think you cracked his heart a little," Susan finally said as Steve drove onto the main road.

"He's a soft-hearted soul," Steve said. "It's just not always easy to see."

"You didn't grow up around him. He terrorized all of us. I've never seen Betsy sweat like the time Deacon Ray came over to speak with her about the length of her dresses."

"We'll be glad for people like him when our own children begin to think wild thoughts."

"Our children..." Susan nestled against him.

"*Yah*," Steve said, smiling down at her. "If *Da Hah* wills it so."

Susan suddenly sat up. "We need to talk with *Daett* and *Mamm* today."

"Really?" Steve glanced sideways at her. "Why?"

"We need to tell them about, well, what we talked about earlier."

"About you becoming my *frau*?"

"Don't say it!" Susan said. "You are making me turn red all over."

"Okay, I won't say it. I'll just think it," Steve said with a laugh.

"There are so many plans to be made, and most of them *Daett* and *Mamm* will be involved in. We can't keep this from them a second longer than we have to."

"You'll have to kiss me first. Then we'll talk all you want."

"I will not. You'll have to wait for the wedding vows. You've had enough kisses. They're getting dangerous."

Steve groaned.

"There is the *dawdy haus* to think of," Susan said, plunging ahead. "And the farm. Plus the expense of another wedding so quickly. We really have to talk to them."

"Okay, okay! We're almost there. I'll behave myself."

"I can't wait, Steve!" Susan said. "When can we get married?"

"Maybe the year after next."

Susan stared at him and Steve roared.

"You really are a tease, you know that?" she said. "Am I going to have to put up with this for the next fifty years?"

"And then some," Steve said as he pulled into the driveway. He stopped at the hitching post and stepped out of the buggy. He tied Toby as Susan climbed out and waited for him. Together they walked to the house. They entered through the front door and hung up their coats. Steve put his hat on the floor by the door. *Daett* was in his rocking chair reading *The Budget*. *Mamm* was sewing on the couch. Both looked up at their entrance, their faces showing their anxiety about what had happened with Deacon Ray.

Daett looked at Steve. "You went with Susan? That was awfully nice of you."

"It's okay," Steve said. "It was the right thing to do."

"So everything turned out all right?" *Daett* asked.

Steve smiled. "Deacon Ray remembered a little something that you apparently know all about. He decided that some things done in one's youthful folly are best left private, provided they affected no one else and that one repents and makes a private apology."

"I see," Menno said. "I'm sure Deacon Ray has made a wise choice."

"What are you talking about?" *Mamm* asked, standing up. "You sound like Solomon dropping hints."

"Don't worry, *Mamm*," Susan said. "Everything's fine." She hugged her. "Now would you please sit down and quit wringing your hands? We have lots of plans to make because Steve and I are getting married this spring! Soon after my baptism." Susan couldn't hold back her smile any longer.

"Well *Da Hah sie lobb!*" *Daett* exclaimed.

"I'm glad someone told me when I'm getting married," Steve said, but no one paid him any mind.

Mamm leaped to her feet again and grabbed Susan in a tight hug. "It's finally happening! Susan's getting married!" *Mamm* waved her hand in front of her face. "Why is it so hot in here? Menno, will you turn the heat down?"

"Sit down, *Mamm*, and take a deep breath," Susan said. "There are lots of things to discuss. But first of all, can we afford another wedding so soon? And then there's the *dawdy haus* to build. And is it okay if we live on the farm? We need a place to stay that's our own. Steve can take over the farm in the spring, if that's okay. That shouldn't be a problem..."

"Hold it a minute!" *Daett* interrupted with a laugh. "One thing at a time. Actually, one thing first, and then you women can do what you wish. So Steve, do you want to take over the farm?"

"If you will sell it to me," Steve said. He named a price without missing a beat. "If this isn't acceptable, you have time to ask the other girls and their husbands if they're interested. If someone wishes to pay a higher price, I would consider going up with my offer."

Susan stared at Steve. The sum he mentioned was more than fair. And Steve had spit out the huge number just like that. He must have thought the matter over often, she decided. But then he'd known he wanted to marry her. She sat down on the couch, trying to catch her breath.

"I'm sure no one will match that price," *Daett* said with a smile. "Besides, I want you to have the place. You will take *gut* care of the fields, and I can rest easy with you in charge."

"Thank you," Steve said. "So we're done then?"

"You're not done," *Mamm* said. "I want to know where I'll be living if you're selling the farm out from under me, Menno."

"In your *dawdy haus*, of course," Susan said.

"I don't see a *dawdy haus*," *Mamm* said. "And spring will be here before we know it."

"Don't worry, it will be built by then," *Daett* said. "We'll start when the weather breaks. And you can have it made however you wish, providing it's plain."

"I know that," *Mamm* said. "But it must have a basement. I won't be without a basement. That something I've always said."

"A basement but no upstairs," *Daett* said. "And Susan is correct. We can easily finish it before the wedding as long as you don't get fancy ideas into your head."

"Come on," Steve said, taking Susan's hand, "let them talk things out." He led her upstairs to her room, where they sat side by side on the bed.

"You know I should be downstairs making plans," Susan protested. "There are all the couples to pick out, and we should start cleaning the barn this afternoon. And..."

"All that can wait," Steve told her. "I want to look at you...at my future *frau*."

"There's just so much to do. Can't you look at me downstairs while we plan?"

Steve held up his hand. "I have to tell you something, and then we can go."

"What is it? You do have a secret!"

Steve smiled. "*Yah*, the secret is that I love you." He stood up and bent over to kiss her. She lifted her face to meet his. She pulled back moments later, gasping. "You tricked me, you naughty boy!"

Steve laughed. "You wouldn't kiss me any other way."

"Well, that's not going to work again," she said. "I'm wise to you now."

"Oh, I'll think of something else," he said, a sly look on his face.

"Steve Mast, you are the most frustrating man I have ever met."

"And the sweetest, I hope." He came close again.

"That's not going to work!" Susan said. She jumped up, ran out the door, and headed down the stairs, laughing all the way.

Mamm looked up when she burst through the doorway, Steve close behind.

"I think we need the wedding vows said for these two—and very soon," *Daett* said with a twinkle in his eye.

"But my house has to be built first," *Mamm* said, grabbing *Daett*'s arm as if she could pull the house out of his shoulder.

"With that, I think I'd better be going," Steve said. "I'll unhitch Toby and put him in the barn. Then I'd better head back to Ada's. It's a beautiful day for a walk." He picked up his hat and put on his coat.

Susan followed him to the front door. "I'll help you with Toby!" She put on her coat.

They went outside and walked to the buggy holding hands. When they reached the horse, they stood together for a long time, reluctant to part.

Finally Toby nickered and nudged Susan, pulling her out of her reverie.

With a laugh, Steve said, "I guess Toby also wants some breakfast!"

Chapter Forty

Susan rode in the back of the surrey, while *Mamm* and *Daett* rode in front. Behind them, Ada and Reuben's buggy followed, staying close. Ahead of them other buggies were coming out of the side roads, all heading to Mose Stutzman's place for Baptismal Sunday.

Today Bishop Henry would ask Susan the baptismal questions, and she would need to answer them once and for all. The time had come. She would now truly become part of the community. Today she would take on the faith *Mamm* and *Daett* had passed down to her. Deacon Ray had been true to his promise, and he never raised the issue of the driver's license again. At the last instruction class two weeks ago, he had even done a most unexpected thing. In front of them all, seated in a circle in the upstairs bedroom with the congregation's singing rising and falling below them, Deacon Ray had told them the story of his time at the *Englisha* hospital and how he had failed to walk in holiness and in the fear of *Da Hah* on some matters.

No mention was made of details, but Susan knew. She was impressed that Deacon Ray was willing to go this far in acknowledging they all had failures in their lives.

"We all make mistakes," Bishop Henry had said when Deacon Ray finished. "And there is forgiveness with *Da Hah*. I'm glad all of you have come to this day and are willing to forsake the devil and the world with all its lusts."

Deacon Ray nodded, as did the other ministers.

Ahead of them the buggies turned into the Stutzman driveway, stopping so the women could get out close to the house. *Daett* had to wait with the buggy still on the main road until the line moved forward. One of the buggies dashed past the walks without stopping, apparently driven by a single young man with no *mamm*, sisters, or *frau* to worry about.

Mamm and Susan climbed out when their turn came, walking toward the washroom with their shawls wrapped over their shoulders. Susan glanced toward the barn where a line of men was forming. Bishop Henry stood at his regular place at the head of the line, deep in conversation with Mose.

Before they turned at the end of the walk, Susan caught a glimpse of Steve coming out of the barn. A hint of a smile crossed her face. He was growing more dear each Sunday night when they visited after the hymn singing. What would it be like when they said the wedding vows? That was still too much to comprehend. She would have to wait.

Already *Mamm* and *Daett's dawdy haus* was underway in the fields lying toward Ada's place. It was the perfect spot, picked out by *Mamm*. The roof had gone on this week, well ahead of the thunderstorm that had hit last night. *Daett* said it wouldn't have hurt to get rain on the subfloor, but *Mamm* was of a different mind. No rain inside her house was the only acceptable option.

Already *Mamm* was dreaming of paint colors and cabinet doors. All of them would be plain, of course, but even then there were options to work with. Thomas, the brazen rascal, had been down last week to speak with *Mamm* about cabinet design. He and his *daett* were the best cabinet makers in the community, so *Mamm* couldn't be blamed for using them. Susan had stayed out of sight upstairs during the visit. Thomas's *daett* could have come just as easily, but that wouldn't have been Thomas's style. Rumors were in the air of a fall wedding for Wilma and him. But one could never be certain when it came to that rogue.

Mamm held the washroom door open for Susan. The women inside were already moving into the kitchen. Susan slipped off her shawl and laid it on the counter. *Mamm* did the same. They went inside and shook hands with the line of women, finishing just in time. Bishop Henry appeared outside the kitchen window, and then led the long line of men into the living room. Susan waited until the married women had left the kitchen before she joined the line of unmarried girls. Soon she would be going in with the married women on Sunday morning, Susan thought, glancing across at the boys' side. Steve was looking at her, a slight smile on his face. Susan returned his smile, ducking her head. It wouldn't be right to give Steve too much attention in public. That time would come this afternoon when he drove her home.

Daett had never allowed both Sunday afternoon and Sunday evening dates for his daughters. At least not until they were close to the wedding and had lots of plans to make. A thrill ran down Susan's back. She had arrived at that time. She was going to be married! She'd found a man she truly loved and who loved her in return.

The girl in front of her sat down on the bench, and Susan almost ran into her. Several girls giggled, and Susan thought what a sight it would be on Baptismal Sunday to trip across the benches, arms and legs flying every which way. She had to get a grip on herself, and the sooner the better! She sat down and folded her hands on her lap, holding completely still. No one seemed to be looking at her, so thankfully her near fall was going to be overlooked. The song leader from the men's section called out the song number, and the singing began. When the boys stood to follow the line of ministers upstairs for this last instruction class, Susan rose to lead the line of girls up the stairs.

Deacon Ray read the last two instruction lessons when they were all seated, adding a few comments of his own. The other ministers did the same. Bishop Henry had the last say.

"I hope all of you have enjoyed this season of instruction as much as I have," he said. "I know you probably think I just say so, considering how many young people I have seen through the instruction classes since becoming a minister. Yet the joy never ceases to affect me. To see people give their lives to the service of *Da Hah* while they're still young is a great thing to behold. You may not think much of sin's influence because you're still young, but as you grow older, you'll understand better what a blessing it is to have *Da Hah* with you early in life. And that will be all I have to say unless someone else has something to add."

Bishop Henry looked around the room at the other ministers. They all shook their heads. The bishop smiled at the group and waved his hand toward the door. The oldest boy stood, leading the way downstairs. Susan followed the boys. They walked up to the benches set apart in the front row for the occasion. Around them the singing continued until the ministers returned.

The preaching started with Minister Emery's opening sermon. Bishop Henry had the main sermon, going over the Old Testament story of the birth of Isaac, the child of promise born to Abraham and Sarah.

"So is given to each of us who believe," Bishop Henry said, "a promise from *Da Hah*. By the Spirit of *Da Hah* in us there will be power over sin, power to live a holy life, power to live a life to the highest standards and pleasing to *Da Hah*, separate from the world and the flesh.

"It may take years of waiting, as Abraham and Sarah had to wait, but in the end the Spirit of *Da Hah* will do His work for all those who believe. In the end there lies the hope of eternal life for us in that land where we will never die, where tears are wiped away, where loved ones gather around us, and where the Son of God Himself will serve His people." He gestured toward the baptismal class.

"It is to such a life that these young people are committing themselves today. Let us join them in a fresh renewal of our own vows and in our own dedication."

The clock ticked on the living room wall as Bishop Henry paused to look down the line of young people. "Now, as many of you who are still willing to make your commitment to the holy vows, please kneel."

Susan waited until the boys had knelt before she bent her knees and settled on the floor. The girls on her right followed her example. Bishop Henry started at the end of the line, asking the pertinent questions, with Deacon Ray following and pouring water from the pitcher after the answers had been accepted. The moments seemed to hang in the air, as they came closer and closer. Finally Bishop Henry was standing in front of Susan.

"Do you, Susan," Bishop Henry asked, "confess that Jesus Christ is the only begotten Son of God?"

"*Yah*," Susan whispered.

"Do you promise to forsake the devil, the world, the desires of your own flesh, and to cleave to the will of *Da Hah*? Will you submit to the Word of God and to the fellowship of the church?"

"*Yah.*" Susan kept her head bowed low.

Bishop Henry's hands came down over the top of her *kapp*. "I baptize you in the name of the Father, the Son, and the Holy Spirit." The water ran down the side of her face and dripped to the floor. "Rise, sister Susan."

Bishop Henry's rough hand clasped her, helping her stand. His *frau*, Ruth, took Susan's hand from Bishop Henry's and kissed her on the cheek. She smiled her welcome.

Susan stayed standing as they moved down the line. When the last girl was baptized, Bishop Henry motioned with his hand, and they all sat down together.

Behind them a song number was announced, and the singing began. When it was done, Bishop Henry pronounced church dismissed. The younger boys dashed for the front door as usual. Susan waited until the boys in the baptismal line had stood before she led the girls into the kitchen.

Betsy and Ada met Susan with hugs. *Mamm* was in tears, dabbing her eyes with her handkerchief. "This is such a blessed day," *Mamm* said as she wrapped her arms around Susan's neck.

The other newly baptized girls were being greeted in similar fashion by their relatives. Finally, Mose Stutzman's wife, Ronda, cleared her throat and announced it was time to prepare the tables. The women broke up, and their chatter filled the house as they worked. Tables were set up in the living room, some jutting into the bedrooms.

The men were taking benches down to the basement where the unmarried boys' table would be set up. Perhaps she should volunteer there, Susan thought. She might catch another glimpse of Steve's smile. While she was deciding, Ronda interrupted her thoughts. "The baptized girls get a place on the first table. A special privilege for today only."

Ronda couldn't be refused, and Susan gave in at once. She would get plenty of Steve's smiles this afternoon. Minutes later Bishop Henry prayed, and the meal began. When it was over, Susan helped serve the next two tables. Out of the corner of her eye she saw Steve leave the group of young unmarried boys and walk toward the barn. He would be ready to leave before long. Making her way to the washroom, she found her shawl and met Steve's buggy at the end of the walk.

"*Gut* afternoon," he said cheerfully.

"*Gut* afternoon yourself," she replied as she climbed in and snuggled against his shoulder.

"Now," he said, as he turned onto the main road, "I think I need a kiss since you're a baptized saint."

"Up to your tricks again, are you?" she accused, not moving away from him.

"Of course. You have to be welcomed properly into church membership."

"Bishop Henry's wife already did that."

"Not the way I will."

"Okay," she whispered.

He bent his head sideways, keeping both hands on the lines to control his trotting horse.

"That's it!" she said pulling away.. "You get no more kisses until we say the wedding vows."

He smiled and looked very smug.

Susan playfully slapped his arm before leaning against his shoulder again.

Chapter Forty-one

The early morning mist had lifted from the road, burned away by the sunlight glaring brightly. Susan stood inside the front door of the house, with Steve right beside her. The last of the buggies had passed the living room window twenty minutes ago, and it would soon be time for them to leave for the barn.

Her dark-blue wedding dress rustled when she glanced down at her clasped hands. The day had finally arrived. She was going to say the sacred vows with Steve Mast. She was going to take her place by his side for their walk through life together, in *gut* times, in bad times, in sickness, and in health.

"It's time to go!" *Mamm* said, her hands fluttering about. "I can hardly stand it! The last of my daughters is getting married! *Daett* and I will be lost by ourselves down at the *dawdy haus*."

Susan reached over to squeeze *Mamm*'s hand as Steve opened the front door. He had on a new, shiny black suit, brushed so not a single piece of lint was to be found. The first set of witnesses went out the door. Steve and Susan followed. Susan took a deep breath before they started across the lawn. Behind them came the soft footsteps of the second couple, who would sit with them in the front row.

All heads turned toward them as they approached the barn door. Every cobweb had been swept off the day before. Every beam was scrubbed. The haymow door had been closed, and every piece of straw picked out of the rough boards. Susan kept her head up, her eyes on the backs of the couple in front of her.

Her heart pounded as the three couples took their places and stood in front of the foremost bench. All of them waited until Steve made the move to sit down. *Mamm* had insisted they practice last night, like James and Teresa had, but Steve said he wouldn't. He wanted the experience to be fresh, he claimed, even if they made a few mistakes. *Mamm* had sputtered protests, but she'd eventually given in. Steve was that way. He was firm when he knew what he wanted. Now all six of them had taken their seats in perfect unison, following Steve's lead. It couldn't have been done better if they had practiced a thousand times.

The singing started, and minutes later the ministers stood to walk to the house. Again Susan and the rest of the wedding party waited until Steve moved before they rose. They left the others walking back to the house, following the ministers upstairs and took their seats on the chairs Susan had placed there this morning.

Bishop Henry nodded toward Steve and Susan. He cleared his throat. "It's *gut* that another wedding day has arrived for us, and I suppose especially so for Steve and Susan." The bishop smiled. "When *Da Hah* first created mankind, he called the union of man and woman a necessary thing because it was not *gut* that man should be alone. We find this to be true even in our day. It's fitting that each man should seek a wife of his own to live with her in humility and tenderness, and to rule his house well.

"Out of this union children are to be born—if it pleases *Da Hah*. If not, then grace will be given to bear even childlessness. We know that such a couple shall not be without blessings from *Da Hah*. So I wish to express to you, Steve and Susan, my joy that you have come this far and that you have been found faithful to the will of *Da Hah* and that of His church. May you continue along this path until the day when time shall be no more, and we are all gathered home to be with the most high God. Now, if the others wish to express themselves, they may do so at this time." Bishop Henry waved his hand at the other ministers.

Susan listened as Minister Emery went first, and then more comments came from around the circle. They gave little pieces of advice. How to be patient with each other. How Steve and Susan thought they knew each other well, but they really didn't. That life lived together had a way of bringing out surprises in the other person—surprises you never expected to find. That *Da Hah* requires faithfulness on each of their parts. He expected forgiveness when harsh words were spoken and forbearance for the weaknesses of the other.

Steve smiled when Deacon Ray told the story of the time his wife used his best work shirt as a rag, thinking he no longer wore it.

"It did have a few holes," Deacon Ray acknowledged with a smile, "but nothing that couldn't have been fixed."

The other ministers chuckled along with him.

"You have to work together. Learn how to work together," Deacon Ray concluded. "Learn to know what the tastes and wants of each are. The years will teach you this, if you allow love to continue growing even in the rough times, as well as in the *gut* times, of course."

Bishop Henry dismissed them when everyone was done speaking. Steve held Susan's hand going down the stairs, but she pulled away from him when they came in sight of people.

"I was enjoying that!" he whispered.

"Someone might see us."

"We're almost married!" he whispered back.

"I was thinking, back there listening to them talking about all your faults, that I still have time to change my mind."

His eyes got big as he stared at her.

"I'm joking!" she said with a giggle.

"This is no time for joking," he said, pulling the edge of his black suit jacket straight.

They quieted as they went out the door, passing two of the women returning to the house to check on something. The singing was in full volume, even though people turned their heads to watch again when they approached.

Teresa was sitting beside her mother. All of Susan's sisters, even the ones from out of state, were scattered around the women's section, but she only caught a glimpse of several. No one was sick or had been called away to a funeral or other event. It was amazing that Donald was here. And he had his mother and Charles with him. *Mamm* had made sure all three of them received invitations. Steve's family was there too. Susan spotted Elizabeth in the women's section and noted she was crying gently.

Steve stood still in front of his chair, waiting for her. When Susan was in place, they sat down together. The ministers returned by the end of the song, and the preaching began. Bishop Henry had the main sermon, stopping just before noon. He turned toward Steve and Susan.

"Now, if our brother and sister still wish to exchange the holy vows, will they please stand?"

Susan kept her eyes on Steve's hands and rose with him.

"And now, do you, Steve," Bishop Henry intoned, "still believe it is *Da Hah*'s will that you take our sister Susan as your wedded wife?"

Steve said, "*Yah.*" His voice firm.

Susan answered the same question, her voice shaking.

"Now do you promise, Steve, to remain faithful to Susan in sickness, in health, in good times, and in bad? That you will cherish and protect her as you would your own flesh?"

Steve said, "*Yah,*" a slight smile on his face.

Susan gathered her courage and said "*Yah*" when Bishop Henry asked her the same question.

Bishop Henry took both of their hands in his. "And now in the name of the God of Abraham, of Isaac, and of Jacob, I declare you man and wife."

The bishop let go of their hands, and they sat down. Susan kept her head down, not looking at Steve. It was done! She was Steve's *frau!* It was almost too much to take in, the wonder of it. Feelings were rushing through her, but she had to stop thinking about it or the tears would come. And tears were not a *gut* thing right now.

Someone started the closing song, and when it was over, Steve stood again. Susan and the other couples followed him outside. Together they walked across the lawn and down the road to Ada's place, where the tables were set up in their new barn.

Steve didn't say anything, even when the couples in front and behind them began chattering about the day. He kept stealing glances at her. Susan reached over to find his hand. He was her husband now, and they could freely do this while people watched.

Susan saw a smile break over his face. She would have kissed him then and there if it weren't for the scandal that would have resulted. Some things just couldn't be done in public even if a couple was married.

They took their places behind the center table, reaching across to shake hands with those who came past to wish them *Da Hah*'s blessing.

Donald and his mother, Ruthann, came together. Both of them were smiling ear to ear. Charles was nowhere in sight.

"It is so good to be here," Ruthann gushed. "I've never been to an Amish wedding before. What a privilege! And you are such a lovely couple."

"Thank you," Susan said.

"We're very glad you could come," Steve assured her.

"And all this food!" Donald said. "I had forgotten how much food there is at Amish weddings."

"I see why you wanted to come back!" Ruthann said with a laugh. They smiled as they moved on to greet other people and find their table.

Bishop Henry announced prayer, and the building became silent. After the words were spoken, the volume rose again, quieting only when the waiters appeared with the bowls of food.

"You look lovely, my darling," Steve whispered into Susan's ear.

She smiled and squeezed his hand under the table.

Many hours later, after supper and the hymn singing had passed, Susan sneaked a glance at Steve's pocket watch as he held it up in the dim light, the hands showing nearly midnight. For an Amish wedding, it was still early—at least for the bride and groom. The hymn singing had ended a long time ago, the young folks scattering soon afterward. But the married couples had stayed around, talking and coming by to give their last best wishes.

Steve and Susan stood outside the barn, watching the last of the old folks' buggies pulling out. Above them the stars blazed. *Mamm* and *Daett* had left minutes ago, their forms still visible as they walked across the fields toward their *dawdy haus*.

"Well," Steve said, "it's down to us, I think." They walked hand in hand toward home.

When they arrived, they paused. Susan looked at the house in the twinkling starlight. The place where she had been born. The house where she had taken her first steps. The door out of which she had run on the first day of her school years. Here she had learned to cook, to sew, to wash clothing, to can food, and to love. Here she had lost so much and gained it back twice over. This was now her place. Their place. Their house, their fields to call home and perhaps someday pass on to another generation, if *Da Hah* didn't return before then. "I'm so happy I could cry," she whispered.

"Then I hope you learn how to be happy without crying because I plan to be very happy with you for many, many years."

"Steve, you're too *gut* for me."

"No, you're too *gut* for me. And do you know what I've been waiting for all day?"

"What?" she teased.

He turned toward her, and Susan threw her arms around his neck as he pulled her into a kiss.

"Mmm…" he said, long moments later. "We may have to stay out here all night doing this."

"*Yah*," she whispered.

About Jerry Eicher

Jerry Eicher's bestselling Amish fiction (more than 400,000 in combined sales) includes The Adams County Trilogy, the Hannah's Heart books, and the Little Valley Series. After a traditional Amish childhood, Jerry taught for two terms in Amish and Mennonite schools in Ohio and Illinois. Since then he's been involved in church renewal, preaching, and teaching Bible studies. Jerry lives with his wife, Tina, and their four children in Virginia.

Visit Jerry's website!

www.eicherjerry.com

A complete list of Jerry Eicher books from Harvest House Publishers...

The Adams County Trilogy

Rebecca's Promise
Rebecca's Return
Rebecca's Choice

Hannah's Heart

A Dream for Hannah
A Hope for Hannah
A Baby for Hannah

Little Valley Series

A Wedding Quilt for Ella
Ella's Wish
Ella Finds Love Again

Fields of Home Series

Missing Your Smile
Following Your Heart
Where Love Grows

Stand-alone Books

My Dearest Naomi
Susanna's Christmas Wish
The Amish Family Cookbook
(with Tina Eicher)

From the home of bestselling author Jerry Eicher (more than 400,000 books sold) and his wife, Tina, comes this warm and inviting peek into an Amish kitchen, complete with…

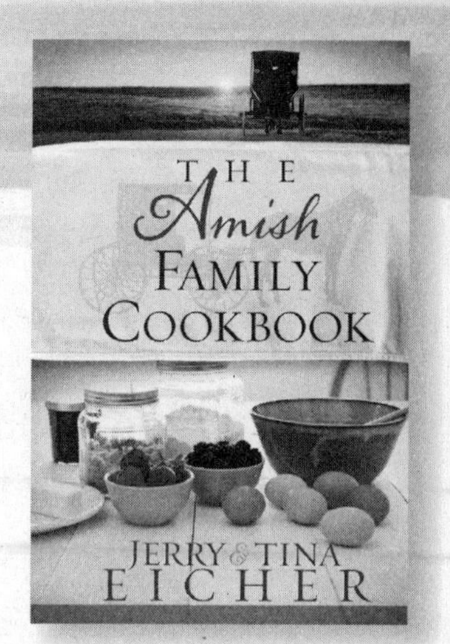

Amish recipes

Hannah Byler's Pecan Pie

Beat on low speed slightly or with hand beater:
3 eggs, 1/3 cup butter, melted, 1 cup light corn syrup
½ t. salt, 2/3 cup sugar
Stir in: 1 cup pecan halves.
Pour into: 1 pie crust.
Bake at 375° for 40-50 minutes.

Amish proverbs

It takes seven to cook for to make a really happy wife.

Amish humor

The *Englisha* visitor suffered through a three-hour Amish wedding service, sitting on the hard, backless church bench.

"Why does it take so long to tie the knot?" he asked afterward.

"Well," the bishop said, stroking his long, white beard. "So that it takes 'em a lifetime to untie it."

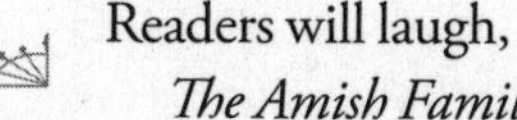

Readers will laugh, pray, and eat robustly with *The Amish Family Cookbook* at their side.